M
9

The ... and

Available in May 2007
from Mills & Boon Intrigue

Riley's Retribution
by Rebecca York
(Big Sky Bounty Hunters)

More Than a Mission
by Caridad Piñeiro
(Capturing the Crown)

Beautiful Beast
by Dani Sinclair

Cavanaugh Watch
by Marie Ferrarella
(Cavanaugh Justice)

My Sister, Myself
by Alice Sharpe
(Dead Ringer)

The Medusa Game
by Cindy Dees
(The Medusa Project)

Stranded with a Stranger
by Frances Housden
(International Affairs)

Strong Medicine
by Olivia Gates

Beautiful Beast
DANI SINCLAIR

First published in Great Britain 2007
Harlequin Mills & Boon Limited,
Eton House, 18-24 Paradise Road, Richmond, Surrey TW9 1SR

© Patricia A. Gagne 2006

ISBN: 978 0 263 85715 3

46-0507

Printed and bound in Spain
by Litografia Rosés S.A., Barcelona

With thanks to Natashya Wilson for the concept, helpful corrections, suggestions, edits and hand-holding as required.

A heartfelt thank-you to Judy Fitzwater and Robyn Pope for plotting assistance, crunch-time reading, terrific suggestions and friendship above and beyond the call.

And for Roger, husband extraordinaire, who listened a lot, offered suggestions, ignored frustration and let me work when other things beckoned. You're the best!

Always, for Chip, Dan and Barb.

Love all you guys.

DANI SINCLAIR

An avid reader, Dani Sinclair didn't start writing seriously until her two sons were grown up. Dani's kept busy writing stories ever since. Her third novel was a RITA® Award finalist in 1998 and she was awarded Best Intrigue of the Year in 2000 by *Romantic Times BOOKclub*.

Dani lives outside Washington, DC, a place she's found to be a wonderful source for both intrigue and humour. Check out her web page at www. danisinclair.com.

CAST OF CHARACTERS

Gabriel Lowe – The solitary soldier has no memory of what happened the day he was forever scarred and branded a liar and a murderer.

Cassiopia Richards – She's determined to clear her father's name and see that his murderer is brought to justice.

Beacher Coyle – He may be a silver-tongued ladies' man, but he's the only person Gabe trusts.

Major Frank Carstairs – He's always been Gabe's chief suspect in the theft of a deadly toxin. Too bad he died the day it was stolen.

Andrea Fielding – Dr Pheng's lab assistant was Gabe's fiancée – even though her brother was anti-military.

Major Bruce Huntington – He didn't like having Gabe under his command. Now he's certain Gabe will get what he deserves.

Rochelle Leeman – The gallery owner is beautiful, determined and bold enough to go after what she wants, no matter the consequences. And Gabe has what she wants.

Arthur Longstreet – The chief of security for Sunset Labs was new to the job when the toxin disappeared from under his nose.

Dr Trung Pheng – The chief research chemist was working to create an antidote to the toxin when his work was stolen.

Dr Powell Richards – His murder started the hunt for the missing toxin. Did the thieves turn on one of their own?

Len Sliffman – The former FBI man is trying to keep an open mind.

Prologue

Unease rode Gabe, but second lieutenants in the U.S. Army didn't question direct orders from a major, even one outside their direct chain of command. When Major Frank Carstairs gave an order, it was obeyed.

Besides, Gabe could hardly call his captain for verification. Everyone knew Captain Bruce Huntington didn't like Second Lieutenant Gabriel Lowe, who had been recently assigned to his military intelligence unit. And the order had nothing to do with Gabe's babysitting job. He was the newest person in the unit, and low man, so he got all the unwanted assignments.

The original orders had been to transport three vials of a deadly toxin from the military base in Frederick, Maryland, to Dr. Powell Richards at Sunburst Laboratory in Urbana, Maryland. Gabe was then to oversee security.

Everything had gone as planned. The doctor had accepted the toxin with no hitches yesterday, and today had been a normal day. The doctor had left early, and

Gabe had made certain the toxin was secured and his men in place before leaving. He'd been on his way home when Major Carstairs had ordered him to pick up Dr. Richards and escort the scientist to the base immediately.

Clearly something was wrong but no one, especially not the major, was going to bother explaining to him what that something was.

While the doctor had appeared stressed and preoccupied when he left for the day, Gabe didn't know him well enough to know if that was normal or not. Dr. Richards hadn't mentioned a problem and none of Gabe's men had reported anything since he left, so what was going on?

Parking the car on the narrow street, Gabe stared up at the Richards house as dusk laid claim to the neighborhood. There was no car in the driveway and no lights to indicate anyone was home.

Other houses sparkled with lights and life as dusk yielded quickly to the press of an early nightfall. A perfectly normal scene, yet Gabe felt something was off.

Uneasy, he stepped from his car trying to determine why his senses were crying an alert for no good reason. He felt oddly exposed. His hand itched for the comfort of his holstered service revolver.

He hesitated as headlights swept up the street. The garage door began to open. The approaching vehicle slowed to make the turn, giving Gabe a clear view of the driver. Dr. Richards appeared even more stressed and distracted than before. He didn't so much as glance at Gabe standing there. Something was definitely wrong.

Gabe's hand still hovered near his revolver as he

followed the car toward the house. He moved more quickly when it pulled all the way into the garage.

Without warning, a giant fireball rocked the neighborhood. Gabe reeled back. Something sliced his face as the garage exploded.

He ignored the warmth running down his cheek and sprinted for the car. A figure struggled to climb out as flames engulfed everything. A billowing wave of heat brought Gabe's hands up to cover his face.

The second, larger explosion sent Gabe sailing through the air. He landed with incredible force amid a hail of raining debris. His last coherent thought was that he should have listened to his instincts.

Chapter One

Frederick, Maryland
Present Day

A slender figure came around the far side of his house and sprinted across the front lawn to disappear in the hedge on the other side. Gabriel Lowe stopped walking. Not CID, FBI, Homeland Security or any of the other official types who watched his house from time to time. Their people would have approached his home in a much different fashion.

Female, based on the swing of nicely rounded hips in figure-hugging jeans. A long ponytail swished against a slender back covered by a fitted jacket. His intruder was obviously looking for a way inside. And in that instant, he knew who it had to be.

His fingers flexed and balled into fists. Jaw clenched, Gabe stepped off the sidewalk and slipped into the nearest shadow. He followed her silently, letting his anger build.

With a low-voiced, muttered imprecation, she battled her way behind the prickly juniper that squatted beneath his dining room window. Identity confirmed, Gabe faded back against the bole of the spreading oak tree a short distance from her.

Cassiopia Richards—the woman who had named him a murderer—gazed up at the window and sighed. She withdrew a ridiculously tiny pocketknife from her hip pocket and hesitated. The small blade was hard to see in the bit of moonlight that filtered between the high clouds, but her intention was clear.

Gabe was reluctant to accost her too soon. Would she actually go through with a criminal act?

She slit the screen and started to reach for the window itself. Abruptly, she stopped.

"Blast."

The utterance was a wisp of discord in the chilly night air. She struggled with the juniper branch that had clamped onto the back of her coat. Apparently, she didn't understand that an illegal activity like breaking and entering required silence and speed.

Not once did she bother to scan her surroundings. She wouldn't have seen him if she had, but she was either extremely sure of herself or totally inept. Watching her struggle with the bush, he was betting on the latter.

FRAZZLED, CASSY JERKED her coat free, half hoping this window would be locked like the others she had already tried. Then she could go home and come up with a new plan. This one was stupid. If she were caught…

She would not think about that. She couldn't afford to turn around and go home. If there was the slimmest chance Gabriel's friend Beacher Coyle had actually succeeded where everyone else had failed, she needed to do something.

She'd been a fool to listen to him in the first place. He'd almost convinced her that they were victims, like her father. He'd persuaded her to listen and now the golden-tongued son of a serpent wasn't answering his telephone. Gabriel had blown her off when she'd contacted him, and now Beacher was avoiding her calls. And if her suspicions were correct, Beacher had brought the results of his search to Gabriel.

They'd found the missing toxin and were going to sell it unless she stopped them. By the time she convinced someone in authority, it would be too late and she was not going to let them get away with it.

Not a sound disturbed the stillness of the night. Cassy had little fear of being observed, given the distance between the houses. The blasted neighborhood was dark enough to give her the creeps. Once more she adjusted the thin bits of plastic over her hands and reached up.

With a scraping, groaning racket all out of proportion to what she'd expected, the window yielded and slid to one side. Startled, she froze. Her heart thundered wildly in her chest. Her ponytail swung as she took a quick look around the yard and at the house next door.

GABE REMAINED MOTIONLESS as her eyes swept by him without faltering and continued on to the house next door. He could have told her she had nothing to worry about from that direction. The family inside would be glued to their television sets at this hour. Nothing less than an explosion would bring them to a door or window.

But what was Cassiopia Richards doing here in the first place? Perhaps he should have heard her out when she called the other day, but her patronizing tone had annoyed him. He'd never forgotten her tirade when he'd been trapped in that hospital bed. Gabe didn't owe her a thing.

She stared at the opening as if trying to screw up her courage to climb inside. Then she cast another nervous glance around. He waited.

THIS WAS NO TIME for paranoia, Cassy admonished herself. There was no one lurking nearby watching her every move, even if the back of her neck was crawling in warning. Gabriel Lowe was at his gym at this hour. While the sound of the window opening had been loud, it hadn't been loud enough to carry inside the house across the yard, and no one moved on the silent street. Not a single car had driven past since she got here.

Well, it wasn't every day she attempted to break into someone's home. Her nerves had a right to be jumpy. She was usually such a practical person.

Cassy gripped the windowsill and levered herself up. The jagged screen snagged on the elbow of her jacket. She yanked her arm back. The screen ripped free of the window and fell, tangling with the bush below. She froze in dismay and swore softly.

So much for hoping he wouldn't notice the torn screen.

ENTERTAINED DESPITE his annoyance, Gabe waited to see what she'd do next. What she did was seek a better grip, even though the weird, loose-fitting clear plastic covering her hands made the task harder than it should have been.

What were those things? They weren't the latex gloves that hugged the skin. These bits of clear plastic fit so loosely she seemed to be having trouble keeping them in place.

Cassiopia Richards had to be the most inept burglar ever. Her thrusting hand tangled in the sheer drape that covered the window. She tried to shove the material aside as she swung her leg up and over but the drape wasn't having any of it. In her attempt to avoid being wrapped in the filmy cloth, her leg apparently collided with the back of a chair.

Gabe nearly smiled. His dining room was small, the furniture too large for the space. He'd kept his parents' old stuff after he bought this place because the pieces served to fill the empty rooms. Since he was pretty much the only one who ever saw them, their relative size had never mattered, but her unexpected contact with the chair nearly reversed Cassiopia's direction. Even from where he stood he could hear the chair clatter against the table.

CASSY STOPPED MOVING half-in and half-out of the window. She stopped breathing as well. She waited for Gabriel Lowe to appear out of the darkness and condemn her. Even though she was almost positive he wasn't home, it seemed an inevitable thing to happen.

She cast another frantic glance around. The yard was pitch-black. She couldn't see a thing. There was no going back now. She expelled the breath of air and forced her other leg over the sill.

The drape swirled around her once more. She wriggled, colliding with the chair again. Cassy wrenched the gauzy fabric to one side in a frantic swipe. Off balance, she tumbled forward. Only pure dumb luck and the mahogany dining room table kept her from crashing to the floor.

Great. He'd never notice *that*. This was not an auspicious start to a life of crime. If she believed in omens, she'd turn around, climb back through that window and go home to bed. She could always get a decent lawyer in the morning.

She should have tried the authorities first. Maybe someone would have listened.

The prickly sensation that she was being watched would not go away. Her hand went to a side pocket and came out with the minuscule pocket flash. The attached key ring jingled as she moved.

If someone *had* been home, they'd have called the police by now. She'd made enough noise to wake the dead. Good thing she wasn't planning on a life of crime. Her nerves couldn't take much more of this.

Get it over with. Call out. See if someone *was* there.

GABE FLATTENED HIMSELF against the side of the house near the open window. He jumped when she spoke.

"Hello?"

Her scratchy voice was barely a whisper of sound.

"Is anybody home?"

And what would she do if he answered?

"Didn't think so, but I wanted to be sure."

Gabe shook his head. The woman was squirrel fodder. He'd been right to not waste time talking with her when she called.

The beam of her small flashlight swung away from the window. Gabe moved to where he could just see her vague outline. Her body radiated tension as she peered around the room. The resonant sound of the grandfather clock chiming the hour sent a tiny shriek past her lips.

"Idiot!"

On that, they were in complete agreement.

Muttering a profanity, she repositioned the chair at the table.

"No way am I going back out that window. When I leave tonight, I'm going out a door like any civilized burglar."

Thoroughly amused, Gabe watched as Cassiopia moved the small ray of light to search out a path to the kitchen. It would almost be a shame to ruin her evening by revealing his presence.

HER FRAZZLED NERVES were playing tricks on her. There was no one here. Gabriel Lowe *was* at the gym. Based on past observations she should have an hour and a half before he returned.

Cassy picked her way carefully through the maze of furniture. Fortunately for her, his tastes ran to the stark. While the heavy old pieces were oversized, he hadn't filled his home with bric-a-brac and clutter. And that seemed a little strange, given that he was supposed to be a sculptor. She'd expected to find dozens of ugly pieces scattered about.

Cassy shook her head. Who cared? The only thing that mattered was finding his home office, doing a quick search for what Beacher had found and getting away before either of them returned. She'd watched Gabriel enough to know that he spent most of his time in his basement. He even entertained Beacher down there, unless they sat around in the dark upstairs when he came to visit. Obviously, the basement was the place to start and she'd better hurry.

Finding a door next to the refrigerator, she reached for the handle. A mop stem hurled out of the darkness and cracked against her shoulder. Cassy leaped back, another small shriek escaping. Dislodged, a plastic pail rocked against the dustpan with a surprising clatter. The broom tipped over. She barely caught the handle in time to keep it from crashing to the floor.

HE WAS GOING TO HAVE to fix that wall mount for the mop and broom soon, Gabe thought, lips twitching. He'd waited until she'd stepped fully into the kitchen before slipping in through the open window without disturbing the drape or the chair. He'd cautiously taken a position near the hall entrance to the kitchen to see what she'd do next.

"I'm going to have a major heart attack before I even find the basement," she muttered so softly he had to strain to hear her. "Gabriel Lowe is going to come home and find my dead body on his kitchen floor wearing stupid baggie gloves. Why didn't I stop and pick up some latex ones?"

Stupid baggie gloves?

She replaced the mop, the broom and the pail and closed the door. The beam bobbled as she sent the anemic shaft of light toward the dining room entrance. He melted back before she shone it in the hall's direction, then moved to observe her when the light swung away again.

Taking a cautious step around the refrigerator, she continued moving until she reached the basement door.

She opened it gingerly and aimed the faint beam of light down the steps. He saw her shudder.

"This is *so* not a good idea."

Gabe agreed. What was she doing here? Didn't she realize his house was searched on a regular basis? The professionals could probably tell her the number of cans and the brand names of the soup in his kitchen cupboard on any given day. This had to have something to do with Beacher.

Gabe's humor dissolved as Cassiopia gripped the smooth wood banister and started down the stairs. He waited for her to reach the third step from the bottom. The board creaked loudly. Her gasp was swallowed by the darkness.

He took a step back from the opening. Sure enough, she sent that stupid little light back up before swinging it in front of her again. What she expected a beam of that size to reveal he wasn't sure. He probably hadn't even needed to move.

"Think of the squeak as an early warning system," she muttered.

That was exactly how he'd always looked at it. The narrow stairs were the only way in or out of the basement. He wondered if she knew that.

Using the flat of one hand and the weakening beam of light, she followed the curve of the wall to her right.

"If that man has a single rodent scurrying around down here I will come back and haunt him for all eternity."

He skimmed down the stairs noiselessly in her wake.

REALIZING SHE'D FOUND another room, Cassy swept her hand over the inside wall until she located the light switch. Waiting for her eyes to adjust to what seemed like sudden brilliance, she gaped in amazement and stepped inside.

The windowless space was filled with shelves and columned pedestals of varying heights. Each held a bronze sculpture or series of small sculptures. Animals, especially lions and big cats, seemed to be his specialty. He'd infused an almost living essence in each subject. They were exquisitely detailed.

Her hand reached out to stroke a deer poised in flight. She stopped before actually touching the lifelike bronze figurine and shook her head reverently. Slowly, she moved about the room in awe. Gabriel Lowe was an artist in the truest sense of the word. His talent was nothing short of amazing.

She paused to squat before a pair of identical, nearly life-sized bronzes. The crouching lions perched on elaborate, ebony wood bases on the tiled floor.

"Absolutely incredible."

"Thank you."

Cassy rose with a shriek and whirled.

Wreathed in the concealing darkness of the hall, deep-set eyes seemed to gleam with a predator's assessment as they surveyed her from beyond the room's pool of light. Panic sent her gaze questing for a nonexistent escape route.

Energy crackled as Gabriel Lowe took a sinuous step into the shaft of light.

Her gaze fastened on the twisted scar that ran from the corner of his left eye to the edge of his strong jaw. Horrible! It added gruesome detail to the sinister, fierce aura he projected.

He was broader and taller up close than she'd expected. Powerful shoulders tapered to a narrow waist. Lean hips and well-muscled thighs confirmed his fitness as he glided forward silently like some large, stalking cat.

Cassy forgot to breathe. The darkness seemed to thicken behind him, creating an impenetrable barrier. His fixed, implacable expression held her silent. Her heart drummed wildly against her rib cage.

There was nowhere to run even if she could have summoned the will to move. Like a cornered mouse, she knew she was trapped. The jig was up.

Gabriel Lowe was going to kill her, too.

Chapter Two

Gabe watched as Cassiopia's shocked gaze traveled the length of his scar before absorbing the rest of him. Well, his features hadn't been all that great even before the explosion. The bright red puckering of the scar had faded to white over time, but he knew its impact was still strong on unsuspecting people.

"Wha-what are you doing here?" she managed to gasp.

He arched his eyebrows pointedly and remained silent.

Cassiopia closed her eyes and groaned. "I knew I was going to get caught." She opened her eyes and grimaced. "I guess I should be glad you aren't a mad rapist."

He waited, keeping his expression blank, still reluctantly amused by her forced attempt at humor.

"You aren't, are you?"

"Which? Mad, or a rapist?"

"I know you aren't a rapist."

He raised his eyebrows. Color singed her cheeks but she pressed forward boldly.

"How mad are you?"

He came away from the door in a motion that brought him across the room in three long strides. Cassiopia took an inadvertent step back, stopping when her heel bumped the base of the nearest crouching lion.

"What makes you so sure I'm not a rapist?"

The silky tone of his words charged the air. Her lips parted without sound while her gaze fastened on his scar once more. She inhaled raggedly.

"Don't be absurd."

Her voice cracked, denying the false calm she was trying to project.

"Are you going to call the police?"

He let his expression darken, then crowded her deliberately, coming to a stop when he was inches from her face.

"Now why would I want to do that? The last thing a mad rapist wants is the police," he told her with silken menace.

Cassy refused to look away. "That isn't funny."

"Neither is breaking and entering."

She dropped her gaze. Gabe sensed it lingering on the scarred backs of his hands and made no effort to conceal the puckered skin. Let her look her fill. There were more scars than these, covered by his clothing.

A piece of burning siding had landed on him in the explosion nearly four years ago. He'd been unconscious, and only the fast action of a neighbor had kept him from burning to death. Any number of times he'd thought the man hadn't done him any favors.

Gabe was close enough to smell a bewitchingly light scent that wasn't some cloying perfume, but was utterly female. He tried to ignore that and focused on the play of color in her hair. Cassiopia Richards was…distracting.

Amazingly, there was neither pity nor horror in her

expression when she lifted her eyes. "You left me no choice," she told him with surprising fierceness. "You could have talked to me when I called you yesterday."

"I did."

Her lips thinned. "You told me to take a hike."

"I'm certain I was more polite than that."

"Stop playing games."

That stirred his anger once more. "I've said all I have to say on the subject of what happened four years ago. I'm not interested in repeating myself."

"Beacher claims you were an innocent victim, too."

Beacher was a fool. His friend was convinced Cassiopia knew something that would help them discover what Powell Richards had done with the missing toxin so he refused to give up his pursuit of her.

As Beacher had pointed out, *"That toxin's somewhere and we're going to find it and prove we had nothing to do with what happened."*

Gabe believed talking with Cassiopia was a waste of time. She'd been away at school when her father had taken the toxin from under Gabe's nose and gotten himself killed. And she'd scored an indelible impression on him that day in the hospital. She was too young, too passionate and obviously too impulsive to be of any help to them.

She summoned up a glare as if he'd spoken his thoughts aloud. "I'm leaving."

"You just got here."

Not many people could hold his gaze when he was in a temper. Given his overall size and his scars, he'd perfected the art of intimidation, but only the quickening leap of the pulse in her neck told him she wasn't as immune as she'd like him to believe.

Gabe stepped back. "Let's go."

"Where?"

"Upstairs."

The widening of those soft gray eyes brought a sudden vision of his bedroom and the two of them intertwined on twisted sheets. It had been a long time since he'd thought about sex and he banished the image instantly. But she seemed to be tuning in to his thoughts.

"I'm not going anywhere with you."

This time anxiety threaded her voice.

"You'd rather remain here?"

"Yes. Go ahead and call the police. I'd welcome them."

The bluster was gone. He'd finally succeeded in frightening her. It made him feel oddly ashamed.

"To the kitchen, Cassiopia," he told her more gently. "To talk. I may be mad—God knows I've been called worse—but I'm no rapist."

He stepped back even farther, giving her space. "Come or stay."

Her chin lifted in defiance. "I'll stay."

"Fine. But you should know that the way you entered is the only way out."

He crossed to the door and waited. She wasn't beautiful in the strictest sense of the word, but he'd definitely call her attractive. That rich brown hair with its hints of gold framed an oval face with high, prominent cheekbones and a long, graceful neck. Under other circumstances…

Who was he kidding? Under other circumstances she'd either take one look at his face and run the other way or cringe in pity. She faced him because she had no choice.

CASSY SOUGHT ANOTHER OPTION and realized there wasn't one. She was not going to cringe like a mouse even if this beast did have her well and truly trapped. She hated feeling afraid. She was in the wrong, but if he'd intended to kill her he'd have done it down here, not upstairs.

With a brief, accepting nod she squared her shoulders and marched over to him.

"Do not call me Cassiopia," she told him, pointing a plastic encased finger at his chest.

"Do you prefer Ms. Richards, or Dr. Richards?"

If he knew she was a Ph.D., he also knew she was a chemical engineer. She brushed aside Gabriel's question with a wave of her covered hand. "I go by Cassy."

He scowled, staring at her hand. "What *are* those things?"

Heat suffused her cheeks. Hastily, she pulled off the silly plastic shapes, feeling foolish.

"They come with packages of inexpensive hair dye."

"Brown isn't your natural color?"

"Of course it is! The hair dye belonged to my roommate."

"So you steal from others besides me."

"Betsy must have forgotten about it. And *I* didn't steal anything!"

He stilled so completely he could have been cast in bronze like the figurines around them. Shaken but refusing to give in to the alarm that charged every molecule of her body, Cassy forced herself to meet whatever retribution he demanded with her head high.

His stillness was so profound it was painful. Abruptly, he turned away.

"What are you going to do?" she demanded as another ripple of fear skated down her spine.

"Probably continue calling you Cassiopia. Cassy doesn't suit you at all."

He flicked off the light, plunging them into darkness.

"Hey!" Before panic could overwhelm her, light winked on at the end of the hall. There was nothing to do except follow, unless she wanted to stay in his basement all night.

The third step from the bottom made no sound for him, yet it squawked like a spitting cat the moment she set her foot on it. Was he even human?

Cassy shuddered. That horrible scar said he was all too human. He must have been an attractive man once. Actually, despite the scar, he wouldn't be bad-looking now if he'd stop scowling all the time. If nothing else, his aura of self-assured power commanded attention.

Cassy wanted to be glad he'd suffered for what he'd done, but Beacher had half convinced her otherwise. What if he were innocent? Could a man who could create such incredible beauty also destroy with such utter ruthlessness?

She'd been so enraged that day at the hospital she'd barely noticed Gabriel as a person. She'd needed a focus for her grief and rage and she'd taken it out on him, ignoring the fact that he'd been swaddled in bandages and attached to wires, tubes and monitors. Wrapped in her own emotions, she'd snuck inside his hospital room without a thought for anything except confronting the man responsible for her father's horrible death.

The memory of being pulled away while she ranted still shamed her. Even then his gaze had been dark and troubling. She'd had plenty of time to think about things since then. Letting go of her anger had been hard, but Beacher had pressed her to listen to him until he finally persuaded her to see that they might have been victims, too.

Gabriel hadn't hurt her just now, and he hadn't called the police. Of course he might be planning to call when they got upstairs, but either he and Beacher were guilty of murder and treason, or they'd been framed, as she was sure her father had been framed.

Had Beacher been playing both of them? Was he even now on his way out of the country with the deadly toxin?

Gabriel flipped on the kitchen light and shrugged out of his black cloth jacket, draping it neatly over the back of one of the two chairs at the tiny kitchen table. The black turtleneck hugged his shoulders and well-defined torso. He was lean and fit and scary in every way.

She'd made it a point to learn as much as she could about both men after Beacher began pestering her. Gabriel seldom left the small house he'd purchased after leaving the military on disability. He never socialized. Beacher was his only real friend as far as she could determine. The two had worked together at the army base, though their friendship dated back several years to when they were neighbors growing up. Gabriel had gone to a military academy. Beacher had gone to college and then joined a private security company. They both ended up working at the same military base and immediately resumed their friendship.

"Sit," Gabriel ordered without turning around. He crossed to the sink and began washing his hands.

"Am I supposed to bark now and wag my tail?"

He slanted her a startled glance. Unexpected humor lightened his dark-eyed stare.

"Skip the bark." And he turned back to the sink.

Outraged, Cassy wished she dared to toss something at him, but the room was immaculately clean. Even if she'd really wanted to, there wasn't a single loose object on the white countertop or the tiny kitchen table. Pale yellow walls and white cabinets did what they could to lighten the space, but it was so small there was barely room to turn around. Cassy would have guessed the kitchen was never used until he dried his hands and began opening cupboards.

Like the rest of the house, the cupboards were neat and orderly and filled with the sort of stuff she saw in her married friends' kitchens. The man even had a rack of spices. She thought of her own empty cupboards and shook her head. She never cooked if she could avoid it.

Gabriel set an electric kettle to boil. With fluid, economical motions that would have suited a laboratory, he removed two large brown mugs and a pair of small, matching plates. An odd-looking teapot in the shape of a dragon joined the rest on the pristine counter.

"What are you doing?"

He didn't spare her a glance. "Brewing tea."

"Tea?"

She'd broken into his house and he was making her tea? What was going on here? Was he stalling for some reason?

"You don't like tea?"

"Mostly I drink it iced."

He made a face and pulled a small cheesecake from a well-stocked refrigerator. Slicing two perfect wedges, he transferred them to the plates without a wasted motion.

"Sit down, Cassiopia."

She gritted her teeth. "I'd rather stand."

His granite face bore no expression as he turned. Hooded eyes focused on her with an unblinking stare that was totally unnerving. Set against the harsh planes of his face, she decided they weren't the tawny eyes of a lion but dark ebony wells of silent turbulence. Gabriel had seen too much of the unpleasant side of life. The impression of barely leashed power lent him a quiet menace that made her tremble. No one looked less like a sculptor.

Cassy knew sculpting had been part of his physical therapy after he was injured, but did he realize what a talent he had? She was pretty sure most people studied for years before they could create the sort of breathtaking beauty he'd captured in the pieces downstairs.

"Do you want to talk or not?" he asked in that deceptively soft voice.

Not. When he gazed at her like that she wanted to run far and fast. Too bad that wasn't an option.

"Yes."

He looked from her to the table without another word.

Cassy conceded defeat. She pulled out the chair that didn't hold his jacket and sat down, glad for the warmth of her own lightweight jacket even though the house itself wasn't cold.

Immediately, he turned back to the counter and measured tea leaves as if scientific precision was called for. Steam drifted from the spout of the dragon, shaped to be its mouth.

Great. Even his teapot breathed smoke. She might be better off if he simply called the police.

Opening a drawer, he withdrew two plain blue place mats and set them on the table. He added forks, spoons and cloth napkins without a word.

His black turtleneck and dark jeans were spotted by stains of what appeared to be mud. However, his hands, including his fingernails, were scrupulously clean. Cassy noticed that his fingers and palms weren't burnt like the backs of his hands.

"Lemon?"

Cassiopia jumped. "What?"

"Would you like lemon with your tea?"

Gabe pronounced each word with deliberate care. She raised her chin.

"No, thank you. Just sugar."

He withdrew a glass sugar bowl from another cupboard and set it on the table.

"Have you had time to come up with a plausible explanation yet?"

She inhaled sharply. Obviously, she hadn't.

"You weren't supposed to be home."

"Oh?"

"You usually go to your gym at this hour."

"Should I feel flattered that you've been spying on me?"

Gabe set a slice of cheesecake and a cup in front of

her and settled in the opposite chair. Instantly, the small room seemed to shrink even further. This had been a bad idea. He did not want to find her attractive.

"Your bad luck," he continued. "I took a walk tonight, instead."

"Isn't it just?"

Her blush told him she hadn't meant to say that out loud.

"What did you expect to find in my basement?"

"Not those incredible sculptures."

She was stalling.

"I didn't realize you were so gifted." The color in her cheeks deepened. She ducked her head and picked up her fork without looking at him.

"Gifted?"

That jerked her face up. "You're extremely talented and you know it."

He inclined his head in acceptance.

CASSY WATCHED HIM fork up a bite of cheesecake. He slid the morsel from his fork to his mouth and chewed with pleasure. She had never realized how sexy eating could be.

She quickly banished the inappropriate thought. There was nothing sexy about Gabriel Lowe. Okay, there was, but he was more dangerous than he was appealing and she'd do well to keep that in mind. Except, surely she didn't have to be intimidated by a man who could create such sensitive works of art.

"Your sculptures look like something in a museum," she told him honestly. "You shouldn't be hiding them away in your basement."

Too late, she clamped her lips shut. What was she doing, lecturing the man?

"I'm flattered." He poured them both a cup of tea without expression.

Gabriel might not be crouching like the lifelike set of lions on his floor downstairs, but the resemblance was still uncanny. Like his metal counterparts, he, too, seemed to be waiting to pounce. Yet she couldn't dismiss the idea that he was silently laughing at her.

"Why are you here, Cassiopia?"

She swallowed hastily. "I want what Beacher Coyle gave you."

He stilled. Though the kitchen lights were on, an ominous darkness seemed to fill the room.

"Is that right?"

The mildness of his tone was a clear rattle of warning. She hoped her quaking was all on the inside.

"We're engaged to be married."

A mistake. She knew it the moment the blurted words were past her lips. She'd never been any good at lying. Why hadn't she thought ahead, prepared something to tell him?

His glance went to where her left hand lay clenched at the edge of the table. "He never mentioned a fiancée."

She wanted to look away but couldn't. Her gaze riveted on that terrible scar. Gabriel and Beacher were close friends. Of course he knew she was lying, but she had no choice now but to keep going or admit the truth.

"We haven't made a formal announcement yet."

If only she'd had a few minutes to come up with something better than a phony engagement.

"He hasn't bought you a ring yet, either."

Her mouth went dry. "No."

"Do you know the password?"

Cold, then heat, flooded her. Was he serious? He looked serious.

"You're making that up!"

She was certain he'd made it up, but his expression never altered. Gabriel waited. Unnerved, she tried to think of something plausible to say and failed.

"Why would he tell you to sneak in through a window?"

"He didn't. But I could hardly call you again and ask for an invitation, now could I?"

Dropping her fork to the plate with a clatter, she glared at him, defying him to contradict her. "You would have hung up on me again."

Was that the faintest trace of a curve to his lips?

"Actually, I wouldn't have answered your call at all," he told her, unperturbed.

He reached for his tea cup and took a swallow. "Why didn't Beacher come himself?"

Danger. This lion was waiting to pounce and tear her to shreds. She took a breath to steady her nerves.

"He couldn't."

"Why?"

Her heart raced. He was toying with her, she was almost certain of it. "I think he's in some sort of trouble."

"You think."

She held his gaze. "Just give me what he gave you."

"Let's both go to see him."

"No!"

"No?"

His misleadingly docile tone sent every nerve in her body clanging in alarm. She'd made a hash of everything.

Gabriel leaned back in his chair with an inscrutable expression, but she knew she'd lost. If Beacher had found the toxin and given it to him he wasn't going to tell her.

He bared his teeth. It was not a humorous smile.

"Want to try again?"

"You don't believe me!"

His mocking expression was confirmation.

Defeat lay like bitter ashes in her mouth. Everyone seemed to agree that her father had taken the toxin and all the research from the lab itself, even though he had no motive. The working theory was that he'd conspired with Gabriel, and possibly Beacher, to steal the toxin and sell it to the highest bidder.

The authorities further decided that Gabriel had double-crossed her father and set charges to kill him and destroy any evidence. They believed her father had come home unexpectedly and set off the explosions before Gabriel could get away. There was no other explanation as to why Gabriel had been at the house that day. As far as she knew, he'd never even offered one.

She wasn't sure where Beacher fit into this scenario, but there were a lot of things no one was telling her. She only knew the consensus was that the three men had conspired to steal the missing toxin and all the research that accompanied it. She assumed the authorities believed Gabriel and Beacher were simply waiting for the furor to die down to sell what they'd stolen. But it never had. The investigation had stayed as active as if the theft had happened yesterday. She couldn't count the number of times she'd been questioned.

"Beacher didn't send you, did he?" Gabriel asked.

"Of course he did." She tried to sound forceful. He might feel sure she was lying, but until he spoke to Beacher he couldn't be positive.

He took another bite of cheesecake and leaned back. She would not squirm under that intense stare no matter how much she wanted to. Instead, she focused on a small scar on his neck that his turtleneck didn't completely cover.

Was he scarred all over? Was that why his fiancée had broken their engagement while he was still in the hospital? Cassy had never spoken with Andrea Fielding, but she'd seen the beautiful lab assistant with Dr. Pheng. Dr. Pheng had sent the toxin to her father in the first place, which wasn't surprising. They were the top men in their field, friends as well as rivals since they had been graduate students together.

Cassy knew Dr. Pheng and Andrea Fielding had come under tight scrutiny as well. Everyone remotely connected to the toxin had, but only her father and Gabriel had had the opportunity to steal it.

With a sigh, she set down her fork. "Are you going to have me arrested?"

"Arrested?" He seemed to savor the word. "I don't think there's any need to have you arrested over some minor damage."

She ignored the heat in her cheeks once more. "I'll send you a check for the drapes."

"And the screen?" he asked blandly.

"Yes, blast it. The screen, too."

"I think we can come up with a more suitable punishment to fit this crime, don't you?"

Cassy moistened suddenly dry lips. She was completely alone in a house with a man everyone believed was a criminal and worse. And she'd let down her guard!

"I'd rather be arrested."

"Do I make you nervous, Cassiopia?"

Did lambs sleep with lions? Of course he made her nervous. If her palms grew any damper she'd drip all over the table, but she'd never give him the satisfaction of admitting as much.

"I'm not afraid of you."

His dark expression lightened. If he smiled at her now she'd toss her cheesecake at him.

"Good," he said neutrally and took another sip of tea.

She released the breath she'd been holding. "I'm going to leave."

"Without what you came for?"

"Are you going to give it to me?"

"No."

So Beacher had given him something! Or was he toying with her again?

"This is a waste of time."

"Not precisely. I rarely have visitors. Try the tea. It's a special blend."

He was definitely toying with her. "To think I was going to apologize. I can see it would have been a waste of breath."

The eyebrows arched once more. "For breaking into my house?"

"No! For that day at the hospital."

Humor vanished in an instant. His jaw hardened.

"Does that mean you no longer believe I murdered your father?"

Cassy wasn't sure what she believed anymore. The authorities claimed Gabriel had had no opportunity to remove the toxin from the lab alone. Only her father could have done so, and *that* she would never accept.

Her father had been understandably devastated by the sudden death of his wife only two weeks earlier. So was she, but no amount of grief would have caused her father to compromise his job.

"Did you kill him?" He wouldn't tell her the truth if he had, but she had to ask.

"No."

She waited until it became obvious he wasn't going to elaborate. "That's all you're going to say? Just 'no'?"

"I said all I had to say four years ago," he told her with deceptive mildness. "Finish your cheesecake."

Cassy shoved her plate aside. "I am finished."

His eyes narrowed. He set down his fork with careful deliberation. "Then it's time for you to leave."

"You're going to throw me out?"

"If you won't go under your own power."

He'd do it, too. She'd successfully roused the beast. Every instinct told her to get up and go, but she couldn't. She hadn't accomplished anything.

"I want what Beacher gave you."

"We don't always get what we want, Cassiopia."

For a millisecond, it was as if she had a clear window into his troubled soul. A lonely beast prowled there. Cassy couldn't help but feel sorry for him.

He stood in a fluid motion that caught her unprepared.

"When you see him, tell your *fiancé* I want to talk with him."

She could have refused to move. She wanted to refuse, but her legs were already drawing her to her feet. The menace in the room was too thick to ignore.

"You're a real bastard."

"Is it my turn to call you a name now?"

He didn't smile.

"Goodbye, Cassiopia. Don't come here again."

Seeing no choice, she walked down the hall toward the front door, aware of him at her back close enough to touch. Desperately, she tried to think of something else she could do or say to change the situation, but nothing came to mind.

He opened the door without a word and waited.

"If even one of those vials is opened a lot of innocent people will die. I wonder if even you could live with that."

Rage flashed across his expression. Cassy stepped onto the stoop, words of apology forming on her lips, but he closed the door in her face.

A chill breeze brushed her skin. Cassy shivered. She couldn't help thinking Gabriel Lowe was innocent after all.

Chapter Three

Anger would get him nowhere. Gabe snagged his coat, pulling it on as he left by the kitchen door. Swiftly, he moved around the side of the house only to find he needn't have hurried. Cassiopia trudged down the sidewalk slowly, her posture showing her dejection.

Unless that, too, was part of her act.

He didn't have time for this. His first commission was waiting on the worktable downstairs. If he wanted it completed on time, he had to finish shaping the clay tonight.

He knew little about Cassiopia Richards beyond the fact that she had a quick temper, made a laughable burglar and was a poor liar. If she and Beacher were engaged he'd eat all his works in progress.

How had she known Beacher had given him anything?

The minute his friend had showed up last night Gabe had known there was trouble, but Beacher had put him off. He'd handed Gabe a small package and asked him to hold it without questions until he returned.

"Don't open it, okay? I'll explain tomorrow when I come back." His expression had been grim. *"I don't*

*have time to explain right now. There's someone I have
to meet and I'm running late."*

He wouldn't say who or what was in the package
and, as of yet, he hadn't returned with explanations.
How had Cassiopia known?

Beacher knew Gabe's house was searched on a
regular basis. He wouldn't have asked Gabe to hold
something that would get them both tossed in prison.
Not when, at the cost of his own reputation, Beacher had
stood by Gabe when no one else would. There was no
one Gabe trusted the way he trusted Beacher so he
hadn't pressed for answers. He regretted that now.

Something was wrong. Beacher should have shown
by now. He'd give his friend until morning, then he was
going to see what Beacher felt needed to be hidden
from the irritating woman.

She stopped beside a small coupe and looked back
at the house. Gabe stilled, willing her to see him as just
another shadow once more.

Slapping the roof of her car in frustration, she
climbed inside and started the engine. As she pulled
away from the curb he made a mental note of the license
plate and hurried to his backyard, bypassing his truck.
The motorcycle started with its usual roar. He picked
her up a few minutes later, traveling at a sedate rate of
speed on the city streets.

Gabe hung well back. If she knew about his habit of
going to the gym in the evening, she knew he rode a motorcycle. Following her was probably a waste of precious
time. He'd take bets she was on her way home and not
on her way to meet Beacher, but he had to be sure.

It was a bet he would have won.

When she turned into the parking lot of a row of modest town houses, he pulled over on the main road and waited. She took her time exiting the car. He used that time to survey the area.

Something moved furtively between two parked cars. Cassiopia had climbed out and was heading in that same direction, a large cloth handbag she hadn't had earlier slung over one shoulder.

Instincts screaming, Gabe kicked the bike to life. He roared into the lot as the crouching figure leaped from between the cars and rushed her. Cassiopia went down. The pair struggled briefly before the hooded figure took off, disappearing around the corner of the building with her bag.

Gabe sent the bike onto the sidewalk in pursuit. Grass and dirt spun under his wheels as he tore after the fleeing figure, only to come to an abrupt halt at a privacy fence blocking his path.

Spotting a gate, he leaped off the bike. The gate was locked or jammed, but the attacker hadn't had time to go anywhere else. Gabe scaled the wood fence. Abruptly, light flooded the small enclosure on the other side. A shape appeared in the sliding glass door holding a gun.

"Police officer! Hold it right there."

Gabe swore under his breath. From his perch on top of the swaying section of fence he saw something moving in the enclosure next door.

"A woman out front was just accosted," he told the cop. "I chased the suspect back here. He's in the yard next door."

"Get down. Slowly."

This cop already had his suspect. Gabe was dressed

in black and wearing a helmet. Until the cop knew for sure what was going on, he wasn't going to listen to anything Gabe said. Jaw clenched, he dropped to the ground, careful to keep his hands in plain sight.

"Flat on the ground," the man ordered. "Hands above your head."

With a sigh, Gabe obeyed. His helmet made the position more uncomfortable than it would have been otherwise.

"Could you at least have someone make sure Cassiopia's okay? I think she was only knocked to the ground, but I saw a knife when he took her purse."

"You know Cassy?" he asked suspiciously.

Not nearly as well as he was going to know her.

"She was just attacked out front."

He suffered through the pat-down and rose slowly when the officer told him to get up. By then they could both hear the approaching siren. The attacker had had plenty of time to disappear.

"Okay to remove my helmet?"

"No."

This man was no rookie. A helmet could be thrown.

Minutes later Gabe was relieved to see Cassiopia standing out front with a pair of neighbors. She appeared shaken, but unhurt. A marked police cruiser, lights flashing, pulled up. The female officer exchanged greetings with the man at his back.

"You can take it off now," the cop told him.

Gabe removed the helmet slowly and waited. They didn't seem to notice Cassiopia's shocked surprise at seeing him. The cop at his back spoke before she could say anything that would have landed him in handcuffs.

"Cassy, do you know this guy?"

Instead of denouncing him, she nodded.

"Gabriel Lowe. He went after the man who grabbed my purse."

Gabe sensed the officer putting away his weapon.

"You can lower your hands now."

Faces continued to appear in windows as a second cruiser joined the first. A small crowd gathered to listen while Cassiopia explained what had happened. Then it was Gabe's turn. The cops eyed his scar and treated him with wary respect as he explained his assumption that the person had gone in through the nearest gate and jumped the fence into the next yard.

"I only saw you," her neighbor stated.

A third unit pulled into the parking area.

"He's probably long gone, but we'd better do a sweep," the female officer suggested.

Eventually, Gabe was allowed to retrieve his bike from the side yard. As he walked it back to the parking lot Cassiopia strode over to him.

"You followed me home!"

"No need for thanks."

"Thank *you?*" She bristled.

"You're welcome. And you might want to lower your voice unless you want to explain to the cops how we know each other."

"You wouldn't dare!"

Gabe waited.

She fumed, but lowered her voice. "Why did you follow me?"

"To see where you were going. Do you know who attacked you?"

"Of course not! You heard me tell the police he was wearing a hooded sweatshirt with a scarf over his face."

There was no use pointing out that the one didn't negate the other.

"Is your roommate home?"

"I don't have a roommate." She blinked in sudden comprehension. "Oh. The hair dye. Betsy moved out last month. She got married."

He scowled. He didn't like thinking about Cassiopia alone and vulnerable inside that town house.

"You might want to stay somewhere else tonight."

"Why? He already got my purse. The house is safe. My keys were in my hand so he didn't get them. It all happened so fast I didn't have time to go for his eyes with them."

She would have done it, too.

"You believe it was a simple purse snatching?"

"Of cour—"

Her eyes turned to saucers. Her voice dropped even lower.

"No one knew I was going to your place tonight."

"Not even Beacher?"

"You think that was Beacher?"

Though obviously shocked by the idea, her words were barely above a whisper.

"No." Gabe shook his head decisively. "Too thin. Most likely a teenager or a woman."

"A woman!"

Gabe shrugged. "Who else knew your plan tonight?"

"No one."

Unfortunately, he believed her. "Then someone is watching you, too."

A flash of fear.

"What do you mean? Why do you assume this wasn't—?"

"Ms. Richards?"

CASSY SPUN TO FACE the approaching officer. In the woman's hand was her large cloth purse. The cut strap dangled limply.

"You found it!"

"This is yours, then?"

"Yes!"

Thank God. Gabriel had been wrong after all. It had been nothing more than a simple purse snatching.

"It was on the ground behind one of the units out back. You want to check to see what's missing?"

The bag was already open. She dug around inside a second before looking up.

"My wallet's gone." No surprise there.

"How much money did you have?"

"A twenty, two fives and seven ones." She knew the exact amount down to the sixty-seven cents in change.

"Credit cards?"

Cassiopia rattled off the name of her cards while the officer wrote the information in a small notebook.

"Driver's license?"

"No. Fortunately, I keep that in a separate folder with my health insurance card. They're still here."

The officer nodded. "You'd better notify your credit card companies right away."

"Yes. Was there any sign of the person who took it?"

"No, ma'am. I'm sorry."

So was she. Had they caught the person, Cassy

would have felt better. Gabriel's suspicions had made her jittery. When the officer finally had all the information from her and left, Cassy turned back to Gabe.

"See? Just a purse snatching."

His expression didn't change. "Maybe."

"You're trying to scare me."

"You aren't stupid."

"I'm not paranoid, either."

His lips twisted wryly, but he gazed at her with a dark frown. "You can come back to my place if you want."

The grudging offer widened her eyes. "Why?"

He remained silent.

"You don't think it was a purse snatching. You think he'll come back." What if Gabriel were right? "But I don't have anything."

"He doesn't know that."

Shaken, she shook her head. "You're in more danger than I am. You're the one holding whatever Beacher gave you."

GABE COULD SEE it was pointless to press her. He'd warned her. That was all he could do.

"I can't go with you," she insisted.

He replaced his helmet.

"I'm not afraid."

His jaw tightened. "You should be."

She stepped back on the curb as he kicked the bike to life. Cursing Beacher and everyone remotely connected to the missing toxin, Gabe turned for home.

Probably, she'd be fine. Tonight's attack could have been exactly what it appeared to be, a kid out to rob whomever fate placed in front of him.

On the other hand, it could have been something else entirely. He hoped he was wrong. He also hoped a little of his paranoia would rub off on Cassiopia. It would be a shame for all that feminine fire to end up extinguished on a morgue slab somewhere.

He didn't doubt for a moment that this was connected to what Beacher had given him to hold. His friend had some major explaining to do.

Halfway home he detoured to Beacher's apartment. He'd only been there a handful of times, but he knew which unit was his friend's. No lights showed and there was no familiar car in the parking lot.

Gabe used his cell phone and called Beacher's number anyway. The answering machine picked up on the fourth ring. Next he tried Beacher's cell phone and was immediately sent to voice mail. Gabe left pithy messages on both and text messaged his friend for good measure. There was nothing more he could do now except worry. He'd had years to perfect that ability.

As he neatened his kitchen several minutes later he debated getting the package and opening it without waiting. The size and shape were about right to hold a hard drive and a few other things, but if Beacher had found the missing toxin after all these years, surely he would have told Gabe. Either he trusted his friend or he didn't.

Gabe went down to the basement and hesitated only a second before turning away from his display room to his workroom on the other side of the stairs. He trusted Beacher. He would wait.

The nearly completed piece he'd been commissioned to do sat on one of several worktables under a cloth.

Working with his hands generally freed Gabe's mind for thinking, but he had to force his thoughts to concentrate on the rose bush and not Beacher.

The bush was proving to be a real challenge. The pair of chipmunks beneath the bush were finished to his satisfaction. So was the general shape of the bush, but Gabe had never tackled individual leaves and roses this small before.

As his fingers stroked a small petal to life his thoughts returned to Cassiopia. Not a day had gone by that he and Beacher hadn't tried to learn the truth of what had happened four years ago. Together and independently they had spoken to, or tried to speak with, everyone connected with the toxin. Beacher had always felt Cassiopia might know something useful, but it had been only recently that she'd agreed to talk with him.

Beacher was nothing if not persistent and knowing him, Gabe suspected his friend had begun to date her in an effort to get her to open up. She was an attractive woman and Beacher liked attractive women—but not enough to get himself engaged to one.

Cassiopia was definitely attractive. Slimmer now than he remembered, her features were more refined, but she hadn't lost any of that temper even if she did have it under better control.

A tiny rose blossomed to full beauty beneath his stiff fingers. Pleased, he moistened his hands and worked another.

Even if they were dating, Cassiopia should have known better than to make such a ridiculous claim. Beacher engaged? Never happen. Not even to someone as interesting as her. Beacher's little black book was filled with beautiful, interesting women. He had more listings than some telephone directories.

Gabe tackled a series of delicate leaves, marking each vein with careful precision.

How had she known Beacher had given him that package unless Beacher had told her? She'd made no secret of the fact that she'd been watching Gabe. Had she also been following Beacher?

Gabe was so used to being watched and followed he barely paid any attention anymore. Open surveillance was part of the government's harassment tactics so Gabe ignored them. That was probably why he'd never noticed her.

His finger flew as he mulled that over.

Cassiopia had implied the package contained the missing vials of toxin. Did she really believe that?

Did he?

Only desperation would have sent her into his home tonight. Surely she knew he was still being monitored by all the forces Homeland Security, the FBI and the United States Army could bring to bear on him.

Was it possible?

He screwed up a leaf in a moment of frustration and had to start again.

He would not give in to paranoia. Beacher would explain everything when he showed up. And he *would* show up. Eventually. For now, Gabe needed to keep his mind on his work.

The bush was coming together better than he'd anticipated. Rochelle Leeman would be pleased. He only hoped his creation wouldn't prove too intricate for Denny and the Bailin Brothers to mold and cast.

Gabe had been fortunate to stumble on Denny Foster when he'd gone looking for someone to teach him how to turn his sculptures into finished bronze pieces. The garrulous moldmaker had been a font of knowledge and connections.

Gabe still wasn't sure how he'd let the old man talk him into showing his work to Rochelle. Even more puzzling was how the stunning gallery owner had managed to convince him his work would not only sell, but sell for big bucks.

The trill of the telephone startled Gabe from his working concentration. The clock on the wall told him it was already 1:40 a.m.

Beacher! Finally.

He wiped his hands while checking the caller ID. A cell phone number, but not Beacher's. Gabe answered anyway.

"Lowe."

"Go ahead and say I told you so," Cassiopia began without preamble.

His stomach gave a lurch at the sound of her stressed voice. "You okay?"

"Yes. I'm outside your front door. Is your offer of a safe haven still open?"

"I'll be right up."

He disconnected and retrieved his gun from its hiding place under a nearby workbench before taking the stairs in twos. Not bothering with lights, he went to the window to check the street before going to the door. Cassiopia's car wasn't in sight and there were no unfamiliar vehicles parked along the street. Neither of those meant a thing, but only one figure was visible on his stoop. He opened the door cautiously, weapon ready.

Cassiopia stared from the gun to him.

"If you plan to shoot me, forget it. I'll go to a motel. I probably should have done that anyhow."

He yanked her inside. "You're alone?"

"No, the marching band is down the street."

"Where's your car?"

"I parked on the next street over. I didn't want anyone to see it in front of your house."

He couldn't decide if she was playing him. "Were you followed?"

"Of course not! I was watching for that."

Given her earlier performance, she wouldn't have the ability to spot a professional tail.

"Stay here."

She gripped his arm. "Where are you going?"

He gave her a hard look. She dropped her hand and followed him down the dark hall to the kitchen.

"Wait," he commanded, heading for the door.

"Sit. Stay. We're really going to have to work on your people skills."

Wanting to smile despite the situation, Gabe slipped out the back door. A thorough search of the neighborhood turned up two prowling cats, one brazen raccoon and a deer munching a neighbor's azalea bush. Cassiopia's car was exactly where she'd said it would be. There were no signs that anyone human lurked nearby.

Returning to the house, Gabe found her still standing in his kitchen muttering under her breath. Once again, she eyed the gun in his hand.

"You took long enough. I kept waiting for shots."

If it hadn't been for the slight tremor in the hand she used to pull back a thread of hair, he'd have thought her annoyed but calm. She wasn't calm. He slid the weapon into his waistband.

"Relax and tell me what happened."

"The two are mutually exclusive."

"Try."

She made a face, then sighed. "I couldn't sleep. It was your fault. I kept thinking about what you said. You know, that maybe someone would come back? So I decided to go downstairs and get a glass of wine to help me sleep. Only, instead of going to the kitchen I walked to the window that looks down on my back-yard."

She shivered.

"Someone was standing there looking up at my bed-room."

He hated that he'd been right.

"You didn't call the police?"

"I started to. I had the phone in my hand, then I realized how much attention that would focus on me."

And why would that worry her?

"I went back upstairs, grabbed a couple of things, slipped out the front door and came here."

She shivered again despite a long dark coat that exposed a pair of slim white calves. Bare feet had been stuffed into a pair of slip-on deck shoes. He couldn't help wondering exactly what she was wearing under that coat. Her hair was a loose, velvety mass that fell around her face and shoulders. In one hand she had a death grip on a plastic shopping bag. The item sticking out of the top appeared to be her broken purse.

He flipped on the kettle.

"I don't want any tea. Thank you," she added as an afterthought.

Gabe shrugged. "No wine."

"That's okay, I'm not thirsty."

He didn't want her here. Even though he'd made the initial offer, he hadn't expected her to accept and now he was stuck. He could always turn her loose. But he knew he wouldn't.

"I'll show you the spare room."

She didn't move when he turned toward the stairs.

"Are you going to bed?"

Despite the darkness he saw her trepidation. It wasn't an act. She was afraid.

"No."

"I'm not sleepy, either."

Inwardly, he cursed. "I have to work, Cassiopia."

"That's okay. I've never watched an artist work. I won't get in your way."

It wasn't okay. She *would* be in the way. She'd be a distraction and he couldn't afford to be distracted any more tonight.

He thought of several responses but dismissed them. She was scared. So was he.

Someone had three vials of a toxin so deadly it could wipe out a city full of people in a matter of hours. The knowledge had eaten at him for nearly four years. Knowing that the authorities were concentrating on the wrong suspects had made it that much worse. Few people knew that *all* the toxin and all the documentation relating to it were missing.

The removable hard drives and Dr. Pheng's research notes had vanished from inside a locked vault on the base. Only a handful of people had access to that secured area and he and Beacher had been two of those people.

They had discussed this over beers in his workroom many nights. The way they had it figured, Gabe had been the designated patsy from the start. Most likely, he'd been intended to die in the explosion along with Dr. Richards. If Major Frank Carstairs hadn't died of a heart attack that same night, maybe they could have proved their suspicions, but as things stood, they had no living suspects, no proof and no trail to follow.

"Did you call Beacher?" Gabe asked her.

Cassiopia hesitated before nodding. "He isn't answering his phones."

So she had called Beacher first—if she wasn't lying. Gabe didn't think she was lying. Her fear was real. He scowled. Reluctantly, he motioned her to follow him.

CASSY GAVE AN EXASPERATED sigh as she tailed Gabriel's broad back down the stairs. She shouldn't have come. It was obvious he didn't want her here. She had plenty of friends she could have called. Why hadn't she?

Because he'd offered. And none of her friends would know what to do if someone came after her again. She couldn't place any of them at risk.

But she could have called the police.

She turned the thought aside as she carefully picked her way down the narrow staircase in his wake. "Forget to pay your electric bill?"

He reached the bottom without making a sound.

"Sometime you're going to have to tell me how you do that."

"Do what?"

"Step on that third step without making any noise."

She suspected he smiled, although she couldn't see his expression as he led her off to the left. She'd turned right before.

His workroom was cluttered and brightly lit. Her gaze instantly fastened on the clay taking shape on the largest table and she inhaled audibly. Even incomplete, the piece was magnificent.

"You have so much talent."

Looking embarrassed, he indicated the ratty old couch and un-upholstered wood chair in the far corner of the room next to an ancient, badly scarred desk and a battered filing cabinet. Exactly what she had been looking for. But if the toxin was hidden in this room, he wouldn't have led her here now.

"I have to finish this tonight."

"Okay." She ignored his impatience and stared around curiously at the crowded workspace. "Go ahead and work. You won't even know I'm here."

RIGHT. CASSIOPIA RICHARDS was the biggest distraction Gabe could imagine. How was he supposed to work with someone in the room? Whenever Beacher came over, Gabe always stopped, got a beer from the basement refrigerator and sat down to talk with him. He didn't have that sort of time tonight.

"There's beer," he told her gruffly with a nod toward the refrigerator.

"Thanks, but what I'd really like is a bathroom."

"Through there." He indicated the door at her back. She turned, still clutching her bag, and disappeared inside. For a moment he wondered if he should have searched the bag. He dismissed that thought as true paranoia and replaced the gun under the table. He must be insane.

He was working when she finally emerged with the coat slung over one arm. Whatever she'd been wearing beneath it had been replaced by the jeans she'd had on earlier tonight and a sweatshirt. Her hair was now clipped behind her ears, flowing down her back to emphasize the graceful curve of her neck.

Right. He was going to have no trouble concentrating now.

Without a word, she crossed to the refrigerator, hesitated over the selection and came out with a bottle of imported beer. Carrying everything to the worn green sofa, she sat on a sagging cushion.

A ton of questions crowded his mind, but the clock discouraged him from starting the sort of conversation they needed to have. He'd be lucky to complete the piece tonight as it was.

True to her word, Cassiopia remained silent. At first it was disconcerting to have her watch, but amazingly, his fingers continued to work, quick and sure, while his thoughts tumbled chaotically. After a while he was lost in the rhythm of his work.

His muscles had started a serious burn of protest by the time the final rose took shape beneath the tool in his tired fingers. It unnerved him to realize Cassiopia had been right. As impossible as it seemed, he *had* been able to ignore her presence.

Looking up, he found her with her head pillowed on her coat, fast asleep. Strands of silky hair covered most of her face. The partially emptied bottle of beer was on the corner of the desk, in danger of falling at the slightest jar.

Gabe rolled his shoulders to stretch tensed muscles and washed his hands before crossing the room to rescue the beer. It was warm and flat. He was too tired to be drinking alcohol, but he finished it, watching her sleep, and tried to ignore the faint stirring of desire.

She wouldn't appreciate his interest. Cassiopia had made her opinion of him clear. She had a lot in common with a rose. Soft and lovely to look at with plenty of thorns.

He couldn't see her with Beacher. Beacher liked his women delicate, plentiful and quick to fade. The thorny ones tended to get tossed back fast. Even ones as appealing as her.

Gabe pinched the bridge of his nose and carried the empty bottle to the recycle bin. Eyeing the finished piece critically he decided it was good. It might even be one of the best things he'd done.

For a moment he debated removing the tiny bee he'd added at the last minute. Somehow, it seemed a little too symbolic sitting on a petal, staring at an unopened bud as if wishing for what it couldn't have. But knowing he couldn't remove it without disturbing the work, Gabe began cleaning up. Cassiopia never stirred, even when he ran the shower in the bathroom next door.

Dumping his dirty clothes in the washer, he wrapped a towel around his waist and called to her gently. No response. There was no way he could carry her up two flights of stairs tonight. He wasn't sure he could carry himself to bed, as tired as he felt. It was going on five and he had to be at Denny's with the bears that were currently cooling in his open kiln by eight.

In the laundry room he found a clean sheet and used it to cover her. A good host would go up and bring her down a blanket. He could live with being a lousy host.

He left a light on for her and headed upstairs. If she decided to search his basement when she woke, she wouldn't be the first. Like the others, she'd be doomed to disappointment.

Chapter Four

Cassiopia was still asleep when Gabe went downstairs to take the cooled pair of bears from the kiln. He scrawled her a note on the back of one of his sketches and left it in plain sight on top of the desk. He hoped she'd have enough sense not to return to her town house.

There hadn't been a word from Beacher and he worried all the way to Denny's place in Hagerstown. The moldmaker was pleased with the bears, but he eyed Gabe with disfavor.

"You look like hell. You sick?"

"No." Exhausted, but there was no point telling the man that the little sleep he'd gotten in the past two days barely qualified as a nap.

"How's that custom piece for Rochelle coming along?"

"I finished sculpting it last night."

"Geez, boy. No wonder you look like that. You don't have to push yourself this hard."

Gabe shrugged. "I have a deadline."

"Didn't anyone tell you artists are supposed to be eccentric? She'll expect you to be late. She knows how hard you've been working to finish the show pieces."

Gabe didn't bother to respond. He'd agreed to Rochelle's deadline, so he'd make the deadline.

"You are one hardheaded cuss, you know that? When are you picking up the ark sets from the Bailin Brothers?"

"Next stop."

Denny nodded and eyed the pair of bears. "I still think you oughta consider doing some of these in cold cast. Resins sell well to the mass market."

"They'd have to be painted."

"Not necessarily, however, I know someone who could help you there. She'd work cheap."

Gabe's lips twisted ruefully. While the old man generally gave good advice and had taught him a great deal about his new career, Denny was a little too concerned with Gabe's lack of social life for comfort. He kept urging Gabe to get out and make new friends. Gabe would take bets the female artist who would "work cheap" was single and attractive, like Rochelle.

"I'll think about it," he temporized.

"You do that, boy. Your work's too fine to be collecting dust in some basement."

The words were uncomfortably close to what Cassiopia had told him only yesterday.

He had plenty of time to worry about her and Beacher on the drive into Pennsylvania to pick up the bronzed ark pieces from Tony Bailin. Tony and his brother, Max, did first-class work when it came to casting and they'd done so once again. Gabe liked the two men and enjoyed their company, but today, he found it hard to concentrate on their friendly conversation.

He decided to stop for a late lunch on the way home and used the time to try and reach Beacher again. Still no answer. Worry had become outright concern. It wasn't like Beacher not to return phone calls. Swinging by his friend's parking lot confirmed that Beacher's car still wasn't there.

Exhaustion vied with worry that was compounded the minute Gabe walked inside his house. Cassiopia was gone. She'd written *Thanks* in rounded letters beneath his note and signed it with a *C*. The sheet he'd covered her with was folded neatly beneath the paper sitting on the desk.

He'd have been surprised to find her still here yet it worried him all the same. He checked his caller ID for the number of her cell phone. When the call switched to voice mail he hung up. She'd probably gone to work. As tired as he was, he needed to do the same. Rochelle's people were due in less than an hour to start loading the show-pieces and he hadn't yet tagged the ones that were staying.

Gabe considered opening the package first, but if it did contain the missing toxin, he couldn't take the risk. As soon as the packers left he'd try Beacher one more time and then he'd see what his friend had in there.

Rochelle's men were friendly and efficient. They'd nearly finished crating and clearing the display room when Rochelle herself arrived and greeted him with her usual exuberant hug.

"I am not letting you have both crouching lions," he warned without preamble.

Rochelle contrived to look hurt. "I didn't come here for that, but I do wish you'd reconsider. Those lions are brilliant. They exemplify you *and* your work."

"No."

"As a pair, they'd be the highlight of the show."

"No."

The flicker of annoyance was accompanied by a toss of her head. "You're just like them."

"Cold and hard?"

"Fierce and determined. Never mind. Denny tells me you finished the chipmunks."

She was giving up far too easily. Nevertheless, he made the switch with her. "The piece will go in the kiln tonight."

"Great! May I see it? Ray and Dave can finish loading while we take a quick look."

He could hardly refuse since she'd commissioned it, however, he pointed out, "You aren't dressed for the workroom."

Despite the fact that it was late afternoon, the white linen suit Rochelle wore still looked crisp and fresh and expensive. While he kept a neat workspace, if she brushed against the wrong thing she'd spot the material. On the other hand, he'd never seen Rochelle anything but perfectly turned-out no matter what she was doing. Maybe dirt was afraid of her.

"Don't worry, I'll be careful."

He knew firsthand that her cheerful, outgoing manner hid a core of solid steel. With an *up to you* shrug, Gabe led her downstairs.

He was surprised by a tension that had nothing to do with getting her suit dirty. He hung back as she strode to the table and stared at the rosebush in silence for so long his jaw ached from clenching.

"I can't give this as a wedding gift."

His stomach plummeted.

"I want it. It's exquisite."

Relief swelled in his chest as his nerves stood down.

"We need to raise your prices."

"Feel free."

She tossed him a gleeful grin. "This is your best work yet, Gabe. I love the bumblebee! Great touch. As much as I adore my aunt and her chipmunk collection, I really think I have to keep this one for myself. I'm thinking a limited edition. Maybe seven. I, of course, want the first cast."

Her features grew serious as she tore her gaze from the piece. "Now then, we really need to talk about your coming to the opening tomorrow night."

"No."

She was one of the few people who could look him in the face without flinching or staring. As she did so now, her mouth pinched in frustration.

"Gabe, the artist needs to be there. My clients like to meet—"

"No."

Her lips thinned. "Have dinner with me."

Amused, he shook his head. "Feeding me won't change my mind."

"I got that. But there's one person you simply must meet."

She held up a hand when he would have refused.

"Before you say no, hear me out. Gretchen Morrison is important to both of us. She's one of my best clients. If she takes an interest in your work you won't be able to produce fast enough."

"My *work*," he emphasized, "not *me.*"

"Gretchen is seventy-two. She's seen it all and she

isn't going to be put off by a scowl and a few scars. Trust me. She's wealthier than Midas and knows everyone there is to know on three continents. If you won't come to your opening you have to meet her tonight. She takes a personal interest in the artists she buys."

An excellent reason *not* to meet her. He already had far too many people interested in his personal life.

"I like my privacy."

"I know, but it's that important. Please, Gabe. She's stopping by the gallery at seven tonight. We'll grab an early dinner, talk about your next project and then you can stop by the showroom so I can go over how I plan to showcase the displays. You don't have to stay. Just say hello, nice to meet you, and then slip away. Please, Gabe," she repeated.

Mentally, he swore. He was dead tired but he owed Rochelle nearly as much as he owed Denny.

"I'm not doing the opening," he warned.

"I'll keep working on that, but this is more essential."

She would, too. She was like a bulldog when she wanted something. The stocky deliveryman called Dave stuck his head in the door before Gabe could refuse once more.

"We've loaded everything and we're heading out, Rochelle."

"Great. Tell Jennifer I'll be back in another hour or so."

The head vanished with a nod.

"You haven't met my new assistant, Jennifer Mackley, yet have you?" Rochelle asked as she started around the worktable.

"No." But he'd talked to the woman and was willing to take bets she was the sort who stared.

Rochelle paused to study the sketches and photographs pinned to the corkboard on the wall.

"Are these for your next project?"

He nodded. The series of wolves stared back at them.

"I want them."

He arched his eyebrow.

"Very commercial," she assured him. "They'll sell in a heartbeat." She stared at his notes. "Scale them down to no more than sixteen inches. I'm having more success with the smaller stuff right now. How soon can you get them finished? Have you thought about doing them in something other than bronze? Let's talk about it over dinner. I'm starving."

He let her sweep him outside to her silver Porsche at the curb. No car had ever looked more out of place in his quiet neighborhood. The truck and its crew were already gone. Rochelle gave him one of her exuberant hugs. His hands automatically steadied her as she leaned into him, smelling faintly of some wildly expensive perfume. He didn't feel even a stirring of desire for her.

"I'm so glad Denny found you for me. You're going to make us both very wealthy. See you at the restaurant. Is the Italian place near the gallery, okay?"

He hadn't agreed to dinner, but it was typical of Rochelle to take his assent for granted. He frowned, not wanting to go, but knowing an argument would take more time than simply going along. At his nod she climbed in and started the engine.

He'd always known Rochelle was beautiful, but until that moment, seeing her features in profile, he hadn't realized how much she reminded him of his former fiancée, Andrea Fielding. The thought was deeply un-settling. He waited until her taillights rounded the corner before he started for his bike.

THERE HADN'T BEEN TIME to run home and change before going to work when Cassy woke up in Gabe's basement, stiff from sleeping on his lumpy couch. Since she didn't have any meetings, she hoped her casual clothing wouldn't matter. Because she arrived at work so late, she clocked out late to make up the time. Not that she should have bothered showing up in the first place. She'd been too distracted all day to get any real work done.

It was almost dark when she pulled into her parking lot and eyed her town house with more than a little trepidation. Making certain no one loitered in the parking lot, she approached her front door nervously. Would she ever feel safe here again?

Of course she would. This was her home. She wasn't going to let some pervert scare her off.

As Cassy stepped inside the foyer something crunched under her shoe. Shutting the door, she flicked on the light and stared in horror at the wreckage of her home. Glass from the hall mirror near the door littered the floor. Mirrors, pictures, vases and ornaments all lay shattered amid the stuffing that had once been her trea-sured couch and chairs.

Shock left her stunned in disbelief. If it could break, it had been broken. If it could be sliced open, its fillings littered the carpeting. In the kitchen, the refrigerator and cupboards had been opened and their contents tossed. The mingled odors of spoiling food made her gag.

The person last night had done all this?

Horror gave way to fury. Marching up the stairs in rage and shock, she was inside her bedroom before the scene registered. The contents of her closet and one of her dresser drawers were scattered everywhere, but the devastation was incomplete, as if the person hadn't finished. The fully made bed looked ludicrous amid the mess. She crossed to it quickly, her hand sliding beneath the pillow, seeking the hard metal weapon she kept there.

Perhaps he made a slight noise, or maybe it subconsciously registered that her bathroom light was the only thing on in the house. Either way, Cassy sensed another presence before her eyes even lifted to the doorway across the bed from her. The figure was nothing more than a silhouette as she yanked her gun from under the pillow.

Cassy didn't realize she'd pulled the trigger until the sound reverberated in her ears.

The bullet slammed into the wall and the figure sprinted for the hall. Cassy glimpsed the blade of a long knife in one hand and fired again. The person continued to run. She started to give chase and stumbled over a pair of shoes on the floor. By the time she was on her feet again, the intruder was gone and the French door leading onto the back deck was standing open.

Fear hit her in a rush of blind panic. Cassy turned to the front door and ran for her car, shoving the gun in her coat pocket. She was halfway to Gabriel's house before she even realized that was where she was going.

Insane. She didn't even like the man, yet he represented safety.

A car horn honked loudly. Jerking the wheel, she

pulled back into her own lane, shaking all over. She was cold. So cold her teeth were chattering.

Reaction. Shock. She shouldn't be driving in this condition.

Cassy pulled the car to the side of the road and gave in to the trembling, but not the tears. She blinked back the angry moisture that filled her eyes. Who had done that to her home? Why?

She should have gone next door. Her neighbor was a cop. Neil would know what to do. Except, if he'd been home he would have heard the shots. He would have come to investigate.

And if she went to the police her employers were bound to find out. Bartlett Inc. had hired her when no one else would. As Powell Richards's daughter, she'd been tainted. No one wanted the authorities stopping by their place of business to ask her questions every few months. And no one wanted to worry about her loyalties. Only Justin Bartlett had been willing to take a chance. Cassy had done everything she could to keep a low profile and prove herself. She would not lose this job!

If she went to the police now her name alone would trigger a new investigation. A mugging was one thing, someone trashing her house afterward was going to set off all sorts of alarms. She couldn't afford to call the police even if it meant her insurance company wouldn't cover the damages.

Gabriel had been right. Someone thought she had the missing toxin. But why now, after all these years?

THERE WERE NO comforting shadows in Rochelle's brightly lit gallery. Jennifer Mackley's wide-eyed gaze of sympathetic horror was about what Gabe had expected. He wasn't surprised when she found a reason to be elsewhere as quickly as possible.

Gretchen Morrison, however, proved to be an outspoken woman with a piercing stare and a military carriage only slightly bowed with age. If Gabe had been into sculpting faces, hers would have been a must. Lined with grace and beauty, her indomitable character was clearly stamped in each feature. She stared hard at his scar and pursed lips thinned by time. She shook a head of soft, silvery hair.

"That must have hurt."

He tried not to show his surprise. Her bird-sharp gaze dropped to his hands.

"How'd you burn them?"

Amazingly, the abrupt question didn't bother him. Though his name was old news as far as the media was concerned, he had a feeling she knew exactly who he was and was testing his reaction. Years of military discipline kept him from giving her any outward reaction.

"Protecting my face."

She sniffed. "Not enough."

He nearly smiled. "No."

"Rochelle tells me you're good."

Unable to think of a suitable response, he twitched his shoulder in a tiny shrug. Approval came and went in those intelligent eyes. Gabe found himself liking the petite woman.

"Self-taught?"

He thought of his grandfather, who'd initially taught him the craft as a boy, and all the books and pictures he'd studied since therapy had opened this new path for him, but he inclined his head.

"The best usually are. We'll see."

The words were a clear dismissal. Gabe nearly went to parade rest. She turned away and began speaking with Rochelle. He gave it a minute, got on his motorcycle and slipped away while they were talking.

Beacher still wasn't answering his home, work or cell phones. Gabe wished he had a key to get into his friend's apartment. Every instinct he had was screaming that something was badly wrong. He might be able to talk his way in past the manager, but then what?

Frustrated and edgy, he changed direction, half tempted to drive over to Cassiopia's town house. That would serve no purpose, either. He'd done what he could for her.

So why was that thought so unsatisfying?

He should go home and open that package. Instead, he turned the bike toward the gym. The meal he'd had with Rochelle earlier was sitting heavily on his stomach. The package wasn't going anywhere and he wanted to give Beacher plenty of time to show up. Besides, he needed a physical release for all his pent-up frustration.

Gabe moved from machine to machine relentlessly, pushing himself until his muscles trembled with the strain and perspiration soaked his T-shirt and shorts. Even his few nodding acquaintances gave him a wide berth. A glance in the mirror after his shower explained why. His features were grim enough to make anyone think twice about approaching. His scar stood out prominently on his cheek, making him appear more dangerous and frightening than ever. No one said a word as he left the locker room.

As always, he was glad to leave the bright lights of

the gym for the welcoming shadows of the night. Though physically exhausted, he felt mentally charged. He'd work tonight. Instead of the wolf set, maybe a baying coyote. It was more suited to his mood.

He was sketching the animal in his mind as he rounded the corner of his street and saw the government car sitting out front. Fear clawed its way up his throat. He should have gone straight home. If they'd made one of their unofficial raids and found the package and it contained what he was beginning to fear it might, he was going down hard and final.

He would not believe that Beacher had set him up. If he couldn't trust Beacher there was no one left in the world he *could* trust.

Gabe swore softly. He'd refused to let Rochelle have both crouching lions for the show. Now he regretted that decision. While extremely well-disguised, the hidden compartment in the ornately carved base of the one would reveal its presence under a close examination. It would have been far better if Rochelle had been the one to find the package.

Gabe was tempted to keep driving, but that would only delay the inevitable. The military was boldly announcing their presence. Did that mean they had a warrant this time?

He drove past the two men inside the parked car and pulled around back. Going in through the kitchen, he didn't have time to remove his jacket before they were ringing the front doorbell.

He'd expected Len Sliffman, but he was startled to see his former superior officer standing there. Time hadn't been kind to Captain Bruce Huntington—now Major Bruce Huntington. The man was thin to the point of emaciation, with less hair on his close-cropped dome than Gabe remembered. The commanding lines that had once framed his mouth and eyes were now unforgiving wrinkles that gave his face a permanently sour expression. Bitter dislike still burned in the pale blue eyes that met Gabe's. Huntington viewed rules with almost religious fervor. Gabe was a frequent sinner in his eyes.

Beside him, Len Sliffman looked years younger than he actually was. Bulky with muscle rather than fat, his thatch of brown hair was neatly combed in a standard FBI cut, even though the former agent had worked with Homeland Security since its inception. He'd been part of the original team of investigators four years ago and, while expected, his presence beside the major caused Gabe's stomach to clench.

The package loomed in his thoughts as he greeted them.

"Got a warrant?"

Huntington's ramrod back stiffened. Sliffman merely shook his head. "We were hoping for conversation without doing this the hard way."

While tempted to keep them standing there, Gabe widened the opening and stepped back. The men crowded into his small hall. He didn't invite them to sit or come in any farther.

"What do you know about Cassiopia Richards?" Huntington demanded.

Gabe's relief was profound. They weren't here because of the package. He tried not to show the fact by so much as a muscle twitch. If they were asking about

Cassiopia, he must have missed a watcher outside the other night.

"She's Powell Richards's daughter."

"Don't get smart."

"You ought to try it some time." With a feral smile that was all teeth and no humor, Gabe slouched back against the wall, both to put himself in deeper shadow and because he knew his posture would infuriate Huntington.

It did. The major's scowl deepened. Hands fisted at his sides. The fact that he ignored the jibe set off a whole new set of alarms in Gabe.

"How *well* do you know her?"

Wrong question. What was going on?

"She believes I murdered her father. How well do you think I know her?"

Huntington spit the next question past a clenched jaw.

"When did you see Beacher Coyle last?"

"Nice of you to be so interested in my social life, Major, but I don't see that it's any of your business."

Fear crawled in his belly.

Huntington closed the distance between them. Gabe allowed the other man to get right up in his face. Déjà vu, except that Gabe was no longer under his command and wasn't the least bit intimidated. He forced himself to remain slouched against the wall while his brain raced to puzzle out the reason behind this line of questions.

"It became my business when he was found dead tonight, mister."

The words crashed over him. Gabe jerked upright,

nearly knocking against the major, who took a hasty step back. Horror and disbelief left Gabe mentally reeling.

"You're lying." He had to be lying.

"You didn't know."

Sliffman's quiet statement barely penetrated the dark haze filling his mind. Gabe stared unseeing at the pair while pain roared through him.

Not Beacher. God, not Beacher.

"It made the news." Huntington turned to growl impatiently at Sliffman. "How could he not have known?"

Gabe glided forward causing Huntington to take several more quick steps back.

"How?"

Sliffman stepped between them. "I'm sorry." The man's features softened. "He was murdered."

"Where have you been, Lowe?" Huntington demanded.

"Let me handle this, Bruce."

"Well, where's he been? Everyone knows he rarely leaves his house. And the two of them—"

"Shut up."

Another time Gabe might have appreciated the way Sliffman dealt with the major, but he could barely think past the talons of grief sunk deep in his soul.

No more beers and conversation to while away the hours. No more handball games at the gym. Beacher was dead. And the cause was most likely inside the package in his basement.

Beacher was dead.

He couldn't wrap his mind around it. How could Beacher be dead? The wrench of pain was intolerable.

Why hadn't he let Gabe watch his back if he was doing something dangerous?

Why hadn't he told Gabe what he was doing?

"He was on the floor in his bedroom. His throat was slit."

Gabe swayed. Sliffman reached out to steady him. Gabe battled to contain the contents of his stomach. He swallowed hard and jerked free.

Sliffman waited until he was steady before stepping back. "Powell Richards's daughter was seen running from his apartment before the police arrived."

Gabe jerked his head like a boxer who'd taken one blow too many. He tried to focus on the words.

Huntington snarled. "They aren't releasing that information, Len."

"Lowe didn't kill Coyle and we need his help."

"The hell we do! We need answers and this bastard is going to give them to us."

Beacher was dead.

"Shut up or leave, Bruce. You're only here in an advisory capacity because the military wanted someone sitting in who knew the principals. I'm in charge."

Gabe shunted his pain aside and focused on Sliffman. "What does Cassiopia Richards have to do with his murder?"

Sliffman shook his head. "We don't know. We'll ask her when we find her."

"You think she killed him?"

"Unlikely."

"Unless you helped her," Huntington added viciously.

Sliffman whirled, an oath on his lips. Gabe stopped him.

"*When* was he killed?"

"The medical examiner will have to determine the exact time of death, but it looks like sometime yesterday."

Beacher had been dead for twenty-four hours and Gabe hadn't known.

"Got an alibi, Lowe?" Huntington mocked.

Gabe forced his brain to concentrate, not feel. "No."

Creases of pleasure bracketed Huntington's features. Gabe addressed Sliffman.

"I worked all day yesterday. I didn't even go to the gym. I took a walk through the neighborhood last night instead."

"Anyone see you?"

Cassiopia. And it wouldn't take them long to learn about his confrontation with the local police at her place. However, if he told them about it now he'd be in for a long night of questioning. He needed to get downstairs and open that package first.

"It's possible I was noticed, but it was dark and I didn't stop to talk with anyone. I came home and worked until nearly five this morning. Around seven I drove to Hagerstown to drop off a piece to be molded. Afterward, I drove to Greensboro, Pennsylvania, to pick up some finished bronzes for the exhibit."

"Exhibit, huh?" Huntington sneered. "Moving up in the world?"

Gabe continued to ignore him and focused on Sliffman. "I can give you names, numbers and addresses. They can supply the times. Who found him?"

"An anonymous caller reported a disturbance," Sliffman told him.

"We're the ones asking the questions, Lowe," Huntington blustered.

Sliffman ignored him. "Coyle's apartment was tossed. Any idea what someone was looking for?"

"No." Gabe pictured his friend's pristine apartment and set his jaw. The killer had been looking for the package. Who else besides Cassiopia knew Beacher gave it to him? Had she murdered Beacher before coming to Gabe?

His mind raced. Technically he didn't *know* what was in the package, but he was walking a razor-thin line until he found out.

"When did you see Mr. Coyle last?" Sliffman asked, still calmly.

"Two nights ago. He stopped by for a beer."

"Was he upset?"

He'd been tense and agitated. Gabe had known something was wrong. He should have pushed Beacher for answers.

"What did he talk about?" Huntington inserted before Gabe could decide how to respond.

"I don't remember. He didn't stay long. He often stopped by." Which they would know from past observation. Beacher had made no secret of his friendship with Gabe despite its effect on his career. He'd lost his security clearance and been forced to resign from his job in the face of their suspicions. He'd been lucky to find another security firm that would hire him.

"He didn't seem upset?" Sliffman pursued again.

"He barely stayed long enough to finish his beer. I think he was meeting someone."

"Who?"

"He didn't say. A woman most likely." And that, too, they would know.

"His fiancée," Huntington supplied with a smirk.

Gabe couldn't mask his surprise. Cassiopia hadn't lied? He risked the proffered thread.

"He never mentioned a fiancée."

Huntington's grin was malicious. "I'm not surprised."

"Bruce," Sliffman cautioned.

"It's been on the news, Len. He might as well hear it from us. Your buddy got himself engaged to your former fiancée, Andrea Fielding."

Chapter Five

Huntington was too pleased with himself to be lying. He believed what he was saying. They would hammer at Gabe for hours if he let them. Gabe had no intention of letting them. The police would come next. Murder, after all, was their jurisdiction.

"Out."

Huntington brightened. "We can take you in right now."

Gabe nodded. "I'm done talking." Jaw clamped, he held Sliffman's gaze, letting the man see he meant every word.

"We need your help, Lieutenant Lowe."

And Gabe knew Sliffman had used his former title deliberately, reminding him of past loyalties.

"I know you don't want to consider this, but Beacher Coyle may have framed you four years ago."

Mutely, Gabe shook his head. His gaze never left Sliffman's, even when Huntington began goading him once more.

"Sure. He had the skills to rig that explosion just like you did. And he had access to the lab. Coyle could have taken the missing hard drives and research notes. He's probably been sitting on everything all this time, laughing while pretending to be your friend. He sells them to the highest bidder and walks away with your woman, your career and your reputation."

"Bruce…" Sliffman warned without looking away.

"But he screwed up, Lowe. The buyer didn't want to pay. You should see the body. Messed him up real bad."

It took every ounce of control Gabe had not to plant his fist in Huntington's face. Both men braced as he began to move. Sliffman's hand started toward his belt and the gun he no doubt had tucked there.

Gabe reached for the knob and threw the front door open before Sliffman could complete the action. Their gazes locked once more as Huntington began to bluster.

"You can't throw us out, Lowe. Under the Patriot Act we can haul your ass in right now and bury you so deep—"

"Shut up, Bruce. Let's go."

"Go? We need to search his house."

Gabe stood mute, letting his expression speak for him.

Homeland Security had lots of room to maneuver, but this situation was tricky and they all knew it. Murder was a police investigation first. Gabe had made it as clear as possible that he wouldn't cooperate with them.

He took what bitter pleasure he could from Huntington's astounded expression as Sliffman gave him a shove toward the open door.

"You can't be serious! We need to—"

Sliffman pulled a business card from an inside breast pocket. "When you've had some time, call me."

Gabe made no move to accept the extended card.

Sliffman let it fall to the floor. With a hard shove at the still spluttering Huntington, they were outside. Gabe locked the door behind them and ran for the basement. They'd be back with the police and a warrant. He had little time.

If Beacher was dead it was because he'd finally found the missing toxin, or someone thought he had. Recriminations were nothing new to Gabe, but thoughts of what he should have done and said to Beacher would haunt him forever. Beacher's death left a hollow void so overwhelming Gabe felt ill.

Ruthlessly, he pushed that aside. He couldn't change anything. But he could find the person responsible.

He raced down the stairs without light, only flicking the switch when he hit the display room door. He jerked to an abrupt stop. Heart thudding, he stared at the empty spot on the floor where one of the crouching lions should have still been waiting for him.

Blind panic assailed him before rational thought kicked in.

Rochelle!

He'd known she'd given up too easily. She'd come in person this afternoon to distract him so her men could carry both lions out to the van. She would claim her men had made a mistake but since she already had them…

Gabe reached for his cell phone then swore. By now her gallery was closed. Even if he got Rochelle to open it for him, he didn't want a witness or questions when he removed the package.

Sliffman was leaning toward believing Gabe had nothing to do with Beacher's murder, but the man was a professional. Gabe would be under constant surveillance from now on. The last thing he wanted was to draw official attention to the lions.

Swearing under his breath, Gabe used his cell phone to call Rochelle's number.

"You took both crouching lions," he told her answering machine coldly. "I want them returned, first thing in the morning. Both of them."

He was fairly certain she wouldn't return his call tonight. She'd do everything she could to keep them for tomorrow's opening.

Assuming the panel they'd built into the ebony base hadn't already been discovered, the package was safer inside Rochelle's gallery than it would be here tonight even if it meant learning the contents would have to wait.

The chain of evidence would be muddied if the lions and the package sat in a public forum for a few days. On the other hand, the person who murdered Beacher was unlikely to sit around and wait. Gabe needed to prepare for unwanted company.

Striding to the workroom he pulled down the gun and spare shells he had taped to the underside of the worktable. He owned two guns that were legally registered to him and had been for over nine years. Unless they were total incompetents, the authorities knew about them and where he kept them. He stuck this one in his belt. The shell casings went into his jacket pocket.

He was too restless and upset to work tonight, but he moved the completed rosebush to the kiln. He was heading for the stairs when there was a muffled thump overhead. Gun in hand, he silently took the stairs by twos.

A second thump and the clatter of a chair against the

dining room table was followed by a soft curse. Gabe returned the gun to his waistband and strode forward to greet his intruder.

"I'm going to have to get that window fixed."

CASSY GAVE A STARTLED YELP. Her penlight flash fastened on the immovable chest that suddenly filled the kitchen doorway. She stopped in the process of untangling her long coat from the chair.

"Gabriel! You scared me! Don't you ever use lights?"

"More often than apparently you use doors."

"That isn't funny."

"I agree."

Her heart continued to leap and thud erratically. "I didn't think you were home. I didn't want anyone to see me standing on your front porch."

"Like the police?"

The flatness in his voice raised goose bumps along her arms. This wasn't simply anger. He was furious, and from the suppressed grief she detected in his tone, he already knew about Beacher.

"You heard. I'm so sorry."

His expression didn't alter by so much as a flicker of emotion.

"You were there."

The words were cold and flat. Cassy shuddered as the horrific memory filled her mind.

"Yes." Bile rose in her throat. She'd had hours to deal with it, but she doubted she'd ever forget a single detail of that room and that smell. They were etched permanently in the wall of her mind.

"Did you kill him?"

"Of course not!"

"Why are you here?" His tone was hard, unyielding.

"Beacher trusted you. That makes you someone I can trust as well."

"One does not follow the other."

Belatedly, she recognized the cold menace in him. Like any wounded beast the lion was fully roused and poised to strike out. Cassy wasn't sure why his anger was directed at her, but she sensed that if she showed the slightest trace of fear he'd rip her to shreds.

"Save your angry lion impression for later." She hated the slight quiver in her voice. "I know you care."

"About you?"

"Hardly. But Beacher was your friend. You want to find out who murdered him as much as I do."

"You're the chief suspect."

"What?"

He ignored her startled yelp. He was serious!

"According to Homeland Security, you were seen leaving his apartment."

Who had seen her there? How had anyone known who she was? Were the authorities following her? That had been the case right after her father died, but she'd thought the shadowing had stopped a long time ago.

"You can't really believe I had anything to do with his murder."

"You'd be surprised by what I believe."

The beam bobbled in her hand. It was shaking. *She* was shaking. She couldn't afford to let his rage get to her.

"I had nothing to do with Beacher's murder. I went to him for help."

"Why?"

Exasperation filled her. "Because of what happened to my house! I've been calling him for days."

And Beacher had been dead at least some of that time. She was angry and scared and tired of being afraid.

"Believe what you want. I drove to his apartment and a couple leaving let me into the building. I was determined to make him talk to me. He didn't answer when I knocked so I tried the handle. The door was unlocked."

She drew a deep breath and tried for calm as the images surged forward. "His place looked like mine, it had been torn to shreds. He was there." She shuddered. "Dead."

"What do you mean—? Never mind. Why come here?"

"I don't know where else to go."

Did he have any idea what it had cost her to admit that? He studied her from the shadows. She was still prey.

"Bad choice," he told her finally. "My house is under surveillance."

Fear fluttered in her chest. He reached for her arm and she realized she'd swayed. She felt the warmth of those firm fingers even through her coat and sweatshirt.

"Come on."

"Where?"

"Away from here."

Well that was clear as mud, but his steely grip left her little choice. He hauled her into the kitchen and released her to open a cupboard. Taking down an opened box of cereal, he dumped half a box's worth of contents into the sink and turned on the disposal. Then he plunged his hand inside the empty box. He withdrew a white envelope that appeared stuffed with cash and shoved it into a pocket.

"Wait here."

Cassy shivered as the past forty-eight hours began crashing down on her. She should leave, but before she could make her legs carry her to the back door he returned.

"Put this on." He held out a man's jacket. "Hurry."

Arguing seemed inadvisable in the face of that grim countenance. She took off her coat and remembered her gun. As he glanced out the back door, she moved it from the pocket of her coat to the jacket pocket, marveling that she was responding without questioning him. Why did he want her to wear the jacket? What was he doing? What was *she* doing? She should leave, but she dropped her coat on the table.

"Let's go."

"Where?" she repeated, tugging on the jacket. His only response was to tell her not to make another sound.

His urgency was contagious. While her mind questioned everything, renewed adrenaline filled her. She'd already been scared. His tension invited a sense of near panic.

"No noise," he warned.

He opened the back door without a sound and reached for her hand. Cassy welcomed his warm touch against her icy skin. Her teeth chattered as he closed and locked the door before leading her into the vast shadows covering his yard.

Cassy couldn't see a thing. A horde of people could have stood there and she wouldn't have known. Clouds obscured what light the night sky might have offered and they were too far from the street and other houses for those lights to reach back here. But apparently lions could see in the dark.

When he stopped moving she bumped into him. He steadied her and she realized his motorcycle was in front of them. He pressed a finger lightly to her lips to indicate continued silence. Then he placed her hand on the back of his jacket. What was he doing?

Gabriel began to roll the motorcycle across the grass of his yard. That made no sense. There was a waist-high fence behind his house. She knew. She'd climbed the thing tonight. She'd found no gate, yet he was heading straight for the fence.

One of them was crazy and she was pretty sure it was her. What was she doing here?

Where else could she go?

She stopped when he stopped. He turned toward her and lowered his head. For a split second she had the insane notion that he was about to kiss her. Her heart skipped a beat but he rested his lips against her ear.

"Hold this."

She quivered as he handed off the heavy weight of the motorcycle to her. It was all she could do to keep it from toppling when he moved away. The clean scent of him seemed to linger on the night air.

She was definitely going insane.

Cassy couldn't see what he was doing, almost noise-lessly, there in the dark, but abruptly Gabriel returned, took the weight of the bike back from her cold fingers and wheeled it through a peeled back section of wood fencing. Cassy followed. Once again she waited with the bike while he replaced the fencing.

She wanted to tell him her car was parked another street over, but she couldn't bring herself to break the silence. They had reached the corner of the yard between two brightly lit houses when a tremendous explosion ripped apart the stillness of the night.

Cassy whirled. Flames licked hungrily at the upstairs window of Gabriel's house.

"Hurry!" he commanded, plopping a helmet on her head.

Her shocked body obeyed automatically. They ran with the bike to the street. She expected Gabe to jump on and start it the minute they reached the pavement, but they continued moving until they came to the street corner. A dim streetlight cast faint shadows from the trees overhead. Only then did he swing onto the bike.

"My car—"

"No."

There was no arguing with that tone and this didn't strike her as a good time to mention that she'd never ridden a motorcycle in her life. She let him haul her up roughly behind him and threw her arms around his waist. Her feet found their place as he started the engine with a deafening roar. There was nothing to do but close her eyes and hold on tight as they tore down the deserted street.

Her thoughts spun, as chaotic as the ride itself. Once they hit the main street he weaved between cars as if they were nothing more than an obstacle course.

Before she realized his intent, they were on the interstate heading south. All she could do was concentrate on staying on the bike. Death seemed the most likely outcome of this crazed ride, but since there was nothing she could do to prevent it, she closed her eyes and prayed the end would be relatively painless.

By the time he pulled onto city streets once more, her entire body felt as numb as her mind. It was anticlimactic when he finally stopped near the entrance to a motel parking lot. She thought they were somewhere in Virginia but she wasn't sure.

"The scars make me noticeable. You're going to have to rent the room. One room. Ask for the ground floor."

One room? That penetrated. If he thought she was sharing a bed with him he was in for a rude surprise. Even as she formed an appropriate protest, he shoved several bills in her hand.

"One night, in cash."

"They'll want a credit card."

"They won't care as long as you pay up front."

He swung her off the bike, scooped the helmet off her head and placed it on his own.

"Go."

Cassy went. What else could she do? She was terrified, confused and too exhausted to think straight. Had he blown up his own house as a diversion? The very thought terrified her.

The two clerks behind the counter were young, female and friendly. Cassy heard herself explaining she and her boyfriend had been robbed while on their way home to Pennsylvania. The women were so nice she felt guilty, but she took the emergency supplies they offered including combs, toothbrushes and toothpaste.

Outside, Cassy handed Gabriel one of the key cards. She couldn't see his features behind the helmet, but she thought he was eyeing the items in her hand.

"What was that all about?"

"I told them we were robbed. They gave me some supplies."

He made no comment and she allowed him to haul

her back up on the bike. He steered them around to the rear of the building where a more dimly lit entrance led inside. The room itself seemed cramped, dwarfed as it was by the huge bed. A scarred table sat between two coarsely stuffed armchairs in front of the bank of windows. Cassy collapsed gratefully into the nearest chair, relieved to be sitting on something that didn't move.

Gabriel immediately closed the drapes. He prowled the room like a stalking beast, checking the bathroom and the small wardrobe. Did he expect someone to jump out at them? Finally satisfied, he tossed his helmet on the bed and finished surveying the room critically.

"Aren't you going to check under the bed, too?"

He glared at her. Cassy didn't care. She was beyond intimidation now. "You want to tell me what happened back there?" she demanded.

His scowl raised the hairs on her arms.

"The house blew up."

That said, he disappeared into the bathroom, closing the door with an audible snap.

As a conversational stopper the move was effective. It also reminded Cassy that her bladder had been shaken thoroughly. She stared at her reflection in the mirror over the dresser. No wonder the clerks hadn't questioned her story. Shadows rimmed eyes that were sunken with fatigue and fear. Her skin had a pallid, blotchy look while her hair was a tangled, listless mop. The ill-fitting black suede jacket was twin to the one Gabriel was wearing. Both were perfectly suited to riding a motorcycle for miles.

Gabriel came out a few minutes later and she seized

the room for her own needs without comment. She was a mature adult. A chemical engineer with a Ph.D. She'd escaped an attacker twice, seen the mutilated remains of a man she'd known briefly and now she was running from the authorities. Sharing a room for the night with a man who didn't even like her would be a piece of cake.

As long as it was on her terms.

She checked the coat pocket to be sure she still had her wallet and the nine-millimeter semiautomatic she'd purchased after her father had died. Once it had given her a measure of security to learn how to use the weapon even though she'd never really expected to need the knowledge.

If Gabriel Lowe thought he had some helpless little woman on his hands, he was in for a surprise.

After running a wet cloth over her face and doing what she could with one of the combs, Cassy decided it was time to face the lion in *their* den.

The room was empty.

She allowed panic to have its moment until she spotted his helmet in the center of the bed. Surely he would have taken it with him if he weren't planning to return. Either he'd gone out to his bike for something or—

The door swung open. Cassy jumped. Her hand went to her coat pocket. Gabriel stepped inside juggling an ice bucket and several canned drinks from the vending machine they'd passed down the hall.

"Limited choices. They don't run to beer or wine."

She expelled a breath and released her grip on the gun while he set everything on the table. He took a glass, added ice and popped the tab on a can of apple juice.

"Have a seat."

"Enough is enough!" She gave him her darkest glare. "I suppose you mean that to be a step up from 'sit.'"

She'd surprised him. Good.

"Did you blow up your house as a diversion?"

She tried not to cringe at the sweep of fury that crossed his face. He gripped the glass in his hand. It was easy to imagine he was picturing her neck there instead.

"No." He took a long swallow of his drink.

"But you knew it was going to blow up."

"No."

"Then why did you rush us out of there right before it happened?"

He folded into the chair nearest the corner without responding. His silence was every bit as unnerving as he probably intended it to be.

"Okay. Enough! I mean it! I'm suitably in awe of you, all right? You can skip the one-syllable answers. They aren't going to raise my fear quotient any higher. I think I topped out when you pulled onto the interstate."

She was positive she saw a flicker of amusement before his eyes returned to their usual impenetrable stare.

"Please sit down and join me," he offered dryly.

"Much better."

Weak-kneed, she took the opposite chair and reached for the can of diet cola. She was proud of the fact that her fingers barely shook at all. She added ice to the second glass and poured the cola over top. He waited until she finished taking a swallow before speaking.

"Tell me what happened," he demanded.

"It was your house."

"To Beacher," he amended.

Cassy took another hasty swallow. The fizzy drink

nearly made her choke. Images of the blood-soaked body caused the trembling to start again. Pretending to be detached was beyond her. She would forever remember the stench of death.

"I didn't recognize him. His throat… There was so much blood. He was on the floor in his bedroom." She swallowed hard.

"Why did you leave my house this morning?"

Cassy scrambled to follow the question. "I was late for work. Your note didn't say when you were coming back."

"You worked all day?"

"I even stayed late to make up lost time. I'm in the middle of an important project right now and… It doesn't matter. I'm rambling."

"You went to Beacher's after you left work?"

"No! No," she amended less shrilly. She took a calming breath before continuing. "I went home. I know it was stupid," she agreed before he could point out the obvious, "but I needed to change clothes. I figured it was long odds that anyone would still be there."

He stilled. "You were wrong?"

She nodded bleakly. "The house was trashed, like Beacher's apartment and…"

"What was he looking for, Cassiopia?"

She clenched the glass more tightly. "It all comes back to that missing toxin, doesn't it?"

Gabriel scowled. "Why would anyone believe you had it after all these years?"

"I don't know."

"Not good enough."

Exhaustion tugged at her. Beacher had finally convinced her that Gabriel might be innocent. His death seemed to confirm that. Either she trusted this grim-faced man or she didn't.

"I think it must be because of Beacher."

"Your fiancé?"

She hated that he was baiting her.

"You know he was never my fiancé."

Gabriel inclined his head. For the first time, Cassy realized he'd turned off all the lights except the one on the table between them. While she'd been in the bathroom he'd positioned his chair so his features were mostly in shadow, as usual. That got on her remaining nerve.

"You really are into this whole creature of the night thing, aren't you?"

"What?"

She waved a hand to encompass the room. "Mood lighting. Shadows to give you a more sinister appearance, a surfeit of silence. What is it with you, anyhow? I've seen your scars, Gabriel. Impressive. Now get over it or go find a decent plastic surgeon. We've got bigger problems. I told you, I passed my scare quotient for the day."

She was pretty sure she saw respect in his eyes.

"Beacher found the vials, didn't he?" she continued. "He found them and gave them to you. Do you know what will happen when the fire department puts water on that fire back at your place?" She couldn't prevent another shudder. "Because I don't, but I can make a guess. They said that stuff multiplies and releases in liquid. If the toxin was in your house—"

"It wasn't."

Relief was a wave that nearly left her giddy. "Beacher didn't find the vials?"

"I don't know."

She slumped. "I was so sure. He looked so excited the last time I talked to him. He wasn't answering my calls so I assumed he took whatever he found to you."

For what felt like a long time Gabriel regarded her. She could almost hear his mind whirling.

"Not to the authorities?"

That gave her pause. "I don't know. I didn't even consider that possibility, but you're right, he would have gone to the military or Homeland Security, wouldn't he?"

"No."

There was no compromise in his tone.

"Why do you think he found anything, Cassiopia?"

"He's dead, isn't he?"

She could have bitten her tongue. She sensed the well of his grief even though it was impossible to read his stern features.

"I'm sorry. I didn't mean—"

"He gave me a wrapped package," Gabriel acknowledged before she could finish her apology, "but it wasn't in the house tonight."

"Where is it?"

"Safe."

"Stop with the cryptic! Did he find the toxin or not?"

"I don't know."

He spread his hands to forestall the blistering words forming on her lips.

"He gave me a package and asked me to hold it without questions. He said he'd explain when he came back."

"You didn't peek?"

"No."

Of course not. She was starting to understand that

Gabriel had a rigid code of honor. Beacher was his friend. Gabriel wouldn't have looked inside without permission.

"I went to check it after I learned he was dead and it was gone."

Panic clawed her throat. "Someone took it?"

"In a manner of speaking. I know where it is."

"Where?"

His expression didn't change. "Later."

"Don't you dare go all cryptic on me again!"

He hesitated a beat.

"Why should I trust you?"

Chapter Six

Satisfied he had her complete attention, Gabe nodded. "Someone is playing for keeps."

"I know that!"

"Do you really?"

"I *saw* what they did to Beacher."

He leaned back in his chair, thrusting aside his guilt and anger.

"Did you call the police?"

"Of course I did! I couldn't just leave him lying there. I called them from my car anonymously."

"From your cell phone."

"Yes, why?"

Gabe didn't bother to answer. The police hadn't needed an eyewitness to her presence at the murder scene. She'd told them she was there with her cell phone call. With a grimace, he changed the subject.

"You said someone trashed your house. Why didn't you call the police tonight? Or your neighbor, the cop."

She looked at him wearily. "Because after that man came out of the bathroom—"

He straightened, leaning forward. "He was still there?"

"Yes. This guy came out of the bathroom in full ninja attire. I nearly had a heart attack. He hadn't finished trashing my room or he'd have found the gun under my pillow. That's why I didn't end up like Beacher."

Gabe stared at her. "You shot him?"

"*At* him," she corrected. "I'm a lousy shot. He ran and so did I. If Neil had been home he'd have heard the shots and come running. He didn't and the truth is, I panicked. I just wanted to get away."

He believed her. Cassiopia was full of surprises. He never knew what she was going to do or say next.

"You're sure it was a man?"

"In that outfit it could have been an alien from Mars. The person was thin but I couldn't even tell you how tall he was."

As descriptions went, it sucked.

"Look, I'm sorry, okay? My goal was to get away. We need to see what Beacher gave you."

"It's out of reach until tomorrow."

"Why?"

He didn't answer, still not sure how much he wanted to tell her. "Why do you think he found the missing vials?"

"Don't you?" Cassy closed her eyes. "Beacher's been after me to talk to him for years now. I wouldn't because…"

"He was my friend."

She sighed. "Frankly, yes. Everyone believed the two of you were guilty and so did I. Do you have any idea how hard it is for me to believe my father was capable of taking something that deadly from his lab in the first place? The authorities implied someone might have been threatening to harm me to coerce him, but no matter what pressure or incentive was brought to bear on him, I would have said he was incapable of such a thing. Yet they are convinced he was the only one at Sunburst who could have removed those things from the vault."

Gabe knew security had been tight at the lab. He'd gone over the procedures himself. Her father must have been the one who removed the vials and the backup hard drive.

"Your father had no ties to any known terrorist group, no bones to pick with the government, so he would have needed a compelling reason to commit an act of treason."

His agreement rocked her back.

"But *would* he have taken the toxin to protect you?"

Her face pinched in pain. "My mother died of a heart attack two weeks before this happened. Dad was devastated. All we had left was each other. As much as I don't like admitting the possibility, I believe he would have done just about anything to keep me safe." She held up a palm. "Anything except steal something like this for a group of terrorists. I cannot—will not—believe he'd do something like that without telling someone in authority."

Gabe tensed. "Me."

"Yes. No!" She took a calming breath. "Dad didn't know you. If someone had threatened me he'd have gone to the head of security at Sunburst Labs."

"Arthur Longstreet?"

Cassy started to nod and stopped. "Arthur Longstreet was new then. I forgot. Frank Zimmer retired before Mom died. I don't think my dad knew the new man very well."

"And he didn't know me."

"No, but he knew Major Carstairs and Dr. Pheng."

"You think he went to Pheng?"

"Dr. Pheng said no when the authorities asked him."

"And Major Carstairs wasn't around to ask anymore."

Cassiopia stared at him.

"How well did your father know Carstairs?"

"They weren't close friends. I know they belonged to the same golf club and played together a few times."

"And Pheng?"

"Dad and Dr. Pheng went to school together."

Pheng wasn't particularly tall, but he was lean and athletic for his age.

"If someone did threaten me, Dad would have wanted protection. Dr. Pheng couldn't have arranged that, so I think he would have called the major."

"And Carstairs would have called me," Gabe agreed.

"Did he? Is that why you went there that day?"

Gabe fell silent. The major might well have ordered him to go to her father's home if there had been a threat, but there were other things he would have done as well and he hadn't.

Gabe leaned farther back into the shadows. He worked to keep emotion from his face and his voice.

"I don't remember anything about that day."

Cassiopia stared in shock. "Nothing?"

"No."

He'd hoped the hard, inflexible tone of his voice left no room for discussion. He should have known better.

"I find that hard to believe."

"So does everyone else," he agreed grimly.

"I've heard of severe trauma bringing on amnesia, but I never met anyone with such a condition."

"Guess I'm your first."

A hint of color deepened her cheeks.

"My dad wouldn't remove those vials and the research from the lab even to protect me."

"Unless he was ordered to do so."

The flat words lay between them.

"By Major Carstairs?"

"The major should have notified me immediately and sent reinforcements if there was a threat. He should have alerted the base commander and my direct supervisor. Homeland Security would have been alerted. None of that happened."

"Because he had a heart attack!"

"Not until after your dad's house exploded."

Cassiopia inhaled sharply. "Are you saying the major had something to do with the theft?"

Gabe picked his words carefully. "I think his death would have been a lot more suspect if Carstairs hadn't recently been diagnosed with heart trouble. He was up for promotion and instead he was going to wash out. You know there are drugs that can be used to encourage a fatal heart attack. Drugs that wouldn't necessarily show in an autopsy unless someone went looking for them."

Cassiopia looked stunned. "You're saying he was murdered? By who?"

"The same person who stole the vials, the hard drives and the research notes."

Cassiopia fell silent for several seconds. "Did you ever wonder about Beacher?"

"No," he lied. Because he *had* wondered at first. Trust

had been impossible for a long time after Gabe had regained enough sense to understand what had happened.

"I know you're friends—were friends—but hear me out. What if Beacher *was* involved? What if that's why he stayed so close to you all these years?"

"No."

"When we talked he suggested my father might have pretended to steal the vials and the research and switched them, hiding the real toxin."

Gabe nodded. "We discussed the possibility. If someone threatened you and he took the threat seriously and called Carstairs, it's possible Carstairs ordered your father to bring everything back to the base."

"Wouldn't he have told you?"

"Unless Carstairs convinced him not to inform me."

Cassiopia shook her head. He didn't blame her. It seemed far-fetched to him as well, but not impossible. Carstairs had left the base during her father's unaccounted hours and returned before suffering his fatal heart attack. No one knew where he'd gone or why.

"If Beacher did find the missing vials, would he give them to you to hold instead of telling you and calling in the authorities?"

Gabe had been asking himself the same question.

"I don't know," he admitted. "Locating the toxin wouldn't be enough. Beacher would want to prove who was behind the theft and why."

She chewed on her lower lip. "Because otherwise you both still looked guilty?"

"Yes."

"He could have been," she added softly.

He knew she saw his anger. "No."

"Let's not go back to one-syllable responses. He was your friend. You trust him. I got that. Let's say you're right—"

"How do you know he found anything?" Gabe interrupted. "The package he gave me could contain anything."

"Neither of us believes that. Why all this sudden interest in the toxin?"

Gabe snorted, "There's no sudden interest. Everyone has been looking for answers since the day it disappeared."

"But no one broke into my apartment or started killing people until now."

Gabe was tempted to contradict her, but these incidents must mean Beacher had become a threat to someone.

"Were you romantically involved with him?"

Her head jerked up. "No!"

"Beacher was drawn to attractive women."

"I suspect there's a compliment in there somewhere, but Beacher and I were not *involved*." Ruefully, she added, "He tried that approach early on."

Gabe nearly smiled at the annoyed censure in her voice. Beacher had probably come away with scorch marks.

"Besides, according to the radio, he actually was engaged."

His amusement dissolved. "No."

She hesitated. "Andrea Fielding was *your* former fiancée, wasn't she?"

"Yes."

"The radio said she was his fiancée."

He shook his head. "No way. Beacher never liked Andrea. The dislike was mutual."

"Well, she must have told someone they were engaged or else where did the rumor come from?" Her eyes widened. "That's why you thought my attacker might have been a woman."

"Andrea was Dr. Pheng's lab assistant."

"That's right!" Her excitement mounted. "Do you think she was behind the theft?"

It was a possibility he and Beacher had discussed many times. "Andrea is impulsive. She came under intense scrutiny due to her position and her relationship with me. She could have been involved, but she couldn't have planned something like this and there's never been a shred of proof against her or anyone else."

"But do *you* think she was involved?"

"I don't know," he hedged. "I wouldn't rule it out." She'd been quick enough to distance herself from him after it went down. "Why do you think Beacher found the toxin?"

Cassiopia set down her glass but didn't release it. "Because I think I told him where to look."

"What?"

"Beacher's a hard person to ignore. I mean, he was."

This wasn't the first time she'd referred to him in the present tense. Gabe still did it himself, but if she'd killed Beacher or been involved in his murder, she wouldn't have any trouble thinking of him in the past tense.

"When I finally agreed to talk to him, Beacher asked me all sorts of questions about my dad. What he liked to do, places he liked to go. You know Dad clocked out early that day. There's a two-hour window that can't be accounted for. Everyone assumes he passed the vials to someone during that time frame."

"Me."

"Yes. But Beacher felt he'd passed off fakes instead and hid the real toxin and research."

"I know. We discussed it." That had been Beacher's favorite theory.

"Yes, but all your assumptions were based on my dad taking the stuff from the lab. What if he didn't? What if the toxin never left the lab?"

Immediately, Gabe shook his head. "Investigators turned that place inside out."

"I know, but—"

"If you're thinking your father switched the toxin with something else, he didn't. They checked everything he had access to and things he didn't. *Someone* would have found the toxin or the hard drive by now."

"True—if they'd stayed in the lab itself. But the facility was adding a wing back then. Dad used to go down to the new gym on his lunch hour and watch them work. When I mentioned that to Beacher, he got this stunned expression."

"No. We talked about that new wing," he refuted. "Every stone, every person working at that construction site was checked and double-checked."

"Right. But did they search the gym?"

Gabe gaped at her.

"Beacher asked me if Dad went to the construction area for any reason. I didn't know. He never mentioned it. Then he asked me what else Dad liked to do on his lunch hour, who he ate with, what sort of exercise equipment he liked best, things no one else has ever asked about."

Why hadn't Beacher mentioned this? Gabe ran his finger up and down the side of his glass of melting ice.

Tempering his rising excitement was difficult. This was the first new lead they'd had in years. Why hadn't Beacher said something?

"That building was searched thoroughly," he told her, thinking it through.

"Sure, but the gym? How much time would anyone spend in there? I mean, where would you hide something in a room full of machines that people use every day?"

"Precisely. Even if your father found a hiding place in there, would he take such a chance?"

Cassiopia shook her head. "I don't know. I never wanted to believe he took the stuff from the secured area in the first place. I can only tell you Beacher thought I'd hit on something."

"So do I," he agreed carefully. "At least, it's an angle no one else ever considered."

"That's why we need to know what's in that package he gave you."

"Yes."

Gabe could find Rochelle and make her let them into the gallery even at this hour. But his original argument still held. The last thing he wanted was to draw attention to the package.

"We can't get it until tomorrow."

"Why not? Where is it?"

Gabe saw no harm in telling her at this point. "Inside one of my pieces at a gallery in Olde Towne, Alexandria."

It was Cassiopia's turn to gape. Embarrassed, he gave a diffident shrug. "They're showcasing my work tomorrow."

"I was afraid all your work was destroyed in the explosion."

He thought with regret of the rosebush and chipmunks. Maybe the kiln had protected the piece. It hardly mattered now.

"I can't believe you hid something like that in one of your sculptures! Are you out of your mind? What if someone finds it?"

He ran a hand tiredly over his jaw. "For one thing, we don't know what Beacher found and, for another, it isn't in the sculpture itself. There's a concealed drawer in the base."

And just in case something happened to him before they got it, someone needed to know where the package was.

"Why would you give it to the gallery?"

Gabe sighed. He was more tired than he wanted to admit. "I didn't. Rochelle wanted both pieces for the show. She kept me distracted while her men took them out to the van."

"Who is Rochelle? Could she be after the toxin?"

Gabe didn't even have to consider that. "No."

"Then why would she take something without permission?"

"She wanted the large pair of lions to be the centerpiece of the exhibition. I only agreed to exhibit one, but Rochelle likes to have her own way." He curbed his annoyance.

Cassiopia brooded over that. "I guess it's just as well. Otherwise the toxin might have exploded along with your house. But why would anyone blow up your house?"

"Good question. First thing tomorrow morning I'll go and—"

"*We'll* go. What gallery?"

He thought about arguing, but it wasn't worth it at this point and there was no reason not to tell her. "First Impressions."

"I've heard of it."

Cassiopia covered a yawn. Gabe noticed the lines of fatigue on her face. He felt the pull himself.

"We should get some rest. We need to be up and moving early."

Her glance flew to the bed and back to him.

"I said rest, not sex." Even if she was the first woman since his accident to stir his libido.

She met his gaze squarely with a hint of humor. "So blowing up the house wasn't just a ploy to get me into bed?"

He could learn to like this woman and her tart tongue. "Maybe next time."

Her expression went from playful to serious again. "How did you know to rush us out of there tonight?"

"I didn't." Gabe rolled his shoulders, which were tight with renewed tension. Fatigue was making him sluggish. "The house was being watched, Cassiopia. When you showed up it seemed prudent to get you out of there right away. I suspected Sliffman was coming back with a search warrant. Whoever he left on surveillance must have seen you climbing through my window."

"Oh." She pushed at a strand of hair. "So who blew it up?"

"I don't know. We'll try to find out tomorrow."

"Okay." Cassiopia stood abruptly. "Which side of the bed do you want?"

She wasn't as indifferent as she wanted him to

believe. That pleased him. If things had been different he might have enjoyed getting her into bed for an entirely different reason.

"Take your pick," he offered.

"This side."

That would put him closer to the door, which was all to the good. If someone came in, they'd have to go through him first.

"Sleep under the covers," he told her, "I'll stay on top."

"That isn't necessary. I trust you."

He raised his eyebrows.

"With my virtue," she amended. "I know you aren't interested in me *that* way."

He stood slowly. Deliberately he let his gaze sweep over her body. "You know nothing at all."

Her lips parted on a silent *oh* of surprise. The pink deepened to red. He didn't know what had prompted him, but he regretted the impulse immediately.

"I told you before, I'm not a rapist, Cassiopia."

"I haven't forgotten. And I'm sure you haven't forgotten I shot at my last attacker."

His eyes crinkled. "You did mention you're a terrible shot."

"Not at close range."

He let his lips curve then. "Truce."

"Absolutely. You should smile more often. You're really not bad-looking when you aren't hiding behind your scar and that glare. I'll use the bathroom first."

Astounded, Gabe watched her stride into the bathroom and close the door. Cassiopia was one surprise after another. Too bad they hadn't met five or six years ago. Except she'd have been too young for him to notice back then.

She wasn't too young now. Good thing he was scarred and jaded. This looked as if it were going to be a long night.

Chapter Seven

Cassy hadn't expected to fall asleep almost the minute she closed her eyes, but she never heard Gabriel come to bed. It was disconcerting to wake and find him watching her from the opposite side of the bed.

His expression was curious, almost tender. He looked years younger with his features relaxed like that. Without thought, she reached out and lightly touched his scar. Instantly, the mask was in place. He rolled off the bed with feline grace.

"Are you one of those people who wake up quick or slow?" he demanded.

She sat up, cursing her stupidity and his manly sensitivity. "When there's a man in my bed, I wake up fast."

Humor touched his eyes. "I think anything I say to that will simply get me in trouble."

"Smart man."

"We need to get moving."

"What time is it?" But she'd already spotted the bedside clock.

"Six thirty-four."

"You've got eyes in the back of your head?"

"Looked at my watch a second ago. You want the bathroom first?"

"Yes." She scrambled out of bed and hurried to the bathroom door, where she paused.

"You know, your scars aren't nearly as off-putting as you'd like to believe." And she stepped inside and closed the door before he could respond.

Showering was probably fruitless since she'd have to put her dirty clothes back on for the third day in a row, but she needed to feel her skin was clean at least.

The events of yesterday had taken on a nightmarish quality of unreality. It suddenly struck her that neither one of them had a home to return to now. She was angry and sad over the loss of a few irreplaceable treasures, but Gabriel had lost far more. She tried hard not to think about Beacher.

Gabriel was a thoughtful male. Not only had he let her use the facilities first, the toilet seat was down and the room was tidy. Although she hadn't heard him, he must have taken a shower last night. Damp towels had been folded neatly and stacked. The tub and shower had been wiped down. The military had left more marks on him than scars and a shattered life. It pained Cassy to think she'd spent so many years hating the wrong man.

The thought stopped her. When had she decided for sure that Gabriel was innocent? Beacher had opened her mind to the possibility, but she couldn't point to any one thing as the defining moment. Still, somewhere along the way the lion image had taken hold and she'd begun to view him as a trapped beast, caged by forces beyond his control.

In a few hours they could be in possession of a

deadly toxin that could wipe out thousands. It was a chillingly sober thought.

Once again the bedroom was empty when she emerged. This time she scanned the room until she spotted his helmet on a chair. She opened the door when she heard the card key in the lock. Gabriel held a tray with steaming cups, breakfast rolls and fruit.

"A woman could get used to this, you know."

His eyebrows arched. There was a flash that was definitely humor in those soft brown eyes.

One cup held hot water, the second coffee. A third cup contained orange juice. Cassy reached for the thick black brew as soon as he set the tray down. Taking a careful sip she let the caffeine seep into her bloodstream.

His lips quirked. He added a tea bag to the second cup and carried it with him into the bathroom. "I'll be ready as soon as I shave."

"With what? A pocketknife?"

"They had disposable razors at the desk."

"Ouch. Aren't you going to eat something?"

"I had oatmeal and juice while you were in the shower."

Of course he had. She almost asked how he'd known she hadn't wanted oatmeal as well, then shuddered at the thought and selected a cream-cheese-and-raspberry Danish. Gabriel closed the bathroom door.

After the toilet flushed she called out to him. "What time does this gallery open?"

Gabriel opened the door. "I've no idea, but I want to be there when Rochelle arrives."

"She's the owner?"

"Yes."

Unselfconsciously, he lathered his face from a tiny

shaving can and opened the packaged razor. Cassy knew she should move away, but she watched with genuine curiosity as the blade carved a swath through the foam. She'd never watched a man shave before, but having nicked her legs often enough she was impressed, even if it did feel uncomfortably intimate.

"Any chance we can pick up some clean clothing first?"

"At this hour?"

He had a point.

"See if you can find a newscast," he suggested.

"Sure. I'd rather not be standing here when you slice yourself with that thing."

The words reminded her of Beacher's throat gaping like a second smile. Queasy enough to lose the Danish she turned away, thankful for something to take her mind from that image. She located the television remote. A local station actually carried news at this ungodly hour and she settled in the chair with her coffee, halfheartedly listening to the troubles of the world. Minutes later, she was jerked out of her complacency when a blazing house came on-screen.

"Recapping our top stories this morning, an explosion inside a house in Frederick, Maryland, took the life of an unidentified man late last night. Police are not saying—"

"Gabriel!"

"—what caused the blast—"

He appeared silently beside her as a camera panned over the remains of his house.

"—that brought neighbors pouring from their homes in this quiet suburban community, but a possible gas leak has not been ruled out. A three-car pileup on the inner loop of the Beltway has left…"

She rounded on him. "I thought we were alone!"

"So did I."

He wiped the remaining traces of foam from his face with a towel and strode back to the bathroom. Cassy hurried after him.

"Then who was killed?"

"Did you notice the two men standing off to one side when the camera panned across the scene? The tall one was Len Sliffman with Homeland Security."

Her stomach gave a lurch. "I remember him."

"The one in uniform was Major Bruce Huntington."

She hadn't noticed either man but both identifications chilled her. There had been a Captain Huntington who'd had something to do with base security four years ago. She didn't think she'd ever spoken with him.

"We didn't turn on any lights in the house last night," he pointed out. "I suspect whoever was watching came to investigate after you climbed through the window. He must have set off the explosion."

"I don't understand. You mean he planted the explosives?"

"No."

"Then why did the house blow up?"

"There are a couple of possibilities. The most obvious is that someone planted claymores on a trip wire on the stairs or inside my bedroom door."

"Claymores?"

"An explosive device. It could have been something else on a detonator, but the trip wire is the most likely. They couldn't be sure when I'd go upstairs and I doubt anyone stuck around to set it off manually."

Cassy shuddered. "How can you say such things so calmly? Why would someone try to kill you?"

"My winning personality? Grab the helmet."

"Gabriel!"

There was no trace of humor in his voice or on his face as he shook his head. "I don't know who or why, Cassiopia. I'm still trying to work through all the ramifications."

His icy tone churned her stomach.

"We need to go. Now. By now they know the body isn't mine. Guess who'll be the number-one suspect."

CASSY REALIZED HE WAS RIGHT. The authorities probably would believe Gabriel had planted the explosives. Hadn't that been her first thought as well?

"Do you have everything?"

She grabbed the jacket she'd draped over one of the chairs and nodded.

"I was out of the house for hours yesterday. Plenty of time for someone to rig the explosives."

Gabe led her to the back entrance they'd used the night before. He slowed his pace as he realized she was practically running to keep up with his longer stride.

"As far as I know, you're the only person who ever disliked me enough to want me dead and I doubt you have the skill to rig an explosion."

"That's not funny!"

"Agreed. Put the helmet on."

"Wait!" She grabbed his arm, jerking him to a halt when he would have mounted the bike.

"Who was killed?"

Gabe shrugged. "Whoever Sliffman had watching the house. I'm guessing someone inexperienced. I doubt he was told to go inside and he should have been watching for traps when he did. Your arrival probably saved my life. I doubt I'd have been watching for a trip wire, either, when I went upstairs."

Her expression was so stricken Gabe didn't stop to think. He tilted her chin and kissed her on the mouth. It wasn't a gentle peck.

For a moment she was rigid in his arms, then she softened, pressing her body into his and returning the kiss in full measure.

He'd wondered what it would be like to taste her, but he hadn't anticipated the wild hunger that raced through his body. He found himself responding greedily to her small sounds of pleasure.

She started to fling her arms around his neck and clunked him in the head with the forgotten helmet.

"Ow!"

"Sorry." She swayed when he pulled back to rub his head.

"All you had to do was ask me to stop."

"No! I didn't mean…"

She hesitated, seemed to realize he was teasing and glared at him.

He wanted her, but he didn't want to want her. She confused him, but he hadn't wanted that kiss to end. He didn't think she had, either. She was unlike anyone he'd ever known. But while she might want to trust him, she didn't. Not really.

"Let's go."

He took the helmet from her hand and set it on her head. Cover temptation. This was no time for the crazy sort of thoughts he was having. On the other hand, he'd wanted to create a diversion for her thoughts and it appeared he'd been successful.

He helped her onto the bike, aware of the wobbly arms she slid lightly around his waist.

He wasn't sure he wanted to know what she was thinking. Cassiopia was the first woman he'd touched in almost four years. How ironic that she still couldn't be sure he hadn't killed her father.

Always nice to know his timing still sucked.

It started to rain before they cleared the parking lot. As omens went, this seemed par for the course. If he'd been home, Gabe would have left the bike and taken the truck. Motorcycles and rain were a dangerous combination.

Gabe swore to himself as he steered them toward the highway. Wind slapped rain into his eyes. He lowered his gaze and the rear tire lost traction. They started to slide on the oil coming to the surface of the road. Gabe dropped his speed even further. Rain began falling more quickly. This wasn't going to work. He couldn't see without his helmet. He'd have to pull over.

No sooner did he have that thought than a pair of deer broke from the trees and darted in front of him. If they'd kept moving it would have been no problem, but they came to a startled stop.

Gabe braked hard and swerved. The bike began to hydroplane. Cassiopia gripped his waist tightly as the bike did a slow slide sideways across the road before spinning completely around.

Gabe struggled to keep them upright and steer into the slide. He thought they'd make it until the back tire reached the slick, wet grass. Even before they plunged into the trees and went down, he knew he'd lost the battle.

"GABRIEL! GABRIEL! Don't you dare die on me!"

Gabe opened his eyes and shut them against the rain and the blurry figure bending over him.

"You all right, lady?"

A stranger's voice. Male and young.

"Help me get this bike off him."

Cassiopia moved out of his line of sight to give orders and a sudden rush of memories swamped him.

A car pulling into a garage in front of him. An explosion. A wall of fire. A second explosion. Pain.

He blinked uncomprehendingly at the trees overhead. Moisture drenched him. Why was it raining? It hadn't been raining.

"Ready? Lift!"

His thoughts cleared. His bike had gone down on the side of the road. They'd missed the trees somehow, but his leg was trapped. The pressure eased as the bike was lifted. Gabe jerked free, scraping skin in the process. Cassiopia gave a soft cry. The bike landed with a thud beside him.

"What's wrong?" the stranger demanded. "Are you hurt?"

"My wrist," Cassiopia replied. "I think it's broken. I must have landed on it."

Gabe struggled to get to his feet. Strong hands reached out to help.

"An' I had to go an' forget my cell phone this morning. If you all have one I'll call for an ambulance."

"No," Gabe told his rescuer. The last thing he wanted was the police and an ambulance. "Cassiopia?"

"You're bleeding."

He touched the back of his head. Warm blood

mingled with the rain. A lump was swelling around the cut. He shut his eyes against a sudden wave of dizziness.

"Gabriel!"

Probably a concussion, he decided as his stomach gave an uneasy lurch. His leg began to throb.

"Easy, man. Lean on me."

"Is he all right? Gabriel, are you—"

"Give me a minute."

"I saw what happened," the stranger was saying. "That was some driving, man. I can't believe you missed all them trees. I can flag down another car and get someone to call an ambulance, but it might be quicker if I just drive you to the hospital. We'll have to leave the bike."

Gabe glanced at his motorcycle. Nothing appeared too badly damaged, but he couldn't tell for sure. Cassiopia pressed her left arm against her middle in obvious pain. His helmet dangled forgotten in her other hand. She looked to be in shock. Even if the bike was okay, she wouldn't be riding it anymore this morning.

"Do you have one of those twenty-four-hour, walk-in emergency clinics nearby?"

Going to a hospital was too risky. He'd just as soon not answer official questions. There was no doubt in his mind that Huntington would believe Gabe had set the trip wire.

Would a walk-in clinic feel compelled to report this accident? Probably not. They should be able to get Cassiopia's wrist x-rayed and get away before anyone official discovered where they were.

"I think there's a walk-in place over on Talbert," their rescuer offered after a moment's thought, "but are you sure you wouldn't rather go to the hospital? I don't know what all a small place like that can do."

"It'll be fine. Mind giving us a lift?"

"No problem, man. Can you make it to my car?"

"Yes." One way or another.

"Those deer are a menace," the man continued.

"They probably feel the same way about us," Cassiopia told him as they started for the road.

While there was pain in her voice, it sounded stronger. She'd cope. He wasn't so sure about him.

Gabe collapsed gratefully onto the front passenger seat of the small sedan that waited on the shoulder of the road. His vision was a little blurred, but the deer, he noticed, had made good their escape.

If he'd been alone, he'd have tried to get the bike back on the road despite his leg and his headache, but he couldn't do it with Cassiopia in pain. He shut his eyes. The world was taking on a bad tendency to tilt and spin. His head throbbed in cadence with the windshield wipers.

"Gabriel, wake up! Stay with us!"

He jerked his eyes open. "'M 'wake."

"Can you hurry?" Cassiopia demanded, leaning over the backseat. She touched his face gently. He wanted to flinch away but it would take too much effort. Besides, part of him wanted to nestle into that hand and savor her touch.

"Not unless you want to end up in the trees again," the driver was saying. "It's coming down so hard I can barely see the road."

A streak of brilliant light was accompanied by the crash of thunder. Gabe tuned it out. It would have been nice to succumb to the inviting well of deep gray that waited whenever he closed his eyes, but Cassiopia's gentle touch prevented it. Passing out would be bad. He had to stay alert.

Gabe roused more fully when their rescuer pulled into a small shopping center. Cassiopia pointed out they'd already made him late for work when the man offered to accompany them inside. She thanked him while Gabe stiffly maneuvered himself out of the car.

He swayed unsteadily. Cassiopia appeared at his side.

"Lean on me."

"'M okay."

"Sure you are. You're a tough guy. Guys always think they're all right. It isn't macho to be in pain. Hopefully if you don't bleed to death you'll be fine."

"Head wounds always bleed."

"There's blood running down your ripped pants, too."

A glance at his upper thigh showed a gash beneath the torn fabric. Now that she'd pointed it out, new pain vied with his throbbing head for attention.

"Just a cut," he told her as they stepped inside what was nothing more than a storefront. "How's your wrist?"

"It's felt better."

The small clinic was bustling despite the early hour. Somewhere out of sight a small child wailed loudly. The keening sound drove splinters of knife-edged pain into his skull.

Gabe decided giving the busy woman at the front desk a phony name would needlessly arouse suspicions. These people were too busy to worry about a pair of fools who'd driven their motorcycle off the side of the road.

The wait was long, but finally a stressed young doctor confirmed Gabe's concussion. X-rays determined nothing else was broken despite considerable bruising, but both his head wound and the cut on his leg required stitches.

Stoically, Gabe allowed them to shave a section of hair on the back of his head in order to stitch the wound closed. Given his looks, he figured another scar or two didn't matter. What he really needed was the ibuprofen they finally gave him for his throbbing headache.

Cassiopia's injuries proved less serious. Besides minor cuts and bruises, her wrist was sprained, though thankfully, not broken. They iced it down, wrapped it and put her arm in a sling, while the small clinic continued to fill past capacity.

"It's always like this when it rains," he heard his nurse grumble to the doctor.

The thunderstorm had passed and the rain had slowed to a steady drizzle by the time they finally limped outside looking the worse for wear. Gabe gazed around the small shopping center and realized they were stranded.

"Do you know how to get back to the bike?"

Cassiopia's expression stated clearly she felt he'd lost his mind. "I wasn't paying attention, but you aren't going to ride it now. You look like you can barely walk."

"Thanks."

"Besides, I wouldn't get back on that motorcycle if I did know where it was. And don't you dare tell me it's like falling off a horse. I wouldn't get back on one of them, either."

His lips twitched.

"We could call for a taxi," she suggested.

"On a Friday? In this rain? We'd be lucky to see one in two hours."

"Okay. Good point. There's a pancake place across the street. We could go there and wait while we figure out what to do."

"Not a bad idea." Except the thought of food made his stomach roll.

"Yeah, except we're covered in mud and blood and grass. Unless you want everyone staring at us, I suggest we stop in there first."

He followed her pointing finger to *there*. A discreet little sign several doors down read New Again. The small, mom-and-pop store apparently sold used everything, from clothing to furniture.

Gabe didn't have to glance at his torn, bloodstained pants to know he made a bedraggled picture. He tried not to limp as they walked beneath the awning to the store's front door.

They'd lost so much time inside the clinic it was far too late to beat Rochelle and her crew to the gallery. She hadn't tried calling his cell phone yet, so she'd probably seen the news about his house. Since they hadn't identified the victim, odds were she believed he was dead.

Two middle-aged women eyed them nervously as they entered the cluttered shop. Gabe left it to Cassiopia to explain their battered condition. The pair tsked like mother hens over her while giving *him* plenty of space. That didn't stop them from making pointed remarks about the dangers of motorcycles. Gabe concentrated on the clothing for sale.

Mindful of the stitches in the back of his head, he located a ball cap to cover his shaved scalp. After a bit of a search he found a pair of dark jeans and a navy shirt in his size. At the last second he spotted a plain navy sweatshirt and carried everything into the make-shift dressing room. Curtains enclosed the space rather than walls.

Deciding everything fit well enough, he used his old shirt to wipe down his jacket as best he could, then stepped outside to hand his torn and stained items to one of the women. Reluctantly, she agreed to pitch them in the trash.

Cassiopia had been gazing at a rack of inexpensive earrings while waiting her turn. A pair of crystal earrings and a matching pendant caught his eye as she carried her bundle into the claustrophobic space. The crystals were shaped to resemble small roses. As he lifted them, the bits of glass reflected the overhead lights.

Questioning his sanity, Gabe paid for them while one of the women helped Cassiopia. Belatedly, he realized it would be difficult for her to use her left arm.

Gabe brooded, gazing around the shop. There were some interesting items for sale. The small painting of a lion captured his attention. He was staring at it when Cassiopia joined him a few minutes later. She'd selected a pair of jeans similar to his, a white blouse and a bright red sweater.

"I like it," she told him. "Good use of color. He sort of reminds me of you with that fierce expression."

"Thanks."

"Don't mention it. Going to buy it?"

"No walls left."

He was sorry for his flip remark when her teasing expression faded instantly.

"You all set?"

"Yes," she agreed.

He strode to the counter, but Cassiopia insisted on paying for her own purchases. Rather than make a fuss, he walked to the door and stared out at the main road. Was it going to rain all day?

"Ready?" she asked, coming up beside him.

"Yes. Here." He handed her the jewelry.

"What's this?"

Gabe shrugged, aware of their interested audience.

"They reminded me of you."

He wasn't sure why he'd done it. He'd never bought a woman a present without a reason before and it felt foolish. She probably wouldn't even like them.

Her lips parted in surprise and her eyes glittered. Gabe hustled her out of the store, but she stopped him outside by laying a hand on his arm.

"Gabriel."

He was startled when she reached up and kissed him lightly.

"Thank you."

He looked away. He'd never been uncomfortable around a woman before. Certainly not when one had kissed him, but then, his face hadn't resembled a Halloween mask the last time it had happened.

"Let me take those," he demanded gruffly.

Those consisted of a bulky shopping bag with her old clothing and some other stuff she must have purchased, including an umbrella.

"Wait. Help me put these on first," she requested, holding out the bits of glass.

It felt intimate, not to mention awkward, sliding the

earrings into the small holes in her dainty earlobes. Just as bad was circling her neck with the delicate chain. Lovers did things like this, not virtual strangers.

"Thank you."

He didn't meet her eyes as he inclined his head. "Hungry?"

"You're supposed to say, you're welcome."

He set his teeth. "You're welcome."

Cassiopia opened the umbrella. A tiny smile played on her lips. "I could eat."

He doubted he could.

The restaurant across the street was conspicuously uncrowded given the hour. It should have bustled with a lunch crowd, but they quickly realized their waitress was more interested in flirting with her coworker than in her two ragtag customers. No doubt that accounted for all the empty places. They settled into a booth, finally ordered and sat back.

"Smile. You'll scare the cook."

"He can't see me." But Gabe felt himself start to relax. "You realize we'll probably get ptomaine in here."

Cassiopia grinned. "I'm hungry enough to risk it. You look different in that cap. Younger. How's your head?"

"Fine."

She made a face. "Right. Why'd I ask? I'm sure it hurts as much as my wrist."

"Sorry."

"Forget it. The accident wasn't your fault. I'd have been more upset if you'd hit those deer. I have something to give you, too."

While her words startled him, he knew what it was even before he looked inside the bag he'd carried for her. How she'd bought it without him noticing he wasn't sure, but he didn't need to unwrap the small package to know it was the lion painting.

His chest tightened painfully. She'd bought this for him. For no reason. He didn't know what to say. No woman had ever given him a gift before.

"For when you get new walls."

Discomfited, he shook his head. "You shouldn't have done that."

"Neither should you, but I really like these crystals." And then with her usual bluntness she added, "Why is this so awkward?"

"I don't know. Do you always say what you think?"

"Most of the time. You should try it. It saves misunderstandings. What are we going to do now?"

Relieved by her change of topic he nodded toward the waitress bearing plates. "Eat."

CASSY MADE A FACE at him, but was secretly as relieved by the interruption as Gabriel appeared to be. The painting had been a spur-of-the-moment decision. She hadn't known he'd bought the jewelry, but there'd been something almost wistful in his expression when he'd looked at that painting. She had a feeling few people had ever given Gabriel gifts, particularly in the last few years. Beacher had said his parents were deceased and he wasn't close to any other family he might have. She knew he had few friends, if any, and it saddened her.

"Lowe is German for lion," he told her.

Her pulse quickened. It was the first time he'd initiated a casual conversation. And the name fit him so perfectly.

"Is that where your ancestors are from? Germany?"

OFFICIAL OPINION POLL

ANSWER 3 QUESTIONS AND WE'LL SEND YOU
4 FREE BOOKS AND A FREE GIFT!

0074823 ||||■|||■|||| ||||■|||| ||||■|||| FREE GIFT CLAIM # 3953

YOUR OPINION COUNTS!

Please tick TRUE or FALSE below to express your opinion about the following statements:

Q1 Do you believe in "true love"?

"TRUE LOVE HAPPENS ONLY ONCE IN A LIFETIME."   ○ TRUE ○ FALSE

Q2 Do you think marriage has any value in today's world?

"YOU CAN BE TOTALLY COMMITTED TO SOMEONE WITHOUT BEING MARRIED."   ○ TRUE ○ FALSE

Q3 What kind of books do you enjoy?

"A GREAT NOVEL MUST HAVE A HAPPY ENDING."   ○ TRUE ○ FALSE

YES, I have scratched the area below.

Please send me the 4 FREE BOOKS and FREE GIFT for which I qualify. I understand I am under no obligation to purchase any books, as explained on the back of this card.

I7EI

Mrs/Miss/Ms/Mr _____ Initials _____

BLOCK CAPITALS PLEASE

Surname _____

Address _____

_____

Postcode _____

DETACH AND POST CARD TODAY!

The Reader Service™ — Here's how it works:

Accepting the free books and gift places you under no obligation to buy anything. You may keep the books and gift and return the despatch note marked 'cancel'. If we do not hear from you, about a month later we'll send you 6 additional books and invoice you just £3.10* each. That's the complete price – there is no extra charge for postage and packing. You may cancel at any time, but if you choose to continue, every month we'll send you 6 more books, which you may either purchase or return to us - the choice is yours.

*Terms and prices subject to change without notice.

NO STAMP NEEDED!

THE READER SERVICE™
FREE BOOK OFFER
FREEPOST CN81
CROYDON
CR9 3WZ

If offer card is missing write to: The Reader Service, PO box 676, Richmond, TW9 1WU

NO STAMP
NECESSARY
IF POSTED IN
THE U.K. OR N.I.

"On my father's side anyway."

"Where did the Gabriel come from?"

"My mother. She liked the sound of it. You're the only one beside her who's ever called me Gabriel. Most people call me Gabe."

"And most people call me Cassy."

His expression lightened with definite humor. "Cassiopia sounds nicer."

"So does Gabriel."

The smile was rueful, but it was still a smile. "Truce?"

"Truce," she agreed. "Now what?"

"We need a car."

The man was exasperating. "I just happen to have one. Unfortunately, it's parked two blocks from your house."

"Too dangerous. The police have probably found it by now."

Cassy set down her fork, no longer interested in food as she thought about the dead man in his house.

"We should go to the authorities."

He lowered his voice even though the last couple seated closest to them had just left. "They'll believe I set that explosive."

"But you didn't!"

"Prove it."

His flat tone was chilling. A shiver moved down her spine. "You can't prove a negative."

He inclined his head, lifted his fork and continued eating. He'd been trying to do just that for the past four years, she realized.

Cassy reached for her coffee to give her shaking hands something to do. Sipping at the bitter brew she tried to think past the creeping fear.

"I could call a friend to lend us a car."

"No. Too dangerous."

"Why would anyone be watching my friends?"

Gabriel simply shook his head and continued to eat mechanically. She was almost certain he didn't taste his food.

"The gallery is open by now," he pointed out between bites. "We can't afford to draw attention to it."

"I could create a distraction."

"No doubt. Then what?"

"What do you mean?"

"If the package contains what we think it does, what do we do with it?"

"Turn it over to… Surely they won't think…" The coffee did a lurch and roll in her stomach. Of course the authorities would think Gabriel had had the vials all along. A few weeks ago she would have thought the same thing.

He set down his fork. "Do you know how to handle the toxin if we find it?"

"You don't handle it. If even a drop of that stuff gets spilled we could have a disaster. Of course, we wouldn't live long enough to bear witness. And what if someone else already found the package?"

"We'd know by now."

For the first time, she saw vulnerability in his expression. For all his take-charge, macho attitude, Gabriel was scared, too.

"We have to do something."

He stared out the window. Suddenly, his expression brightened. "I know how to get a car. We'll buy one."

"Of course. How simple. Why didn't I think of that? We'll just buy one. You've got deeper pockets than I do."

His lips curved. "Not so deep, but we don't need to ride in style. There's a used-car lot right down the street."

"You're just going to march over there and buy a car."

"Not on this leg," he agreed, "but I can limp."

"You're serious."

"Watch me."

Chapter Eight

Gabe found the cheapest car on the lot and made a ridiculous offer. The resulting transaction took longer than Cassy would have thought, given they were paying cash, but eventually they climbed inside a small white sedan that had seen better days.

"Are you sure this thing will run? Shouldn't we at least have given it a test drive?"

"It's been state inspected. It'll run."

"Gabriel, it's eleven years old!"

"That's why we got it so cheap."

"Cheap? I wouldn't have given him five dollars. Did you see how much mileage it has on it? And look at this interior! It's in horrible shape."

"It's transportation."

"Only if it runs! You're crazy, you know that, right?"

"Sanity's overrated."

His rakish grin stopped her mid-rant. The man had a killer grin. He'd be devilishly appealing if he set his mind to it. And this was not the time to be thinking how attractive he was.

"How is it you have an envelope stuffed with hundred-dollar bills anyhow?"

She'd seen him pull the envelope from the box of cereal herself, but her mind had been on other things at the time. Gabe started the engine and Cassy quickly reached for her seat belt.

"I set money aside for emergencies. I think this qualifies, don't you?"

Without being told, she knew the emergency he'd expected was being arrested and charged. He would not appreciate her pity.

Rain had begun again. The windshield wipers squealed in protest as they sluggishly swiped at the glass.

"You aren't really going to take this thing on the highway, are you?"

"Would you rather stop and pick up my bike?"

He'd do it, too. "No. What are you going to do about your motorcycle?"

"We'll go back for it later."

Not if she had anything to say. "Someone might steal it."

"Then I'll report it missing."

Cassy sat back and didn't say another word until they were in Olde Towne, Alexandria. She stared out at the small shops as they drove down the busy streets.

"Hey! Wasn't that the art gallery you just passed? First Impressions?"

"Yes."

He continued driving.

"Where are you going?"

"Sliffman and Huntington were going inside."

Cassy inhaled sharply. "You saw them? Do you think they'll find the package?"

"We can only hope."

Her lips parted in astonishment. "You *want* them to find that package?"

As they came to a red traffic signal, Gabriel twisted to look at her. "I *want* that stuff back where it belongs. I'd *like* to see it destroyed along with all research of that type. But then, I'd like a perfect world, too."

As he faced forward again and started into the intersection, Cassy tried to get her mind around an entirely new assessment of Gabriel Lowe.

"I never pictured you as an environmentalist," she ventured. "I mean, being former military and all."

"My lawyer arranged for the military service to keep me out of jail."

Cassy forced her gaping mouth shut. His expression was sardonic.

"A pair of buddies and I got drunk one night. One of them decided to get even with a rival who'd made a move on his girl. Unfortunately, we were so wasted he picked the wrong house."

"What did you do?"

"Actually, I don't remember doing anything besides throwing up, but I was there when the cops arrived to find them smashing in the windshield of a car. The three of us were arrested. Since I had good grades and had been in ROTC, someone pulled strings. I was told I had leadership potential if I could lose the attitude." He gave another shrug. "You can see how well that worked out."

Cassy was torn between amusement and shock. "What did you want to be?" she asked after a moment.

"Good at something."

"You are," she told him softly, thinking of his incredible sculptures. "Why don't we just park and wait for them to leave?"

"Odds are they'll have someone stick around to keep an eye on the place. We'll come back."

"Okay. What are we going to do instead?"

"I'm going to drop you somewhere while I go and have a talk with…an old friend."

"Andrea Fielding?"

He shot her a startled glance and she shrugged.

"It was either that or Dr. Pheng and somehow I don't think the two of you were ever buds."

"You're sharp."

"Thank you, but the possibilities seemed limited. I know everyone's been investigated up one side and down the other, but the media is saying Andrea was Beacher's fiancée and we both know she wasn't."

"Very sharp."

It didn't sound like a compliment.

"That's why I'm sticking with you. Two heads and all that, remember? And don't remind me they're playing for keeps. I'm one of the people they're playing with. I'll feel a whole lot safer next to you."

"Why?"

"Because I trust you."

Gabe jerked as if he'd been sucker punched. Good, he needed a few jolts if that's what it took him to see he wasn't alone. He was a scary person on several levels, but he was no killer. Hard to believe she'd ever thought differently.

The legal system might not have placed a physical prison around him, but Gabriel had been tried, convicted and sentenced in the eyes of the public. He'd been in solitary confinement a long time now and like any other trapped beast he wouldn't trust easily. That was okay. Cassy had learned the need for some patience while waiting for a desired result.

"Do you know where Andrea lives?" she asked.

"I know. It would be best if I drop you off somewhere."

"Maybe from your perspective, but that isn't going to happen. You're stuck with me."

A muscle twitched in his jaw. "Are you always this obstinate?"

"Pretty much."

Cassy expected an argument but he didn't say anything more. She wasn't surprised that he knew where Andrea lived. She'd be willing to bet he could find everyone connected with the events of four years ago.

They drove back into Maryland, where he did surprise her when he pulled off the interstate in Montgomery County instead of continuing on to Frederick.

"It's Friday," Gabriel explained even though she hadn't asked. "She'll be at work."

Where Cassy should be at the moment. She hadn't given work a thought. She should have called in sick, but it was too late now. She'd have to come up with a story on Monday. The thought made her cringe, but at least her boss was taking a long weekend. No one should be looking for her.

"Doesn't Andrea still work at the base?"

"No. She took a position with a private lab that does genetic research. I don't see her car." He slowly cruised the parking lot of a low brick building.

"Late lunch?"

"Very late."

"Maybe she rode in with someone else today. Or she could have left early."

As he pulled into a visitor's spot Cassy laid a hand on his wrist and felt his tension. He was far from the calm he projected. "Why don't you let me ask for her? If she hears your name, she might not talk to us."

"Good thinking."

The cheerful receptionist told them Andrea hadn't come in today.

"Now what?" Cassy asked as they climbed back in the car.

"Her condo."

"You're worried."

"Things are coming to a head."

Cassy frowned. "That's good, isn't it?"

"Depends if we survive."

"You're so reassuring."

He didn't smile.

Andrea's condominium was in a nice, well-kept neighborhood that to Cassy's eyes looked rather pricey for a mere lab assistant. Gabe scanned the mostly empty parking area and pulled in beside a late model sporty-looking red car. Leaving their car running, he climbed out with a terse, "Wait here."

It took Cassy several seconds to realize the red car was occupied. Gabe favored his leg slightly as he hurried around to the driver's side where dark hair was the only visible sign of the person slumped over the steering wheel. Dread sent Cassy out of the car.

Gabe jerked the door open and stopped. He touched

the person lightly. They didn't twitch. The bleakness that stared from his eyes as he lifted his head froze Cassy in her tracks.

"Get back in the car."

Cassy obeyed without a word. Gabe shut the car door and used his jacket to wipe where his fingers had touched the metal. Fear speared cold talons down her spine.

An expensive looking SUV pulled into the lot and parked a few spaces away. The pair of young women who got out sent them a curious look from beneath a pair of brightly colored umbrellas.

This was the wrong neighborhood for a clunker like the one they were driving. And Gabriel, well, his forbidding expression gave Cassy chills.

"Andrea?" she asked as he got back inside the car.

"Her throat was slit from behind." His voice was utterly devoid of emotion.

Cassy began searching through her bag for her cell phone.

"What are you doing?"

"We need to call the police. Those women saw us. They're going to remember us. If we don't call, we're going to look guilty." She was surprised at how calm she sounded. She was shaking so bad she doubted she'd be able to punch in the number.

"I'll do it." He whipped his own cell phone from a pocket and dialed. "I want to report a suspicious death."

Calmly, he gave the dispatcher the location then hung up and put the car in reverse. The women had disappeared inside the building.

"She's been dead for hours," he told Cassy in that emotionless, stranger's voice. "Her killer must have waited in the backseat, yanked her head back by her hair and slit her throat before she could struggle."

"My God!" She pictured Beacher and wanted to throw up.

"I doubt she even marked him. It was a professional hit."

"What does that mean?"

"Her assailant knew how to kill. Military-trained, at a guess. There was no hesitation. Andrea must have been the inside person after all."

Cassy inhaled sharply. "What?"

"She was involved in the theft of the toxin."

And Andrea was the woman Gabriel once loved. Maybe he still did. He might be an expert at hiding his emotions, but that didn't mean he didn't have them. Cassy would never forget the bleakness in his eyes when he first looked up.

She rested a hand on his arm and felt the steel of bunched muscles. "I'm sorry."

He didn't respond, but he didn't shake off her hand, either. Cassy squeezed lightly and withdrew. Pain twisted her heart. Everyone he cared about was dead and she didn't know how to comfort him.

"Beacher always believed she was the one who stole Pheng's notes and the hard drives from the safe on the base. He kept trying, but she wouldn't talk to us. Recently we learned her brother died shortly after the toxin went missing."

Cassy frowned. "What does her brother's death have to do with anything?"

"Ron was very intense and very anti-military. He hated that Andrea worked on a military base. He and I didn't exactly hit it off, but I never saw much of him even though he lived with Andrea. Their parents were dead. Both were ex-military, and their dad died in a training accident."

"Accounting for Ron's dislike, huh? How did he die?"

"He fell from the top floor of a parking garage and broke his neck after leaving a popular D.C. club one night."

"Oh, geez."

"He was underage, but his blood alcohol level was well over the legal limit. There was no sign that he was pushed or forced over."

"You don't think it was an accident."

"It *could* have been an accident, but the timing bothered us."

He didn't take his eyes from the road. The rain was heavy again and the wipers were struggling to keep up. He reached for the defroster.

"Stupidity happens, Gabe. People do die. What makes you think there's a connection?"

He shrugged. "Beacher and I began looking at Ron's close friends. Before he died there was a core group that used to hang out at Andrea's house. It occurred to us to wonder if someone had convinced them they should show the world what the government was doing behind closed doors. They were all college kids, antiestablishment, pro-environment, typical dissident types. Teenage idealists are easily manipulated. That's why so many get caught up in cults."

"They were in a cult?"

"No, but they could have been manipulated."

"Into stealing the toxin?"

"Or helping someone else do it."

"That sounds pretty far-fetched."

Gabe nodded. "I believe I mentioned grasping at straws. We'd exhausted every other lead and to our surprise, it turned out Ron's girlfriend quit school immediately after he died and moved to Chicago."

"So?"

He shot her a quick glance. "She disappeared on her way to a job interview shortly after moving. She hasn't been seen since."

Cassy felt the start of goose bumps. "Do the authorities know about this?"

"Beacher has…*had* an inside source. Supposedly they took a hard look at Ron's death. Nothing came of the investigation but they also searched for the girlfriend. Don't forget the authorities already had a strong suspect."

Him. Her nails bit into her palms and she forced her fingers to relax before they drew blood.

"Everyone remotely connected with the toxin was put under a microscope, Cassiopia. Even you."

"So?" she prodded when he fell silent.

"All of those kids are dead."

Cassy was stunned. "That can't be a coincidence! You need to tell someone!"

"They know—" he smiled without humor "—but in their shoes, I'd still suspect me, too."

Cassy inhaled.

"I was engaged to Andrea. I knew her brother. And can you see your father responding to a threat from a group of college kids? I can't."

"Then what did they have to do with this?"

"You know how you said Beacher was hard to ignore?"

"I think I said he was easy to talk to."

"That, too. He went out drinking with the brother of one of Ron's friends last month. The kid supposedly committed suicide by slashing his wrists after washing down a bunch of pills in some alcohol. The brother doesn't believe the kid committed suicide."

And Beacher and Andrea had had their throats slit.

"The brother still had the kid's laptop computer so Beacher bought it from him. Want to guess what we found?"

Cassy realized she was holding her breath.

"Information on making bombs and rigging explosives."

"Gabriel, you have to tell someone!"

He didn't look away from the road. "The explosives used to kill your father came from a secured area on the base. Andrea didn't have access, but I did. So did Beacher. Someone had to give them those explosives."

Cassy was momentarily deflated. "I'm so confused."

"Welcome to my world."

There was no humor in his smile. The muscles in his neck were knotted. His hands gripped the steering wheel more tightly.

"But the computer—"

"Doesn't mean a thing since we had the opportunity to tamper with it. We learned that Ron and two of the others had been arrested at a military protest rally a year before the toxin was stolen. I think someone convinced them they could make a bigger statement by stealing the toxin."

"They'd kill millions of people to make a point?"

He shook his head. "That wouldn't have been their plan. Steal it, destroy the hard drives and research notes and get the public to help them demand stuff of that type be destroyed for good."

"But Dr. Pheng was probably using the toxin to work up an antidote!"

"I doubt the kids knew or cared. Idealists tend to have one-track minds."

"You think the kids killed my father?"

"If they did we'll never prove it now."

"There has to be *something!*"

His lips curved wryly. Chagrined, she realized her frustration was nothing compared with his.

"Beacher and I played 'pin the guilt' on every person we could think of and we kept coming back to Carstairs. The timing of his heart attack, the fact that he was away from the base during your dad's missing hours, that he had easy access to most places on the base and my presence when your father's house exploded all point to him, but it's all conjecture. We have no proof."

"There has to be a way to find some." Cassy fell silent trying to assimilate his words. "Is there any chance Beacher and Andrea actually were engaged?"

"No." The word was firm and uncompromising.

"Why would she tell the media they were?"

His jaw hardened. "As his fiancée, she'd gain information on the investigation into his death. She's always been impulsive."

"She's a lab tech!"

"I can't speak to her work ethics, but she'd get all

enthused about something for a while and then it would fizzle out."

Like their engagement?

"Marriage was her idea," he told her without inflection as if he'd heard her thoughts. "I doubt she'd have gone through with ours even if this hadn't happened."

"Then why…? Sorry. None of my business."

"She was attractive and the sex was great."

His voice was utterly flat, as if he were reporting the weather.

"It seemed like a good idea at the time."

There was nothing to say to that. "What are we going to do now?"

"Go shopping."

"But we have to see if Beacher found the toxin!"

"The opening tonight is semiformal."

Her lips parted in shock. "We're going to the gallery opening? We can't retrieve the package in front of a lot of people! Can we? Besides, if Rochelle thinks you're dead, won't she cancel the show?"

"Not a chance. Dead artists sell better than live ones."

"That's just wrong."

His lips curved slightly. "That's commerce."

"Shouldn't you at least call her?"

Gabe shook his head. "If I call Rochelle I draw attention to the exhibit. Sliffman and Huntington know I'm not dead. If they told her I'm alive, I'm sure she's been told to let them know if she hears from me. Whether they found the package or not, they'll be at the opening or have someone there in case I do show." He shot her a darkly amused glance. "Should be an interesting evening, don't you think?"

Cassy studied his expression. "I think you've watched too many James Bond movies."

He flicked on the radio with a grin.

"No radio?" Cassiopia asked dryly when nothing happened.

"Apparently not, but the roof keeps the rain off and the car runs."

"Small mercies. If Andrea was murdered because she knew something, why did someone try to kill you? They must have known you didn't have the vials or they wouldn't have blown up your house."

"Unless they didn't care."

"You think they *wanted* to release that toxin in that explosion?"

"That's one possibility. If they searched my house and didn't find it, they might have decided it was worth the risk as long as they were far enough away at the time to be safe."

That theory made a chilling sort of sense. "Everyone would believe you'd had it all along. The authorities would stop looking for anyone else."

"Not necessarily."

"But whoever's behind all this might think that!"

He shrugged. "I'm a loose end, Cassiopia. There's nothing anyone can use as leverage against me and I think someone feels they're running out of time. The authorities have never let up the pressure. Neither have Beacher and I. That stuff's out there somewhere. Sooner or later it's bound to surface and point fingers at the guilty party. If our thief has done his homework he knows I won't rest until I find out who killed Beacher."

He might be wounded, but this was one beast with

enough pride and fierce loyalty to drive him to complete whatever task he set for himself.

"I'm going to help you."

"I appreciate the offer, but it would be better if—"

"Don't say it! Like it or not, we're partners Gabriel. My dad is at least partly responsible for this situation. I will not allow thousands to die. Remember, someone wants me out of the way, too, so let's hit the mall."

THE LADY WAS A FORCE to be reckoned with. Gabe left her in the women's department and headed for the drugstore for a supply of ibuprofen. His cuts were throbbing and his headache had returned with aggravating intensity. Cassiopia's wrist probably hurt as well.

They were laden with packages and a suitcase apiece when they headed back to the small car. He dumped their parcels in the trunk and offered her the second bottle of cold water he'd purchased along with the ibuprofen.

"Mind reader."

He eyed her sling. "You all right?"

"I've been better. Now what?"

His cell phone rang before he could answer. Caller ID showed a number he wasn't familiar with. He had a feeling he knew who would be on the other end.

"Lowe," he answered.

"Len Sliffman. Don't hang up, Lieutenant."

Gabe waited in silence.

"You called in Andrea Fielding's murder."

Fast work. "Yes."

"Is Dr. Richards the woman who was with you? She's missing. We're concerned about her."

There was no point lying. "Yes."

"Do you know who killed Ms. Fielding?"

"No."

"We need to meet, Lieutenant."

"No."

"I don't believe you had anything to do with her murder. Or the explosion at your house," he added quickly.

"Who died?"

Cassiopia's anxious expression turned frightened. Sliffman hesitated.

"That's one of the things we need to talk about."

"No."

"All right, don't hang up! One of the men assigned to watch your place was a rookie. He saw someone enter through a dining room window and called for backup. When no lights went on he decided not to wait and went inside. He hit a trip wire on the stairs."

Exactly as Gabe had figured.

"Yours, or meant for you?" Sliffman asked.

"Not mine."

"We need to work together. Do you have the toxin?"

"No."

"Do you know where it is?"

"No."

Frustration filled Sliffman's voice. "Why would someone try to kill you?"

"When I find him, I'll ask."

Cassiopia worried her bottom lip. She gazed at him fretfully.

"Do you know why someone would kill Ms. Fielding?"

Gabe hesitated. "No, but you might take another look into the deaths of her brother and his friends."

This time the silence on Sliffman's end lasted several seconds.

"Talk to me, Lowe. What do you know?"

"Nothing I can prove."

"Believe it or not, I want to help."

"I've had enough government help."

Sliffman changed tactics. "Do you know why Ms. Fielding was getting ready to run?"

A hollow, sinking feeling filled his chest. Andrea had been dead long enough that rigor mortis had set in when he found her. He hadn't known she'd been about to rabbit.

"Her suitcases were in the trunk of her car," Sliffman continued. "She had an e-ticket for Tampa, Florida, in her purse. One way."

Sliffman had been Homeland Security's prime investigator when the toxin went missing and unlike the others Gabe had dealt with, Sliffman's questions had been direct and without malice.

Gabe knew all about good cop, bad cop, and he knew which role Sliffman had played and was still playing. But he also understood the job and respected it and the man. Still, Gabe wasn't prepared to put his welfare into the hands of anyone right now. The minute his freedom ended, so did his chances of solving this thing.

"I can't do much from a jail cell, Sliffman."

Cassiopia's eyes widened.

"What if I promise not to arrest you?"

"We both know you can't make that stick."

"If you aren't guilty, you won't go to jail."

"That's how it's supposed to work," Gabe agreed dryly. "Doesn't always."

Gabe closed his phone, dropped it to the pavement

and kicked it away as hard as he could. The phone sailed beneath a minivan. Cassiopia yanked on his arm.

"What are you doing?"

"Get in."

"Gabriel—"

He gave her no choice but to scramble around to the passenger side when he slid behind the wheel. She was still putting on her seat belt when he pulled out of the parking space. With any luck some poor fool would pick up the phone and use it, sending Sliffman's people on a wild-goose chase.

"It's possible to use global tracking to triangulate on a cell phone," he explained to Cassiopia. "Make sure yours is turned off. If it's emitting a signal it's a beacon to us. Sliffman got my number when I called 911. It will take him a little longer to get yours, but he'll get it, particularly now that he knows we're together. We can pick up new phones and pay for individual minutes if we need them."

Cassy fumbled in her purse and glared at him. "Why didn't you turn yours off, then?"

He pulled out of the parking lot. "I want to lead them to a dead end."

"Maybe you should have talked to him."

"I will when I have something to tell him."

"He didn't find the package?"

"I don't think so. He did tell me Andrea was leaving town."

"Why?" She closed her phone and put it back in her purse. "Why now? Why didn't she run when her brother was killed? Why would her killer wait all this time?"

"He appears to be cutting his losses all around."

"And we're on his list." Frustration laced her voice. "But we don't know anything!"

"He can't be sure of that. People with guilty consciences can make some wild assumptions. In this case I think he's making the same assumption we are, that Beacher found the toxin and gave it to me."

They were overlooking something and he knew it.

Chapter Nine

Gabriel was tired and he was hurting. Cassy saw it in the tight lines around his mouth and eyes. She wished the aspirin would kick in to stop the throbbing in her wrist. Trying on clothes had been difficult and she was tired.

She stopped talking, even when he drove into D.C. instead of Virginia. At least they were going against rush-hour traffic. He didn't offer an explanation and she decided not to ask until they pulled up in front of a costume store.

"You're kidding, right?"

A touch of humor lit his eyes. "You don't see me in a bunny suit?"

"You'd scare the heck out of all the other bunnies. A knight," Cassy corrected. "Dark, brooding, mysterious, but ready with your sword to smite the enemy."

Instantly, his expression closed down, becoming remote.

"Don't get fanciful. I'm no one's hero, Cassiopia."

"No? The armor's tarnished, but the image still fits." She reached for the door handle and stepped out into the light rain before he could reply.

Having never been inside a costume shop before she was fascinated, despite her aching wrist. While Gabriel walked over to speak with the older couple behind the counter, Cassy strolled between the rows of costumes. She paused near the back of the store at a display of wigs. A pretty, golden red one caught her eye. She was reaching out to touch the long strands when Gabriel came up behind her.

"I've always wanted to be a redhead," she said, grinning at him impishly.

"Try it on."

He didn't look as if he were teasing. "You're serious."

"I'm going for blond."

Cassy stood there with her mouth open as the owner began sorting through boxes of wigs underneath the display. She could hardly ask Gabriel what he was thinking with the older couple hovering nearby, especially when the wife walked over and offered to help Cassy try on the red wig.

Gabriel's flat look told her nothing. Bursting with curiosity, she allowed the woman to settle the long red strands on her head. In a nearby mirror, her gray eyes blinked back at her in surprise. The look wasn't bad, but it was different. In fact, it changed her entire appearance.

"We'll need to change your makeup, of course," the woman said seriously. "Hold on. I'll be right back."

"Looks good," Gabriel told her.

Astounded, she gaped at his own transformation. The man had helped him don a masculine, thick blond wig.

"You look like a surfer." She brushed back a strand of hair. "You can't be serious."

His lips curved. "I think it suits my playful side."

She very nearly asked what playful side but bit it back in time. She would have known Gabe's features anywhere no matter what color his hair was, but from the back, even from the side, it would take a second look and then recognition would be mostly because of the scar. The woman returned with a tray of makeup and handed her husband a jar of something.

"Now you just sit back and let me see what I can do," she suggested, pointing to some chairs at a counter off to one side.

Gabe was already taking a seat. Uncertainly, Cassy joined him at the small mirrored bar. He was going to let the man paint his face? This was too weird.

The woman was deft and sure as she worked on Cassy's face. "I used to be a makeup artist before Zeke and I retired and opened this place. Mostly theater in New York, but we worked more than a couple of movie sets, too. You've got good bones, honey, not like some of the people we've had to do. Good coloring, too. It makes it so much easier to change your look. You could have gone blond, you know. Most would, but not many can. I think you made a good choice with the red. The color suits you."

Cassy didn't know what to say. Fortunately, she didn't have to say anything. The woman chattered on about plays and the movie sets she'd worked on. At one time, she informed them, Zeke had been a costume designer. The two had met at the Kennedy Center some years ago where they'd both taken jobs.

"Your boyfriend says you want to fool some friends tonight. I think this should do it. What do you think?"

Cassy stared in the mirror at the transformation. While it wasn't a stranger who stared back, it wasn't her, either. She never wore eye makeup. In fact, she seldom wore more than lipstick and blush. The transformation was astounding.

"Wow."

The older woman beamed. "Always nice to know I haven't lost my touch."

Glancing at Gabriel she got another jolt. His scar was gone. A wiry blond beard, neatly trimmed, now hugged his jawline as if it had always been there. His eyebrows had been lightened and with the blond wig looking so natural, she'd take bets his own mother wouldn't have known him.

"I don't believe it."

He flashed her a genuine smile. "Zeke and Janet know what they're doing."

The older man looked pleased.

"I don't think anyone will recognize us tonight, what do you think?"

"I'm speechless."

The couple beamed, sharing smiles. Cassy watched Gabriel pay in cash, trying not to wince at the cost while she kept sneaking glances in the mirrors around the room to reconcile their new looks. Gabriel chatted easily with the couple about the surprise they were going to give their friends before they announced their engagement.

The last bit startled her so much she nearly gave them away by gasping out loud. A funny tingle in her midsection became electric when he slid his arm around her as naturally as if he did it all the time.

Cassy barely managed to go with the flow. It was all

she could do to pretend his easy conversation was something she was used to hearing when she'd never heard him talk so much. She couldn't help thinking this was probably the man he'd been before the toxin was stolen. It made her sad to think how badly that one incident had changed their lives.

Without thought, she leaned her head against his chest and let him talk them out of the shop when three new customers entered. The rainy day had given way to a dreary evening.

"What do you think?" he asked when they were in the car.

"Is that beard going to stay on?"

He grinned and her stomach fluttered. "The problem's going to come when I try to take it off. Itches like the devil."

"The beard?"

"And the wig."

Her own wig didn't itch exactly, but it was a strange feeling having something tight covering her scalp. She had to fold her hands to keep from touching it.

"How did you know about that place?"

"I dated a local actress once."

Of course he had. The old Gabriel must have been a ladies' man, like Beacher. He could be devilishly attractive. She'd thought so even when he was scaring the daylights out of her. And when he smiled one of those rare smiles, a woman didn't have a chance.

"Where are we going now?"

"You're going to rent a car," he told her.

"Why?"

"We're confusing our back trail."

"It's working. I'm confused."

Again the flash of humor that did disturbing things to her insides appeared.

"Why are we renting a car when we have this wonderful little wreck?"

"Because by now Sliffman knows about this car. Remember the two women in Andrea's parking lot?"

"Oh. Well, why didn't we rent a car in the first place?"

His lips twisted wryly. "Because I didn't think of it at the time. The used-car lot was right there. Can you drive with that arm?"

"If I take off the sling, but I'll need to use my driver's license. If they know I'm with you—"

"That won't matter. The people watching the gallery will be looking for this car. I plan to be in and out before they run this rental plate and make the connection." He hesitated. "You don't have to do this."

"No, but we both know I will."

Feeling strange in the wig and makeup, and minus her sling, Cassy walked to the rental place alone after he dropped her at the corner. He hadn't told her what sort of car to get so she rented a sporty, bright blue coupe and prayed she'd be able to drive it around the corner to the shopping center where he'd said he was going to park.

Part of her wondered if he'd be there or if this was a ploy to walk away from her. But she told herself he would have rented the car *before* taking her to the costume shop if that had been his intention.

Cassy tried not to use her left hand as she drove cautiously to the arranged spot and found him there, parked beneath an overgrown tree in the farthest, darkest corner of the lot. Despite the blond wig and makeup that covered his scar, Gabriel was still seeking out the shadowy places of the night. It made her heart ache for him.

She moved to the passenger's side while he transferred their packages to the backseat and small trunk of the rental.

"Did this thing come with sunglasses?" he asked.

Puzzled, she glanced at the light mist falling around them in the dark before she realized he was referring to the car's color.

"I like blue."

"So do I but this neon color stands out."

"Then you should have specified, or rented it yourself."

He scowled. "I don't match my driver's license picture at the moment."

"In case it's escaped your attention, neither do I, but they barely glanced at it."

"You're a woman," he pointed out, sliding behind the steering wheel.

"There's a typical masculine response."

"Here's your sling."

"Thanks." Cassy welcomed the material cradling her arm once more. Her body had begun complaining about this morning's tumble from the bike. Stiff and achy muscles accompanied her throbbing wrist.

"Now what?"

"Now we go back to the mall and use a restroom to change clothes for the reception."

"Why not check into a motel?"

"We want to stay a moving target. The minute we

settle we risk being found. Sliffman isn't going to roll over and wait for us to talk to him. He'll have people actively looking for us."

Cassy fell silent until they left the parking lot. "What time do we need to be at the gallery?"

"The reception's from seven to nine."

"We're going to be late. And won't we need an invitation to get in?"

"Technically, yes."

"Technically?"

There was irony in the curve of his lips. "We're going to fake it."

"This just keeps getting better."

"You could always wait outside," he offered.

CASSY HAD CHOSEN her outfit with care but there was no way to change without causing her wrist more pain, especially now that she didn't dare disturb her wig and makeup. The wide-legged black silk pants had an elastic waistband that pulled on easily, but required both hands. The full material looked like a skirt until she moved. She'd chosen it for the slash pockets deep enough to conceal a gun. A black satin, button-down blouse and matching jacket with a pair of satin heels rounded out the look. She wished she'd opted for flats instead, but the outfit required heels to complete the sophisticated look she was going for.

In the ladies' room mirror she barely recognized herself. The crystals Gabriel had given her were the perfect accent as they sparkled in the overhead lights. The black outfit set off her new red hair and the only thing that marred the look was her cloth sling. Cassy decided she could stuff it in the other pocket and hold her wrist against her waist. However, until they reached the gallery she'd keep the sling on for support.

She studied her reflection looking for an awkward bulge from the gun. Relieved when there wasn't one, she went to join Gabriel and found him waiting in the hall between the restrooms. Behind a pair of spectacles, his eyes gleamed in masculine approval the minute he saw her. Her heart beat a little faster when he strode forward to claim the bag of old clothing from her good hand.

"You look…perfect."

His voice sounded rusty. "Thank you. You look pretty good yourself."

While the dark sports coat, black turtleneck and slacks weren't a big departure from his normal attire, the outfit made a dramatic statement with his blond beard and hair. The look suited him.

"Where did you get the glasses?"

"At the drugstore when I picked up the ibuprofen."

"Nice touch. Can you see through them?"

"Well enough."

Cassy was aware they drew several eyes as he led her outside to the car. The force of his personality would command attention anywhere he went. Even if it was a farce, she felt good being escorted by him.

"We're running awfully late."

"Intentionally," he assured her. "We need to arrive at the height of things so we'll be less noticeable."

Women would always notice Gabriel, but she didn't tell him so.

"It won't take us long from here."

He had just enough time to rehearse her role for getting them inside and they were there.

GABE WAS FAIRLY CERTAIN the man checking invitations at the door would be one of Sliffman's people. He'd spotted a dark sedan with a view to the entrance and someone inside who was probably backup. Sliffman might or might not be here himself, but for certain, others would be.

They moved quickly to fall in behind another well-dressed older couple who appeared to be walking toward the door.

"Did you bring the invitation Gretchen gave us?" Cassy asked in a carrying voice.

"I thought you brought it."

"I told you I wasn't going to carry a purse tonight."

Gabe let annoyance show in his voice. "I didn't realize that meant you weren't going to bring the invitation."

"Since when was I put in charge? It probably doesn't matter anyhow. Surely Gretchen will have given them our name."

"Don't bet on it," he told her glumly.

"Oh, Perry, don't sulk. I know you didn't want to come in the first place, but what's the worst they can do? Send us away? If they do, we'll come back another time. If Gretchen hadn't said this sculptor was so good we wouldn't even be here. Tell you what, if they don't let us in we'll go over to that new place you've been wanting to try for dinner."

The older couple paused at the door to show their

invitation. The woman cast a sympathetic look Cassy's way while Gabe grumped about her blasted art collection.

"May I see your invitation?" the attendant asked in a bored voice.

Gabe scowled as he studied the man, looking for the telltale bulge that would show where he kept his gun. "My wife forgot it."

"I did no such thing, it was your fault. And it wasn't even our invitation. Gretchen Morrison offered us hers because she couldn't come tonight. Hopefully, she gave Rochelle Leeman our names. Perry and Bonnie Sturbridge?"

The man glanced at a clipboard. "I'm sorry, you're not on the list."

"I told you so," Gabe groused. "Now can we leave?"

The older couple had paused nearby. The woman, obviously listening, came back. "I'm certain you'll find Gretchen Morrison on your list," she told the man. "This couple is friends of hers."

He glanced down again and frowned. "I'll have to check on this."

"Do so. There's Rochelle now." She made an imperious motion to Rochelle, who hurried to obey the summons.

"Deborah, how good to see you! And Eric, so nice of you to come."

Gabe knew this was the moment when it could all fall apart but the flustered woman eyed Gabe and Cassy without a flicker of recognition.

"Is there a problem?"

"No invitation," the man told her, indicating them. "And their names aren't on the list."

Cassy stepped forward quickly.

"Ms. Leeman, I'm Bonnie Sturbridge. Gretchen Morrison is my godmother. She offered us her invitation but we left it at home. She told me I had to come and check out this new sculptor you're featuring. I don't remember his name."

"Gabriel Lowe. Yes, of course. It's all right, Ned. Please do come in. Gretchen was quite taken with Gabe's work. Are you a collector?"

"Newly started, I'm afraid. Perry just came into a generous inheritance and I'm trying to find some display pieces for our new house. Gretchen got me enthused and suggested we come tonight."

"Of course. I'm so glad you did. Come in and look around. If you'll excuse me for just a second…"

Rochelle turned to greet a man who'd entered behind them. The first couple had faded away and Gabe put his hand on the small of Cassy's back to steer her clear of the door.

"Nice," he whispered in her ear. She glowed up at him, eyes bright with relief and excitement.

"I was scared to death," she admitted, "but she didn't recognize you."

He turned down a glass of champagne from a passing waiter and Cassy did the same. "Don't get cocky."

"I'm too nervous for cocky. Look! That's one of your pieces over there, isn't it? And it's marked sold!"

Gabe felt a strange thrill as he stared at the sold sign on the Noah's Ark set he'd picked up only yesterday.

"I wonder how much she got for it?"

His eyebrows lifted in amusement even though he wondered the same thing. He couldn't believe it when they found a second piece also marked sold. This affirmed his talent in a way nothing else could have done.

The crouching lion held center stage in the second room and his heart lurched. *One* crouching lion.

"What's wrong?" Cassiopia whispered as he neared the sculpture and ran a hand along its flank.

"Where's the other one?" he muttered.

Her eyes widened. She cast around the room looking for the second lion, but he'd already seen that it wasn't there. Before she could say anything the couple they'd come in behind joined them.

"Amazing, isn't it?" the woman asked. "His work is so realistic. The artist was extremely talented."

"Was?" Cassiopia asked.

"You haven't heard? Oh, my dear, it's been all over the news. That house that blew up last night belonged to him."

Gabe listened even as he inspected the piece carefully.

"No way," Cassiopia exclaimed, putting just the right amount of shocked emphasis in her tone.

"I'm afraid so. Either he's the one who was killed or he's in very serious trouble. Rochelle doubled the asking price on his work as a result."

Gabe worked to control his reaction to that.

"You do know Gabriel Lowe is the man the FBI believed stole that deadly toxin five years ago. You must remember the case. The toxin was never recovered. I must say it makes one wonder."

It was on the tip of Gabe's tongue to ask her "Wonder what?" but she changed the subject with barely a pause for breath.

"Your husband seems very fond of this piece. Are you going to buy it?"

"Oh, no. It's too big for the space."

"Maybe," Gabe answered at the same time.

Cassiopia sent him a worried look. "Darling, where would we put it? We're just starting to collect. I wanted something more along the lines of the Noah's Ark pieces," she told the woman.

"Yes. Those *are* spectacular. I do hope more than one cast was made. I wouldn't mind owning that set myself. If there's only the one, the buyer's price will really jump with the artist being dead."

Cassy shuddered. Gabe moved quickly to her side. "We ought to think about the lion for the back garden," he told her.

"Surely you're jesting," the older woman said. "You don't put works like these outside."

"No?" He tapped the lion's head. "You think it would rust?"

Humor danced in Cassiopia's eyes. The woman made an excuse and hurried her husband away from them.

"That was mean," she told him.

"Yeah, well, we have to work our way over there. I need a look in the back room. Pretend an interest in that painting."

"Not that orange monstrosity!"

Gabe inclined his head. He pointed to the piece, urging her in its direction. "Rochelle's back room is beyond that door."

"I thought we were going to—"

"New plan. If anyone asks, I went in search of a bathroom."

Cassiopia bit at her lower lip as they made their way across the room, dodging waiters and guests alike. Gabe had been keeping his eyes peeled for Sliffman or Huntington, relieved not to see either of them. He didn't think his disguise would fool a professional like Sliffman up close.

Gabe halted them before the large blob of orange paint. The minute he saw an opening, he reached for the door handle beside it, and found it unlocked.

Slipping inside he turned on the light switch immediately. If he were caught, it would look more natural than if he pretended to be fumbling around in the dark. He didn't think he'd be long. Given the way things had been going so far, he had a sinking feeling he wasn't going to find the other lion.

He was right.

When he emerged he found Cassiopia chatting with an intense, birdlike woman in a scarlet dress who bobbed her head a lot and flung her arms about like a pair of broken wings. She was enthusing over the ugly painting. Gabe suspected she was the artist. Rochelle was heading in their direction and Gabe wasn't sure if she'd seen him come out of the room or not. While she hadn't recognized him yet, he wasn't about to press his luck.

"That wasn't the bathroom," he announced, interrupting the woman. "We have to leave."

"We just got here," Cassy protested on cue.

"Something I ate disagreed with me."

"Are you sure, Perry? I was just talking with—"

"Not now. I'm going to be sick. Sorry," he told the woman as Rochelle reached them.

"Are you enjoying the show?" she asked perkily.

"Very much," Cassiopia responded, "but I'm afraid my husband is ill. It's his own fault. I told him not to eat all that shrimp at lunch today, but would he listen? No. I told him it tasted a little off."

Gabe tried to look ill and groaned.

"Honestly, Perry," Cassiopia scolded. "This is so embarrassing. I'm sorry, Ms. Leeman, but the truth is, my stomach is a little upset as well. We're very interested in several pieces including this brilliant painting of Ms. Weissel's, but we're going to have to come back. Will you excuse us, please?"

"Of course."

With a perplexed frown, Rochelle stepped aside while Cassiopia continued to berate him as they hurried toward the entrance.

"Next time will you listen to me? If you throw up in front of all these people, Perry, I will never forgive you. Do you hear me? Never!"

"The whole block can hear you. I'm going to be sick and all you can do is complain."

They were past the alert attendant and out the door without being stopped, but Gabe didn't drop his role in case anyone was watching or listening.

"I think I may have ptomaine," he complained as he hurried them down the sidewalk. "Maybe I should go to the hospital." And in a barely audible whisper he added, "Keep going."

Cassiopia was so quick on the uptake he could

have hugged her. She stepped up the pace and continued her harangue.

"This is humiliating. I hate to think what Ms. Leeman will say to Gretchen when they talk. I hope you've learned your lesson. Next time, show some restraint at a buffet. You are such a pig when it comes to shrimp. This serves you right. I wasn't ready to leave and if someone buys that painting before I can get back here tomorrow, I'm going to be furious with you."

"I'm dying and all you can think of is some stupid painting?"

They reached the car and he handed her the keys. He knew her wrist was hurting. He'd seen the way she kept her arm pressed against her middle while she was listening to the artist, but it couldn't be helped.

Questions and fear were in her eyes, but Cassiopia said nothing as they pulled away from the curb. Gabe watched the mirrors. There was no sign anyone had followed them.

"Pull into that lot over there and we'll switch places," he told her. "We need to get back to the shopping center where we left the other car in case they run these plates."

"What about this car? And what about the lion and the package?"

"We'll leave this one on the rental lot and lock the key inside. The lion is gone."

She braked to a halt and stared at him wide-eyed. "What do you mean, gone?"

"That's the wrong lion on display."

Chapter Ten

"Are you sure?"

"Positive. Beacher and I built those bases. If you believe in the power of prayer, now would be a good time for one."

"Do you think the authorities have the other lion?"

Gabe scratched at his jaw where the spirit gum was irritating his skin. He felt drained and achy and scared at the same time. "No. I think Rochelle sold it."

"What are we going to do?"

"I don't know," he admitted. "Let me think about it."

Neither of them spoke as they drove to the parking lot where they'd left the car they'd purchased earlier. Gabe transferred their clothing and purchases back again.

"You're going to have to return this rental to the lot," he told her. "Park it in front of the door, put the key under the mat, lock it and walk to the corner. I'll wait there for you. It probably won't matter, but if the lot has surveillance cameras I'd rather not have our license plate show up on them."

She looked as drained as he felt, but nodded gamely.

When she joined him a few minutes later it was obvious they had both run out of steam. She didn't even ask where they were going.

Gabe headed north, keeping to the city streets. As soon as they crossed into Maryland he started looking for motels. When he spotted a likely candidate he pulled into a nearby chain restaurant.

"I'm not hungry," she protested.

"Neither am I. Wait here. I'll be out in a few minutes."

HE WAS GONE MORE THAN a few minutes. Cassy was about to go in and check on him when he came striding out, a bag of food tucked under one arm. The beard and wig were gone and he was carrying his jacket. He'd put his glasses back in place, mussed his hair and retained the putty that covered his scar. Once again his look was altered just enough that anyone who didn't know him well would have had to look twice to recognize him.

She hadn't been hungry, but now the scent of roast turkey woke her sleeping appetite.

"I needed an excuse to use their restroom so I hope you like turkey and coconut cream pie. I'll get us checked in over there and we can eat in the room."

She took the bag and tried not to salivate as the smells reminded her that lunch had been hours ago. The room proved to be remarkably similar to the one the night before. Different colored paint, paper and bed-spread, but the layout was much the same.

While Gabe went to the drink machine in the hall, Cassy laid out their meals.

"Not exactly gourmet fare," he told her around a bite of turkey.

"Good, though. I was hungry after all. Your face is red, you know."

"The spirit gum irritated the skin."

Gabe turned on the television set and they ate in silence. An inane sitcom kept them from thinking too much. Halfway through her slice of pie, Cassy put her plastic fork down.

"What are we going to do?"

Gabriel took a long swallow of his bottled water before answering.

"When Rochelle introduced me to Gretchen Morrison she said Mrs. Morrison was a very important customer."

"Uh-huh. That's why we used her name."

"Right. The lions weren't crated. They must have gone on the truck last. I'm guessing Rochelle showed them to Mrs. Morrison and she bought one then and there."

"But wouldn't Rochelle have waited to let her take it until after the show? You said she wanted them for the centerpiece."

"I doubt she'd argue with a good customer, especially since she was never supposed to have had both lions in the first place."

"Then we'll have to go see Mrs. Morrison."

His surprised expression would have been comical another time. "I'll go see Mrs. Morrison. You get some rest."

"I don't think so. It will seem less threatening if we both go to see her."

"I wasn't planning to visit her exactly."

"You're going to break into her house?" Of course he was.

"Don't worry about it."

"I'll worry if I want. I'm going with you."

"No, you aren't. I can do this better alone."

"No doubt." She grinned up at him, remembering her inept attempt to enter his house. "But I'm going anyhow." She held up a hand to stave off his next protest. "I'm a quick study. I won't get in the way. Do you really think I could sleep while you go over there alone?"

"No."

He stood, his features hard and uncompromising.

Cassy glared right back. "You walk out that door and I'm calling Sliffman."

"You won't."

"Wrong." She put all the conviction she could into her voice and her glare. "I've done nothing they can arrest me for and if you aren't going to protect me, he will."

She saw at once that she'd fully roused the beast and he was most intimidating. Still, she refused to flinch or back away despite every instinct that urged her to sit down and make herself as small as possible.

"Tonight, I proved I can be an asset," she told him, proud that her voice didn't quaver.

"Yes, but this time I'm breaking in to a house, not a party. And that *is* a criminal act."

"I can live with it if you can. I've already broken in to your house. Twice."

She shouldn't have reminded him. He didn't need ammunition for why she shouldn't go with him.

"But this time you'll go to jail if we're caught."

"Then make sure we don't get caught."

For a minute she thought she'd pushed him too far. Gabriel could have posed for one of his crouching lion sculptures. Every muscle and sinew was tensed to strike.

"If you were a man I'd deck you."

"If I were a man we wouldn't be having this conversation." She wasn't sure where the courage to face him down was coming from but she could not afford to relent. "You'd take Beacher along, wouldn't you?"

"You aren't Beacher."

"No, but I'm the best you have. While you look up her address, I'll put my jeans back on."

She started to push past him. He grabbed her shoulders firmly enough to hold her in place, but not hard enough to bruise.

"Why?"

She reminded herself that he was a wounded beast with no reason to trust. But he needed someone to trust and she wanted that someone to be her.

"Because I'm scared and I'm tired and I want this over. And we both know it won't be over until we know what Beacher found."

"It may not be over even then."

"But we'll have tried. *I'll* have tried."

"Because of your father?"

She hadn't given any thought to her father, but said, "That, too."

His eyes bore into hers. She held that gaze. There was only an instant to recognize the change in his expression before he lowered his face, drew her body against his and claimed her mouth.

Once again it was not a gentle kiss, but Cassy didn't want gentle from him. The fluttery feeling in her stomach became a warmth that quickly blazed. She used her good hand to pull him even closer and kissed him back. Her legs turned to jelly while her insides melted. She felt the press of his erection against her leg and was elated. She wanted him just as much.

GABE PULLED BACK, struggling for a control that should have come easily. It was anything but. Touching her had been a serious mistake. He wanted her with a hunger that blunted common sense. And she wanted him, too, scars and all. That knowledge was heady.

The bed was right there. A simple nudge and she'd be flat on her back, as open, needy and willing as him to sate this driving urge.

"You're playing with fire," he growled.

She shook her head. Her silky hair tumbled about her shoulders. "A lion."

"Lions maul their mates," he warned. "I don't want you getting hurt, Cassiopia."

"That's not high on my list, either, but I make my own decisions."

He was pretty sure they were having a conversation on two levels at once. The words applied to tonight's planned activity as well the one they were close to having in the large bed that beckoned them.

He kissed her again. She made a slight mew of protest and he gentled the kiss, all desire to punish her gone. This kiss asked, rather than demanded, and she responded instantly.

Gabe thought he might never get enough of the taste and feel of her body against his. He groaned, low in his throat, and forced his hands to set her aside. Humming with unfulfilled desire he found he was shaking. Shaking!

She took an unsteady step back. Her mouth had a bruised, just-kissed look, her gaze sexily slumberous.

"I'll be right out."

Her voice wasn't close to steady.

"Wait for me."

Gabe groaned and turned away. She made her way into the bathroom, trusting him to do as she demanded. Torn, he stood there. She came back out to reach for the bag of clothes they'd purchased earlier.

He could still leave, but he knew he wouldn't. She amused him, angered him, tantalized him and in general drove him crazy, but he wanted her like no one else, ever. And he wouldn't be able to forgive himself if anything happened to her.

Only a fool would let her come along tonight but if he hadn't been a fool he never would have touched her in the first place. So much for military discipline. His emotions were a tangled mess.

Her father's death would always be there between them. She might want him physically, but once her passion ebbed and she started thinking again she'd be appalled. As long as Gabe remembered nothing of what happened that day, even finding the toxin wouldn't prove his innocence.

Why hadn't Beacher told Gabe what he was doing? Why had he gone off on his own to play hero?

Wasn't that exactly what Cassiopia accused Gabe of trying to do?

This time his groan of frustration came for an entirely different reason. He reached for the phone book tucked beneath the nightstand and wished he could get the taste and feel of Cassiopia out of his head.

THERE WAS NOTHING like a little sexual tension to make a woman forget all her other aches and pains, Cassy decided. She managed the stretch jeans with their elastic waistband, but thought better of the white blouse. If they were going to break into a house she needed to wear dark colors, so she left her fancy blouse on.

She was about to commit a felony. Again. Yet all she kept thinking about was what would happen here in this motel room *after* they got back.

Assuming they didn't get caught.

Gabe was waiting when she entered the room and reached for the jacket.

"You do what I say, when I tell you or you stay here. Clear?"

Cassy gave him a curt nod, afraid to trust her mouth with words. This was no time to argue. Gabriel didn't look satisfied, but he led her back out in the rain to the car without a word.

Gretchen Morrison's house was huge and tucked away among the trees on top of a hill. The only way to get there was up a steep, narrow driveway. Gabriel made a U-turn and parked on the exposed side of the road down below.

"This car will stand out in this neighborhood," she warned.

"I know, but it's not like we can leave it at the end of the block."

No, the block was close to a mile long in the direction they'd come from and who knew how far down it continued. Each estate had acreage and all of it wooded.

"The car would have never made this hill," she huffed as they trudged up the incline. "I'm not sure I will. I'd hate to live here in winter."

There was a flash of teeth, as he must have smiled.

Moisture dripped from the canopy of trees overhead. The rain had stopped again, but thanks to the trees they were thoroughly wet by the time they reached the house, where fear stopped her in her tracks. Gabriel also halted as they stared at the black Jaguar parked in the turnaround out front. Few windows faced this side of the house and most of those were on the second level. All were ablaze with light.

"That's not good."

"No," Gabriel agreed. "Wait here while I check the sides and back. Call out if anyone comes up the drive."

Privately, Cassy was relieved. She had no desire to get any closer to this solemnly intimidating structure.

Gabriel vanished, becoming one with the shadows. He was entirely too good at doing that. The military should have put him in covert operations. He was a natural.

Cassy studied the parked car in the weak glow from the porch light. A dented scrape along the front fender marred the car's pristine finish. She was about to move closer for a look at the license plate when the front door swung open.

Cassy pressed against the nearest tree. A figure hurried outside and ran straight to the waiting Jag without giving her a glimpse of his face despite the additional light spilling from the front door. The dome light didn't go on as he climbed inside and started the engine.

Frozen in place, Cassy held her breath. Headlights swept past within inches of where she stood. The car didn't slow. It rolled down the steep drive with more speed than sense.

Gabriel emerged out of nothing beside her. The scream of his name choked in her throat unuttered.

"I saw. Did you get a look at him?"

She shook her head.

"Come on."

Quaking, she followed. They were at the front door before her stunned brain kicked in. Surely he didn't intend to go in there? Couldn't he see something was wrong?

He nudged the door open with his foot. It bounced back against something on the floor out of sight. Gabe swore beneath his breath.

"Wait."

Cassy had already stopped moving and was racked with uncontrollable shaking now. She glimpsed a pale thin arm stretched out against the cold, hard slate floor and her stomach rebelled. The last time she'd entered an unlocked door, she'd found Beacher's body.

REGRET HIT HIM as Gabe took in the scene, and summoned a professional detachment. Gretchen Morrison had supported her last artist. Her frail body was sprawled in a pool of her own blood. The coppery smell of death clung to the air. Her throat had been slit so deeply that the cut had nearly severed her head.

From the position of the body and the blood splatters, Gabe was fairly certain she'd opened the door to her attacker. She'd either turned her back to him or he'd forced her around to strike the killing blow. It wouldn't have taken much force. She had been a fairly small woman.

But her killer had been sloppy. He'd stepped in her blood on his way down the hall. Several clear, running footprints led away from the scene. He must not have noticed them against the dark stone floor.

Going inside would compromise the crime scene, but

Gabe had no choice when he spotted the crouching lion in the foyer to his right. His sculpture had obviously been positioned to stand guard at the bottom of the open stairway that led to the second floor. Someone had pushed the piece over on its side.

Gabe removed his wet shoes and stepped inside, quickly moving to the lion. He was careful not to step where the killer had. There were blood smears on the cold metal, but the hidden compartment was still closed, giving him hope.

Gabe opened the hidden panel at the back of the base with trepidation. He fully expected to find the package gone, but it was still nestled inside. He scooped it out, wiped where he had touched, closed the panel and stood.

His heart landed in his throat as his gaze traveled down the opposite hall to a wheelchair sitting there. No wonder the killer had gone to his left first. Gretchen Morrison hadn't died alone.

Gabe didn't have to cross to the victim to see that the man slumped there had tried to flee. He must have called out to Gretchen and summoned death instead.

Sickened, Gabe returned to the front door and handed Cassiopia the package before he stepped outside and put his shoes back on. She gazed at him with eyes that were too wide and filled with horror. He was thankful she hadn't seen what he had.

He took her arm and hurried her back down the steep driveway. Not until they reached the car and began driving away did she speak.

"I didn't get his license plate number," she whispered.

He glanced at her, worried she might fall apart, but her bleak gaze was steady. She'd hold it together.

"I did."

"We need to report this."

"We will."

"I'm going to be sick."

"No, you won't."

She shut her eyes and leaned her head back, swallowing hard. She was trembling. He felt shaky himself. There might have been other people inside that house. He should have checked, but it was too late now. Bitterly, he drove well away from the area before he started looking for a public telephone. They weren't as plentiful as they used to be now that everyone carried a cell phone, but a brightly lit gas station on a busy corner had one and he pulled over.

Cassiopia said nothing when he got out and made the call. Minutes later they were back on the road. Her eyes were shut, but Gabe knew she wasn't sleeping. He pulled into a beer-and-wine shop. She merely nodded without opening her eyes when he told her he'd only be a minute and went inside.

Her silence worried him, but he didn't feel much like talking, either. As soon as they arrived back at the motel she handed him the package and went into the bathroom and closed the door.

Gabe listened for the sound of retching that never came. After a few minutes he heard water running and relaxed. He poured her a glass of white wine and opened a bottle of beer. The alcohol wouldn't help rid him of the taste of death, but he needed it all the same.

THE WATER HELPED SOME, but Cassy still felt ill as she left the bathroom to face Gabriel. He was waiting in one of the chairs, an open bottle of beer in his hand. The wrapped package sat on the table beside him. He'd opened a bottle of wine as well and poured her a glass.

Such a small thing, it shouldn't make her want to cry. She moved forward, lifted the glass and drank it straight down. The wine churned in her stomach.

"You'll get sick," he cautioned.

"Probably. Are you going to open that?" The package was the right size for a thick, oversized paperback book.

"I thought I'd let you do it."

She poured another glass of wine but didn't drink it. "This isn't a lab."

"Do you need one?"

For an answer, she reached for the package. Her hands were surprisingly steady. The toxin needed liquid as a catalyst. They should be safe. Nevertheless, she unwrapped the box with care.

A white envelope with *Gabe* scrawled across the face had been taped to the outside of a black box. Cassy removed the note gently and handed it to him without a word.

Gabriel stared at his name for a second. The pulse in his temple throbbed. He turned the envelope over and opened it with care. There was a single sheet of paper inside.

"Buddy," he began to read aloud, *"if you're reading this I'm in big trouble or dead."*

Cassy swallowed hard, forcing the image of death aside.

"Dr. Richards outsmarted the bastards, but his daughter pointed me in the right direction."

She caught her breath.

"I left the toxin where I found it, but here's the documentation. The hard drive is encrypted but the notes aren't. I'm leaving this with you because I think Andrea followed me to Sunburst. If so, she knows I found something. I need to go talk to her."

Gabriel's jaw clenched. The vein in his forehead throbbed with life.

"If something happens to me, dig at her. Dr. Pheng might know if she was involved with Carstairs or anyone on base besides you, but here's something interesting. I learned Huntington's wife is spending big all of a sudden. Where's all that money coming from on a major's salary?"

Cassy heard growing anger in Gabe's voice.

"The word is that Huntington's going to be passed over for promotion and plans to retire. We both know he has no love for you so be careful. I spotted a black Jag following me twice now."

Cassy inhaled sharply.

"Find out who owns one or has access to one. I'm sure you're pissed at me right now, especially if I got myself killed, but things fell into place fast after I talked with the daughter. I had a hunch and it paid off. You couldn't have come with me into Sunburst so I didn't bother to tell you about it and I'm not going to tell you what I'm doing now, either, because you'd insist on coming with me, and Andrea won't talk if you're there. She knows something. I know she does. I'll explain everything tonight. You know how much I always wanted to be a hero, but if I don't make it back to pick this up…"

Gabriel's voice suddenly faltered.

"...it's my own damn fault, not yours. Don't get yourself killed trying to avenge my stupidity. Go out and live your life, Gabe. Do it for me, buddy. You're the brother I always wanted. I hereby make you personally responsible for the contents of my not-so-little black book. There's bound to be someone in there that can put up with a loner like you. Love ya, pal. Beacher."

GABE COULDN'T SWALLOW past the tight constriction in his throat. The hollow pain of loss was so acute his vision blurred. He stood abruptly, dropping the note to the table. He didn't look at Cassiopia as he walked out the door. He needed space. He needed to move. He wanted to hit something or someone. He wanted Beacher alive, that friendly, boyish face beaming at him as Gabe trounced him at handball or sat with him over a beer.

CASSY WATCHED HIM GO, tears threading their way down her cheeks. She didn't call out or try to stop him. He needed to grieve in private and she understood. She sat in the chair and cried for the dead and for Gabriel. When she finished, she splashed water on her blotchy face and organized their earlier purchases, changing into the sweatpants and shirt she'd bought to sleep in.

The box sat where they'd left it. She tossed the wrapping paper in the wastebasket and neatened the room. When there was nothing left to do, she pulled off the sweatsuit and climbed into bed naked.

She was wide-awake and waiting when Gabriel returned, his cold, remote mask solidly in place. He smelled of sweat and despair. She guessed he'd been running. As a stress reliever, she approved, but her heart ached for him. He was so alone.

He said nothing as he took clothing from his bag and went into the bathroom. Cassy settled when she heard the shower start up. The worst was over. He was grieving in his own way, but at least he wasn't bottling it up completely. She was pretty sure he'd been crying.

Even though she'd pulled back the covers on his side of the bed, Gabe didn't use them. He came out in yet another turtleneck pullover and pair of jeans, turned off the single light she'd left on for him and laid flat on his back on top of the blankets.

His voice came out of the dark, husky, with a tight edge. "As of now, you're out of it."

She rolled to face him, though she couldn't see his features in the dark room.

"You want me to end up like the others? I'm safer with you."

"I can't protect you, Cassiopia."

There was such pain in him. She touched his face and his body went stiff.

"You're the only one who can," she told him softly.

"Don't." He drew her hand away.

"I need to touch you. I need to feel alive. I need *you.*"

"No!"

She gripped his hand, feeling the puckered skin of his burns. She lifted it to her mouth and kissed it tenderly.

"No."

But he didn't pull free.

"Fate made us partners, Gabriel. I'm going to make us lovers."

Chapter Eleven

Gabe knew he should roll away from the temptation of her, but God help him, he didn't want to. He craved her touch like a starving man. Beacher's note had ripped him to shreds and the run had left him exhausted. And while his grief seemed overwhelming, her touch brought him to life in a way he hadn't felt in years.

No woman had ever made love to him before. He'd always taken the lead. And as her lips and hands moved over him, it took massive control not to reach for her. When she touched his burnt skin with tender, almost reverent lips, Gabe tried to pull back. He'd actually forgotten about his many scars for a moment.

"No," she demanded. "Let me. They're the scars of a hero, not something to be ashamed of."

"I'm no one's hero," he growled. Beacher had wanted to be a hero and now he was dead.

"Mine," she whispered.

The word had the sound of a vow. He trembled inside but there were too many conflicting emotions to sort. Too much to feel, to taste, to hunger for.

"Stop, Cassiopia." But he didn't want her to stop. Not

ever. He held her away with unsteady hands. "These aren't the only scars." He couldn't bear her knowing how much damage had been done. Even without the light on she would know what his clothing hid if she continued.

"Let me see."

"No." He pulled away and rolled to his side.

"Do you really think I'm that shallow, Gabriel? Do you think the sight of a few scars will send *me* running?"

No, she wouldn't run. She would stay and her pity would be worse. Much worse.

"There's more than a few scars," he told her gruffly. "A section of burning siding landed on me while I was unconscious. I'm not a pretty sight."

"I'm sorry for what you went through, Gabriel. I can't even imagine how awful it must have been, but physical beauty isn't the measure of a person."

He shifted uncomfortably. She didn't understand. She couldn't possibly. "Look, just forget the whole thing and get some sleep. We have to be out of here first thing in the morning."

She sat up. Before he could stop her she'd turned on her bedside light. The blanket and sheet pooled at her waist revealing both silken breasts, the nipples hard and pointed.

"No. We need to talk about this."

Gabe groaned.

"I want you and you want me, too."

He didn't want to be having this conversation and he wished she'd pull up the blanket and cover herself.

"Don't push me aside, Gabriel. I'm not Andrea."

"Andrea has nothing to do with this!" Frustrated and angry, he glared at her.

She didn't even flinch at the lash of his words.

"Of course she does. She rejected you when you needed her the most, but it's been almost four years. Time to move on, Gabriel. You have to lower those formidable barriers you put up to keep everyone at a distance. It's time to let go and take a chance. With me."

Bitterness twisted his insides. "What gives you the right to judge me? You want to see scars, lady?" He reached for the hem of his shirt. "I'll show you scars."

"No! Not like this!"

She yanked on his hands before he could get the shirt up and over his head. They struggled briefly before she winced and drew back. The sight of her tears wrenched something loose inside him.

"I don't want to cause you more pain. I never wanted to do that." Her voice was thick with the tears starting to trickle down her cheeks. "I know I'm outspoken and pushy and I usually say the wrong thing, but this is about me, too. This is about how you feel about me! Whether you admit it or not, you're comparing me to the woman who walked away from your pain while you were in a hospital bed. But if you're going to keep judging every woman by her standards then I hope you enjoy living the life of a hermit."

With a sob, she started to leave the bed. He reached for her, pulling her back down, careful this time not to hurt her when she struggled briefly. She wouldn't look at him as she began to cry in earnest. His own cheeks were damp, but he couldn't stand her pain.

"I'm sorry. I'm sorry."

Because she was right. He *was* afraid to take a

chance. He was afraid she'd be so repulsed that she'd leave, but if he didn't try he'd lose her and he didn't want to lose her.

Gabe held her against his chest, resting his head on her silky hair, barely feeling the tears that soaked his shirt and streaked his face.

She was right. He was afraid.

There's bound to be someone that can put up with a loner like you, Beacher had written. Even Denny had tried to force him from his self-imposed isolation. Did he really want to live the rest of his life alone?

He and Cassiopia couldn't have forever. Unless his memory miraculously returned she could never be entirely sure what role he'd played in her father's death and neither could he, but it didn't matter. Not right now. Not tonight.

She pulled back, rubbing at her eyes furiously. Her face was puffy and blotchy. Hair tangled about her face. Tenderly, he regarded her, lifting her chin with his knuckle.

"Can we start over?"

"Why?"

"Because I need you to teach me how to trust again."

He dropped his hand when she said nothing. He'd blown it, and he'd lost something important. Something he hadn't even known he'd been missing.

"Take off your shirt."

Her voice was low, still clotted by the aftermath of tears. His gaze slid to the light and back to her face. She waited impassively. He could do this. He had to do this. For both of them.

Without rushing, he eased the shirt over his head.

He'd thought he'd been prepared for any reaction. But she examined him in silence, giving him no idea what she was thinking. And when she leaned toward him and placed her lips gently against a puckered ridge of skin, his eyes welled with fresh moisture.

"That wasn't so bad now, was it?"

He didn't know how to express the rush of emotions he was feeling. "What are you doing to me?"

"Loving you."

Gabe pulled her to him, saying with his lips and tongue what he couldn't with words.

He had to help her with his snap and zipper. Mindful of her wrist, he shucked pants that had become too tight, still uncomfortable as he bared even more scars on his hip and leg. Cassiopia insisted on kissing each one.

He couldn't put names to all his emotions, but she was going too slow with her tasting and touching. Barely trying, she was leading him ever closer to the brink. He wanted her now. And when she took him in her mouth, he nearly lost all control.

"My turn," he demanded gruffly, setting her aside.

Her smile of feminine satisfaction edged him another step closer. He paid homage to her mouth and throat and breasts, before working his way down her belly until her sweet cries became demands matching his own.

Gabe rolled on his back, pulling her with him, struggling to allow her to set the pace. She mounted him with exquisite slowness. Exerting every ounce of control he had left, Gabe let her settle, slick and tight and abruptly, as eager as he to release the incredible tension.

He swallowed her soft cry as she clenched around him. Control vanished in driving need and exquisite release.

For a very long time they lay together while their bodies cooled and their heartbeats mingled. Gabe thought he might be willing to hold her like this for the rest of his life. But after a while the back of his head and his leg began to throb. Cassiopia rolled off to one side, wincing as her bandaged wrist hit the mattress.

"Are you all right?"

She gazed at him and her smile lit his soul. "Never better."

And she curled against him trustingly and closed her eyes. After a few minutes, he closed his as well. He should get up and turn off the light, but it seemed like entirely too much effort.

He awoke to find the light still on and her pressed against him spoonstyle. His hand rested on the flatness of her belly while his arousal pressed against the rounded cheek of her butt. Gabe couldn't resist the impulse to slide his hand over the globe of her breast. Instantly, the nipple budded beneath his palm, rigid, tempting him to rub and pinch it to hardness.

Her breathing changed the moment he touched her. She made a soft sound of acceptance and pressed back against him, moving in invitation. Gabe swept aside the spill of her hair to reveal the long, smooth length of her neck. He kissed her there while pulling her more tightly against him until he could slide inside her. She sighed in welcome as she tightened around him.

In the soft gray light of early morning, augmented by the softly glowing bedside lamp, they made love slowly, learning each other's bodies with gentle eagerness until they were damp and too spent to move.

"GOOD MORNING TO YOU, TOO," Cassy told him some time later. "We left the light on all night."

"I noticed."

She didn't want to move, but she was stiff and sore all over and her wrist was throbbing painfully.

"Did I hurt you?" he asked.

"Do I look hurt?"

"You winced."

"Because my bladder is going to explode and I'm too comfortable to move."

"Yes."

She couldn't help grinning. "Don't revert. Complete sentences, remember?"

His eyes twinkled. "Too much effort."

And she was just thinking how much younger and relaxed he looked when his eyes began to cloud. Their idyllic moment was over. He rolled off the bed in a fluid motion.

"Do you want the bathroom first?"

"You're up. You can go ahead."

He entered the room without another word.

Now she did wince. Gabriel was an intensely private person. She suspected he hadn't always been that way. Given the extent of his injuries it was surprising he was even alive. She'd pushed him to reveal something painfully private last night while he was still grieving over the death of his best friend. She needed to be patient now. He needed time to accept all that had happened. Her wounded beast had begun to heal, but the process wouldn't happen overnight.

When Gabe came out a few minutes later she scooted past as he reached for last night's discarded jeans.

"I'll load the car while you take your shower," he called after her. "We can grab something to eat on the way."

"Deal," she agreed, wondering *on the way* to where?

Why did the morning after have to feel so awkward? Nobody needed all these stupid insecurities. Was he sorry? Could they both accept the night for what it was? Great sex.

Okay, stupendous sex. But sex. Not a lifetime of commitment. It wasn't as if she had never gone to bed with a man before. However things shook out, she was not going to regret what had passed between them last night. Or this morning. She smiled at the memory. She would take things one day at a time and try not to worry.

Or think the situation to death.

He had a steaming cup of coffee waiting when she came out.

"You are a god," she told him gratefully. And she would swear his neck reddened. He stepped quickly inside the bathroom and shut the door without replying. It would take time to teach him how to relax and have fun again.

And it wouldn't happen while they were in hiding for their lives.

Ignoring the television, she lifted the box that sat on the desk. After a moment's indecision, she opened it. One of the small notebooks her father had favored whenever he was working on a new project sat on top of the hard drive. Her father always claimed he thought better when he could scribble notes out in longhand before transferring them to the computer.

Love for him mingled with the sadness of her loss. She remembered all the times she'd seen her dad poring over notebooks like this one in his office at home and she suddenly missed him so much. She had a feeling he would have approved of Gabe.

Her coffee sat forgotten as she idly began scanning his notes in their neat, precise small script. While his field wasn't her area of expertise, she understood the basics. Apparently, her father had been doing a peer review of Dr. Pheng's work.

She began flipping through the pages. Her dad tended to write personal asides in his private journals as he thought an idea through. These notes weren't meant for others, they were a way of organizing his thoughts, but words like *ridiculous* and *preposterous* jumped out at her.

This was so typical of him, and yet the more she read, the more puzzled she became. Sequences had been underlined. Her dad's impatience and annoyance came through as clearly as though he were speaking.

Taking up the small pad of paper the hotel provided, she began making her own notes. She wasn't a chemist, but even she could see why her dad had been puzzled. "You're right, Dad, why would this have that result?"

"What result?"

Startled, Cassy looked up to find Gabriel standing there with his neatly combed hair still damp. He was dressed in yet another dark turtleneck shirt, pants and a sweatshirt that didn't hide the breadth of his shoulders or the trimness of his waist and hips. He was every inch an alpha male and his scars only enhanced the effect.

She sucked in a breath and let it out again at the flash of renewed desire. His eyes darkened as if he sensed her thoughts.

Arrogant male. He probably had.

"Dad was doing a peer review of Dr. Pheng's work.

That's not surprising given they're the leading experts in their field. From these notes I'd say they were working on possible antidotes to the toxin in the event it was ever used." She tapped the notebook lightly with her nail.

"I don't have a security clearance so I shouldn't even be looking at this."

She began putting things away. "I need to burn the few notes I did make so I don't get in real trouble. You wouldn't happen to have a match or a lighter, would you?"

"No. And this isn't the place." He nodded to the overhead sprinkler system.

"Good point."

"We'll burn them outside."

"Only if you find a match."

"Wait here."

Alpha male indeed. She really was going to have to work on his communication skills.

Her stiff muscles had loosened in the shower, but they were beginning to make themselves felt once again. Her wrist throbbed and she was aware of a multitude of bruises and new aches.

"Where should we put this box with the hard drive?" she asked as soon as Gabriel came back through the door.

He nodded toward his suitcase. "Unless you want to hold on to it."

Cassy had purchased a large shoulder bag when they'd gone shopping. She thought it might fit inside and it did.

"I thought of a way we can get rid of this hard drive that won't lead back to us," she told him. "What if we buy a shipping box and stick it in the mail? We can address it to Homeland Security and let them deal with it. We could even enclose a note telling them where to look for the vials. The authorities might suspect you were responsible but if we don't leave any prints they won't be able to prove anything."

Gabriel didn't look enthusiastic. "It has merit."

"But?"

"The minute we turn that hard drive over to anyone we lose the only edge we have. Are you all set?"

"Yes, but I don't understand. Aren't we in danger? Holding on to this seems like a really bad idea."

He nodded, but waited until they were outside to explain further. "If the killer suspects the toxin is out of reach, he's going to disappear. Right now he's desperate, making sloppy mistakes."

"He seems pretty efficient to me."

"You're still alive," he reminded her, "and you saw him."

"I never saw his face."

Gabriel opened the car door. Sandwiched between the car door and a privacy fence at his back, he pulled out a book of matches with the hotel's logo imprinted.

"Give me the notes you made."

Cassy peered around nervously before handing them over. Gabriel produced a small tin ashtray he'd appropriated from somewhere and burned them one sheet at a time. He even burned the rest of the hotel pad that was still blank. And as each page finished, he dumped the ashes in a small mud puddle and ground them beneath his foot.

"That was effective."

Gabe offered her one of his rare smiles. Cassy walked to the passenger's side feeling inexplicably good. As soon as they were moving she resumed their conversation.

"What sort of mistakes is the killer making, Gabe?"

"He killed the wrong person at my house."

"But he doesn't know that, does he?"

"Unless Huntington is our killer. Otherwise, if Sliffman's as good as I think he is I suspect he'll ask the media to downplay their coverage temporarily. Gretchen Morrison's murder will work to our advantage by giving the media a new focus. That's where the killer made his biggest mistake to date. He left evidence at the crime scene."

"What evidence?"

"Footprints in the blood."

Cassy swallowed hard.

"He set the bloody knife on top of the crouching lion and probably left more evidence throughout the house. I didn't go any farther than the foyer because once I realized he hadn't found the hidden compartment I took the package and left. I suspect he missed it because he was rattled by the presence of the man in the wheelchair."

"What man in a wheelchair?"

"Mrs. Morrison wasn't alone in the house. There was an older man in a wheelchair."

Thankfully, he didn't say more. Cassy didn't need details. Her stomach wanted to revolt. The image of Beacher was still fresh in her mind.

"We have to stop him."

"We will." Flat and uncompromising.

"How did he know to go after the lion?"

"He's trying to tie off loose ends. He knows or suspects Beacher recovered something and passed it to me. He turned over the lion to be sure the base was solid and nothing was hidden inside. Only a few of my pieces are large enough and have the right shape to conceal a hard drive and the missing vials. What bothers me is how he got close enough to take Beacher out in the first place. Beacher was no fool. He wouldn't have stood by passively and let someone slit his throat."

"Is that what he was going to do to me?"

Gabriel's knuckles whitened on the steering wheel.

"I don't think your attacker in the parking lot was our killer. I think it was Andrea."

"Andrea!"

"Beacher said she followed him to Sunburst. What if she saw you coming out of my house that night?"

"You did ask if my attacker could have been a woman."

He nodded. "The person in the parking lot wore a hooded sweatshirt with a scarf over their face. Is that the same thing the person wore in your bedroom?"

The attack in the parking lot had been so sudden, but she saw what he was asking. "No. In my bedroom he wore…I'm not sure what it was exactly, but it wasn't a hooded sweatshirt. It reminded me of those ninja outfits in movies, but it still could have been the same person."

"Uh-huh, but let's say the attacker in the parking lot was Andrea. She might have returned later, but when you saw her and ran she couldn't know that you wouldn't call the police. Knowing her, I'd bet she cut her losses, went home and decided it was time to leave town."

Cassy considered. "That's a lot of supposition."

"But it fits."

"Maybe."

"The killer needed a reason to search your house."

"I did call Beacher several times and left messages.

He could have listened to one." If so, she'd led him right to her. "But why didn't he tear your house apart?"

"Because if I'd come home to a disaster I would have gone through the house with extreme caution."

"And spotted the trip wire."

"Exactly. He did search my house or it's unlikely he would have known about the gallery showing. I think he decided if he could kill me and blow up the toxin at the same time all his problems would be solved."

"Is that why he didn't slit your throat, too?"

"Maybe, but as everyone keeps pointing out, unlike Beacher, I have a well-earned reputation as a loner. I can't think of one person I'd let close enough to use a knife on me."

"Me."

He returned her smile with a wry twist of his lips. "You don't need a knife to do me in."

Chapter Twelve

Gabe pulled into a fast food drive-thru.

"I'm not hungry," Cassiopia protested.

"Neither am I, but there's no telling when we'll have time to stop again."

They ordered breakfast sandwiches and pulled over to eat without getting out of the car. She nibbled on hers without enthusiasm.

"I still don't see how he made the connection to that poor old woman last night."

"When he searched my house he would have seen that most of my work had been removed and the gallery invoice was sitting in plain sight on my desk."

"Then wouldn't he go to the gallery? And how would he know about Mrs. Morrison?"

"Who says he didn't go to the gallery?"

"I'm pretty sure someone would have noticed a hooded man dressed in black."

Gabe nearly smiled. "He didn't need to be hooded to walk into the gallery earlier in the day. No one there would know him as anything but a potential customer wanting to browse."

Cassiopia crumpled the paper that held her half-eaten sandwich.

"Either he was there when Mrs. Morrison bought the lion, or he heard Rochelle discussing its delivery."

"But why kill her and the poor man in the wheelchair? Why not wait until they went to bed to break in?"

"The Morrison house had an alarm system. There was a sign out front. Given the neighborhood, he would know that alarm was likely being monitored."

"And the last thing he'd want is the police arriving," she agreed. "Still, why would she open the door to a masked...oh. He wasn't wearing his hood when he went to the door, was he? That's why he killed her."

"That's the way I have it figured. He's driving a Jaguar," Gabe continued. "Exactly the sort of car she would take for granted in that neighborhood."

"And not the sort of car your common criminal runs around in."

"No." Gabe crumpled his wrapper.

"What is it?"

"We need a pay phone."

"Why?"

Gabe gathered up the trash and dumped it without answering. He was still thinking through the ramifications. Calling Sliffman was dangerous, but not calling him might get someone else killed.

"You're going to call Sliffman, aren't you?" Cassiopia asked as he got back in and started the engine.

Gabe wasn't surprised that she'd followed his train of thought.

"Are you going to tell him what we found?"

Gabe hesitated, weighing the risks. Any admission

on his part could end up with him in jail unable to prove his innocence. "I don't know. I'm playing this by ear."

Cassiopia didn't press him, for which he was grateful. His mind was still sorting options, but one thing was clear—he needed to get to the gallery ahead of Rochelle.

"I have my cell phone," she offered.

Regretfully, he remembered the business card Sliffman had tried to hand him. "I don't have Sliffman's phone number."

"What's wrong with the police? I can phone in an anonymous tip that I saw a black Jaguar driving recklessly as it left her driveway last night. It will certainly get their attention."

Gabe was so used to being on his own he hadn't even considered calling the police for help. And, he admitted ruefully, he didn't want their help. He wanted to nail the bastard himself. But not badly enough to see another person die.

"Go ahead. They'll trace the call back to you, but they won't have our location."

Cassiopia bit at her lip then fished for her phone and turned it on. After trying for several seconds, she turned back to him in frustration.

"The battery's too low. I can't call out."

Gabe increased his speed.

"Why did he kill Andrea Fielding?"

"Remember Beacher's note? I think she knew or suspected who he was."

Cassiopia shook her head. "But if she was a threat now, she was a threat four years ago, wasn't she?"

"I don't know. Maybe he's just trying to get rid of loose ends."

"Like us."

"Yes."

"You're worried."

Gabe spared her a glance. "He was in a hurry last night. He didn't find anything and he's taking bigger and bigger risks."

"You think he'll try the gallery again this morning?"

"Yes."

"Oh! You think he'll hurt Rochelle."

"I think he'll hurt anyone who stands in his way."

"What's he going to do when he doesn't find the toxin?"

"Increase his efforts to find you."

"Me?"

As he stopped for a traffic light he held her gaze, knowing it was important that she understand the danger she represented.

"He needs to know what you told Beacher. He wants to know where that toxin is, Cassiopia."

"But I don't know!"

"Not specifically, but you told Beacher about your father using the exercise equipment. It's a good bet you were right about the toxin not leaving the building. Beacher made friends with someone who works there. I'm not sure how he talked his way inside, but you know his silver tongue."

"It was probably a woman."

He grinned. "You're probably right. As soon as we get to a phone you're going to call Sliffman to pick you up and place you in protective custody."

"Try again."

"Several people are already dead, Cassiopia. You're next on his list."

"You think I'd feel safe with the authorities babysitting me? People get killed all the time in protective custody."

"That's in the movies."

"So you say. I'm not willing to take that chance. What if Huntington is the one behind all this? No, thanks. I'm sticking with you. I know *you* won't let anything happen to me because I'd come back and haunt you forever."

He'd known she wouldn't agree and he didn't really want her someplace where he didn't know what was happening to her. "You'd do it, too."

"Believe it. What are you going to tell Rochelle Leeman?"

Gabe frowned. Since he couldn't be sure what Sliffman had told her the conversation would be tricky, but he needed to impress on her that she and her staff might be in danger.

"Shouldn't we also go see Dr. Pheng?" Cassiopia asked.

"Pheng won't talk to me. I've tried before."

"He'll talk to me."

Gabe didn't respond because they were coming up on the gallery. Being a Saturday morning, he'd made excellent time. The sleepy streets were just starting to wake with people and they still offered plenty of parking. He ignored the empty spaces and cruised slowly past the gallery. The light was hitting the display windows, but he thought he glimpsed a shadowy figure moving around inside.

He drove around to the delivery area. The store's

van and three cars were parked near the rear entrance. Rochelle's car wasn't there, but a black Jaguar with damage to the front fender was.

Gabe swore. It had the same license plate.

"Find a phone. Call the police."

He slammed the gearshift into Park and leapt out, running for the back door.

Locked.

Gabe pounded on its surface before sprinting around to the front of the building, drawing his gun as he ran.

HEART IN HER THROAT, Cassy watched Gabriel tear off. She climbed behind the wheel, but before she even settled in her seat, a hooded figure in black erupted from the back door and ran toward the Jaguar. In one hand, a long knife dripped splatters of blood. The opposite hand cradled a hefty-sized bronze animal on a wooden base.

Cassy froze long enough for the ninja to climb inside the Jag and start the engine. She pulled forward intending to block the other car, but the driver never hesitated. With a squeal of tires he plowed into her with enough force to shove her lighter car to one side and kept going.

Stunned, it took her a full second to realize the loud popping sounds were gunfire. Gabriel was sprinting toward her, a smoking weapon in his hand. He reached the car and flung open her door before she could move.

"Are you all right?"

"Yes."

"Stay here!"

GABE SPRINTED FOR the now open rear door of the building. Inside, a woman with dark hair sat on the floor of the workroom bent over a man. From the pungent, coppery scent of blood, Gabe knew what he'd find even before he approached the pair. The woman was making tiny broken sounds of distress.

"Rochelle!"

But it was Jennifer Mackley who lifted her head to stare at him without comprehension. Blood ran from a gash across her throat. Since it wasn't spurting, Gabe knew the artery hadn't been severed. That was probably due to the unconscious man on the floor.

There were obvious signs of a struggle. Spotting a bin of cloths they probably used to clean display pieces, he grabbed several and gently moved Jennifer to one side.

"Hold this against your throat."

Obediently, she pressed on the cloth he wrapped around her neck. Her eyes were wide and staring in shock.

Gabe turned his attention to the deliveryman Rochelle had called Dave. The large man was bleeding profusely from several wounds to his chest and abdomen and he was unconscious. His arrival may have saved Jennifer's life at the cost of his own.

Cassiopia ran inside and jerked to a stop. This was one time he was glad she hadn't listened to him.

"We need an ambulance."

She was already moving past him toward a wall phone near the door to the main room.

Gabe unzipped the man's jacket. Yanking up Dave's shirt, he used another cloth to apply pressure to the worst of the stab wounds.

"They're on the way," Cassiopia announced.

"Hold this," Gabe commanded. Her eyes were also wide, but her hands were steady as she took over for him. Jennifer had fallen silent. Gabe stood.

"Where are you going?"

"Get to Sliffman," Gabe told her. "He'll keep you safe."

"Get back here! Gabriel!"

He didn't answer. If he hurried, he still might catch the Jag and bring this nightmare to a close.

CASSY DECIDED she would throttle him at the earliest opportunity. Meantime, she was stuck. If she wasn't mistaken, the man on the floor was dying.

Abruptly, a large figure blocked the light as he stood silhouetted in the door's opening.

"What th—? Who are you? What's going on here?"

He wore jeans, not black pants, and he was much larger than the person she'd seen running from the building. He lumbered inside looking confused and annoyed.

"Go out front and let the paramedics in," she ordered.

"Is that Dave?"

"Yes." She didn't know if it was or not, but it didn't matter. "He's hurt. Hurry!"

The man swore then raced past her through the gallery to open the front door for the police and paramedics whose sirens shrilled out their approach.

Minutes later the room filled with people. Cassy was moved aside for the paramedics, but a uniformed police officer stopped her when she tried to leave.

"What happened here?"

"I don't know." She didn't have to fake the shrill tone

of her voice. She was quaking all over now that help had arrived. "A man dressed in black came running out the back door. I think it must have been a robbery. He was holding a knife and a statue. He jumped into a black-colored Jaguar and took off."

"A Jaguar?" the officer asked incredulously.

Cassy couldn't blame him, but she nodded wide-eyed. "The front fender was all smashed in. He left this door standing open so I looked inside. These poor people were bleeding all over."

"Take it easy. What's your name?"

"Janice Culpepper," she lied. "I work a couple of doors down. I used that phone on the wall to call for help."

"Did you get a good look at the man?"

"No. He was dressed like a ninja."

"A ninja?"

She bobbed her head. "Like in those movies where they dress all in black and know karate and stuff."

"Okay. Wait over there please, miss." She heard him mutter under his breath, "A ninja and a Jaguar," before he turned to the big man who was crowding the ambulance attendants in his concern over his friend. "Sir, you're going to have to stand back and let the paramedics work."

"But that's Dave! Is he gonna die?"

Cassy inched toward the back door again. People had begun to gather as the shopkeepers arrived for the start of their business day. Rochelle Leeman pushed her way inside.

"What's going on here?"

"Ma'am, you'll have to step outside."

"This is my gallery! What happened here? Good

God, is that Dave? And Jennifer?" She moved toward them with admirable speed. "What happened?"

While the police officer's attention was on her, Cassy stepped outside. She walked away quickly shaking her head and muttering, "Horrible," for the benefit of those clustered near the door.

No one stopped her. She hoped the officer would assume she'd returned to her own shop. That would buy her a couple of minutes before he raised a hue and cry.

As soon as she rounded the corner she broke into a run and crossed the street. Her purse banged against her side. She didn't even remember taking it from the car. She'd jammed her sling inside on top but if she was stopped and searched, she'd have a hard time explaining why she had a box with a government classified hard drive in her purse.

She would kill Gabriel for leaving her stranded like this. *She* wasn't carrying a nice fat envelope full of cash. Her wallet contained a little over twenty dollars. And her hand was sticky with blood. Great. Just great.

He would suffer when she found him again. A slow death, she promised herself. She rubbed her hand on her slacks in an effort to wipe the blood away.

Her teeth were chattering, but she didn't have time for hysterics. What would happen if Gabriel did catch up with the Jag? The ninja could have a gun as well as a knife. And Cassy needed to get off the street before the police started looking for her. But where could she go?

A horn honked sharply and repeatedly. Cassy glanced around. Gabriel was blocking traffic on the opposite side of the street, motioning to her.

An SUV nearly ran her over as she crossed to reach

the car. The passenger door was dented shut from its impact with the Jag, but she was able to get the back door open. The minute she was inside, Gabe pulled away from the curb.

"I could kill you!" she yelled.

"Later."

Police were fanning out from the side street. Cassy lay down across the backseat, pretending she was invisible. "Get us out of here."

"Workin' on it."

"Work faster! Why'd you come back?"

"It's Saturday."

No matter how she thought about that, she couldn't derive any sense from his statement. "So?"

"Even Sliffman gets days off. You would have spent a lot of time answering questions from people whose reactions I can't predict before someone actually called him."

"And you were going to do what? Sacrifice yourself to get me out of there?"

"No. I'd have thought of something, but you got yourself out of there. You can sit up now."

"What are we going to do?"

"Retrieve the toxin, talk to Dr. Pheng and take everything we have to Sliffman."

Cassy shook her head. "How do we get inside Sunburst? Even if we do, we still don't know exactly where to look."

"True."

"People are being killed, Gabriel. We need to talk to Sliffman first."

He pursed his lips but nodded. "Sliffman it is. We need a telephone book."

But when they located a phone book they discovered Sliffman wasn't listed. Huntington was.

"We're going to his home?" Cassy asked in surprise when Gabriel told her what he intended. "Is that wise? What if he's the one behind all this?"

"There's only one way to find out. Don't worry, I'll take some precautions. He won't risk killing us in his own home."

"Are you sure about that?"

"You want to wait while I see him alone?"

Yes! "No."

"Then what choice do we have?"

GABE STARED AT the modest house in the Frederick suburbs as he parked across the street. A brand-new green Lexus sat in front. The garage door was open and a pair of shiny new bicycles leaned against the wall inside. Two young girls spilled from the house and went running across the lawn.

Gabe had known Huntington was married, he just hadn't expected the dour major to have a young family.

Huntington himself appeared and began moving around in the garage. Gabe had never seen him dressed in civilian clothing before. He was never going to like the man, but it made him more human somehow.

"I don't suppose you'll wait here in the car?" he asked Cassiopia.

"Good guess." She bit uneasily at her bottom lip. "Maybe we should wait until we can reach Sliffman."

"We can't afford to wait."

Gabe slipped his gun into his hand. "If this goes wrong. Leave."

"You can't shoot him!"

"No. As tempting as it might be, this is to keep him from getting ideas about shooting me."

Cassiopia looked as if she were going to object further, but Huntington had pulled what appeared to be a new lawnmower onto the driveway. Gabe stepped from the car as he began to fill it with gasoline. Huntington looked up. Shock stiffened his spine. Gabe let him see the gun and watched fear send his gaze roving in search of his children.

"I don't plan to use it," Gabe told him.

"What are you doing here?"

"We need to talk."

Huntington's gaze went to Cassiopia, who spoke quickly.

"We have something to tell you. Please give us a chance."

Gabe kept his eyes on Huntington. "Two civilians were murdered last night. Two others were attacked this morning."

Huntington narrowed his eyes as Cassiopia moved to stand at Gabe's side. "They were killed by the same person who murdered Beacher Coyle and Andrea Fielding."

"Why?"

"Because someone believes Beacher found the toxin," he told the man.

"Did he?"

Gabe ignored the question. "I told Sliffman to look

at Andrea's brother." He watched Huntington's gaze narrow. "Did he?" For a long minute, Gabe thought he wouldn't get an answer in return, but Huntington finally gave an abrupt nod.

"The brother got drunk and fell to his death in a parking garage in D.C.," Huntington told him grudgingly. "His former girlfriend disappeared in Chicago. His best friend died in an apparent robbery. Another one committed suicide while another OD'd on drugs."

"All neat and tidy. Was the one who died in a robbery stabbed?" Gabe read the answer on the major's stern face. "Our killer likes knives. He's had combat training."

"Come inside. We'll discuss this."

"I like it here."

Huntington scowled. "You always did have a problem with authority."

"Yep, and you're a military man." The scowl deepened. "Pheng's ex-military, isn't he?"

"What do you want, Lowe?" The low growl was a warning.

"Have Carstairs exhumed."

That broke through Huntington's stoic facade. "He had a heart condition!"

"And everyone knew it. With access to the right drugs…" Gabe let him fill in the blank. "Think it was coincidence he died that same night?"

"You're still suggesting the major was involved in the theft?"

"He had access to the vault." Gabe allowed a tiny shrug. "He also had access to the missing explosive."

"So did you."

"And you," Gabe agreed, "but Carstairs left the

base during the doctor's missing hours, and someone sent me to the Richards house that night."

"You still maintain you don't remember?"

"I'd like nothing better than to remember."

Huntington's scowl was fierce. "Those orders would have come through me."

"Yes, sir. I made a convenient scapegoat, didn't I?"

"Spit it out, Lowe. You think I was involved?"

"Were you?"

Huntington swore.

"Nice new lawnmower. The Lexus looks new, too. Hit the lottery did you?"

For a second, Gabe thought the man would swing at him. Huntington kept his fists at his side with obvious effort.

"My wife's mother died, you little bastard."

"Sorry to hear it. She must have been loaded. That will make losing your promotion a whole lot easier to take, won't it?"

Cassiopia interrupted before the major forgot Gabriel had a gun and went for his throat. "Gabriel did not kill my father."

Watching Huntington control his temper was enlightening.

"I see you made a convert," he snarled. "Why civilians?"

"Someone thinks I have the toxin," Gabe told him.

"Do you?"

"No."

Cassiopia interrupted once again. "We think my dad took the toxin and the research to protect me."

"Where's your proof?"

"Have her mother's body exhumed as well as Carstairs," Gabe suggested.

Cassiopia drew in a sharp breath. "Gabe! She was cremated. You don't think—?"

"The killer needed leverage against your father," he explained without looking away from Huntington. "Telling your dad that your mother was murdered, whether she was or not, would give your father a strong incentive to protect you."

Huntington muttered under his breath.

"Dad still wouldn't have given the toxin to anyone," Cassiopia objected.

Gabe nodded. "He didn't. He pulled a switch and gave Carstairs a fake. By the time the person behind this realized what he'd done, Carstairs and your father were dead and he didn't have what he wanted."

Huntington stiffened.

"Carstairs was career military," Gabe continued. "He was going to be cashiered out because of his heart condition. Maybe he was promised money to retire in style. Maybe the killer had something on him. The motive doesn't matter. Once Carstairs sent me to the Richards' place and turned over what Dr. Richards gave him, Carstairs's usefulness was over. The authorities would focus on me while the killer cleaned up loose ends."

Huntington's eyes narrowed dangerously. "That's quite a tale you're spinning."

"Isn't it?" Gabe agreed.

"It makes terrifying sense, Major," Cassiopia put in. "Andrea's brother and his friends were loose ends."

"Why?"

"Backup scapegoats," Gabe answered.

Huntington huffed out a breath. When he spoke, it was grudgingly. "We looked into them before."

"And now they're all dead," Gabe reminded him.

"Let's go inside." It was an order.

Gabe stiffened. "As you've pointed out, I've got a problem with authority. The toxin is still at Sunburst."

"The place was searched," he argued coldly.

"Search again." He grabbed Cassiopia's good arm when she would have added something. "We're leaving."

He thought she'd argue but Huntington started to step around the lawnmower and Gabe flashed his gun in warning. The approach of two giggling little girls stopped Huntington in his tracks. Fury and the promise of retribution filled his expression.

Chapter Thirteen

Cassy allowed Gabe to hustle her toward the street, but once there, she yanked her arm free, furious with his high-handed antics.

"Why didn't you tell him about the gym?" she demanded as soon as they were in the car. "You told him everything else."

Gabe had them moving down the street before he answered. Huntington had vanished inside while the little girls claimed their bicycles from the open garage.

"If he's the killer, he already knew everything else," Gabe answered.

"Do you really think he's the killer?"

"He didn't ask the right questions."

"What are you talking about?"

"He asked *why* civilians, not *which* civilians. How did he know who I was talking about?"

She thought about that.

"Huntington gets off on authority. Until I know for sure we aren't misreading what we do know, I'm not going to trust that son of a bitch."

"Then why did we go there?"

Gabe shot her an unreadable look. "To add a piece to the puzzle."

"Okay, I missed that. What did we add?"

"That depends on what Huntington does with the information we just gave him. If he calls Sliffman, he's innocent. If he goes to Sunburst alone, he isn't."

"Oh."

Gabe smiled without humor. "What you don't know, because the information was never made public, is that the hard drive and toxin aren't the only things missing. Other classified drives were stolen from the base at the same time."

"What else was taken?"

"I don't know, and couldn't tell you if I did, but all of the existing toxin along with every scrap of data pertaining to it is gone. That isn't true for the other items, but a person who didn't know the system wouldn't have known for sure which hard drive went with the toxin."

"You think Huntington took them and sold them?"

"Actually, I always thought Carstairs took them."

"Could either of them simply walk off the base with a stack of classified hard drives?"

"Nope. But someone did."

She released a deep breath. "This just gets more and more complicated."

"Welcome to my world. Huntington was transferred a few months after the theft. He was reassigned to the base just recently. I wish we could run a check on his mother-in-law to see exactly what sort of inheritance she left her daughter."

"Is that what we're going to do now?"

"No. First we'll see if my bike is still there and in

drivable condition. Then we'll have a go at Dr. Pheng. I'd give a lot to know what the doctor had to say to Beacher about Andrea."

Cassy fastened on the words that brought her brain to a halt. "Your bike?"

His expression was not reassuring. "I want an alternative form of transportation available."

"Rent another car," she demanded. "That bike isn't an option."

"It's not raining," he pointed out.

"I don't care. It's a deathtrap on wheels. I am not riding on it again."

"That's okay, you can use the car."

DR. PHENG OWNED a stately home in a pricey section of town. He lived with his wife, his mother, one of two grown sons, his daughter-in-law and two grandchildren. The artistically landscaped grounds held an impressively large fountain, which graced the lawn in front of a covered portico flanked by roman columns. A pair of elegantly cut wooden doors and two urns of flowers guarded the opening. A number of expensive-looking vehicles filled the curved driveway. None of them was a black Jaguar, but Dr. Pheng was obviously entertaining.

Cassy waited for Gabe to climb off his death machine and join her. It was unfortunate that the bike had only sustained cosmetic damage. She'd seriously hoped it had been damaged beyond repair, stolen or towed away.

"Maybe we should wait. It looks like he has company." A whiff of burning charcoal told her why.

"All the better. Come on." They started up the long driveway. "Impressive," Gabe allowed, staring at the large, white structure.

"Old family money," she told him.

"Obviously. He didn't buy this on a research chemist's salary."

"No. His mother actually owns the house. Her family is quite wealthy. Textiles, I think. Dr. Pheng's only daughter married a pediatrician. His oldest son is a successful importer. The son that lives with them is studying to be a lawyer and he's got a brother who's a cardiologist, another brother who's a respected mathematician and a sister who's a seismologist."

"You seem to know a lot about the family."

"Christmas cards over the years," she explained. "Dr. Pheng comes from a long line of successful overachievers. My dad told me he and Dr. Pheng were always competing with one another in school for top honors."

"Who won?"

Cassy grinned. "He never said, but they remained friendly adversaries."

Gabriel didn't return her smile. "Let me direct the conversation, okay?"

"Why?"

"You're too trusting."

That shocked her. "You don't trust Dr. Pheng? It was his research that was stolen!"

"I don't trust anyone."

"Thanks a lot."

His features softened. "You're the exception."

"That's better, but don't you think you're being a little paranoid?"

"Yes."

At least the man knew his faults. "Okay. You're in charge."

His grin was fleeting, but genuine. "Bet that cost you. Come on."

Cassy didn't know whether to laugh or hit him, but her nerves took over as they approached the expensive double doors. "I still think we should wait and come back."

"Too late," Gabe pointed out as he pressed the fancy doorbell.

A young woman answered the soft chime a few minutes later.

"Yes?"

"Dr. Cassiopia Richards and Gabriel Lowe to see Dr. Pheng," he told the woman.

"Oh." Her puzzled features frowned. "Is he expecting you?"

"No, ma'am, but it's important or we wouldn't bother him on a Saturday evening."

"Please, come inside. He's out back. We're having a family barbeque."

"This will only take a few minutes," he assured her.

She did not look happy. "One moment, please."

They were left standing in an impressive foyer of marble and gilt. Overdone for Cassy's taste, but she had no doubt the marble inlay table alone cost a fortune. The centerpiece was a profusion of yellow roses in an exquisitely cut lead crystal vase.

For a house where there were a number of people, it was oddly silent. Cassy looked at Gabriel. His expression was unreadable as he watched Dr. Pheng stride down the hall toward them.

The doctor had aged considerably since Cassy had seen him last. His hair was mostly white now, his features lined. His expression was inscrutable as he ignored Gabriel and walked straight toward her.

"Ms. Richards, it's been a long time."

He hadn't used her title. Normally that wouldn't have bothered her, but Cassy felt certain the slight was deliberate. She had no idea why, but there was something cold in his manner. She reminded herself they were the intruders here and interrupting a family gathering. Besides, she might be misreading him completely.

"Hello, doctor. I believe you know Gabriel Lowe."

"Yes."

Just that. The two men faced one another like opponents seeking a weakness.

"Beacher Coyle came to see you," Gabriel began. "Will you tell us what was said?"

"Why?"

"Because he's dead. We believe he discovered where your missing toxin went."

"Then you should be speaking with the authorities."

"Doctor, please," she interrupted. "Gabriel had nothing to do with what happened four years ago. He's trying to help."

"Even if I believed that, Ms. Richards, there is nothing he can do."

"You're wrong."

Gabriel squeezed her arm in warning without lifting his gaze from the doctor. "Beacher left me a note. He said he planned to talk to you about Andrea Fielding. We're fairly certain she was involved in the theft."

"Then you know more than I. Ms. Fielding was a barely competent lab assistant."

"Whose brother disliked your form of research," Gabriel added just as coldly.

"I know nothing about her family or her personal life. I have told the authorities everything many times. Despite the fact that I have moved on they continue to badger me. I can't help you."

Cassy found it hard not to feel angry with him here in his ostentatious home. "You mean, you won't."

"If you wish to put it harshly, yes."

Her anger rose. "Your life wasn't the only one affected by what happened."

"I regret the death of your father, Ms. Richards."

She realized to her shock that she'd been thinking of Gabriel, not her father.

"It's *Dr.* Richards," she told him evenly. Gabriel touched her arm, but she ignored him. "I'd think you'd be jumping at the chance to help us recover your data."

"I no longer work for the military. The data belongs to them, not me. I'm sorry, but I told Mr. Coyle exactly what I'm telling you."

There was a ring of truth to his words.

"Now if you'll excuse me, my family and guests are waiting." He held open the front door in clear dismissal.

Cassy fumed while Gabriel's expression remained neutral as he stepped outside. "One last thing, doctor. Do you know anyone who owns a black Jaguar?"

The man didn't blink or hesitate. "Yes. Several people. Good day. I'm sorry I couldn't be of more assistance."

"No," Cassy told him bluntly. "You aren't."

Seething, she strode toward the battered car without looking back.

"That arrogant, uncaring…how can he be so, so… awful?"

"Because he's lying."

Cassy stopped dead. Gabriel climbed astride his motorcycle. He was looking toward the closed front door of the big house.

"How do you know?"

"Intuition. Follow me."

"Do I salute first?"

His lips curved slightly. "Only if you want. Sorry, but we shouldn't stand here talking."

"Fine." Fuming, she turned back to the car. Gabriel's arrogant manner wasn't intended to get her back up, but she was nervous. And scared. And her wrist throbbed despite the tablets she'd swallowed this morning. Unfortunately, she couldn't put her arm back in the sling and still drive.

When Gabriel pulled off the road a short distance later, she pulled in behind him. He came to stand at her open window. "We need a look inside his garage."

"You can't be serious."

"Picture him in black. Is he the right size to be your ninja?"

Her heart began to thud heavily. "Why would you even think such a thing? You're talking murder here, Gabe. The man is a respected scientist. And what would be his motive?"

"I don't know, but do you know anyone else who was involved four years ago that can afford to drive around in a black Jaguar?"

"No." Fear rose up, threatening to choke her. "You can't go back there! He's got a house full of people!"

"Relax. I'm not going back right now."

She couldn't possibly relax. "I thought it was Huntington you didn't trust."

"I don't. Did you notice the shiny new Lexus in *his* driveway? Could *he* have been the man you saw?"

Trying to picture the officious major in a ninja outfit was impossible. "I don't know. Both men are thin."

"Dr. Pheng is considerably shorter. And he was wearing a pair of black pants just now."

The major had been dressed in jeans.

"That doesn't mean anything. They both had plenty of time to change clothing."

He waited.

"I just don't know."

"Okay. We rattled their cages. The Jag has major damage now and the driver knows we can identify it. His first step will be to get the Jag out of sight."

"Won't he try to have it repaired?"

"Repairs can be traced. Unless your ninja knows a chop shop, he's got an expensive liability on his hands."

"Maybe the Jag was stolen."

"Undoubtedly it will be reported that way."

"That alone would tell us, won't it?"

"Sure. If he doesn't kill us first."

"Thank you. You've just made a bad day perfect."

"I won't let that happen," Gabe promised.

Her smile held the slightest wobble. "Of course not. You're just trying to scare me. Congratulations, I'm scared. What do we do now?"

"Do you think you can get us in to Sunburst Labs?"

"Sure. No problem. Do you want a tour of the White House, too?" Her sarcasm edged on hysteria. "I don't have those sort of connections."

"Relax. You know the people who worked with your father."

"A number of them, yes, but they can't just take me in to a secured lab on a Saturday evening. What am I supposed to tell them?"

"Let's try the truth. We passed a phone booth at that gas station back there. Let's go."

Cassiopia's look plainly said she thought he'd lost his mind, but she followed him back to the gas station and waited while he fished for change and called information to get Arthur Longstreet's number.

"You're going to call the head of security at Sunburst Labs?" she asked, when he disconnected.

"No, you are. Tell him you suspect your father left the missing toxin inside the building and you've thought of a place where it might be."

"He'll tell me to call Homeland Security."

"Fine. Get him to give you Sliffman's phone number."

"Why do I think this is a really bad idea?"

Gabe shrugged. "It's all I have unless you want to go back and stand watch while I break into Pheng's garage."

"Pass."

"We can't keep running and hiding in motel rooms."

"I like motel rooms. You don't even hog the blankets."

He grinned as she reached for the phone and punched in the number he gave her.

"See if he'll meet us at the lab."

She rolled her eyes and began speaking as someone on the other end answered.

"This is Dr. Cassiopia Richards. I wonder if I might speak with Arthur Longstreet? Yes, I will. Thank you." She didn't look at Gabe as she waited. "Mr. Longstreet? I don't know if you remember me... Yes, it has been. I'm sorry to trouble you on a Saturday, but I wonder if I could have a few minutes of your time this evening."

She forced excitement into her voice.

"I think I know what may have happened to the missing toxin.... Yes, I know, but I'd rather call the authorities *after* we see if I'm right. I'll feel pretty foolish if I'm wrong. I'm not far from Sunburst right now.... Uh-huh. Yes, I do.... I know, but I'd rather not go into detail on the phone. This won't take long if I'm right. I know it's a huge imposition.... Yes. Thank you. I'll wait for you there."

She disconnected with a mixed expression. "He's going to meet me in the parking lot."

"Excellent."

"What if we're wrong?"

"What if we're right?" he countered.

"I'm scared."

He bent and covered her mouth. Her lips were incredibly soft but receptive as he kissed some warmth back into them.

"I'm scared, too," he agreed gently, "but I promise I won't let anything happen to you."

"I know. I won't let anything happen to you, either."

He smiled because he could see she was serious. "You're an easy person to care about, Cassiopia. Let's go." Before he did or said something utterly stupid.

He climbed on the bike while worry hammered at him. Would Longstreet show or would he have the authorities meet them there? Gabe wished he could have left Cassiopia out of this. Despite his promise, something could go horribly wrong and he was ill-prepared to protect her.

As he pulled into the parking lot of Sunburst Laboratories Gabe spotted security cameras positioned around the building and tried to relax. Whatever came next, he'd be just as happy to have on camera.

Cassiopia joined him and he slid his arm around her shoulders. Her hand circled his waist. Neither of them spoke as they waited beneath an electric light pole.

Arthur Longstreet should have been tall and thin given his name, but he wasn't either one. As the beefy man stepped from his midsized sedan, Gabe watched the experienced ex-cop approach them cautiously. He remembered Longstreet. The man was older now, but still fit and alert. He took his job and his responsibilities seriously.

He recognized Gabe and he did not look surprised. That gave Gabe a measure of hope as he approached them with wary confidence.

"Dr. Richards?"

Cassiopia stepped forward. "Thank you for coming. You remember Gabriel Lowe?"

"Yes. You're looking pretty lively for a dead man."

Gabe inclined his head. "Right house, wrong victim," he agreed. Longstreet didn't offer to shake hands and neither did he.

"As I told you on the phone, Mr. Longstreet, we think we know where my father put the missing toxin."

"You didn't mention Mr. Lowe."

Gabe answered for her. "I was afraid you wouldn't come if she did."

"Gabriel was as much a victim as my father was," Cassiopia told him stoutly. "The only way to prove that is to find the toxin. Please help us. I know Sunburst has been searched repeatedly, but what about the gym? I'm not talking about the locker room, I'm talking about the room with all the equipment."

"There isn't anyplace in there to hide something."

"I think you're wrong. My father liked to work out on his lunch hour. The one place no one would expect to find something like the toxin is in an open gym."

Longstreet continued to look skeptical. "Dr. Richards, we've been over the building repeatedly."

"Humor me. Please?"

"Beacher Coyle already found the toxin here at Sunburst," Gabe told him. "He left me a note saying he left it here because he was afraid to remove it."

"Beacher Coyle is dead."

"Yes, he is," Gabe agreed. "And his murderer wants Cassiopia and me dead as well. Show him the hard drive in your purse."

"Gabe!" she protested.

At the same time, Longstreet stiffened. His hand went to his jacket pocket. "Hold still, Dr. Richards. Keep your hands were I can see them. Both of you."

As he pulled a gun, Gabe nodded, unperturbed. "I'm armed, too," he told the man. "You can have the gun, but understand that someone has already tried to kill us."

Moving slowly and keeping his hands clear, Gabe took the position against the battered car. Trusting

Longstreet was a risk, but the man was built wrong to be Cassiopia's ninja.

"There's a gun in my purse, too," she offered.

Gabe wished she'd kept silent about that.

"Set the bag on the ground and turn and face the car like Mr. Lowe."

Longstreet was thorough. He removed Gabe's gun and stepped back before turning to Cassiopia's purse. He took her gun as well but didn't touch the hard drive although he eyed it for several seconds.

"Any other surprises?" Longstreet demanded.

"No, but I'd feel a whole lot more comfortable inside than standing out here in the open."

With a quick glance around, Longstreet nodded agreement.

There were security cameras, locks to be swiped, a metal detector to walk through and an armed man at the reception desk. Longstreet signed them in, issued them temporary badges and told the guard to have someone named Jason meet them at the gym.

Jason proved to be a tall black man with ex-military in his carriage who eyed Gabe and Cassiopia with alert curiosity. Longstreet didn't bother with introductions and Jason opened the gym door, turned on the lights and stepped to one side.

It wasn't a large space but it was comfortably packed with all sorts of exercise equipment. One wall was covered in a bank of floor-to-ceiling windows. The grounds outside were dark enough that Gabe could barely make out the building addition across the court-yard from them.

"What are we looking for?" Longstreet asked.

"Space where a person could stow a package about this big," Gabe replied, indicating the size with his hands.

"In here?" Jason asked skeptically.

"Look for loose tiles, panels, flooring, whatever. What was your father's favorite equipment, Cassiopia?"

"I don't know. He used the bike and treadmill, but probably everything else in here as well."

"We'll start with them first. How often is this stuff moved for cleaning?" Gabe asked.

Longstreet looked grim. "Let's find out."

"Wait a minute. What about up there?" Cassiopia pointed toward the cold air return high up on the ceiling.

"Why there?" Longstreet asked.

"Dad would have wanted someplace simple and quick that wasn't apt to be examined by anyone," Cassiopia explained. "He always carried one of those all-purpose knives. You know the kind with enough heads that you can build a house from scratch?"

"There's a ladder in the storage closet," Jason told his boss.

"Bring it."

"Brilliant," Gabe told her.

She flushed, but demurred. "Wait until we see if I'm right."

Jason brought the ladder and positioned it beneath the opening. It turned out that he also carried one of those all-purpose knives, suitable for removing screws. Longstreet stopped him as he started up the ladder.

"Hold it, Jason. Dr. Richards, if the toxin is there, does it need special handling?"

"It should be in some sort of safety container. Just don't drop it."

"But no pressure, right?" Jason's smile was wry as he continued up the ladder. "This thing's been opened recently," he told them, removing the loosened screws that held it in place.

"Beacher," Cassiopia and Gabe said at the same time.

Jason removed the grate and passed it down. Pulling a flashlight from his belt, he shined it around inside. "I'll be darned. There's a case of some kind up here."

Gabe flashed her a grin. "Brilliant."

Cassiopia smiled back.

"Bring it down carefully, Jason," Longstreet ordered.

"Yes, sir."

When he would have handed the case to Longstreet, the security man indicated Cassiopia should take it. Inside were three vials marked with serial numbers. The clear liquid that filled them could have been anything at all. Gabe handed the grill back up for Jason to replace.

At the sound of a shot, Gabe flattened Cassiopia against the floor behind the stationary bike. A volley of shots followed the first through one of the windows. The case lid went flying as she fell, still clutching the case itself. Arthur Longstreet collapsed to the floor beside them. Blood spurted from a wound in his chest.

"Stay down!" Gabe yelled. He crawled to the man's side. Longstreet was clawing for his weapon. Abruptly, the room plunged into darkness. Jason had cut the lights. Gabe hoped the man had tripped the alarm as well if the broken window hadn't already.

Longstreet shoved his gun at Gabe. The older man's breathing was labored. Blood bubbled at the corner of his mouth. Gabe guessed the bullet had caught a lung.

"Stay still," he whispered. Cassiopia crawled over to him as the barrage of shots continued.

"The door. Get help."

The large window collapsed, sending shards of glass everywhere.

Chapter Fourteen

With the case of vials clutched protectively in her bad hand, Cassy tried to crawl along the floor toward the door. Her fingers encountered human flesh. The man called Jason was sprawled on the tile floor and he didn't move under her touch. In the dark, she couldn't tell how badly he was injured, but she felt the sticky warmth of blood seeping from somewhere.

Horrified, she tried to go around him, but his body was blocking the entrance. Unexpectedly, everything went eerily silent. Cassy bit back Gabriel's name and stilled.

Glass crunched underfoot. She didn't need light to know the gunman was inside with them.

Sudden flame licked the blackness as someone fired again. The room erupted in another barrage of shots that pinged off the metal equipment. Cassy tried to make herself as small as possible. There was a thud and the room went still once more. Terrified, she waited.

Someone shoved against the door from the hall outside. Jason's body pushed against her as the light flooded the immediate opening. Another burst of gunfire and another body fell, this time in the hall outside. The door swung closed.

Running footsteps came within feet of her. The overhead lights came on as the gunman located the wall switch. Cassy stared up at her hooded ninja and the gun gripped firmly in his hand.

"Give it to me," he demanded.

She knew that voice. "Dr. Pheng?"

The gun vanished. He dove at Cassy. There was no time to move. He yanked her hair and lifted her head up and back to expose her neck. A large knife appeared in his hand. She felt the blade bite her skin and stilled.

"I will kill her," he promised. "Drop your weapon."

Gabriel was on his feet, his weapon aimed at them. Blood ran down the side of his face. He didn't seem to notice.

"Drop it," Pheng ordered once more.

"That's not how it works."

"Then she dies."

Gabriel shook his head and swayed. "No. No one else dies."

The knife bit deeper. She felt blood well and begin to trickle down her neck. The case containing the vials dropped from her numb hand. Two rolled harmlessly toward Gabriel. The third hit metal and broke open.

Cassy gasped in horror. Dr. Pheng released her to toss his knife at Gabriel. He ducked and the room erupted in more gunfire. But these shots came from the shattered window.

Dr. Pheng jerked as a bullet slammed into his shoulder. Gabriel lunged for him. Major Huntington erupted through the shattered window, gun in hand. He was not alone.

"Get back!" Cassy yelled at them. "The toxin's been spilled!"

Everyone stopped moving except Gabriel and Dr. Pheng. Gabriel smashed his gun against the side of the other man's head. At the same time, Cassy scrambled to stop Longstreet's blood from reaching the spilled liquid. She was too late. Blood mingled with the toxin.

Horrified, she drew in a breath and held it, knowing it was futile. They were already dead.

"Get a containment unit in here!" Huntington yelled.

Cassy expelled her breath. "It's too late." But she didn't feel any differently. They should already be dead. Why weren't they dead?

Gabriel moved to her side. "How bad are you hurt?"

She touched her neck where the warm slide of blood was flowing down her throat. "It's a scratch."

"Why aren't we dead?"

She shook her head. The cut began to throb. "I don't know. Maybe it's inert in blood."

Huntington yanked the mask from Dr. Pheng's face. The doctor faced him with angry eyes. Huntington pulled out a pair of handcuffs and yanked his arms behind his back.

"Why aren't we dead, doctor?" he asked the man.

Dr. Pheng smiled coldly.

Gabe walked out of the wreckage of his house for the last time carrying the plastic box he'd been using all morning to collect the few items he'd been able to salvage from the burned-out shell. This time, it held the miraculously intact rosebush sculpture.

He should have been surprised to see Cassiopia

standing beside his truck, but he wasn't. He'd known she wouldn't let him put her off forever, but he wished she didn't look so unbelievably lovely standing there.

"It wasn't ruined!" she exclaimed as he placed the open box on the floor in the back of his truck.

"The kiln protected it," he explained.

"I'm glad. I hated thinking it had been destroyed."

The moment was as awkward as he'd known it was going to be.

"You've been avoiding me."

He saw no point denying the obvious.

"Why?"

"I've been busy. And it looks like I'm not done yet."

She followed as he inclined his head toward the street where a car was pulling up to the curb. Sliffman and Huntington stepped out and strode toward them. Gabe hadn't spoken to either one since his release from the lab more than a week ago.

Hazmat teams had isolated Sunburst, and the people exposed, for days while they tried to contain, assess and clean up the damage. A team of doctors had been brought in to treat the wounded while a team of scientists tried to determine why the toxin hadn't reacted with the blood. No one had become ill or showed any signs of contamination.

Cassiopia moved to Gabe's side in a show of solidarity that warmed the cold places inside him, while at the same time making him wish for the impossible.

"Lowe," Sliffman greeted. "Dr. Richards."

Cassiopia stiffened. "What do you want now?"

Gabe touched her in warning.

Huntington's scowl deepened, but Sliffman only

smiled. "We come bearing information, not asking more questions. A preliminary report is being pulled together right now and we felt you deserve to know the results of the findings. This information is not for public dissemination, however."

"The toxin?" Cassiopia asked.

Sliffman's lips pursed and he shook his head. "There was no toxin, Dr. Richards. Dr. Pheng faked the whole thing."

"What are you talking about? How do you fake a deadly toxin?"

"*Why* would he fake it?" Gabe demanded.

"Did he tell you this?" Cassiopia asked anxiously.

"Pheng won't be telling anyone anything," Huntington told them. "The sneaky little bastard managed to slit his wrists. The how is being looked into. Someone's head is going to roll over that."

Cassiopia made a small sound of distress. Gabe glared at him. "Did he talk?"

It was Sliffman who answered. "No. He never said a word to anyone. We've made a few assumptions based on what we do know. Four years ago the base was making cuts in outside contractors. Dr. Pheng held a senior position at the lab, but it was felt that his work could be absorbed by other, lower-paid scientists there."

"He was being fired?" Gabe asked.

"More or less. His research projects were going nowhere despite pressure to produce results."

"He was an overachiever, Gabe," Cassiopia inserted. "His reputation was everything."

"Too true, doctor. He must have guessed his name was on the list when several vials of an unidentified substance were sent to him for a priority analysis. I'm not at liberty to tell you where the vials came from or anything about them. Suffice to say there was a great deal of new pressure to determine what the substance was."

"He told them it was some new, deadly toxin," Huntington added.

Cassiopia shook her head in denial. "He lied?"

"Yes, doctor," Sliffman agreed. "As near as we can determine, he lied. Not only did he assure those in command that the toxin was a massive threat, he convinced them that with a little time he could come up with an antidote that would counter its effects."

"I don't believe it," she protested. "He had to know he'd be found out."

"That's why he set out to make everything disappear, including all his research."

Huntington laughed without humor. "The cold bastard was actually negotiating for a new job with his current employers while he set up the whole thing."

"Unfortunately for Dr. Pheng, a peer review was arranged before he was ready to implement his plan. We believe he intended for the theft to happen before the toxin was sent to your father. It appears that Ms. Fielding, her brother and his friends were initially supposed to take the blame when everything disappeared."

"How did he manage to clear out the vault?"

Huntington looked pained. "We can't discuss that."

"But," Sliffman added, "we believe your assumption about Major Carstairs was correct. When the timetable was moved up plans had to change quickly. Dr. Richards couldn't be allowed to complete his examination of the toxin or Dr. Pheng's research."

"For my father to be the one to uncover his hoax would have been intolerable," Cassiopia agreed.

Sliffman nodded, but Huntington's expression was hard. "The guy was a nut case."

Cassiopia shook her head sadly. "He wasn't insane, Major. His culture would demand that he not lose face."

"Even if he had to kill a lot of people?" the major grumped.

Her eyes clouded. "Even then. I don't excuse him. No one can. But I'm not surprised he killed himself. I'm just grateful that thanks to your timely arrival, we weren't numbered among his victims and neither were Mr. Longstreet or his coworker."

"How *did* you arrive in the nick of time?" Gabe asked.

Huntington grinned. "You called Longstreet, he called his boss, his boss called Sliffman—"

"And I called the major," Sliffman completed.

"I never liked you, Lowe. I still don't, but I do owe you an apology."

"We owe you our lives. I'd say that makes us even."

After a moment, Huntington nodded.

Cassiopia slipped her cold hand into Gabe's. He clasped it gently. "Is it over?" she asked.

"Yes, as far as the government is concerned." Sliffman handed her his business card. "We just wanted you to know. Best of luck to both of you."

"Thanks for telling us."

Silently, Gabe watched them return to their car. The crisp, fall afternoon cast sharp shadows on the ground. For the first time in a long time, he didn't have the urge to stand in one of them.

Cassiopia inhaled and exhaled deeply before turning to look up at him, when he dropped her hand. "New beginnings are good. Speaking of which, that's a new look for you, isn't it?"

Gabe ran his hand over his clean-shaven head. He'd removed the bandage from the left side where one of Pheng's bullets had creased his scalp. Since they'd had to cut away more of his hair to put in new stitches, he'd shaved the rest of his hair off. The change gave him an even more sinister look than before, but Cassiopia didn't look suitably alarmed.

"There's always the blond wig," she told him lightly.

"Why are you here?"

"I came to find out if I was a one-night stand after all."

He managed not to flinch. "What are you looking for, happily ever after?"

"Always."

Her hopeful expression was so open it took all his strength not to gather her in his arms.

"But I've discovered happily ever after is frustratingly elusive," she added.

Like her. She was a breath of spring sunshine on this crisp fall day while he stood there frozen like old man winter. How was it she could twist his insides like a pretzel? If things had been different…but they weren't.

"Maybe you keep looking in all the wrong places."

HE DIDN'T WANT HER. Cassy had begun to suspect as much but she would not let him see her cry. She'd known coming here like this was a risk. He wasn't ready to love or be loved and it was going to break her heart.

Her chin lifted in outward defiance. "So you're going to go back to hiding in the shadows again?"

She could see her question stung, as it was meant to.

They would tear each other apart at this rate, but she felt helpless to prevent it from happening.

"It's what I know best," he told her honestly.

"No. What you know best is how to create beauty out of clay." Why couldn't he see that? "Someday, maybe you'll accept that truth. Have a good life, Gabriel." She heard the pain threading her voice. "*I* intend to."

GABE WATCHED HER TURN and walk away with an ache that was physical.

You just going to let her go, pal?

It was as though Beacher stood beside him. He could hear his friend's mocking tone in his head.

You're pure magic when it comes to a ball of clay, but a real idiot when it comes to a woman.

"I don't know how to be what she needs."

Don't tell me, pal, tell her.

She'd reached her car and was opening the door. Her head was bowed in a way that reminded him of the first time he'd sent her away.

He was a fool, but he didn't want her to go.

"Cassiopia! Cassy! Wait!" He ran after her, more afraid now than he'd ever been in his life.

She swiped at her face before turning toward him. If she'd been crying, there was no sign of tears now.

"What did you call me?"

He paused, several feet from her. His chest felt as tight as if he'd run a marathon.

"That's the first time you've ever called me Cassy."

Gabe swallowed, wishing he didn't feel like an adolescent about to ask a girl out for the first time.

"I'm no good at personal stuff." Not anymore.

Maybe he never had been, but it had never been this important before. "Why would you want me?"

HIS VULNERABILITY struck her full force. Cassy fought an urge to fling herself against his chest and hold him tight. Instead, she worked to keep her voice even.

"That's certainly blunt and to the point. I'm a fool, I guess. I love you. I don't know why. You certainly don't deserve me."

She saw shock and more in his somber eyes. Was that hope?

"I know I don't. Cassiopia, I still don't remember what happened that day with your father. I get brief flashes, but I probably won't ever remember exactly what happened."

Relief left her knees week. "Is that what's bothering you? I thought we decided Carstairs sent you to the house for some reason."

"But I don't *know!* I'll never know for sure."

"So? I don't blame you for anything that happened. I wish I could take back my initial reaction, but I can't. I can only apologize."

He shook his head. "I'd have felt the same way in your place. You're like sunshine, Cassiopia—bright, open, giving. You said it yourself, I live in the shadows."

"You don't have to. Not anymore. Sun and shadows go together. See?"

SHE POINTED TO their mingled shadows on the sidewalk. Then she reached out to touch his scarred face. Gabe couldn't prevent a flinch as her soft fingers delicately traced the line of his scar.

"Each scar is a mark of honor and courage. You got this, and these—" she lightly touched the back of his hand "—trying to save my father. I believe that, even if you don't remember. You got this one—" her finger skimmed over his scalp near the spot Pheng's bullet had grazed "—saving me." Her eyes suddenly twinkled. "The one on the back of your head, however, is because you ride an idiot death machine, but I'll work on that one."

And he laughed. He couldn't help it. He loved this woman, every inch of her sassy, infuriating, gorgeous being.

"I love you."

The words sounded as rusty as they felt.

"It's about time you realized that."

He swooped her up then, kissing them both breathless.

"We're going to make a new start," she told him.

Warmed by what he saw in the depths of her eyes, he smiled back. "Right now?"

"Why not? I know where there's a room with a large bed. Of course, if you need to drive the rosebush to your friend Denny first…"

"I can be late. I'm told we artists are supposed to be eccentric and that would take too long."

"Hmm. We'll take it later then."

"Much later."

* * * * *

Debra Webb's
COLBY AGENCY: NEW RECRUITS
returns next month in
The Hidden Heir.

*Turn the page for an
exclusive extract!*

The Hidden Heir

by

Debra Webb

Victoria Colby-Camp sat in the coffee shop on the first floor of the building she called her second home. The place where the Colby Agency had been born, where it thrived more than twenty years later.

Located mere blocks off Chicago's glorious Magnificent Mile, coming to work every day was a treat for the senses. She loved the excitement of the city. Her city. The sounds and smells; the good and the bad that went along with living in an ever-expanding metropolis.

She should be getting back to the office. Lucas—she smiled—would be wondering where she'd gotten to. Every woman who had loved and lost, whatever the circumstances, should have a second chance at the kind of love she had found with Lucas Camp.

Victoria thanked God every day for him, as well as for the health and well-being of her family.

She sipped her Earl Grey and studied the patrons

swarming in and out of the small coffee shop. There were only six tables, each with two delicately formed wrought iron chairs. The seats weren't cushioned, most likely to prevent anyone from growing too comfortable. The owner needn't have worried; most who entered the shop were in a hurry. They were either in a rush to get to work or simply needed to get away from the office for a few moments. Smoking was no longer permitted in the building, so those who partook were forced to go outside to do so.

Of course, there was coffee and tea of all sorts in the lounge on the fourth floor just down the hall from Victoria's office. Or Mildred, her secretary, would have been happy to see after her refreshment needs. Each morning when Victoria came to work, she found coffee, her favorite blend, waiting for her in an elegant carafe. Mildred had a kind of sixth sense when it came to anticipating the needs of most everyone at the agency. This one had been no different.

But, like those with cigarettes and lighters in hand, this morning Victoria had come down to the lobby for a different reason. Escape, for only a minute or two. She couldn't say precisely why she had felt the need. All was well at home and in the office. She simply needed a few moments, not necessarily alone but to herself.

She watched the men and women rush through the main entrance and across the expanse of polished marble floor only to have to wait in line while security scrutinized their possessions as well as their persons. To move beyond that checkpoint, one had to have proper identification and be thoroughly screened for anything that might be used as a weapon.

It was a nuisance, but unfortunately a necessary one in today's climate of unrest.

Victoria settled her attention back on the swiftly cooling tea. Maybe the reason for her desire to have a moment alone was more apparent than she realized. For the first time in almost two decades, everything in her life was exactly as it should be. Her son Jim and his wife Tasha, were at long last happy, and the first Colby grandchild was on the way. The horrors that had haunted Jim since his return home were now finally under control.

A smile toyed with the corners of Victoria's mouth. And her other baby, her agency, was better than ever. She'd hired more new recruits, bringing the total to five. The energy from those young men and women had provided just the transfusion of excitement the agency had needed recently.

Unstoppable.

That was the one word that truly defined her agency as it moved toward its third decade of operation.

She felt completely satisfied for the first time in far too long a time. Satisfied and extremely lucky.

That smile that had tickled her lips now spread

across her face as she caught sight of her husband in the lobby. Confidence radiating from him, Lucas strode straight into the coffee shop. He didn't glance her way, but she knew he was aware of her presence. When his turn in line came, he placed his order— coffee, the strongest Colombian blend, no doubt. Cup in hand, he bypassed the side counter holding various sweeteners and creamers and headed directly for her table. That determined gaze settled on hers and that special connection that bound them so inextricably hummed at its full intensity.

"Is this seat taken?"

She looked up at the man she loved more than life itself and let her smile speak for her. Her husband's own lips quirked as he lowered himself into the seat. The tailored pin-striped suit he wore was her favorite. The blue shirt and deeper navy tie turned his silvery eyes to a warmer hue of passionate gray, making her feel warm and safe inside.

Lucas surveyed the dwindling comings and goings, then rested his full attention on her. "It's kind of early for a break, isn't it?"

That much was true. It wasn't even nine yet. This man had spent the past twenty plus years worrying about her. Even now, when life was as good as it gets, he didn't relent.

"It's been a long time, Lucas, since I've sat and watched life happen around me. I've been so busy trying to keep my world from shattering at every turn that I couldn't risk taking note of anything else." It felt good to be able to step back and just enjoy life as it happened.

He nodded knowingly. "You're afraid it won't last."

Victoria frowned, performing a quick inventory of her feelings. "To some degree, I suppose that's a fair assessment." She picked up her tea, held it with both hands and relished its warmth. However strong she might be, no one was exempt from worry now and again. "Who doesn't worry?"

"You could always retire," he suggested with a mischievous twinkle in those sexy eyes. "We could spend our mornings watching the world go by and our evenings admiring the sunset from anywhere in the world that pleases you."

She couldn't say his offer wasn't tempting, but Victoria understood that she would never be happy doing *only* that. Retirement was not for her. "I can't say that I haven't considered just that," she admitted. Especially since Lucas had stepped down from his high-powered position in D.C., choosing to serve as a consultant when needed and usually via a telephone conference. Once in a while, he still had to fly to the District to take care of highly classified business personally. Then there was the pending arrival of their first grandchild.

In spite of all those seemingly logical reasons to

choose retirement, she knew herself too well. "But you know that would never be enough."

"I would be shocked if you had proposed otherwise." Lucas leaned forward and gave a covert look around to ensure no one was within hearing distance. "Speaking of work, Mildred wanted me to give you a message."

Victoria lifted an eyebrow skeptically. "Did Mildred send you to bring me back?" She hadn't intended to stay this long; time had gotten away from her. It amused her immensely that Lucas didn't mind playing messenger. Just another indication of how very much he loved her.

"You had a call from a client she felt you wouldn't want to miss. The appointment is scheduled for half an hour from now."

Her calendar was clear this morning. An unexpected appointment wouldn't be a problem. "Who's the client?" Someone in a hurry, obviously. Someone who wanted to see her personally rather than one of the two men who served as her seconds-in-command.

"Desmond Van Valkenberg."

Surprised, she tried to remember the last time she'd had Mr. Van Valkenberg or his representative in her office. Three years? Four? A corporate profile request, if her memory served her correctly. She didn't know Desmond that well, but she had known his father quite well. Hershel Van Valkenberg had been a giant in finance, a man of his word until the day he passed away twelve years ago. He preferred doing business the old-fashioned way, himself and in person. His son had proved to be a vastly different businessman, with numerous representatives to see after his interests while he remained reclusive and as far from the limelight as possible.

"He's sending his representative, a Mr. Lance Brody, to see you."

Mr. Brody was his personal attorney, not one of the corporate team he usually sent. Victoria had met the gentleman once at a reception she had attended and where Van Valkenberg had made one of his rare appearances. Brody was a very formal man. He gave new meaning to the term stuffed shirt, but had quite the stellar reputation as an attorney.

In any event, she should prepare for his arrival. She stood. "Under the circumstances I suppose we should get back."

Lucas pushed to his feet with effort. Some days, the fact that he wore a prosthetic for a right leg was more pronounced than others. Her heart squeezed at the memory of how he'd gained that at times unwieldy appliance. His sacrifice as a prisoner of war had saved her first husband's life long, long ago. Lucas was not only a wonderful husband, he was also a man of unparalleled courage. He'd proven to be her savior more than once.

He offered his arm. "Shall we?"

Victoria looped her arm in his and thanked God again for this wondrous man. To have known and loved two great men in her lifetime was truly a blessing few had the good fortune of claiming. "Absolutely."

A few minutes later, Victoria sat in her office reviewing the Van Valkenberg file Mildred had already pulled for her convenience. The work the Colby Agency had done for this client, and for his father before him, generally involved background searches on potential employees and profiles of companies targeted for potential mergers. She had every reason to anticipate that the coming meeting would be more of the same. But she was puzzled that he had chosen to send his personal attorney.

A light rap on the door alerted her to Brody's arrival. Mildred opened the door and announced him. Victoria, though strangely preoccupied with her own thoughts this Monday morning, couldn't help noticing her longtime secretary's glow. Another weekend with her beau, she supposed. Victoria felt certain those two would be setting a wedding date soon. And why not? Life was too precious to waste.

Victoria rose from her chair. "Thank you, Mildred." She shifted her full attention to her visitor. "Mr. Brody, come in, please."

Lance Brody crossed the room in three long strides and, shifting his briefcase to his left hand, extended his right across her desk. "Mrs. Colby-Camp, it's a pleasure to see you again."

Victoria shook his hand, acknowledging his greeting with a nod. "Why don't we sit and you can tell me what it is that Mr. Van Valkenberg requires of my agency. We're anxious to be of service."

Brody sat, his shoulders as stiff as the freshly starched gray suit he wore. "Our needs are quite different this time I'm afraid. This time is…personal."

A new kind of tension rippled through Victoria. *Personal.* Desmond Van Valkenberg was not the kind of man who often allowed anyone outside his most intimate circle close enough to know his most personal business.

"I see. Why don't you start at the beginning and give me the details." Victoria settled into her chair and waited for the representative of her client to proceed as he saw fit.

Brody crossed his long legs and appeared to settle in. "Some ten years ago, a female companion of Mr. Van Valkenberg's, a Miss Ashley Orrick, gave birth to a son while living here in Chicago with him. The two had been involved for just over one year."

Victoria was surprised to hear this. She wasn't aware that Desmond had any children. "Was proof of paternity obtained?"

The lawyer nodded. "Certainly, but the trouble ultimately proved unnecessary. There were a few minor complications at birth and the child's blood type confirmed the truth of his parentage. Mr. Van Valkenberg has a very rare blood type. The child has the same."

"Has there been contact with the child or the mother recently?"

"Not since the child was about three months old. The woman, Miss Orrick, left abruptly and took the child with her."

The idea that Van Valkenberg would simply permit her to leave with his son in tow surprised Victoria. "Did Mr. Van Valkenberg attempt to stop her or to exercise his rights as the father at that time or since?"

"No," Brody explained carefully. "There were problems with the woman. She threatened to blackmail him, using the child as leverage. At one point, she went so far as to contact one of his rivals in an attempt to undermine an ongoing business deal." Brody shrugged. "Frankly, I'm convinced she was unbalanced. Her irrational behavior only worsened as time went by."

"And yet," Victoria interrupted, "you allowed her to leave with the child."

"Actually," he said pointedly, clearly somewhat offended by her suggestion, "she took the child and disappeared. *After* stealing a considerable sum of money from Mr. Van Valkenberg, I might add. This woman was a gold digger from the outset, I'm afraid."

"Mr. Van Valkenberg wishes to find the child now," Victoria guessed.

"Yes." Brody opened his briefcase and took out a file. He leaned forward and offered it to Victoria. "You'll find all the information we have on Miss Orrick in this file, including numerous photos, but, unfortunately, the photos are ten years old."

Victoria accepted the file, considered the contents a moment before asking, "Why now? After all these years?" She needed to know the rest of the story. The Colby Agency prided itself on discretion, both in the cases they accepted and in the way they conducted their investigations. However long Van Valkenberg had been a client, she needed clarification on exactly what he wanted and, equally important, why.

Mr. Brody leveled a solemn gaze at her. "As you're well aware, Mr. Van Valkenberg has always been a man dedicated to his work and inordinately reserved in his social agenda. He hasn't taken the time to develop or nurture any sort of real personal life. However, he recently learned news that has forced him to rethink his past decisions."

Victoria braced herself for what came next. Judging by the man's expression as well as his somber tone, the news was not good.

"Mr. Van Valkenberg has given permission for me to share this information with you, but, as you will see, the public cannot know, for obvious reasons. He's dying. According to the team of specialists working on his case, he has five or six months at best. He feels he has accomplished all that he'd set out to in the business world for a man barely forty. However, he knows that not acquainting himself with his only child would be a disgrace on a personal level. This is his greatest wish. We must locate the boy before it's too late."

CONTENTS

4 *Acknowledgments*

6 *Series editor's preface*

8 *Foreword*

12 *Chapter 1* Democratic design

28 *Chapter 2* Ingvar Kamprad: the grand designer

46 *Chapter 3* The E and the A of Ikea – Elmtaryd farm in Agunnaryd

60 *Chapter 4* Småland, stone walls, and the language of Ikea

80 *Chapter 5* Innovative materials

98 *Chapter 6* Flat pack city

116 *Chapter 7* Chuck out your chintz

136 *Chapter 8* The Furniture Dealer's Testament

154 *Chapter 9* Tour of the Vikings

172 *Chapter 10* Ikea in the global village

188 *Notes*

192 *Bibliography*

ACKNOWLEDGMENTS

Many people have helped me during the research of this book. Unfortunately most of them cannot be named as they spoke to me off the record. For my contacts within and close to Ikea – many thanks – you know who you are and I wish I could thank you by name.

I would also like to thank all those individuals who gave me a colorful insight into Sweden and Scandinavian culture. Niclas Ljungberg, Rassami Hok Ljungberg, Thomas Gad, Nicholas Ind, and Bo. Alexander von Vegesack, director of the Vitra Design Museum, Weil am Rhein, and Dr Viviana Narotsky, senior research fellow in the history of design at the Rotal College of Art, helped place Scandinavian design in context.

John Simmons has written some excellent pieces for me in *Brand Strategy* magazine and I was delighted to be given the opportunity to write something for him. Martin Liu, Pom Somkabcharti, and Linette Tye at Cyan books remained enthusiastic and supportive even when the book changed shape – thank you.

I'd also like to thank Ruth Mortimer, who helped set up some essential interviews for the book, and also the rest of the *Brand Strategy* magazine team who've been patient when I've been distracted at work – Becca, Jo, Morag, Howard, and Nigel.

Thanks to my close friends – Liz for reading proofs and providing encouragement, Rhi for providing lodging and interviewing skills at very short notice and the other Deneke East girls for not getting bored with my Ikea stories.

Most of all I'm grateful to my mum for providing tea, advice, and windswept walks in Lulworth Cove while I was writing. And my constant thanks to Simon for patiently accompanying me on endless trips to Ikea, making me lots of tea, and tiptoeing around the house for three months. I couldn't have written this without you.

PREFACE

We've all been there and done that. We've wound our way through Ikea, emerging with an item of flat pack furniture that we've taken home to swear at. Where is the Allen key? What do they mean by dowel B that fits in hole C? If I manage to put it together, will it stay together?

Shopping at Ikea comes surrounded with a lot of challenges. Often the biggest of these challenges is the queue of cars to get into the car park. But that in itself is a sign that we see something special and irresistible in Ikea, something that overcomes all the barriers that they seem to erect to make this anything but an easy experience.

The "something" is the brand. In this book Elen Lewis describes the ideas, principles, and history that lie behind Ikea, a brand that has changed the way we live. On the one hand Ikea has democratized the whole business of home making, making furniture and household goods affordable to all – such great value, as customers say. On the other hand Ikea has made furniture a disposable fashion item, a symbol of the way modern consumer society has corrupted our sense of value – no one buys an item of Ikea furniture to hand down to future generations.

There is a dilemma here not just for Ikea, but for all of us. Elen Lewis is a fan of Ikea, but a thoughtful, questioning one. Her questions go to the heart of issues that face many brands. All brands that survive for any length of time have to face the questions that come with success. Is this brand sustainable? Is the idea behind it capable of further development? Will the customers that love it today fall out of love tomorrow? If so, how do you replace them? Are the brand principles that pulsed so strongly at foundation still able to beat strongly when people, time, and geography take the brand further and further from its origins?

So far Ikea has found ways to answer these questions but, as with any brand, they never quite go away. To even attempt answers you need to understand the story itself. In this book Elen Lewis has told the story of the Ikea brand and, whether as professionals or as consumers, we can all learn from it. And perhaps, in keeping with Ikea tradition, enjoy a dish of Swedish meatballs at the end. But to do that you'll need to visit Ikea – take this book with you, it will be the best way to get greater understanding from your visit.

John Simmons
Series editor, *Great brand stories*

FOREWORD

> As soon as Hialmar was in bed Ole Lukoie touched
> all the furniture in the room with his little wooden
> wand, and everything began to talk. They all talked
> about themselves except the spittoon, which was
> silent and much annoyed that they were all so vain
> as only to talk about themselves and to pay no
> attention to him, standing so modestly in the
> corner and allowing himself to be spat upon.
>
> Ole Lukoie, the dustman, from
> *Hans Christian Andersen's Fairy Tales and Stories*

Writing a book on Ikea is like assembling flat pack furniture. There are so many different pieces to craft into one. So many snippets of information, urban myths, fascinating tales, and characters to speak to – the difficulty is putting them together and making sure nothing vital is missing.

This is not the book I thought it would be. When I first chatted to John Simmons, Martin Liu, and Linette Tye at Cyan Books, we always presumed that Ikea would cooperate wholeheartedly with the project. Although Ikea initially agreed, to the extent of drawing up a detailed itinerary of all the people I'd be meeting in Sweden, it later changed its mind.

At the time I was disappointed and puzzled, but I now see this book is more interesting because of it. It's an independent account of a Swedish furniture dealer, not told by an official storyteller but more of a sleuth.

I thought it would be quite simple – a trip to Sweden to interview key personnel, which I would then turn into a story. Instead I was tracking down ex-employees, traveling around Europe speaking with Ikea co-workers away from their workplace, persuading people close to the company to speak to me in confidence, and spending hours and hours watching and talking to Ikea customers and co-workers. I hate to think how many meatballs I've eaten in the last three months.

I applied for about 10 different Ikea jobs but got no further than an acknowledgment letter. I fired off correspondence to customer services, individual stores, the store cards, and the website using different names and addresses. I had my camera wrestled off me in one Ikea store as I took photos of sofa beds.

Many people I spoke to either inside or close to the organization spoke to me in confidence, off the record. (Any errors are my own.) They wanted the Ikea story to be told well but were scared of going behind the back of their headquarters. They brought me tea light holders fashioned out of electricity pylons and sang Swedish drinking songs into my Dictaphone.

As I've learnt more about Ikea I've begin to understand some of the reasons behind their decision not to cooperate. Ikea is incredibly secretive and it doesn't like outsiders getting too close. It's also a humble organization. In Scandinavia, it's very important not to be seen to be boastful or better than anyone else – a sentiment that Ikea is very true to.

In one trip to Ikea late one Monday evening, in a feeble attempt to avoid the crowds, the store was looking a little shabby. The room sets were looking very lived in – dirty carpets, rumpled bed covers, sofa cushions scattered on the floor. I suppose it resembled how Ikea looks in our own homes.

There was a tile missing in one of the bathrooms and I peered into the hole. I don't know what I thought I'd see. Perhaps a group of Swedish designers toiling away creating affordable furniture, or Ingvar Kamprad, Ikea's eccentric founder, addressing a group of co-workers. I thought I'd snatch a glimpse of Ikea's back stage but there was nothing – just a cavernous expanse of darkness.

The saga that follows is my attempt to make sense of the Ikea behind its yellow and blue veneer. It is a brand punctuated with myths and legends. And I hope that after reading Ikea's story, assembling flat pack furniture will never feel the same again.

Ikea in numbers

1 million customers visit Ikea every day.

3.5 store visits a year by the average Ikea customer.

28 million Billy bookcases have been sold since 1978.

42 is the average age of an Ikea customer.

60 percent of Ikea's visitors are female.

150 million meatballs a year are served in Ikea restaurants.

10,000 products live in the Ikea range.

365 million visitors went to Ikea last year.

12.8 billion euros in sales was made by Ikea in the 2004 financial year.

84,000 co-workers in Ikea.

20 percent of Ikea's sales came from Germany.

12 percent of Ikea's sales came from the United Kingdom.

145 million Ikea catalogs were printed in 48 editions and 25 languages.

179 Ikea stores in 23 countries and 202 in 32 countries if you include franchises.

Source: www.ikea.com and author research

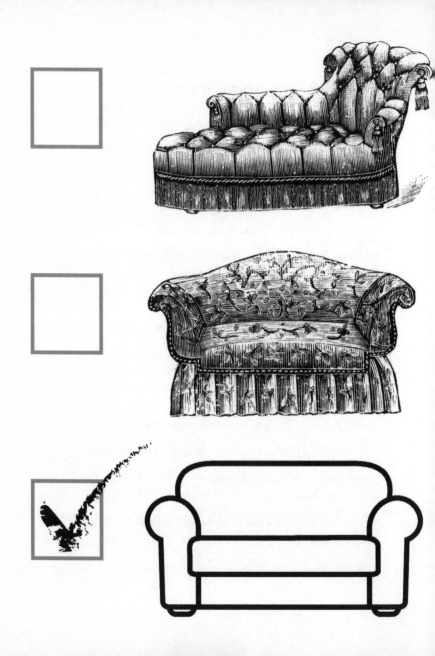

1 Democratic design

> Life is like assembling Ikea furniture: it's hard to
> understand what the purpose is, you are unable
> to put the pieces together, an important part is
> always missing and the final result is never at all
> what you'd hoped for.[1]

There are very few brands that can change your life. Ikea can. The Swedish furniture dealer peddles the intoxicating promise that the addition of an Ektorp armchair, a Tuvull travel rug, and a carefully positioned Tajt vase and Issjo lamp can transform your dowdy home into a vision of Swedish stylishness.

It is rare for a brand to have such an impact on society. Many brands think they do, but they don't. Ikea persuaded us that fashion is no longer what you wear, but how your home is decorated. It has played a crucial role in driving the rise and rise of fashion in the home.

Before Ikea, furniture was handed down from grandparents and parents. People used to save up their whole lives for stuff for the home. We bought a sofa for life. Now there's a "Top Shop" fashion mentality, furniture has become disposable and transient. Ikea is a brand that gives you an opportunity for self-expression.

We live in a world where transforming the home has become very important. We no longer judge people by the car they drive, the clothes they wear, where they go on holiday, or the size of their house. But when you visit someone's house, you know everything. We use our homes to project our personal identity. Perhaps it's a post-9/11 occurrence. You can't control the outside world, but you can control inside your home and make it look nice.

Ikea has made designers of us all. We are the "*Changing Rooms generation*" who update our interiors with trendy, low cost, Swedish furniture every year or two. Ikea enables us to get excited about being able to transform our living space with a carrier bag of small things. It's like not being able to afford a new outfit, but buying some accessories and feeling like you've made a whole difference.

The invention that revolutionized furniture

The saga of Ikea begins with an accidental but momentous invention. In the early 1950s, Gillis Lundgren, Ikea's fourth employee, was struggling to squeeze a table into the trunk of his car. So he took its legs off and flat pack furniture was invented. This discovery meant that furniture could be transported without shipping vast quantities of air across the world with it as well. It also meant that the costly part of putting the furniture together could be offloaded onto the customer.

It meant Ikea could make things so cheap that furniture would no longer be burdened by the accumulative emotions of handing it down generation by generation. It meant that furniture could seem disposable and transient. And it meant that we would now buy things for the home that we don't really need, because they are so cheap.

It would lead to overheard, stolen conversations in an Ikea anywhere in the world between mothers and daughters, husbands and wives, lovers and friends, as they struggle to balance desire, need, and ridiculously low prices.

"So this would be perfect if you wanted to make a quiche."

"Why would I want to make a quiche?"

"OK, for one of your vegetable pies."

"Why don't I put it straight on the oven tray?"

Or the bickering couple, locked in furious whispering combat, sat on a Malmo bed in an achingly trendy bedroom. They're examining a white bedside table called Corras, a steal at just £15.

"You won't let me buy anything for the house."

"We've already got a bedside table."

"It's not expensive."

"But we don't need it."

"It's so cheap."

Or the two men stalling as they wheel a trolley towards a seething crowded check-out. There's a gargantuan yucca plant in a steel pot precariously balanced among towels and curtains and picture frames and tea lights. "You know I haven't got oven gloves and that's what I came for," says one.

Or there's Edwina Hejazian, a 40-something woman who works for Glasgow City Council. She and her husband visit Ikea twice a week and bought a new car so they could fit the flat packs in. "I'm Ikea mad. I buy and decide what I want it for later. Valentine's Day two years ago, Jim says, 'Where would you like to go?' I say, 'Edinburgh.' 'What do you want to go there for?' he asks. 'Ikea. You can buy me dinner in Ikea.'"[2]

There are the Ikea fans that communicate on web blogs on the Internet, exchanging gossip, news, and experiences of the Swedish furniture dealer. In America, a web designer called Jen Funk Segrest is an Ikea fanatic intent on persuading Ikea to open a store where she lives in Ohio. Her blue and yellow website (www.verybigdesign.com/ikea) has a revolving banner that continually repeats: "Not too proud/ to beg/ Ohio wants Ikea."

Or there's Wang Jian Shuo in Shanghai who used his first month's salary after graduating to buy a Billy bookcase for 840 RMB ($100) in 1999. It's more affordable for him now and his web blog tells how he loves visiting Ikea for its free underground parking, cheap ice cream, and no questions asked return policy.

Ikea is a phenomenon. It has overtaken Abba and Volvo as Sweden's most famous export. Over 347 million people visited Ikea's 202 stores in 32 countries and we're prepared to drive 100 miles to visit one. Over a million customers visit every day. In Britain, on some Sundays more than twice as many people visit Ikea as attend church. One estimate suggests that 10 percent of Europeans were conceived on Ikea beds.

Ikea's reclusive founder Ingvar Kamprad has become the world's richest man, according to one Swedish newspaper. Ikea's profit margins are staggering – on average 18 percent compared with around 6 percent for Tesco. Ikea's group sales increased by 13 percent to €12.8 billion in 2004, and in the last decade its sales have trebled. Meanwhile its prices have been reduced by 15–20 percent over the last five years.

The Ikea generation

You know a brand has made it when it is stamped into public consciousness and name checked in popular culture. Ikea has become a cultural signpost for a certain attitude or way of living. Douglas Coupland, the author of the 1991 book *Generation X*, refers to "semi-disposable Swedish furniture" in a reference to Ikea. It is the official furniture supplier to post baby boomers – those born in the 1960s.

In the 1999 David Fincher film *Fight Club* starring Brad Pitt and Edward Norton, the narrator Jack played by Norton lives in an Ikea world. "Like everyone else," he says, "I had become a slave to the Ikea nesting instinct."

Jack is an insomniac who becomes addicted to joining support groups for crippling or terminal diseases he does not have. In one of the film sequences his apartment becomes a walk-through Ikea catalog as descriptions, prices, and ordering information appear on the screen next to the narrator's furniture. He also asks, "I'd flip through catalogs and wonder, 'what kind of dining set defines me as a person?'"

Or there's the comedy band I hear about in northern England that performs a song called "Ikea" to the tune of "Maria" from the musical *West Side Story*. The lyrics are: "Ikea – my boyfriend's discovered Ikea. And suddenly my flat is filled with lots of tat, you see. Ikea – it's all made of chipboard veneer. Ikea – I'll never stop paying, Ikea."

Two Swedish artists Anders Widoff and Stig Sjolund used Ikea objects in their art. Ikea art has since spread further afield. In the United States, installation artists – Andrea Zittel, Jason Rhoades, and Clay Ketter all use Ikea furniture in their installations.

Democratic design

Ikea has brought design to the masses. It has helped people realize the value of well-designed furniture – this is contemporary design in a digestible way. It's the equivalent of taking wine and putting it on the supermarket shelf.

"We have decided once and for all to side with the many," are the opening words to Ikea founder Ingvar Kamprad's 1976 book *A Furniture Dealer's Testament*. "What is good for our customers is also, in the long run, good for us." His aspiration was to "create a better every day life for the majority of people."[3]

It's easy to be snooty about things that are popular. But Ikea is excellent for the general public. Alexander von Gesack, director of the Vitra Design museum, Weil am Rhein, Germany, explains why:

> Anyone who can't compete with Milan first-rate
> design can buy a reduced version of extravagant

design – it's not just cheaper but cleverly reduced without losing the principle of the idea. It's a clever way to popularize inventions and fashions and it helps you to build up your own likes.

Internally, Ikea talks about its brand as being for people with "the thin wallet." A trip to Ikea is always full of those surprise moments when you can't quite believe how cheap something is. Or later at home you'll have one of those conversations with friends.

"Do you like this mug?"
"Yes."
"20p – Ikea."

It's the post-purchase Ikea rationale, which is – "how unbelievable was this price!" And that's why Ikea is democratic. Ikea means that you can furnish an interior for £800 that structurally looks the same as an interior that cost £20,000. The quality will be different, but the homes will look similar.

Dr Viviana Narotsky is a senior research fellow in the history of design at the Royal College of Art. She believes that: "The differences in taste and furnishing between income groups used to be more defined – they liked different things. Now they like the same style. It's a measure of popularization of taste," she explains.

Ikea and post-modernism

Dr Narotsky believes that Ikea reflects post-modernism. The domestic space has become a closed expression of individual identity and is ever-changing. "An invasion of uncertainty, transformation and change has become very close to the hearth. In some ways it's unsettling but it can also be creative. It's one more area that's opened up to easy, low range consumer culture," she adds.

The home used to be a solid core where things were stable and known – your grandmother's armchair would always be in the corner of the kitchen, next to great uncle Harvey's corner cabinet. But now we live in a society of spectacle and Ikea has helped us to stamp our own transient identity onto the home.

There's a supermarket mentality about furniture nowadays – it's disposable. The home fits into the shopping cycle like food and fashion. We no longer buy furniture because we need to but we shop in Ikea at the weekend to see what's around. Our homes can be themed, redecorated from a "Zen-style" bachelor pad to a "girly" boudoir at the flick of a trip to Ikea.

Internally, Ikea believes that it has impacted social change. Employees are quite clear that they have educated the masses about how to furnish their homes. They keep describing a bare light bulb in the middle of the room hanging bleakly above a stark dining room table. "This is what it was like in Europe 20 years ago," they say. "We've taught people about symmetry, getting the dimensions tight and about lighting and knowing where to place objects."

Dr Narotsky is not convinced that Ikea has impacted social change:

> It affects taste because there's no way around it. You end up liking the stuff you can afford. When most is very affordable its influence spreads further. There is a popularization of taste through market prices but I'm not sure I would call it social change.

But will my generation pass furniture down in the same way as my parents and grandparents did? I suspect not. We're the Ikea generation. We buy sofas and tables for a quick fashion fix, like shoes and dresses. Each home, each room set reflects a certain moment in time – there's the student pad, the bachelor flat. Or the first shared apartment that juggles and struggles to reconcile different tastes – rosebud duvet covers with mammoth stereo speakers and pastel colored crockery with shiny chrome appliances.

Our parents had a very different relationship with furniture. The things I inherit from my parents I'll pass on. But it won't be Ikea because their furniture doesn't pass the test of time. That's not what it's made for. I have a friend who sold some Ikea furniture on eBay, the online auction site. The buyer came to his house to collect the wooden shelving units. He paid for them and my friend said he'd help him put them in the car. By the time they got to the car, both units totally fell apart and were completely broken. My friend refunded his buyer who offered to take them to the tip instead.

Ikea: the anti-marketing brand

Ikea – we love it and hate it, lean on it, and shun it; but we keep coming back for more. Ikea is an anti-marketing brand. On paper it doesn't work. It never asks its customers what they want, but tells them instead. The barriers to purchase are extraordinary. We're expected to get into our cars, drive out of town, become gnarled up in traffic, be herded around a spaceship of a shop with a thousand other followers, collect our own stuff from the warehouse, and then build it – with missing screws and unintelligible instructions.

"Yes, Ikea is crowded but you always come back," counters one co-worker (the name given to Ikea employees internally). "Everyone always buys white napkins and tea lights. If you can't make your mind up about a £2,000 sofa you can get something for £300."

Internally Ikea is driven by the missionary zeal of its founders and co-workers, to provide design for the many. This vision is larger than Ikea. Whether you love or hate the Swedish ministry of furniture, be sure about one thing – Ikea loves you. That is, as long as you're prepared to work for its affection – by assembling your own furniture, fetching your stuff from the warehouse, and buying another 100 tea lights that you don't need.

Customers become part of the Ikea cult, because we have to participate in the process. Ikea thinks it's good for us if we learn to build our furniture, collect it from the warehouse, and haul it onto our roof racks to take home – ourselves. Its roots lie in the Swedish protestant work ethic of Ikea's history. This participation means we belong more to the Ikea brand than other brands in our lives. We are intrinsically part of Ikea's brand and business model. We're one of the reasons its prices are so low.

In a way this is one of the key ideas behind Ikea, this is why it's different from other furniture retailers. Ikea's way of shopping, of putting your stuff together and taking it home – this is an innovation that Ikea owns. This is why it's so cheap and this is what differentiates it from the competition.

There was a theory inside the company that Ikea is good for people's sex lives, because it's about the man being able to regain his hunter gatherer instincts in a modern world of equality. So his manly instincts drive him to put furniture together and be perceived in a different, more traditional light than is normal in his home.

It's certainly true that shopping in Ikea gives you a feeling of being useful and practical – you're doing something tangible for your home, and not just going to a shop and buying something. Ikea offers us a possibility to get away with being not so practical and still getting a result we're proud of. So, in front of your kids you can assemble the Billy bookshelf, with the illusion of being an accomplished carpenter.

Ikea is a company with a belief system and living, breathing values that pump around the global furniture dealer like blood through its veins. This is the reality of the company and you either understand it and join the cult, or you don't.

Smoke and mirrors

But behind the bright yellow and blue façade of Ikea lies a secretive and private organization. When you shop in an Ikea store it's like going backstage: you feel as if you might be seeing the inner working of the furniture dealer – but you're not. Ikea doesn't let you look behind the curtain. It's all smoke and mirrors. There are so many stories and so many urban myths about Ikea, many of them perpetuated within the organization. It's not like other companies or brands where you're faced with the same concrete veneer every time you hear about them.

Behind the relaxed, Swedish image is a tightly controlled and highly efficient organization. This brand is carefully played and supervised by its puppet masters. After initially agreeing to cooperate and provide access to Ikea's senior decision makers for this book, Ikea nervously changed its mind. Books had a long shelf life, it said. It didn't want to become a target for anti-globalization protesters, it said.

So my camera was wrestled from me in Ikea in Croydon (UK), by a smiling yellow-shirted co-worker, who told me that all photography inside Ikea required special, written permission from head office. My request to interview two Swedish authors who were close to Ikea in the 1960s was politely and persistently turned down. My numerous interviews with Ikea co-workers and people close to Ikea were furtive and whispered and all off the record. I was advised by a Swedish business journalist when interviewing fellow Swedes to tell them I was writing a newspaper article and not a book.

What follows is the saga of Ikea. It's an independent account that scrapes beneath the surface of an ambitious Swedish furniture dealer. It discovers tales of how shopping trolleys are made into sofas, how the invention of flat pack furniture revolutionized an industry, and how one man's vision created a phenomenon that furnished the world.

To the checkout

2 Ingvar Kamprad: the grand designer

No one has made more mistakes than I have.

(Ingvar Kamprad)[4]

Ingvar Kamprad is not the face of Ikea but he is its soul and conscience. He is not a household name but his vision and values are the lifeblood of Ikea. The initials of his name form the first two letters of Ikea followed by the first letters of Elmtaryd and Agunnaryd, the farm and village where he grew up in the pine forests of southern Sweden.

Kamprad is notoriously secretive and private. Since 1986, when he stepped into the background of the company he founded and obsessively grew, he rarely gives interviews. The grand designer himself, who furnished the world with contemporary Swedish design, has become a living legend.

His reclusive silence perpetuates the myths. He is half cranky hermit, half high priest. He is also, allegedly, the world's richest man with a personal fortune of $53 billion, compared with Microsoft's Bill Gates' paltry $47 billion.

Veckans Affärer, the Swedish business magazine that reported Kamprad's wealth in April 2004, came up with the estimate from digging around in the available information on Ikea's profitability to calculate its value. But as it is a Swedish private company, much of Ikea's comings and goings are shrouded in secrecy. And much of Kamprad's wealth depends on whether he still owns Ikea.

Ikea is unhappy about being owned by the world's richest man because that does not fit its folksy, thrifty image. It immediately released a statement:

> Ingvar Kamprad does not own the Ikea Group.
> Since 1982, it is owned by the Stichting INGKA
> foundation. Therefore it is totally incorrect to
> estimate Ingvar Kamprad's personal fortune
> based on a valuation of the Ikea Group.

Interestingly, on the fifth of April, just a few days after the news of Kamprad's wealth was released he sent one of his "letters" to Ikea's staff and agencies. The email begins with an underlined question: <u>What does it feel like to be so rich, Ingvar?</u> This is followed by a robust attempt to deconstruct these claims of Kamprad's untold riches. "Pretty darned good, to tell the truth! The greatest riches I have are my health, my family and the wonderful co-workers at Ikea."

"As you know, neither my family nor I have a reputation for being 'consumerholics'. Being careful with money is firmly rooted in my Småland soul." Kamprad continues by pointing out that this "wealth" is tied into Ikea's 200 stores and stock, which are not for sale. He says that the calculations have been made as if Ikea was a public company, which it isn't.

"But, if you ask me, I think they've underestimated the value of such a fantastic company as Ikea, with fantastic co-workers, a fantastic business idea and such a fantastic corporate culture!!!" Kamprad signs off, as he always does. "As I always like to point out when concluding my message: We've only just begun. A glorious future awaits!"

Extracts from Ingvar Kamprad's letter
5 April 2004

Despite the fact that, since the 1970s, I don't own a single cent in Ikea, I still feel a strong affinity with all of you who have "grown up" together with the company and I'm delighted that I still have the privilege of being able to poke my nose in just about every aspect of our business. I often feel that I still have something to give by being involved and making my voice heard....

The money we make, we need. We need it to continue to develop, to serve as a financial buffer for rainy days, and to be able to work with long-term intentions in markets which make losses to start with, but which we know can produce good results over a longer perspective. Russia and China are two good examples of this. At the end of March I spent the entire week in Russia when we opened our new store in Kazan, and I was overjoyed at the positive reception from both customers and the authorities alike. You get the feeling that we are doing something really big for the many people there, and I'm sure that, in a few year's time, the financial results will be good for us too....

A happy Easter to you and the entire Ikea world.

Yours truly
Ingvar Kamprad
5 April 2004

However, despite Kamprad's protestations, he is a wealthy man. He lives in a large chateau in Lausanne (Switzerland) for tax reasons and he also owns a vineyard in the south of France. He first moved out of Sweden in 1973 to Denmark, where he stayed with his young family for four years. Kamprad has said that his move from Sweden to Denmark, and then Switzerland, was not only because of Sweden's large taxes but also because he was concerned that if he stayed in Älmhult (Ikea's HQ) he could risk becoming a nuisance to the company.

Keeping a hand in

Despite the distance Kamprad placed between himself and Ikea's heartland in southern Sweden, he's still involved. He may not actively participate in the day-to-day running of Ikea any more but he hasn't let it go. In his words, "I'm delighted that I still have the privilege of being able poke my nose into just about every aspect of our business."

If you see a 78-year-old man walking slowly and deliberately around Ikea on your next visit, it could be Kamprad. Myths reverberate about him turning up at stores unannounced to ensure his vision is in place. He might be checking the prices on items to make sure they're low enough or vigorously questioning shoppers at the checkout about their purchases.

A British documentary[5] shows silent, grainy black and white footage of a man in his sixties. Clean-shaven with defined cheekbones, chin, and a pair of large square glasses, his lips are tightly closed. He's wearing a polo neck jumper, baggy trousers, and an anorak. His hands are folded behind his back and he is strolling around; deliberately, slowly. He's in an Ikea store and his beady eyes are never still, looking up and down, up and down and left and right.

Internally, Kamprad is famous for playing a game during his arduous 15-hour visits in Ikea stores. He pretends that he is a customer shopping with his wife, Margaretha. (Kamprad plays both parts.) So during these inspections he'll walk around pretending his wife is with him, talking to her, asking her opinion. At every room set and display he checks these imaginary shoppers have everything they need. He will be saying things like: "So Margaretha, what do you think of these sofas and where is the pen where we could write down notes about it?" It's as if he's fine-tuning a violin.

When Kamprad visits a store officially, he's announced, but only a few days in advance, so staff have little time to prepare for his inspections. He witnesses the real life of the stores; from 6 am when the first trucks rumble in, to 10 pm when the last customer leaves the store. Kamprad knows the details of the business as intricately as he did 50 years ago. He will make exhaustive notes – often 15 pages detailing the basic design of the store from the size of the price tags to the placement of posters.

Economy class

Kamprad's most lasting contribution to Ikea is the way that his own frugal lifestyle embodies Ikea's own cost-consciousness.

Some myths and stories about Ingvar Kamprad

- He travels on public transport whenever he can, and uses his pensioner's free bus pass in Sweden.
- He buys his fruit and vegetables from the market in the afternoon, because it's cheaper.
- When he takes a drink from a mini bar in a hotel, he visits a supermarket to replace it.
- He recycles his tea bags.
- Sometimes he drives from his home in Switzerland to Sweden to save money.
- He dries out three times a year to keep his drinking under control.
- When he eats out in the evening, he likes to spend under £5.
- He would rather sleep in his car than stay in a posh hotel.
- He pretends he's shopping with his wife, when visiting an Ikea store.
- He carries a plastic spoon in his back pocket to stir his coffee with.

Myths about Kamprad's eccentric, economical ways are whispered among staff. That he wrote an important message on a scrap of serviette to save paper, that he travels in a rusty Volvo and that he ate a 35p hot dog instead of lunch in the restaurant.

There are so many of these myths and stories, and in a way it doesn't matter whether they're true or not. They help inform the internal culture – what Ikea stands for and believes in. So you'll hear someone from Ikea recall the time when Kamprad visited a store and was scrutinizing the mugs, which are priced at just 90p. He would say they were too expensive and kept asking the staff, how can we make these cheaper?

There's another story that during one store visit Kamprad took a piece of furniture, a chair from the shop floor and took it down to the waste room. He then asked all the staff to go there for a meeting once the store had closed. He stepped up on a ladder so he could survey the people below him and admonished them for throwing out a chair which he dramatically pulled from the huge rubbish bin. Waving the chair above his head he told them, "Even if this chair was scratched or damaged we should never throw things away, but we should sell them cheap."

On a separate store visit, there's a story of Kamprad questioning Ikea customers as they queued for the check-out. Seizing items from their trolley and basket he kept asking them how much they paid for their things. Apparently everyone just thought he was a bit crazy, a bit of a grumpy old man – they didn't realize they were being questioned by the Ikea founder. Then he would ask them, "Well, is this worth it? Is this item worth the amount you're paying for it?"

One woman, under much duress, admitted that she thought one item in her shopping basket was overpriced. Kamprad used this to teach the staff of the store a lesson on the importance of pricing. He said it showed that Ikea must always keep track of the value for customers, and that the Ikea price should always be perceived to be correct. If Ikea customers didn't have the satisfied feeling of buying a bargain, then Ikea needed to change the price until they did.

Kamprad is constantly modeling the virtue of extraordinary value that is central to Ikea. So when he takes a drink from a hotel mini bar he'll visit a local supermarket to replace the drink, because it's cheaper than paying the hotel. He always goes shopping to the fruit and vegetable market in the afternoon, because it's cheaper. When Kamprad hires a car, he always hires the cheapest. So in Sweden he's often slaloming around the snow in the freezing cold because he won't hire a car with snow chains or snow tires on the wheels.

In London, I speak with someone else who'd had a meeting with Kamprad the week before. They were supposed to be meeting at 6 am but the Ikea founder was 20 minutes late because the bus was held up. So Kamprad, allegedly the richest man in the world, had taken a bus in London at 5.30 in the morning. London public transport is unreliable at the best of times, and it's almost non-existent at that time of day.

There's also the time that Kamprad traveled to the United Kingdom to visit the Brent Park store in north London. He flew economy class and then jumped on the London Underground and traveled through the city. Meanwhile, no one at the Brent Park store knew where Kamprad was and when he might arrive. They all waited for him in the welcoming party. Eventually he arrived after catching a bus to the store. Traveling by bus is one of his favorite ways of getting around Sweden, as he now benefits from free travel thanks to his pensioner's bus pass.

The Brent Park store in north London is almost impossible to reach by public transport; it's towards the end of the tube line and a long walk from the station through subways and over motorway bridges. Before my visit to Ikea's UK office, which perches on the top level of the multistory car park at Brent Park, I was warned to take a taxi from the closest tube station or drive myself. Ikea HQ's last female visitor had intrepidly walked and been mugged on her way there.

Kamprad was invited to Älmhult, the tiny town in Småland where the first Ikea store opened in 1953. A statue of Kamprad in the town center had been erected and Kamprad was supposed to attend to cut the ribbon and officially inaugurate his statue. When the moment came, instead of cutting the ribbon, Kamprad carefully untied it, rolled it up in his hand and handed it back to the mayor, saying: "Now you can use this ribbon again."

Kamprad's violent distaste of overspending means that Ikea is one of the leanest companies in business. Staff must fly economy class or with budget airlines, and stay in box-like cheap motels when they're away, often sharing rooms with their colleagues. Sometimes Kamprad will drive from his home in Switzerland to Sweden to save money.

An ex-Ikea employee recalls a business trip to a factory in Poland with some other managers, Ingvar Kamprad, and one of his sons. They were traveling in three cars but got lost and couldn't find a cheap hotel. The only hotel free in the area was a Marriott, an expensive chain that Kamprad immediately vetoed as it cost too much. They all slept in their cars that night.

People at Ikea talk in apocalyptic language about waste. They will say things like, "Unnecessary expenditure is a disease, a virus that eats away at otherwise healthy companies." There is a fundamental rationale that their business depends on lower costs that can only be realized with significant internal spending constraints.

"No one has made more mistakes than I have"

Kamprad has always been an idealist and sometimes this idealism has got him into trouble. In 1994 he was forced to confess to links with a pro-Nazi organization when he was young. Kamprad's revelations shocked fellow Swedes and Ikea fans. Kamprad said he bitterly regretted what he called "the worst mistake in my life."

In the 1940s, Kamprad was a member of Nysvenska rörelsen – the New Swedish Movement – which openly supported Nazism; he became friends with its founder Per Engdahl who idolized Hitler and Mussolini. The two men were so close that Engdahl attended the wedding of Kamprad to his first wife, Kerstin, in 1950.

Kamprad said he was influenced by his grandmother, a Sudeten German who had been persecuted while growing up under

Czech rule. The Sudeten Germans were a German-speaking ethnic group who were based in Bohemia and Moravia before their homeland became part of the newly founded Czech Republic in 1918. Kamprad's grandmother fled Czechoslovakia's Sudetenland for Sweden before the war and before her grandson was born. "She was very dominating and very pro-German. She set me off on the wrong path," Kamprad explained in an authorized and sometimes melodramatic biography of himself by Swedish journalist Bertil Torekull.[6]

Torekull details how Kamprad wrote a letter to each of his employees suggesting that his early involvement in Nazism had simply been an error. "You have been young yourself. And perhaps you will find something in your youth you now, so long afterward, think was ridiculous and stupid. In that case, you will remember me better."

The letter worked. Hundreds of Ikea staff signed a letter of support and faxed it to their leader's office. "INGVAR, WE ARE HERE WHENEVER YOU NEED US. THE IKEA FAMILY." Then according to Torekull, "The father of the family broke down and wept like a child."

There's a grainy fragment of a BBC documentary with the camera zooming into Kamprad's lined face, until he fills the screen.[7] He speaks slowly and quietly and does not look at the camera until he says the word Nazi and then he looks straight at you: "When I was a young guy I made a big mistake. I was a bit influenced by the Nazis. So I asked my co-workers to excuse me. It was a mistake, I was young but it was 50 years ago and I was not alone."

Helan går: a Swedish drinking song

It's not the only skeleton in Kamprad's closet. In 1998, Ikea's founder admitted that he had been controlling a drink problem for the last 30 years. In a press conference, he told journalists that he abstains from drinking alcohol for three times a year for three to four weeks at a time, to ensure he does not become a full-blown alcoholic. "There are a lot of people in Sweden in my situation. I have to clean out my kidneys and liver, and they should do the same."

His problem with alcohol began in the early 1960s when Ikea first started sourcing materials from Poland, where it was "almost compulsory to take vodka …" It was also around the same time that his first marriage to Kerstin was disintegrating.

However, a drinking culture was also part and parcel of growing up in the countryside. The young Småland men would often drink blodder, a fermented mixture of honey, sugar, and potatoes, before they went dancing. I spoke to one woman who grew up in the same place as Kamprad and whose family knew him when he was a young man. She recalls that they describe him as "a very primitive guy who drunk a lot and was not very sophisticated."

Kamprad's addiction may be under control, but alcohol is now banned from the Ikea Sweden offices. One co-worker recalls having to leave a bottle of wine he bought in his car, because of "his history." Yet despite this, Kamprad's co-workers regard him affectionately and are forgiving towards their "great leader."

Many of them refer to the struggles and harsh environment of his youth as way of explanation. "He was a lot tougher then than he is now. It must have been touch and go at some point and it was impossible and he had three kids to support at the same time," one says. Another describes him as half entrepreneurial, half psychopathic. "So he's half creative but he's also obsessed."

Every Ikea co-worker seems to have his or her own story to tell about Kamprad: that he carries a plastic spoon in his back pocket to stir his coffee and that he recycles his tea bag. "He's a funny fellow. He's unassuming and you wouldn't know it was him. We'd have big meetings of around 30 people and he'd come in and preach to us. He's a good speaker – passionate and thoughtful – everyone listens and respects him," says one.

A snapshot of Habitat, owned by the Kamprad family

1964   Terence Conran opens the first Habitat store on Fulham Road in London. It becomes the décor darling of the university-educated middle classes in the mid-1960s, offering new design at prices below Heal's and Harrods.

1965   Habitat launches a mail order catalog.

1966–7   New Habitat stores open in Tottenham Court Road London, Kingston, and Manchester.

1973–6	Stores open in Belgium, France, and New York.
1981	Habitat launches on the London Stock Exchange.
1982	Habitat merges with Mothercare to form Habitat Mothercare plc.
1983	Habitat Mothercare plc acquires Heal's and Richards.
1985	Habitat has stores in eight countries.
1986	Habitat Mothercare plc merges with BHS to form Storehouse.
1989	Terence Conran's new corporate responsibilities mean Habitat is suffering. He spends his last year in the business, leaving to focus on his restaurants.
1990	Storehouse sells Conran and Heal's.
1992	Habitat is sold to Stichting Ingka Foundation and the IKANO Group by Storehouse. Later all stores are sold to the IKANO Group which is owned by the Kamprad family.
1994–7	New Habitat stores open in Germany, Italy, and Thailand.
1998	Tom Dixon is appointed head of design of Habitat.
2000	Habitat's 78 European stores turn over €417 million.

Stepping down

When Kamprad retired as Ikea's group president in 1986, Anders Moberg, his successor, had to put systems in place within the company for the first time. Kamprad was also Ikea's corporate memory. He would literally be able to remember facts and figures of products ordered 10 years ago, down to the details of when a particular factory owner's daughter got married. One executive, interviewed by the Harvard Business School, recalled that in a group of 600 items, Kamprad would ask about a particular product and know its price, source, and cost, and he would expect his colleagues to know it too.[8]

Officially Kamprad is not active in Ikea any more and has taken a back seat. In reality, he knows everything and every new development has to be presented to him. If he doesn't know it, or he doesn't like it, then he can make things change. One co-worker tells me how he received official guidelines from Ikea Sweden to change an aspect of the layout in the stores. Everything was changed. Then one year later, another official memo was sent saying that the founder didn't like the new layout, so it was changed back to how it was before.

This is not an isolated example. A European store manager tells me: "We received new official rules that we had to follow, so we started changing things around. Then we had a new memo saying we had to stop and ignore the mail we received two weeks before as Kamprad had said 'no way.'"

"The group who are normally responsible had presented the idea to him two weeks late and he just said, 'No, we've got to keep this way of working and that's it.' When that happens they don't try to argue, they just say OK, the founder doesn't want it. It was embarrassing for them. They were the people who are supposed to decide all the rules."

Even when Ikea outmaneuvers Kamprad, he figures out a way to get back on track. I hear a story about him becoming frustrated with the length of time it was taking designers in Ikea Sweden to come up with new product ideas. So Kamprad set up his own product development business.

It was founded under the umbrella of IKANO, a company owned by his family, which also owns most of Habitat, the British home furnishings chain launched by Terence Conran. With just five people based in Switzerland, it existed to compete with the new product development teams in Älmhult. In some cases Kamprad's IKANO team managed to launch new products in half the time, for half the cost. "So you shouldn't relax, you've always got to try harder or he'll just stir things up," confirms one co-worker.

Even if Kamprad is no longer in Ikea's official meetings, he hovers above his furniture dealers like an omnipotent presence, overseeing every little detail. "Ingvar Kamprad is still the President," jokes one Ikea lifer. Kamprad will always want to know everything about Ikea; it is a vision he has created and nurtured for over 60 years. And despite his retirement, he's still obsessively involved in the business.

3 The E and the A of Ikea – Elmtaryd farm in Agunnaryd

Ingvar
Kamprad
Elmtaryd
Agunnaryd

Ingvar Kamprad's grandparents Achim Erdmann Kamprad and his wife Franziska immigrated to southern Sweden from Germany in 1896. They came with their two sons, the three-year-old Franz Feodor, who was to become Kamprad's father, and Erich Erwin who was 12 months old. Achim had bought a Småland forest he had never seen through an advertisement in a German hunting magazine.

Timber ran in Achim Kamprad's blood, as it would through his grandson's veins, because Achim's father had also worked in forestry. However, the young Kamprad family could not speak a word of Swedish and the large forest needed a lot more invest-ment. Just one year after arriving on the shores of Sweden, Achim was refused a vital loan from the local bank. Devastated and desperate, Achim shot his dogs and then himself, leaving his pregnant widow and two young sons alone in a foreign country.

The estate was not lost, as Achim's bereaved mother traveled from Germany in order to help her daughter-in-law and ensure her grandchildren did not become destitute. When the eldest grandson Franz Feodor turned 25 he took over the running of the estate. He then married Berta Nilsson, the daughter of the owner of a local store. Ingvar Kamprad was born in 1926 in the White Cross Maternity Home on the boundaries of Älmhult, according to Bertil Torekull's *Leading by Design*.[9]

Kamprad developed an entrepreneurial instinct at a very young age. When he was just five years old, his aunt helped him buy 100 boxes of matches from a store in Stockholm that he then sold on individually at a profit. As he got older he sold Christmas cards, wall hangings, lingonberries, fish, and ballpoint pens. Inside Ikea there's a joke that the young Ingvar could ride his bike faster than the old lady who had traditionally sold Christmas cards, so he got to everyone's houses first.

There's a black and white photo of Ingvar Kamprad when he's a small, skinny boy aged around ten. Dressed in shorts and a bare chest, with a beaming smile at the camera, he squints at the sun. He is crouched on the bonnet of a toy wooden car while his little sister Kirstin (four years his junior) sits in the driving seat.[10]

But Kamprad wasn't always driven and hardworking. A story in an Ikea internal newsletter published in the English newspaper the *Guardian* explains that he used to be a lazy teenager, until he was given an alarm clock as a present. Written in the style of a children's fairy tale, typical of Ikea's moralistic internal communication, it states:

> As a youngster, Ingvar Kamprad was always reluctant to drag himself out of bed to milk the cows on his father's farm. "You sleepy head! You'll never make anything of yourself!" his father would say. Then, one birthday, Ingvar got an alarm clock. "Now by jiminy, I'm going to start a new life," he determined, setting the alarm for twenty to six and removing the 'off' button.[11]

Just like timber ran through his paternal grandparent's blood, trading was in Kamprad's maternal grandparent's blood. Carl Bernard Nilsson, Kamprad's grandfather, ran the largest country store in Älmhult, called C B Nilsson. Although the store no longer exists, in the 1960s Kamprad bought the property and the site around it from his uncle and built the Ikea office on its foundations, immediately opposite Älmhult station.

Timeline of Ikea in the early years

1926   Ikea founder Ingvar Kamprad is born.

1943   Ikea is founded by Ingvar Kamprad. The name is formed from the founder's initials (IK) plus the first letters of Elmtaryd and Agunnaryd, the farm and village where he grew up.

1945   The first Ikea advertisements appear in local newspapers.

1948   Furniture is introduced into the Ikea product range.

1949   *Ikea News*, Ikea's first brochure, is sent to farmers as a supplement in their weekly newspaper.

1951   Ingvar Kamprad decides to focus on low-cost furniture and the first Ikea catalog is published.

1953   Ikea opens its first furniture showroom in Älmhult, southern Sweden.

1955   Ikea suffers as its rivals pressurize suppliers into boycotting the cheap furniture dealer. Ikea begins designing its own furniture. Flat pack furniture is invented.

1958   Ikea opens its first store in Älmhult. At 6,700 square feet it is the largest furniture display in Scandinavia at this time.

1963   Ikea's first store outside of Sweden opens in Norway.

1965   Ikea's second Swedish store opens in Stockholm.

1973   Ikea's first store outside Scandinavia opens in Switzerland.

1974   Ikea opens a store in Munich, Germany.

Ikea news

In 1943, at the age of 17, Ingvar Kamprad founded Ikea using the money his father had given him for doing well in his studies. He juggled his entrepreneurial ambitions with study at the School of Commerce in Goteberg where he began to learn the importance of distribution and finding the simplest, cheapest way of transporting products from the factory to the customer.

There's a shed in Älmhult. It's small, around 2 square meters, and is painted green with a white painted door and a curved roof. It's the sort of shed that would have been used to store milk churns. This was the spot where Kamprad ran his business in the early days. It stored fountain pens, wallets, picture frames – whatever the young Kamprad could find that he could sell on at a reduced price – as well as table runners, cigarette lighters, watches, jewelry, and nylon stockings.

In 1945 Kamprad began to struggle to make individual sales calls, so he started advertising in local newspapers and operating a makeshift mail order catalog from his shed in Älmhult. To save money he distributed his products via the local milk float, which delivered his goods to the train station.

Three years later, Kamprad decided to introduce and advertise furniture for the first time, using small, local furniture manufacturers close to where he lived. His first pieces of furniture were an armless chair called Ruth and a coffee table. Later, Ingvar added a sofa bed and a cut glass chandelier which were all published in a mail order brochure called *Ikea News*. The furniture was a success and Kamprad's parents and relations had to start helping him packing up the orders.[12]

Although Kamprad's fledgling business was reaping the benefits of a postwar boom, Swedish society was changing. The traditional practice of handing down custom-made furniture through generations was giving way to young homeowners looking for new, cheap furniture. Demand was growing but Swedish manufacturers and retailers were keeping prices high. Between 1935 and 1946 furniture prices rose 41 percent faster than the prices of other household goods.[13]

By 1949, Kamprad began sending out *Ikea News* as a supplement in the farmers' national weekly paper, which was read by 285,000 people – Ikea's first mass audience. The brochure holds hints of Ikea's future direction and vision, as it appeals to the farmers' common sense and need to save money. It was also the first Ikea catalog in embryonic form, which was launched two years later.

"To the people of the countryside," it begins. "You may have noticed that it is not easy to make ends meet. Why is this? You yourself produce goods of various kinds and I suppose you do not receive much payment for them. And yet everything is so fantastically expensive. To a great extent this is due to the middlemen.... In this price list we have taken a step in the right direction by offering you goods at the same prices your dealer buys for, in some cases even lower."[14]

In 1951, Ingvar Kamprad made the momentous decision to become a furniture dealer. He decided to discontinue all other products and focus purely on low-priced furniture on a larger scale. He managed to sell the rest of his other stock aside from around a dozen dried-up fountain pens and some Christmas cards, which he still keeps in his cellar at home.

It was one model of ironing board that made Ingvar begin to think about adapting his business model. Ikea became embroiled in a price war with its main competitor Gunnars over the Melby ironing board. One season Ikea sold the ironing board for 23 krona, then Gunnars lowered the price to 22.50 and Ikea lowered it to 22 and the spiral continued. The same began to happen with furniture. The price wars trickled down to affect the quality of the products and consumer complaints poured in.

Kamprad and the first Ikea employee Sven Gote struggled with how they were going to pull Ikea out of the vicious low price/low quality circle and regain customers' trust. They decided to open a furniture showroom in Älmhult so that customers could touch, feel, and see the furniture before they bought it. On the back of the latest catalog they wrote, "Come and see us in Älmhult and convince yourself...."[15]

The furniture exhibition opened on 18 March 1953 in an old Älmhult joinery, which Kamprad bought for just 13,000 krona. It was laid out on two levels, with free coffee and buns upstairs. Over one thousand people turned up to the opening, walked around with catalog in hand and then wrote out an order.

The coffee and buns became the template for Ikea's successful restaurants, which now sell over 150 million meatballs a year. Kamprad firmly believes that "no good business is done on an empty stomach." Quite quickly, Ikea became Älmhult's most popular tourist attraction and was being visited by people from all over Sweden. Ikea arranged a discount for its customers with Swedish Railway and also built a hotel and a restaurant on site for its customers.

The boycott

One year later Ikea's turnover had soared to 3 million krona, doubling the following year when half a million copies of the catalog were sent out, proclaiming "Dream home for a dream price." Ikea's success had not gone unnoticed, and Sweden's furniture dealers became incensed with Ikea undercutting their prices. One rival took an ad in the *Smålands Posten*, a local newspaper, saying, "If your dream house at a dream price becomes an overpriced magpie's nest then come to us next time."[16]

Ikea's rivals pressurized suppliers into boycotting it. Some suppliers flatly refused to do business with Kamprad, while others would use false delivery addresses or deliver wares under the cover of darkness or in unmarked vans. The National Association of Furniture Dealers sent an ultimatum to some suppliers threatening to stop buying from them if they continued to sell to Ikea. Both Ikea and Kamprad personally were banned from trade fairs. Kamprad smuggled himself into one, hiding in a rolled-up carpet in the back of a Volvo.

It was a tough time for the young company. Kamprad persistently managed to sidestep the restrictions by setting up new companies so that he could continue to sell furniture at trade fairs. The boycott also led to Ikea designing its own furniture rather than relying on existing ranges in order to continue working with suppliers.

Around this time, Kamprad employed a young designer from an advertising agency in Malmo (southern Sweden) called Gillis Lundgren – he was Ikea's fourth employee. He helped Kamprad lay out the furniture and take pictures for the new catalog, and he also sometimes sketched furniture designs. This way Ikea could sidestep the boycott as the manufacturer would not be making exactly the same furniture for Ikea as it was for everyone else.

Lundgren's most important contribution to Ikea was the invention of flat pack furniture. Frustrated by the space a table took up as he tried to squeeze it into his car, Lundgren took the legs off and flat pack furniture was born. From then on, Ikea's designs tried to incorporate those items that could be flat packed. The 1953 catalog included a table called Max – Ikea's very first self-assembly table. The separate pieces of Ikea's business had been designed – now they just needed to be screwed together.

Swedish invasion

In 1958, Ikea opened its first store in Älmhult. At 6,700 square meters it was the largest furniture display area in Scandinavia at that time. By 1961, from this unlikely location, Ikea's business was booming. Its turnover was over 80 times larger than an average furniture store. Four years later, a second store on the outskirts of Stockholm was opened, which set a template for Ikea stores. It had lots of parking space and was a cavernous cash-and-carry style showroom where customers had to serve themselves.

In 1963, Ikea opened its first store outside Sweden. It was based in Norway, just outside Oslo. This was followed in 1969 by the first Ikea store in Denmark. Between 1965 and 1973 Ikea had opened seven new stores across Scandinavia. But Kamprad had his eyes and ambitions fixed further afield. He wanted to sell Scandinavian living to the rest of the world too.

German-speaking countries became his priority, as they were the largest furniture market in Europe. Mythology says that Kamprad then chose Switzerland as Ikea's first market in 1973, because he knew it would be the toughest to crack. If he could persuade the Swiss with their traditional, dark wood, sturdy furniture to shop with him, he could persuade anybody.

To back the launch Ikea promoted itself with offbeat advertising, making a joke about "Swedes with strange ideas." It worked and the following year Kamprad opened his first store in Munich, West Germany. Using similar advertising and promoting low prices and immediate delivery, 37,000 people visited the store in its first three days.

At this time Germany was not only Europe's largest furniture market, it was also the largest producer and exporter. Unsurprisingly, Germany's retailers complained vigorously about Ikea's launch. They took legal action challenging the truthfulness of Ikea's aggressive advertising and complained that the Swedish furniture's seal "Mobelfackta" did not require such stringent standards as its German equivalent. Despite these setbacks, Ikea boomed in Germany, opening ten new stores over the next five years.

Entangled web

Perhaps it was the hostile reception that Ikea faced first in Sweden, and then in Germany, that led Kamprad to construct such an entangled and opaque business structure. Ikea and the businesses surrounding it are shrouded in secrecy and complexity. Even Ikea co-workers don't quite seem to understand the labyrinth depths of the company. The model was thought out in the 1970s and implemented in the 1980s.

The Ikea group is owned by the Stichting Ingka Foundation – a charitable foundation registered in the Netherlands. The foundation owns Ingka Holding, the parent company for all Ikea Group companies. Ingvar Kamprad, his son Peter Kamprad, and then Hans-Goran Stennert, Jan L Carlsson, Goran Lindahl, Carl

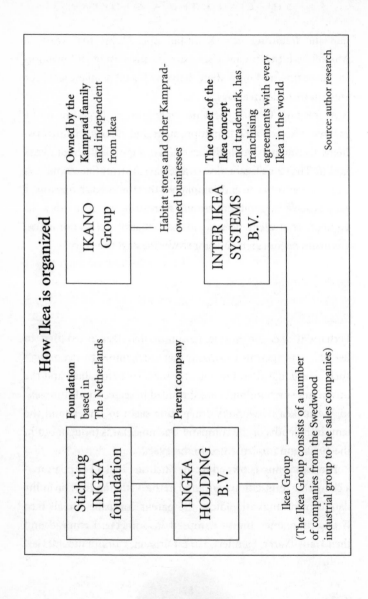

How Ikea is organized

Stichting INGKA foundation
Foundation based in The Netherlands

INGKA HOLDING B.V.
Parent company

Ikea Group
(The Ikea Group consists of a number of companies from the Swedwood industrial group to the sales companies)

IKANO Group
Owned by the Kamprad family and independent from Ikea

Habitat stores and other Kamprad-owned businesses

INTER IKEA SYSTEMS B.V.
The owner of the Ikea concept and trademark, has franchising agreements with every Ikea in the world

Source: author research

Wilhelm Roos, and Bruno Winborg all sit on the Ingka Holding board. Stichting Ingka also owns 25 percent of Habitat, the furniture retailer founded by Terence Conran. The rest of Habitat's shares are owned by the IKANO Group, which is owned by Kamprad's sons.

There is a separate company called Inter Ikea Systems that owns Ikea's intellectual property – its concept, its trademark, and its product designs – which it franchises out to every Ikea store in the world. A store manager would have to write to Inter Ikea Systems to gain permission for deviating from the standard concept, say for example if he or she wanted to get rid of the children's playroom or build a smaller restaurant.

Stellan Bjork, a Swedish journalist who has written a whole book on this topic, says the difficulty lies in finding out who actually owns Inter Ikea Systems. In *Leading by Design*, Bertil Torekull reveals that it is owned by a parent group in Luxembourg called the Inter Ikea Group that also owns an internal bank and a property company. He also writes that Kamprad's three sons sit on the board of Inter Ikea Systems' parent company, which is confusingly not Inter Ikea but System Holdings. However, because it is a foundation, although Kamprad's sons can control the Ikea concept, they cannot own it.[17]

The intricate construction of Kamprad's empire is yet another potent example of the founder's resilience and strong sense of survival. This opaque structure is a means for him to protect the company from flotation, hostile takeovers, and inheritance taxes. It also, despite the smoke and mirrors, keeps the concept within the family. Unlike the furniture that Ikea sells, Kamprad's vision is probably impossible to dismantle.

4 Småland, stone walls, and the language of Ikea

Småland
It is silence
It is forests dominating the landscape
A small lake hidden behind tree trunks
A moose sipping fresh water
Lingonberries waiting to be picked
Stonewalls. Stubbornness.
Hard work and a strong will to create a better life
It is the heart of small scale business in Sweden
It is Småland

Småland, in the countryside of southern Sweden where Ingvar Kamprad grew up, is etched with clues about the company's values and identity. Småland is a windswept, harsh, sparse environment with pine forests as far as the eye can see. Älmhult, a small town in Småland, is Ikea's Mecca.

Outside of Sweden, it's easy to presume that Ikea is all about Swedish or Scandinavian values. But it is, of course, more complicated than that. If Ikea had been founded in Stockholm, Sweden's urban metropolis and capital, it would have been very different. Imagine instead, a global retailer that was founded in an undeveloped region in the middle of nowhere. It's like Habitat being launched from Sunderland in the north of England.

The poem above appears on giant posters in Ikea stores. It is written across the backdrop of clear blue skies and rocky landscape punctuated by dry stone walls. Småland is Swedish for "little land." It was historically an agricultural community where farmers struggled against the elements to make a living from their small pieces of land.

Even today, the land is carved up by the boundaries of dry stone walls. Ingvar Kamprad has said that Småland's old stone walls, a monument to human perseverance and optimism, symbolize Ikea's soul. He says they help remind the international retailer of its humble beginnings.

Swedes from other parts of the country joke that the Smålanders are frugal and stingy with their money. One Swedish myth says that the Smålanders cry when they blow their nose because they don't like to lose anything. The Smålanders are also known for being entrepreneurial. "Ingvar is by no means unique, he embodies Småland," explains one Swede. "There are lots of little businesses there, he's just unique because his has become international."

It's a poor part of Sweden with hard land to farm, and set high so it is often quite cold and snowbound. Many Smålanders struggling to make ends meet emigrated to America at the beginning of the 20th century, hoping for an easier life. In 1910, 20 percent of the Swedish population lived in the United States, and many of these were from Småland. Ikea's internal business values seem to be carved from the soil – cost consciousness, team spirit, informality, egalitarian relationships, and making do with what you've got are Småland values.

Where did this rural entrepreneurialism come from? It's not restricted to Sweden, there are businesses founded in the middle of country fields in Denmark too, like Danfoss, an engineering company, or Lego, the toy brick brand. The founders of Tetra Pak (the packaging company) are two brothers who were also farmers in southern Sweden. Perhaps Småland farmers needed to become more entrepreneurial and source other streams of income because of tough farming conditions. These companies seem to be born from a mix of Lutheranism (where the thrift comes from) and entrepreneurialism (so how do we make money from these things?).

Älmhult – Ikea's Mecca

No one had heard of Älmhult before Ingvar Kamprad founded his business on its doorstep. It's an old, remote farming town, with two main streets and a railway station; it's an odd place, in hindsight, for a revolution in domestic design. Today the Ikea offices in Älmhult have around 3,000 employees in a village of just 6,000. It's very likely that in every single Älmhult household lives at least one Ikea co-worker.

On the outskirts of town, near the station, there's Ikea's first store, the offices of Ikea Sweden, which is in charge of Ikea's design, and Swedwood, one of Ikea's manufacturers. Most of the people who work and live in Älmhult are Ikea designers or those in charge of putting the catalog together. You may be more familiar with the Ikea Älmhult staff than you think. It is often them and their families who smile up at you from the pages of your Ikea catalog.

Within Ikea, it is a real honor to be offered a job in Älmhult, as this is where the important decisions are made. For international Ikea workers, Älmhult is the hub, the Mecca. It is where they go for training, to meet people, to watch the catalog being photographed, or to be talked through the new ranges. The town is always full of extra Ikea staff, who stay at the Ikea hotel opposite the station.

The hotel used to have a swimming pool, but they had to build more rooms there instead, because of Ikea's growing staff. Ikea's hotel, as you would expect, is very simple and kitted out entirely with Ikea furniture. The Ikea museum consists of three rooms in the hotel's basement, showcasing Ikea furniture through the ages.

Although Kamprad has moved to Switzerland, he still has a large family house in Älmhult. It has a big garden, an indoor swimming pool, a sauna, and a housekeeper who stays there all year round and cooks for visitors. Sometimes if the hotel is full, Ikea co-workers get a chance to stay there instead, but they must still pay for the privilege. In the garden there are three small houses for each of Kamprad's sons.

The Ikea store in Älmhult, the first Ikea ever built in 1958, has become something of a joke among co-workers, who jest that it is more of a museum than a real shop, as its sales are not very high. Unlike other stores it is not used to test new products or new retail innovations, perhaps because of the low volume of sales. However, it is the number one tourist attraction in the village.

Some Ikea workers find Älmhult a little claustrophobic. It's a small town. Aside from a few restaurants and a pizza place, there's very little to do there, nothing apart from Ikea. It's the only big business in the area aside from a scrap metal specialist. "Ikea is everything there and everyone just sits around dinner tables talking about Ikea or furniture," admits one Älmhult Ikea worker. "People who live there enjoy it because they can indulge in their work." Copenhagen in Denmark, however, is just a few hours away by train across the Oresund Bridge connecting south Sweden and Denmark, for those who need to escape.

Billy, Sultan, and Varde

There are two women in Älmhult who probably have one of the most important and influential jobs in the business. They choose the silly Swedish names for your furniture, from Billy the bookcase, to Sultan the mattress, to Varde the kitchen. Kamprad named the very first chair he sold in the early 1950s Ruth, because as a dyslexic, he found it difficult to remember order numbers. The naming of Ikea's products has continued ever since.

The 10,000 products in the Ikea catalog have the same names the world over, but sometimes this can get the Swedish retailer into trouble. A few years ago, a wooden bed called Gutvik, the name of a small town in Sweden, caused ripples of interest in Germany. "Gutvik" means "Good f***" in German – so Ikea's ads for the bed were hastily withdrawn from windows and newspapers, when Ikea realized its error.

Blogs and chatrooms on the Internet across the world are trying to crack the code of Ikea's naming; even the co-workers seem a little in the dark. There is an Ikea game on one website which provides an Ikea name and gets people to guess what the product is. For example, is a Gustav a CD rack, a dining room table, a clock, or a cushion? Is a Trall a dining table, box with a lid, clock, washstand, or gate leg table?

The Ikea game

1/Is Gustav?
a/ desk
b/ light
c/ blanket
d/ highchair

2/ Is tecken?
a/ candlestick
b/ kitchen
c/ mug
d/ bunk bed

3/ Is Kasted?
a/ shelving unit
b/ rug
c/ chair
d/ lamp

4/ Is Tajt?
a/ vase
b/ basket
c/ mirror
d/ soap dish

(Answers: 1a, 2c, 3b, 4a)

There is a system – bathrooms are named after Norwegian lakes (for example Mallen), kitchens are named after boys, bedrooms are named after girls, and beds after Swedish cities, according to an article in the English newspaper the *Guardian*.[18]

Kamprad's biography adds to the confusion with a different system. His female cousin I-B Bayley, who worked as Kamprad's secretary in the early days and later became product range manager, says suites, sofas, and chairs should have city names, bookcases boys' names, curtains girls' names, and duvets bridges' names. Nothing is ever allowed to be called Ingvar.[19]

Critics of Ikea suggest that persuading us to speak their language is a subtle technique for encouraging compliance. Joe Kerr from RCA told the *Guardian*:

> In following them you become evangelists for Ikea. If you look at police interrogation techniques, for example, you see that one of the ways you break somebody's will is to get them to speak in your language. Once you've gone and asked for an egg mcmuffin or a skinny grande latte or a Billy bookcase, you're putty in their hands.[20]

Viking nosh

A plate of meatballs and a Swedish cake has become a rite of passage for Ikea shoppers – it's part of the experience. During a trip to Oslo in Norway in the 1960s, Kamprad had been fascinated by a shop selling "Viking nosh" and had immediately wanted to sell something similar at Kungens Kurva. After discussion with his colleagues it was decided to offer Småland specialities, rather than Swedish food. One dish offered in Stockholm was Isterbrand, a Småland sausage, recognized by the city dwellers as food from the country.

A classic menu was developed which has been adhered to. Meatballs with lingonberries, potatoes in white sauce, apple pie with vanilla sauce, and crayfish salad are all familiar staples at the Ikea restaurant. In 2003, Ikea sold 112, 606, 368 meatballs.

The Swedish delicacies in the restaurant and in the food shop at the end of the store are all part of the Ikea experience. The Swedish shop proclaims, "try a taste of Sweden," and sells jars of sliced beetroot, lingonberry jam, Blekinge salmon, and Wasa crispbread. Many Swedish expats just visit Ikea to stock up on their favorite food. "We leave with a great nostalgia for Sweden, a few candles, some jars of Abba fish, and a stomach full of meatballs and salmon," says one Swede from London.

Shopping at Ikea offers a slice of Swedish life. One disgruntled international customer jokes that, "Ikea is Swedish for out of stock". The blue and yellow stores and uniform reflect the colors of the Swedish flag and the snapshots on the walls portray an idyllic image of Swedish country life. (In Sweden the stores and the uniforms were always red and white because it signals low price.) The blue and yellow Swedish box has done a lot to place its founding country on the map.

It's a total immersion – the Swedish food, the Swedish names of the products – there are even Swedish books in the room sets in store, no matter what country you're in. Stroll into an Ikea living room set in London, Madrid, Toronto, New York, or Moscow and you'll see tomes such as *Skolans Historiebok* by Folke Dahlquist, *Olof Mohlin* by Tidensgang, *Bilder av Bildt* by Lars Lundberg or *Scania and its vehicles 1891–1991* by Bjorn Ericlindh on the bookshelves.

Swedish history lesson

There are also many clues to Ikea's way of working in the history and beliefs of Sweden as a nation. Sweden has always been a very democratic and non-hierarchical society. Sweden enabled its farmers to own their own land at a very early stage compared with most other countries especially Russia, a geographical neighbor that still had the serf system until the 1830s.

Ask a Swede to tell you about Sweden and he or she will soon tell you about the Scandinavian model of social care. The basic idea of paying high taxes for a generous level of public services seems to enjoy wholehearted support, even among young voters. The architects of the welfare state were the Social Democrats, traditionally the dominant political force in Scandinavia, although today they only occupy the prime minister's office in Sweden. Social Democrats formed the government in 1920 and redefined socialism to mean achieving a larger shared prosperity in a society where no one is better than anyone else.

"The Social Democrats built the folkhem – Ingvar Kamprad furnished it," says Miriam Salzer, an associate professor at the

Stockholm School of Economics (Salzer's PhD was based on Ikea[21]). The Swedish welfare state was born from a shared sense of a "people's community", known by the Swedish term "folkhemmet." Much of it grew out of a protestant–Lutheran culture, in which care for the weak is the responsibility of society as a whole.

The history of Swedish social democracy

Sweden enabled its farmers to own their own land from a very early stage. These farmers were a political force and could not be controlled by the king; although they were a threat, they also supported him. These independent farmers had a political system that grouped them into communities. Their leadership was circulated within the group so they were different from traditional tribes where fathers passed on their titles to their children. This was where the very basic Swedish democratic and equality principles began.

The Swedish Social Democrats formed the government in 1920, and although they were the traditional political force in Scandinavia, today they only govern in Sweden. They redefined socialism as a shared sense of a "people's community" (folkhemmet). However, for the social system to thrive Swedes need to continue paying high taxes. *The Economist* pointed out that Swedes increasingly move money offshore to avoid paying taxes.[22] It estimated the total being kept overseas as a hefty SKr 500 billion (US$65 billion). Ikea is one Swedish company that has moved its headquarters abroad. Similarly, its rich founder Ingvar Kamprad lives in Switzerland.

Kamprad's decision to move abroad was not very popular among Swedes, but they were more concerned with Ikea shifting production and offices out of the country. "We all suffer from the taxes," explains one. "It's usually frowned upon if you're rich and move away." Kamprad is thought of as a grumpy old man, who is not very well liked but who is respected and grudgingly admired by the Swedes.

The heavy inflow of migrants into Sweden means they need to learn to live with big social changes. Roughly 1 million of Sweden's 9 million people were born outside the country; and if you add in those with at least one parent born abroad, nearly a quarter of the population are outsiders. In time, Swedes are likely to accept that the folkhemmet can include people born in other countries. Sweden also needs to decide whether to reduce the inflow of asylum seekers – now around 40,000 a year, according to *The Economist* – or allow more legal migrants in.

As more foreigners enter and settle in Sweden, they may in turn help to change their host country's values. The Swedish population may demand more choice within the welfare state and become more reluctant to pay such high taxes. If so, the yellow and blue boxes of Ikea scattered around the world may become a snapshot of another past, another country, where things were done differently.

Swedish stereotypes

What do outsiders think of the Swedes? Often they lump Nordics (Sweden, Norway, Finland, Denmark, Iceland) together as one. The list of stereotypes ranges widely: they are good looking, hard drinking, heavily taxed, and prone to suicide.

Binge drinking may soon become a thing of the past. Although Norwegians and Swedes have traditionally caused more injuries per liter of alcohol drunk than other Europeans, drinking patterns seem to be shifting away from violent binges.

Other stereotypes are that they are taciturn, perhaps a little boring, but when they do open their mouths they speak good English. These generalizations may not apply, but proficiency in English does seem to be the case. In Ikea, although English is the language of business, Swedish is said to be the language of the culture, and non-Swedes are encouraged to learn.

A survey by the Economist Intelligence Unit on the best places to do business in the next four years ranked Sweden in eleventh place. A book called *Inspiration* by Nicholas Ind pointed out that Sweden also scores number one on an Innovation Scoreboard published by the European Commission. Other countries that score highly in the study are generally northern European, protestant countries and those that perform below the norm are often southern European, catholic countries.[23]

Although the Swedish government is concerned that it has not spawned any great, international companies since the 1970s, Ikea is just one of a handful of global Swedish companies – Volvo, Ericsson, Tetra Pak, H&M, Saab, Absolute Vodka, Gant, and Electrolux. Sweden is the fourth largest country in Europe in terms of square footage, with just 22 people per sq km as opposed to 300 in the Netherlands. It's interesting that in a country with a population of just 8.9 million, Sweden has created so many international brands. Compare it with a country of a similar size such as Austria, for example: aside from Red Bull, it's difficult to think of any more Austrian brands.

Before Ikea gained momentum internationally, Sweden seemed to be represented abroad by stereotypical Swedish things like saunas, hot tubs, and Abba. Internationally, it feels as if there is a great clarity about Sweden and Swedishness because of all of its international brands. It would be much harder for an American to define Norway, for example.

Sweden's neutrality means that it is well liked abroad and its "Swedishness" has been a help rather than a hindrance during Ikea's international expansion. Called a "moral superpower" by one of its leaders, Sweden is a proactive supporter of peacekeeping, and has provided 90,000 soldiers to UN armies since the country took part in the Korean War. Sweden's defense spending is among the highest in Western Europe, so it is not as pacifist as it might appear.

However, compared with American brands, for example, Ikea never has to be concerned that its country's foreign policy could damage business abroad. It is ranked number 43 in a list of global brands with a value of US$6.92 billion. The top 100 global brand list by brand consultancy Interbrand is dominated by American brands. Ikea is one of just ten European brands in the top 50, and the only retailer to be listed.

Scandinavian living

Aside from meatballs, Ikea's most potent export has been transporting Scandinavian design to the rest of the world. A recent article on the satirical American website The Onion joked about Ikea's pervasive influence:

> This epidemic of self-assembled, clean-lined modernist furniture is still largely contained to densely populated urban areas, but the danger exists that it will spread to other areas throughout America. At the rate it's moving it could suffer European levels of Scandinavian design within a decade.

In Ingvar Kamprad's evangelical pamphlet for his employees, *The Furniture Dealer's Testament*, he states that: "In Scandinavia, people should perceive our basic range as typically Ikea. Elsewhere, they should perceive it as typically Swedish."[24] No other company aside from Ikea has promoted the concept of Scandinavian design so widely.

By the late 1950s, Scandinavian design had become widely popular, characterized by elegant and functional domestic products that most consumers could afford. Using the natural color of wood, Scandinavian design created a version of modernism that focused on clean lines and comfort. It was popularized through exhibitions like the seminal "Design in Scandinavia" show which toured the United States and Canada from 1954 to 1957.

The background to Scandinavian design is very pertinent to Ikea's own mission and values. The most obvious inherent characteristic of Swedes that relates to design is practicality. For centuries, the home had been the focus in Scandinavian life – partly as shelter from the hostile climate, with its nine months of dark wintry cold; and partly because it frames family life.

Self-sufficiency was common in remote rural communities, such as Småland, so the design focussed on the practical and functional. Historically life has been a struggle in Scandinavia, with a limited range of raw materials. This led to a culture of minimizing waste wherever possible.

It was also intrinsically linked to social democratic ideals. Since its birth in 1920, modern Scandinavian design was underpinned by a democratic ideal to design that seeks the enhancement of life through affordable products and technology. It all sounds remarkably similar to Ingvar Kamprad's own proclamations in *The Furniture Dealer's Testament*: "We have decided once and for all to side for the many."[25]

Social democratic ideals in design were emerging before the 1920s, though, according to *Scandinavian Design* by Charlotte and Peter Fiell. They explain how as early as the beginning of the 19th century, a Swedish writer and feminist called Ellen Key (1849–1926) suggested that design standards could be raised to help bring about social reform, with a call for "Skonhet at alla," which translates as "beauty for all." Similarly a Swedish society for craft and design called Svenska Slojdforeningen, founded in 1845, was guided by the conviction that design could and should be used as a catalyst for social change.[26]

Kamprad had a rich Swedish design history to draw his values from. "Vackrare Verdagsvara" was a catchphrase used in the early 19th century, which translates as "more beautiful everyday objects." The catchphrase was coined by Gregor Paullson who published a pamphlet aimed at manufacturers that identified a large, overlooked group of consumers – low-wage earners. He concluded that manufacturers could benefit financially by using design as a competitive marketing tool, a conclusion that Kamprad obviously agreed with.

Much of Ikea's early furniture seems to be inspired by Carl Larsson (1853–1919), one of Sweden's most famous artists. The Larssons' home at Sundborn was decorated in a minimalist and homely style. Larsson published *Ett Hem* (The home), a collection of his watercolours with accompanying text in 1899, which conjured up the rustic idyll of flaxen-haired children scampering over striped rag rugs on scrubbed pine floors.

When the Social Democrats formed the government in 1932, they regarded design as a tool for social change rather than an exercise in aesthetics – to fulfill their vision of folkhemmet (people's home). At this time there was a preoccupation with cleanliness because of cholera epidemics sweeping Swedish cities, which well suited the cleaner, uncluttered lines of Scandinavian design.

After the Second World War the idea of the "people's home" translated into a welfare state with a state-controlled housing policy. Modernism became a potent symbol of the postwar home-making dream. The traditional Swedish practice of handing down custom-made furniture through generations was giving way to young householders looking for new, inexpensive furniture.

Although demand was growing, Swedish manufacturers and retailers kept prices high, and between 1935 and 1946 furniture prices rose 41 percent faster than prices of other household goods. Kamprad could see that this social problem offered Ikea a business opportunity.

Part of the furniture

Scandinavian design differs from Italian design. Milan-based design is about elegant, complicated, high-quality design, and is unlikely to meet the interest of the general public. In contrast, modest Scandinavian design is simple, colorful, and public – which meets the needs of a larger audience. It's more democratic.

As it has grown internationally, Ikea feels less associated with Scandinavian design and more carved from modernism. "I don't see specific Scandinavian things in Ikea designs," says Dr Viviana Narotsky, a professor of the history of design at London's Royal College of Art:

> Scandinavia has a very organic relationship with its material but it's not there with Ikea. The furniture is designed simply, but it could be any wood. It's designed to be manufactured in a way that could be flat packed. In terms of classic, modernist, Scandinavian design, there's not much left aside from modernism.

But what do the Swedes think about their home-grown global furniture designer? They tell me Ikea is part of the furniture, they barely notice it. If they invited a colleague round to the house he or she wouldn't notice the Billy bookshelf, but comment on the books. In Sweden Ikea is translucent, it's nothing.

In Sweden everyone seems to have worked in the stores, at some point. Everyone has been indoctrinated, brought up with Ikea. Like Sweden, Ikea is very democratic. Swedes like the way that all those who go there get treated the same poor way and have to do it themselves. The social democratic vision in Sweden means you're not supposed to be better than anyone else. It's not polite to brag, it's not polite to be better or richer. Ikea fits snugly into that vision.

They're proud of Ikea, but they also have a love/hate relationship with the retailer – the queues at the weekend, the lack of stock in the warehouse. Ikea in Sweden used to struggle with its image. It was thought to be cheap and poor quality, the place where you furnished your first home before upgrading to something better. It's still working on its image and becoming more respected by its home market.

In Sweden everyone used to joke about the self-assembly and how difficult it was to put together Ikea furniture. It was quite typical during Swedish stag and hen nights to be set the difficult task of assembling a piece of Ikea furniture at the end of the evening as a forfeit. Ikea has become part of the social fabric.

5 Innovative materials

> To create a better everyday life for the many people...We shall offer a wide range of well-designed products at prices so low that as many people as possible will be able to afford them.[27]
>
> Ingvar Kamprad,
> *The Furniture Dealer's Testament*

Twelve words changed the world of home furnishings. They were uttered in 1951 by a young Ikea designer called Gillis Lundgren from Malmo, South Sweden, as he struggled to fit a table into the back of his car. "God, what a lot of space this takes up," he muttered, before saying, "Let's take the legs off and put them under the table top" – and flat pack furniture was invented by accident.

Ikea's 1953 catalog included a table called Max – Ikea's very first self-assembly table – and by 1956 the flat pack concept was an integral part of Ikea's system. The invention of flat pack furniture has revolutionized the sector. Flat pack is a major contribution to design history and consumption because it affects everything – the design stage, the manufacturing stage, and the distribution stage. It allows huge economies of scale at the buying end and the user end.

Designing products that could be flat packed and assembled by customers enabled Ikea to cut costs significantly. Flat packed furniture meant Ikea no longer wasted money transporting empty space with its products, and lowered both its storage and transport costs. Ikea could ship more items in one truck, store more products in its warehouse, and avoid transport damage.

Similarly, if you consider that Ikea has to pay for two things to form a product – the material and the workmanship – flat pack and the subsequent self-assembly by the customers means that some of the workmanship comes for free. It cuts labor costs. The furniture industry has not been the same since Ingvar threw his wrench into the system.

Gillis Lundgren still works at Ikea. He appears in the front pages of the 2005 Ikea catalog standing tall next to the Lunna swivel armchair, one of his inventions. The 77-year-old Ikea veteran has played an important role in its history. The fourth employee at Ikea, he became its first full-time designer, creating, among other things, Tore, a storage system inspired by kitchens. He also spent 15 years in charge of the catalog as well as being responsible for the product range.

In the late 1950s, Kamprad also recruited Bengt Ruda and Erik Worts who were designing furniture for self assembly for a rival firm, which had yet to cotton on to flat pack's commercial potential. The Regal bookshelf (1959) was one of the first items to be sold as a flat pack. At the same time Ikea's designers were also developing the concept of modular components and interlinking systems rather than one-off products. This led to a coordinated product range and the promotion of integrated home furnishing – an early and important example of lifestyle retailing.

Ikea reminds Alexander von Vegesack of a German furniture designer called Michael Thonet (1796–1871), who was a simple cabinet maker. Von Vegesack is the director of the Vitra Design museum in Germany, and curated an exhibition of Ikea in 1999.

"Ikea improved the Thonet system and updated it. I don't know if Ingvar knew about Thonet when he started Ikea but he'll know about him now," said von Vegesack.

Thonet developed a new technique to bend wood using steam, and was then able to make the round-backed chair – an art nouveau design that he mass produced. It's often cited as an example of that wonderful moment when mass production is aligned with great design and tied into an industrial capability, just as the invention of the flat pack was an industrial solution that allowed a market to expand.

Kamprad's lens

Ingvar Kamprad visited the Milan Furniture Show in the 1950s, and when he came back to Sweden he began to question why everyone couldn't have beautiful, simple furniture that was well put together. In *The Furniture Dealer's Testament*, Kamprad's quasi-religious pamphlet, he states that: "Any architect can design a desk that will cost 5,000 krona. But only the highly skilled can design a good, functional desk that will cost 100 krona."[28] His genius is to make us look at beautiful things and realize we can afford them.

The lens through which Kamprad regards furniture design is fascinating as it always begins with price and driving costs down. Ikea's innovation lies not only in designing for the mass market, but also in its production. Ikea's mission "to improve the everyday life of the many people" drives everything it does and leads to astonishing feats of low cost, good design. One Ikea Swedish advertising slogan states: "I slot och koja …," which means, "in palaces as well as in tenants' cottages.…"

One of the main reasons why Ikea is so innovative with its production is because in the early days it had to be. It reminds me of the story of Swatch, which revolutionized quality time-keeping into something disposable. In Switzerland, in the beginning, all the Swiss watch manufacturers refused to deal with Swatch because they could see it was revolutionizing the process. Swatch had to break the established price cartel of the industry and find a way to circumnavigate that in order to drive the price down.

The similarities between Swatch and Ikea don't end there. Like Ikea, design played a key role in Swatch's success. Swatch's founder Nicholas Hyatt realized that timekeeping didn't need to be restricted to your grandfather's watch, but that people could wear multiple and cheaper watches that they kept changing. It was the same insight that drove Ikea forwards.

In the 1950s, the National Association of Furniture Dealers in Sweden sent an ultimatum to suppliers urging a boycott against Ikea. By the late 1950s, despite some brave suppliers who would deliver their wares under the cover of darkness, the boycott was becoming painful. Kamprad needed to find more suppliers outside Sweden.

Denmark was investigated first, but then in 1960 Kamprad heard that Poland was keen to form partnerships with Swedish companies, and a year later he was scouting the communist bloc country himself, accompanied by the secret police. It was in

Poland that Kamprad developed a taste for alcohol, sealing deals with factory owners with a celebratory shot of vodka. Ikea's first order from Poland was for just 69,000 krona (US$8,625); by 1998 it was exporting goods worth almost 2 billion krona (US$300 million).

Poland's prices were low, and Kamprad was able to pay around half the cost of corresponding Swedish manufacturers by developing long-term relationships with the suppliers. Ironically, it was a price lead that the Swedish furniture market could never catch up with. By the mid-1960s, half of the pages in the Ikea catalog were showcasing goods made in Poland.

However, Ikea's relationship with Poland was not always smooth. *Leading by Design* details how after the fall of the Berlin Wall some Polish suppliers attempted to raise their prices, and Ikea turned to other countries in Eastern Europe to fill the gap. The fall of the Berlin Wall also led to some manufacturers failing to honor old agreements with Kamprad; and, using the machinery he had invested in, to instead fulfill orders from new clients.[29]

In 1991 Ikea acknowledged that it needed more control over its suppliers and manufacturers, and bought a Småland company called Swedwood. Today, the Swedwood Group has 32 factories in nine countries – across Sweden, the Baltic countries, Central Europe, and Canada. It has an annual turnover of around 5 billion krona (US$755 million) and 11,000 employees.

Ikea now produces its furniture using a mixture of outsourcing and its own manufacturers. While it makes sense for high volume, regular product lines to be made within Ikea companies, outsourcing outside the core range gives more flexibility. Now very few of Ikea's products are made in Sweden; they are made instead in Poland, Bulgaria, and Asia. Countries are chosen that are best equipped with primary sources such as timber, and factories with skilled employees. Ikea has around 2,000 suppliers in 50 countries.

Innovative materials

The pressure of the early days and the Swedish boycott also led Kamprad and Ikea to become more innovative with materials than they had been before. There are stories of Kamprad visiting wood factories and examining the offcuts to see what could be made from them. He knew that by taking materials that were not just cheap, but also of no value to the current owner, he could produce extraordinarily low priced products.

In *Pirates Inside*, brand consultant Adam Morgan tells the story of Kamprad at an open food market in China. Ikea is in the furnishing business yet Kamprad is mesmerized by the rows and rows of plucked chickens. What he wants to know is what they are going to do with all the feathers. He discovers that they are discarded and are not regarded as something of value. As a result Ikea is able to make millions of Ikea feather duvets at discount prices, well below those stuffed with duck or goose feathers.

Ikea's materials

- A sofa is made from a shopping trolley.
- A table is made from some skis.
- Table legs are made by a window factory.
- Bed headboards are made by a door factory.
- Cushion covers are made from shirts.
- A chair is made from a plastic bucket.
- A metal bin is made from a tomato tin can.
- A tea light holder is made from an electricity pylon.
- A photo frame is made from some rubber car tires.

There are scores of examples of Ikea sidestepping a traditional furniture manufacturer and using an unconventional supplier to drive prices down, and also in the early days to avoid the supply boycott. Ikea uses a lot of manufacturers that didn't previously make furniture, and it went to them because they could make the product more cheaply.

There's an Ikea sofa called Moment, designed in 1985, which is made by a shopping trolley manufacturer that produces its wire framework. A matching table, designed in 1987, won the Swedish prize for excellent design. There's also an Ikea table that is made by a ski supplier; a window factory that makes Ikea table legs; a door factory that makes bed headboards; and a cushion cover made by a shirt manufacturer with excess capacity. In the 1990s, Ikea sold one line of picture frames fashioned out of rubber cuts from a Volvo factory.

In 1974, a plastic hardwearing chair called Skopa was designed by Olle Gjerlov-Knudsen and Torben Lind – it was one of the first Ikea products to be designed using modern plastics. After months of fruitless searching for a suitable manufacturer, Ikea struck a deal with a factory that made plastic bowls and buckets.

In the 1990s, Kamprad was keen to start offering his customers circular, stylish metal bins that had become fashionable. He wanted to be able to sell them for around US$10, as opposed to the US$40 they were retailing for on the high street. He instructed his team to try to source a factory that could make these bins for a reasonable price.

Nobody seemed to be able to do it for such a cheap price. Some said they could make them for $20, but no lower. During a discussion about the problems they were facing, Kamprad led his team into the Ikea kitchens and pointed to an industrial-sized can of tomato soup. The next day, the soup can manufacturer was approached by Ikea, and agreed to make stylish metal bins that could be sold for $10.

Often Ikea designers think about the material of a product before they consider a design. For example, Ikea sourced a new material from Poland that was traditionally used to insulate electricity pylons and switchboards, and asked its designers to create a suitable product. They came up with a tea light holder, which looks as if it's made from white china, and can be linked together to make a shape. There's also a range of ceramic lamps that are made from the same material.

Design economy

It's not easy being an Ikea designer. The designers must always consider form, function, and price – and price is sacrosanct. It is Ingvar Kamprad's obsession. When he sees a mug in Ikea priced at £1, he wants his designers to make that mug for 50p.

Ikea's 11 in-house product managers are based in Älmhult, southern Sweden. They must walk the tightrope daily, balancing low prices and quality. "They are truly passionate," acknowledges one Ikea worker. "They try really hard to get the best design with a tiny budget and cut corners, but they also try to maintain the quality. I'm not envious of the product managers. It's really tricky."

It's even more of a struggle to maintain the quality of furnishings like sofas and bookshelves while continually shaving off costs. Ikea workers from the stores get a chance to view the designer's new products in Älmhult, but their questions are always about price. "Our first reaction is, that's nice, and then how much?" reveals one. "If it sounds too expensive, we say, make it half price. We know the market; you can't have something expensive at Ikea. They take our input and go back to the designer, who feels very frustrated. Sometimes Ikea Sweden says, 'You'll have to wait two weeks because the designer is calming down or thinking about it.' It's nice to have beautiful furniture but only if it sells. Design is important but only if it's for a large public."

Ikea's reputation in the design world has improved over the last decade. Designers now want to work at Ikea because they know it will teach them how to design furniture for the mass market. In the beginning, Ikea's designs were considered to be ugly and purely functional objects, mainly for the lower classes, but slowly Ikea in the last 20 years has been able to create more beautiful products too.

Ikea has over 20,000 products, of which 9,000 form the core of simple, functional items common across its stores worldwide; plucked from these are 3,000 products displayed in the catalog. In order to keep costs down and maintain long-term relationships with suppliers, designers must work two to three years ahead. Annually, 2,000 new products are added to the range, but some successful Ikea products pass the test of time. Over 28 million Billy bookcases have been sold since it was designed in 1978.

Ikea has always battled against accusations of design plagiarism, as the traditional furniture industry rails against its cheap prices. Just last year, Ikea tapped into the design trend of Brazilian shantytown chic led by the Campana brothers who exhibited at London's Design Museum. Ikea created the Fargglad chair with metal frame and plastic woven seat and back, for the shanty-town price of £9, which compares favorably with the brothers' own expensive designer chairs.

Ikea designers are not design innovators in the traditional sense, but they are deftly accomplished at designing a chair that will sell for £5. It's the same skill that enables Spanish fashion retailer Zara to borrow trends from the Milan catwalk and reproduce design chic for high street fashion prices. However, it's debatable whether Ikea should be applauded for original design, as it does seem to copy design standards.

Design highlights

1951   Gillis Lundgren invents flat pack furniture as he struggles to squeeze a table into his car trunk.

1953   Max, Ikea's very first flat pack table, is designed.

1963   Marian Grabinski, an architect, designs the MTP wooden bookcase, which encouraged Ikea to forge relations with Polish suppliers.

1969   The Privat sofa is designed by architect Ake Fribyter using a particleboard base that saved on wood and weight.

1974   The Skopa chair is designed by Olle Gjerlov-Knudsen and Torben Lind using modern plastic.

1978   The Billy bookcase is designed – over 28 million have been sold since then.

1982   Lack shelves are created.

1997   Children's Ikea is launched.

Hot dog prices

Everybody always has a moment of surprise while shopping in Ikea. Sometimes, it's very difficult to believe or understand that an Ikea item can be so cheap. It's jaw-dropping and a technical piece of ingenuity. Inside Ikea, these ridiculously cheap items are called "hot dogs," named after the 50p sausages you can buy at the cash till. One of Ikea's entrenched competitive advantages, difficult to replicate, is quite simply that the product itself looks more expensive than it is. This is in tune with what the general public wants – we want to appear stylish but we don't want to have to pay for it.

Sourcing cheap materials is essential for Ikea's low prices. Ikea designers and buyers are always looking for less expensive, good quality alternative materials. In the early 1960s, Ikea led the trend to replace traditional teak with less costly oak, and in the 1970s Ikea helped to win a broader acceptance of inexpensive pine furniture.

In the 1960s, the arrival of particleboard made a big impact on Ikea. In 1969 the Privat sofa was designed by architect Ake Fribyter. It had a particleboard base with a white lacquer finish, and brown floral cretonne covers. Similarly, "board-on-frame" products which replace solid wood with chipboard sheets built onto a frame like a sandwich, saving on wood and weight, have been a great success for Ikea and are mostly manufactured in Poland.

Another reason for Ikea's low prices is the enormous scale at which it manufactures its products. Economies of scale bulldoze prices down. Lack, a best-selling small coffee table, is a good example of this. In 1990, Ikea was producing around 242,000 tables and selling them for €25.70, but by 2004 Ikea was producing 2 million tables and was able to sell them for just €9.90. Ikea differs from most retailers because it passes its savings onto the customers.

You would think that Ikea's profits on individual items would be tiny. In fact its profit margins are huge. Between

17–18 percent of the price of an Ikea product is pure profit, which is staggering considering most rival firms operate on single-figure margins. Even Tesco, the British supermarket that has successfully expanded abroad, only operates on margins of around 6 percent.

Demand on supply

Ikea needs to place tremendous pressure on its supply chain to lower costs. Although it has been generous to fledgling factories in Asia and Eastern Europe – by investing in technology and safety equipment so the manufacturer can supply the volume Ikea requires – this often means its supply chain is very dependent on Ikea. This dependency makes it easier for Ikea to drive down prices, which is common practice in retailing.

Some of Ikea's suppliers have little choice but to lower their prices. This is especially true of those factories that used to make doors, for example, but now make billions of Ikea bed headboards with peculiar measurements instead. They are completely dependent on Ikea's business. Ikea's scale, a blessing for some manufacturers, is double-edged.

"The key to Ikea's success is logistics, I can't think of anyone who does it better," confirms one ex-Ikea worker. "Ikea will move in and push hard on price – but they have to." Ikea also always doubles up its production facilities across different countries – Poland, Bulgaria, China, Russia, Sweden, and Hungary – to make sure there's less risk of running out of products.

Ikea's supply chain is highly mechanized. It was a pioneer of the automated warehouse and the first company to have a warehouse run by robots. Ikea owns 27 cavernous hangars where products rest between factory and store. These warehouses span 10,000,000 cubic meters across the globe, from Shah Alam in Malaysia to Peterborough in the United Kingdom. They're dark, high-ceilinged chasms where squadrons of robotic cranes twirl and pirouette, stealthily propelling boxes from shelf to shelf.

In theory the system is designed to operate in mathematical precision. Let's say you buy an Applead kitchen in the Warrington store in the United Kingdom. Your new kitchen will be logged by the cash till and the purchases of Applead will add up until they trigger a warning of low stocks. An electronic message is passed on to the closest distribution center, which will dispatch more kitchens. It sounds slick. In practice, things can go wrong.

Kamprad's frugal system means that the tiniest human error can cascade through the system, causing chaos. Perhaps someone forgets to pick up the shipment of Applead units languishing at the warehouse; perhaps a warehouse worker forgets to mark down damaged work tops that have been thrown away – the system can collapse.

We've all experienced the mayhem and queued in a chaotic Ikea warehouse for a piece of the Pax fitted wardrobe, which was out of stock last time. You stand shoulder to shoulder with a troop of angry customers baying for Sultan mattresses, Komplement shoe racks, and Pax sliding doors.

The most creative part of Ikea's story is how it revolutionized the production process. Did you know that Ikea has its own rail company? Ikea Rail was launched in 2002 to help Ikea physically build rail tracks and trains in China to shuttle its goods across the vast country.

It is not the first time Ikea has built its own transport infrastructure. When it first pinpointed Russia as a valuable source of timber, the Russian roads weren't good enough for Ikea to get its products back out. So Ikea built a motorway enabling its trucks to go back and forth with timber. I can't think of another retailer that has created its own transport infrastructure.

Ikea's ambitions for democratic design seem to hold no boundaries. In the late 1990s, it experimented with prefab apartments. The pilot programme was called BoKlok, which is Swedish for "Smart Living," and Ikea partnered with an international developer Skanska. These small buildings expanded Ikea's design agenda, beyond metal bins made from tin cans and sofas made from shopping trolleys, to cover whole communities. By 2000, Ikea had built over 1,000 prefab apartments across four countries in Scandinavia, bringing democratic design to a logical conclusion.

To the checkout

6 Flat pack city

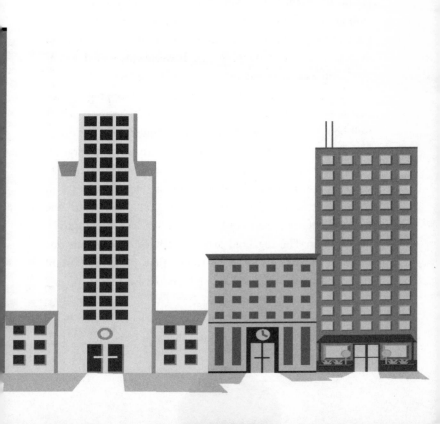

On Palm Sunday, American cousin went to Ikea
assuming that the store would be empty because
the English would be in church...Soon she was
stuck in her minicab in a three-lane jam on the
North Circular. "There must be a terrible accident
ahead," said cousin to the driver. "No," said he.
"They're all going to Ikea."[30]

Ikea is the new church. More British families worship at the
shrine of Swedish furniture design on Sundays than go to
church. It has become a ritual entwined into modern society –
arguably as potent and as routine as the weekly outing to mass
40 years ago. Over 310 million people worldwide visited Ikea in
2003, and we're prepared to travel over 100 miles to get there.

Ikea is about being as much as buying. It's a shopping journey
that hopes to lull you into the Ikea belief that an inner self of
well-being can be achieved through a combination of low prices
and design. The Ikea world is half warehouse, half cathedral.

Ikea is like a museum of the modern world. Herd-like
instincts are encouraged. Yellow shopping bag in hand, we all
follow the arrows into the labyrinth, shuffling from one
covetable lifestyle snapshot to the next. It's very difficult to be
an explorer. The big bold arrows push you around in one
direction. Bedrooms or living rooms first, the all-important
sofa purchase, a table, a chair, and a bookcase; before moving
on to kitchens and bathrooms....

There's something about the Ikea experience. You're being
pulled along a journey. It's a quest that you can't pull yourself

out of. It becomes a dream-like state – following the arrows at your feet around the store. But it's a maze, and beware the intrepid shopper who attempts to stray off the path. Moroccan bazaars, Syrian souks, and Egyptian camel markets have nothing on Ikea.

Kungens Kurva

All of the retail and product innovations that we're familiar with at Ikea today were tested and founded in Sweden. On June 18, 1965, seven years after the opening of the first Ikea store in Älmhult, Kamprad and his young team opened a flagship store just outside Stockholm in Kungens Kurva (King's Kerb – named because the King had an accident at that spot). The 48,500 square feet store dwarfed the first Ikea store of just 6,700 square feet and it was expected to make four times more money.

The new store's circular design was inspired by the Guggenheim Museum in New York; customers started at the top and spiraled their way through the whole store. The queue for the store on its first day wound its way around the building like a ball of string. Around 35,000 customers turned up on the first day, and Ikea staff at Älmhult had to race to the capital to help their colleagues.

It was chaos. The whole store was organized so people could walk around the store by themselves, write down what they wanted, and then pick up the goods after paying and handing their list to the helpers. Writing out long orders and not enough checkouts caused huge queues. Some customers sick of waiting in the rush left without paying, while others simply took matters into their own hands and walked into the warehouse to pick up goods themselves.

At one point, Ingvar's wife called him up to tell him about the chaos. He told her to give the customers free coffee, buns, and hot dogs to keep them happy. He was also intrigued to see some customers walk into the warehouse themselves to collect their furniture. Indeed, he thought it was a good idea and liked the notion of getting the people to help themselves. So the concept of self-service was born.[31]

Kamprad was disgruntled by the number of customers who were wearing out his carpets gazing at the inspirational room sets but not buying anything. He considered charging an entry fee. Then it was decided that there needed to be something at the end of the trail, something smaller, so you always have to buy something, so you always leave with some knick-knack that you didn't know you needed – and the Ikea marketplace was born.

The rationale is explained in "Ikea's history book," *The Future is Filled with Opportunities*, which was distributed to all employees:

> The growing stream of customers soon created problems.... But the maintenance costs for the store went up still faster. What to do? Increase the prices? Out of the question! Why should those who bought be punished because others came to look?

> Entrance fee? Well, it wasn't a very appealing idea
> for a retailer to perhaps annoy or stop his
> customers at the door. The solution to the problem
> was, as usual, unconventional....[32]

Ironically, it wasn't until the Kungens Kurva store burnt down and was rebuilt that Kamprad was able to expand and modernize the store to improve the shopping experience for customers. The store burnt down in 1970 when a faulty electrical sign ignited the whole building, leading to the largest insurance claim in Swedish history.

The store was reopened in March 1971 with a playroom for children by the entrance and an open warehouse where customers could collect their own purchases. It was also the first store to develop Småland cooking in a restaurant.

The Ikea concept

In every Ikea across the world there is a kid's playroom located just inside the entrance. Most major corporations don't provide on-site childcare, yet Ikea does – for free. Local managers have to ask permission if they don't want to have one in their store – it's part of the Ikea furniture. Across 202 stores in 32 countries (including franchises), you'll see children playing in the colored ball parks, leaving their parents some freedom to shop in peace, aside from the occasional announcement asking Mr Smith to go and collect naughty baby Rose from the playroom.

It's also replaced the family day trip. Why go to the seaside when you can go to Ikea? Why visit a theme park when there's fun for the whole family at an Ikea near you? Going to Ikea at the weekend is the new family outing. Visiting Ikea is like a surreal fairground ride.

There is a set pattern for all Ikea stores. Each one begins with five living rooms. At one time, stores had to ask permission if they wanted to change the order of viewings. Ingvar Kamprad was reportedly most dismayed by a Frankfurt store beginning its journey alternatively. However, he must be getting tame in his old age, as Ikea in north London begins with bedrooms.

Each room set has been carefully crafted by an Ikea designer to appeal to a certain type of person. There is a Scandinavian style, a country style (which works well in England), a modern style, and a "young Swede" style. When the Ikea designers prepare a room set they have got a detailed picture of customers in their head: what kind of clothes they wear, what kind of car they drive, what kind of taste they have – every detail.

The Ikea pathway makes it almost impossible to stick to a list. Even the most disciplined shoppers will find it hard not to be tempted into buying something they didn't even know they wanted until they saw it in an Ikea display. It's a clever selling device, and manipulates people into buying things they hadn't previously considered without making them feeling pushed to do so. "It's a very dangerous shop for someone like me," admits one fan. "I always buy things that I never would have bought if they hadn't been under my nose."

So we end up with another 100 tea lights, a penguin ice tray, a frothing device for our lattes, three martini glasses, a wooden spoon, and a huge black and white photograph of three pebbles. This is part of the appeal for some shoppers. "You never know what you are going to come home with. You go for some curtains and arrive back with a shoe stand and a bedside table," says one.

Ikea people always say that their range is their identity. American booksellers like Barnes & Noble use the term "authority of range," and this is what Ikea has too. It's a mountain of choice rather than a carefully edited selection. Ikea stores generally do around ten times the business of a superstore competitor, and they have an enormous range of items rather than a focus on a few key lines. Rather than get people through the store quickly and conveniently, they march them past every single item.

Gavin Rothwell, retail analyst at Verdict Research Ltd, says Ikea has a "category killing format." He points out that the average Ikea store is 190,000 square feet. No other retailer (in the United Kingdom certainly) has such big stores. Asda supermarket's biggest store is around 100,000 square feet, while DIY operator B&Q has a largest store of 130,000 square feet. Ikea stores are like space ships.

I'd heard a rumor about a secret passageway. Savvy Ikea-goers told me about an unmarked door for intrepid shoppers who want to walk their own way and circumnavigate the store. Whispered rumors in online chat rooms and a detailed description from my work colleague Jo helped me find it. I pushed my way through an unmarked door like Alice through the looking glass, and emerged blinking in the market hall. I'd managed to miss out the kitchen, bathroom, and office.

Writing home

Ikea's little brown pencils have become an integral part of the shopping experience. They have other lives aside from being used to scribble down the serial numbers of the Ikea products. They've been spotted on cruise ships in the Mediterranean being used by bingo players to mark their cards. A football referee in Scotland has even been seen marking his notebook during a match with the miniature brown pencil. Golfers use them to mark their scorecards and teachers keep some spare in their desk to hand out to pupils. One pencil even ended up on online auction site, eBay – although the opening bid was just 1p.

Insiders at Ikea's Scottish stores suggest that customers are pilfering millions of pencils. One customer makes special "restocking trips" wearing tracksuit bottoms that can hold handfuls of the wooden engraved Ikea pencils, according to one staff member.

Part of the family

As you pass through the Ikea world, you become part of the family. You have to move the furniture yourself, you have to assemble it yourself, but 75,000 yellow-shirted Ikea faithfuls believe this is good for you. Inside the retail operation they call us pro-sumers rather than consumers because we have to be proactive.

Ikea is an anti-service retailer. It asks a lot of its customers. Ikea's flat packed philosophy encourages customers to build their own furniture, to find their own way around stores, to get into the car, and drive out of town. Then loaded with goods, a line of squat concrete bollards stops you wheeling your trolley to the car. The lone shopper has to abandon his or her wares and make a run for it.

Ikea's out-of-town location means it can wrap customers up in an experience – its crèche and cheap restaurant encourage them to stay for longer. Some people visit Ikea for the restaurant alone. One friend used to go there with his Swedish girlfriend to stock up on her favorite food from home at the deli at the exit. Another reveals that her five-year-old girl thinks that: "Ikea is a brilliant restaurant with some boring furniture stuck on the side."

I quietly watch the comings and goings in the restaurant. It's early Saturday morning and Ikea's restaurant is swarming with excitable shoppers, all fueling themselves before the marathon shop ahead. There are grandmothers and babies, teenagers and young families, gay couples, newly weds, pregnant mothers, and fathers and sons – wearing trainers, stilettos, sandals, flip flops, Jimmy Choos, and Caterpillar boots. It's a microcosm of society in one café – everyone united by the £1 breakfast, the bottomless coffee cup, and a big, yellow shopping bag. It caters for all.

Some people struggle with the Ikea system. One grand-mother is trying to spoon coffee out of the old tea bag bin; another is perplexed by fact she has to pay for an empty glass and then fill it with Cola once she's paid her bill. She brightens up when she realizes she can keep topping up. Shopping with her granddaughter and daughter, she is propelled around the store and café by them. She doesn't realize I'm writing a book. "It's revolutionized this country!" she exclaims as we wait in a long queue, while staff bang and knock a coffee machine that's playing up. "My son used to live in Sweden and he said it was wonderful and now it's here!" We reflect on how lucky we are as the coffee machine grumbles into action.

Ikea forces customers to do things in an Ikea way, even if they don't want to. You have to clear your own dishes away – very Ikea, but customers are told on the wall that "At Ikea clearing your own table at the end of the meal is one of the reasons you paid less at the start." That seems quite reasonable considering we all paid just £1 for an English breakfast.

There's a giant tomato ketchup dispenser in the middle of the café. It seems to symbolize people's complex relationship with Ikea. Myriads of customers are queuing and then jamming the lever up and down, up and down to get some ketchup on their sausages, but nobody's getting any ketchup because the dispenser is broken. No one complains. It reminds me of the way we all resign ourselves to that wobbly Ikea coffee table in the living room, steadying it with last year's catalog. Ikea introduced a transparency to pricing and customer service that hadn't been seen before – we love the cheap prices so we have to be prepared to do more of the work.

Seven levels of hell

We all have a love/hate relationship with Ikea. Many people are Ikea maniacs – they're often drawn to visit the stores and go shopping there but also get frustrated with the long queues, the hassle, 20,000 bickering couples, and swear to never go again – until next time. Missing items, seething crowds, poor customer service…. The tiniest human error cascades through the system, leaving another customer cursing Ikea bitterly as he or she drives back home with boxes piled on the roof rack.

"Ikea is absolute hell," rants my friend Ryan:

> You've gone to buy a bookcase because it's good quality, cheap, and stylish and you might want to look at a rug. Instead you're forced to tread a two-foot wide path between ludicrous kitchens of the future, nasty futons, and novelty storage solutions while a pushy bride-to-be drags her poor bloke over to look at a nicely colored patchwork blanket because it's only a fiver.
>
> I never know whether to pick up things there and then or whether you're supposed to note down its number and pick it up in the warehouse, and end up pushing my trolley the wrong way back. You leave in a two-hour traffic jam through Croydon (UK), vowing never to go back again. The products are good though, so two months later when you need a wardrobe you repeat the whole joyless experience.

This is not an isolated reaction. "Never again, I think I'll reclaim my chintz after the amount of stress they cause," says one frustrated shopper on a DIY online chat room. Another says Ikea gave him an attack of claustrophobia when he couldn't find his way out – one customer who could have done with finding the secret passageway. My friend Caroline's mother nearly fainted in the store, and referred to it as the seven levels of hell because you can't get out once you're in.

My colleague Rebecca recalls a particularly painful trip for her boyfriend:

> John once accompanied his sister to Ikea. She was moving into a new place after living in a van for a year and needed a lot of new stuff. After about three hours he left her to carry on shopping while he sat waiting in the restaurant. After five hours, he found her again and told her he was walking home and would leave her with the car. Walking home from an out-of-town Ikea is not easy. His sister returned home after 10 hours shopping in Ikea.

You would think that after all this queuing – for breakfast, for lunch, for kitchen advice, for bathroom advice, at the checkouts – we would all want to leap in our cars as soon as we've bought our goods. Not so – there's a Swedish deli brimming with lingonberries, meatballs, and rye biscuits, and a hot dog stand selling hot dogs for a remarkable 35p each. A queue of 50 shoppers complete with trolleys and flat pack furniture snakes it way behind the tills, wanting a reward at the end of their journey – something cheap and Swedish to eat.

There's also the self-service Mr Whippy ice cream machine. What better indulgence fits the end of a marathon shopping trip? "It's great to have these low-cost rewards at the end of a long shopping trip," says Ruth, the researcher for this book. "That dismal experience didn't put me off. Perhaps the Mr Whippy at the end is more important to me," she confirms.

The Ikea way of doing things can also aggravate customers as when it goes wrong the systems crunch to a halt. Amy (a friend) moans:

> On Friday we were assembling our Ikea wardrobe only to discover that they'd given us the wrong door ... so off we trotted back to the store. The returns department only had one till open so had to wait half an hour and then trail through the store again to the wardrobe department to reorder the right door. Then we had to go down and wait another 30 minutes for the door to be brought out of the warehouse.

There are those who've mastered the Ikea system. Morag (a colleague) reveals:

> I largely enjoy my trips to Ikea because I've learnt from experience. It can be frustrating if you don't

know how to work the bare bones service system. And there always seems to be some new inconvenience. If you figure out that they open the store an hour earlier than advertised on Sundays to browse and call to check that certain items are in stock and buy huge quantities of bulbs and plugs that don't seem to be sold anywhere else – then you're laughing.

The crowds mean we go shopping at times we'd never previously have dreamt of. There are those who've become Ikea night-time shopping fanatics. They arrive at the store at 10 pm, fuel up with hot dogs and a glass of wine, and shop till midnight. Ikea in the UK is lobbying for 24-hour opening – we wait with bated breath.

Furniture makers

A lot of new industries crop up around Ikea, like cattle egrets, the white birds that follow herds of elephants. There's a man with a van based in north London who'll take orders from the catalogue and do your shopping for you. In Scotland before the Glasgow Ikea opened, a man and his lorry used to travel down to the Gateshead (England) branch to buy furniture for the Scots – he was doing thousands of orders a month. In Ireland, there's a coach that will drive Ikea fans across the Irish Sea to visit the store in Warrington (England).

Just outside the complex of Ikea Brent Park in north London there is a battered poster for a company that puts together self assembly furniture. I wonder how many weary shoppers buy Ikea furniture to save money and then go straight over the road to have someone else do the hard work? They save a lot of sweat and tears in the process, but Ikea does not approve.

Creating the furniture when you get home is intrinsically tied into the Ikea brand, ranging from the incomprehensible diagrams in the box, which never quite make sense, to the lottery draw as to whether you'll get an Allen key in the package or have to resort to using a kitchen knife instead.

But this process can make you more attached to your purchase than you would be if it arrived as it was shown in the store. The sense of pride is more than the excitement of buying new furniture. Ruth reminisces:

> I really love my futon because it was quite compli-
> cated to make. But now people sleep on it so I
> managed to create something with real use in my
> life. And all the parts were there.

One friend left her husband in charge of buying the marital bed. He bought a king-size bed frame for a double-size mattress. Their house was so small that they were unable to open their wardrobe doors as a result. "That's just the result of combining men, shopping, and pick-your-own furniture," she laughs.

I remember my first television cabinet, bought for a tiny, grimy London flat – the first time I'd properly lived alone. It felt monumental that my television was no longer going to be balanced on the *Complete Works of Shakespeare*, an *Oxford English Dictionary*, and the *Yellow Pages*. I put it together back to front, and for the next two years stared at shelves of unfinished plywood rather than birch veneer. Then there was the Billy bookcase – so tall and exhausting to assemble that I neglected any nails that didn't seem essential. It always required a gentle kick each time I passed it in the corridor, to pull the shelves together again.

There's more to self-assembly furniture than another Ikea cost-cutting measure. It becomes a tool of evangelism, another moral crusade that teaches you the value of good, honest, Swedish hard work. And that's why we feel attached to our Ikea furniture – the ritual ties us closer to our purchases.

7

Chuck out your chintz

Chuck out your chintz, come on do it today,
Prise off those pelmets and throw them away,
Those sofas are too twirly, too silly, too girly
That flower trimage is harming our image.[33]

Ikea people often call themselves the quiet rebels. One thing they've always had to do is confront and shake up entrenched, existing social attitudes. Ikea's advertising plays a crucial role in urging this social change because of the need to persuade people to change their behavior.

Ikea is asking a lot of us – that we drive out of town to go shopping, that we collect our own furniture from the warehouse and put it together, and replace our traditional, chintzy décor with a modern, Scandinavian interior. Advertising also needs to cajole consumers to accept the possibility of disposable, fashionable furniture. This is furniture that you change and swap when you get bored; you don't buy a sofa for life any more.

In the early days, Ikea used its Swedish provenance in advertising in new markets. The retailer was promoted as typically Swedish, with a cheerful, laughing moose that became a long-lasting symbol and one that Ikea has been desperately trying to suppress ever since. Similarly, in France around 15 years ago, a television advertising campaign for Ikea used the strapline: "Ils sont fous, ces Suedois," which translates as "They're crazy, these Swedes." Ikea has never been afraid of taking the mickey out of itself.

A more serious press ad about Småland appeared in Sweden in 1981, where Ikea's philosophy was explained below a photograph of a dry stone wall in the southern Swedish countryside. The ad was produced by Swedish advertising agency Brindfors, and the idea was to show a typical Småland landscape to symbolize the soul of Ikea. It stated: "Ikea's soul is in the right place. Like Småland's farmers, our values are down-to-earth. We have toiled hard in a difficult field to produce sweet harvests ..."[34]

Challenger brand

Ikea has three choices when it launches into new markets. It could accept that they do things differently overseas and write off certain countries as unsuitable for expansion, it could compromise on what it believes in to make its offering more acceptable to foreigners, or it could stick to its guns and challenge local beliefs and tastes.

Unsurprisingly, Ikea always opts for the third option. It positions itself as a challenger brand, an outsider that has been parachuted in to shake up the status quo, sometimes leaning on Swedishness, but sometimes not. There was a German campaign which proclaimed: "Verdammtes IKEA – geliebtes IKEA" and another which said: "IKEA, Swedish for common sense." In Switzerland, they ran a campaign that simply stated: "Stop being so snobbish."

As an idealistic, challenger brand, Ikea can take more risks in its advertising than other brands might. Similarly, the fact it is a Swedish brand in a foreign country gives Ikea license to say things that other brands can't say. So, in the United Kingdom in the late 1990s, the Swedish furniture dealer could say: "Stop being so English." A local furniture maker couldn't have said that. Being an outsider means Ikea can get away with more.

In the United States, Ikea was the first brand to use a gay couple in its television advertising in 1994. The 30-second ad showed a 30-something couple debating which dinner table to buy. "Buying a table leaf together means staying together," jokes one. "We've got another leaf waiting for when we really start getting along."[35]

Ikea was typically blasé when questioned about its "daring" advertising in the American press. Peter Connolly, Ikea's marketing director, said: "We've showed a family with kids, one with a new baby, a divorced woman, and a couple setting up home. This time we thought: what other households exist? And we decided to do a gay couple, a middle-aged couple, and a retired one."[36]

Ikea may be global, but it does not use one global advertising network to create its marketing. Relationships are more likely to be forged with small, independent agencies that are able to tap into local customs and humor. It's fascinating that a brand which uses a cookie-cutter approach in its business model and retail environment, prefers to stay local in its advertising.

Changing British taste

Ikea has spawned many award-winning ads across the world. However, one British television ad from the late 1990s is

A selection of Ikea's advertising strap lines

France – 1981 launch campaign "Ils sont fous ces Suedois" (They're crazy, these Swedes).

Germany – "IKEA, Swedish for common sense."

Switzerland – "Stop being so snobbish."

UK – 1996 "Chuck out the chintz."

UK – 1999 "Stop being so English."

America – "America's a big country, someone's got to furnish it."

America – 2002 "Many of you feel bad for this lamp. That is because you're crazy. It has no feelings. And the new one is much better."

especially interesting because it shows how Ikea successfully persuaded people to change their taste. Seventeen years ago, the first ad introduced Ikea to the British public and raised awareness of the first Ikea store in Warrington, northern England. The 1987 ad showed a woman in her nightwear on a bed, as a voiceover observed: "The bed cost less than the pajamas."

A later campaign showed minor UK celebrity Keith Chegwin bouncing on an Ikea bed shouting that although it was cheap, it was good. These price-focused ads felt apologetic. Ikea's best advertising is created when the retailer doesn't just focus on its cheap prices but attempts to change entrenched attitudes by being rude and brave.

Ten years on, and Ikea's UK advertising and its focus on price wasn't working. Ikea's British growth was stagnating. In 1996, there were seven stores in the United Kingdom, with permission to open four more, and Ikea was concerned the demand wasn't there.

Ikea's thriftiness infiltrates its marketing budgets too. Ikea does traditionally spend less on advertising than its competitors. In the UK, its ad budget equated to around 8 percent of the total marketplace as opposed to MFI, a local competitor that had around 30 percent. It spends around €11 million in the United Kingdom and 4.3 million in France, for example.

Every agency executive that I interviewed informed me that Ingvar Kamprad does not approve of marketing – he views it as a cost. Ikea wants to tell people a new store is opening, but internally it doesn't subscribe to the fact that you have an image. Ikea prefers to let the world come to its own conclusions.

Ikea's small advertising budget meant the retailer was being dwarfed in communications. Because its furniture ads were formulaic and following the rules – always show a product, always show a price, use a lot of press ads and poster ads, and spend a small amount on television – Ikea had become invisible.

Ikea decided to hold a pitch for its advertising account in the UK to St Luke's, BBH, Mellors Reay, and AMV. All four ad agencies seem to have been chosen on their creative credentials. BBH was one of the London agencies of the moment, and produced award-winning work for Levi's; AMV, an award-winning agency whose work included *The Economist's* print campaign and the Guinness surfer campaign; creative hot shop Mellors Reay, which has since been merged with Grey, a global ad agency; while St Luke's had recently been formed from a group of agency execs from TBWA who wanted to found a new kind of ad agency that would be co-owned by all of its workers.

The pitch lasted for two months and was presided over by Anders Dahlvig, who was made Ikea president in 1999, and Matti Naar, a UK marketing director who now heads up Ikea's marketing in the United States. According to ad agencies that attended the pitch, it felt as if the Ikea people were less interested in the work they were presenting and more interested in whether they could work with the people. Most agencies that pitched for the business suggested that Ikea should tweak its product in order to appeal to the British public; St Luke's suggested Ikea tried to change people's taste.

Middle England versus Scandinavian living

Ikea, with its modernist, Scandinavian take on home living, was trying to expand into middle England, where two-thirds of people didn't like modern décor. Focus groups at the time were telling Ikea that people wouldn't shop there because it was too modern and too cold. They wanted it to be more British, with warmer colors, chintzy patterns, and floral patterns.

Ikea refused to budge. As far as it was concerned, Ikea was a global concept that couldn't be changed. Ikea's philosophy was that if you can't change the product you've got to change people. That's all you can do. It was a tough advertising brief – persuade people that modern is good for them and change their taste. Ikea's advertising always works best when it has an enemy. In 1996 in Britain, it was chintz.

St Luke's imagined a war between Ikea and UK style. The most potent symbol of British taste in the home was chintz – a floral, country-house-style fabric that dresses English sofas, cushions, beds, and windows. "Chuck out your chintz," an ad that urged women to spring clean their homes to make room for some Scandinavian style, was launched in autumn 1996. The main television ad features a housing estate where a crowd of women are throwing out all their old flowery and traditional furniture, curtains, and doilies – to replace them with modern Ikea furniture and furnishings.

The soundtrack features a 1960s protest-style song written specially for the ad, which starts: "Chuck out your chintz, come on do it today, prise off those pelmets and throw them away, those sofas are twirly, too silly, too girly, that flowery trimage is harming our image ..." and then cuts away to an Ikea home which is "spacious and airy and light, loose and informal and stripy and bright."[37]

In *The New Marketing Manifesto*, John Grant, a co-founder of St Luke's, recalls a research group held in an Ikea manager's house, to see how British people reacted to its décor. One woman, who was staring at a creative arrangement of twigs and red apples in a vase, revealed:

> See that. Now that looks great. And I might even
> copy it. But it's something I'd never come up with

on my own. I might as well put on my wedding
dress, tuck it in my knickers, put a bowl of fruit on
my head, and run down my road singing.

Ikea had a lot of educating to do.

Before the television ad was aired, St Luke's showed it to a
group of women in Birmingham, which was perceived to be the
heartland of British housewives, to gauge what reactions it
might provoke. They hated the ad and were furious and angry.
They felt it was a dig at their taste and their own home. During
the focus groups they were looking around their own home to
see if they had any offending items like doilies or net curtains.
They said things like, "If you put that ad out I'm going to have
to chuck away all my furniture and you're telling me all my taste
is wrong."

Ikea and St Luke's were nervous about the television
campaign, but they decided to run it anyway. It was self-
confident, it told people what to do, and it set a standard for how
Ikea advertising could push the boundaries of being rude and
brave and bossy without damaging its business. It questioned
British people's taste, and Ikea started selling a lot of furniture.
The ad nearly doubled Ikea's British sales in the process.

The ad seemed to tap a nerve in the British public. "These
women had left behind nearly every traditional idea of the role
of women – in their careers, their clothes, their relationships –
but were still reverting to quaint ideas in décor," says Grant.
The slogan, "Chuck out your chintz" was like burning your
bra.

The campaign struck a nerve with the British media. The right-wing broadsheet, the *Daily Telegraph*, wrote a column in defense of chintz, while "Chuck out the chintz" was used in word play by other journalists. One newspaper writing a profile of the Blairs used a headline satirizing the famous Blair policy – "Tough on crime, tough on the causes of crime" – "Tony Blair – tough on chintz, tough on the causes of chintz." After the 1997 election, when Tony Blair and the New Labour party were voted into power, one minister was interviewed outside Number 10 Downing Street. "What's Tony doing now?" asked the reporter. "I expect he's chucking out the chintz," came the reply.

Out with the old and in with the new

It's difficult to know whether Ikea influenced a sweeping change in social behavior or if its advertising cleverly tapped into something that was inherently there. In the 1960s and 1970s some British décor was very modern, with purple beanbags and low pine coffee tables, then in the 1980s, with Thatcherism, dado rails and old fireplaces were uncovered again. By the mid-1990s this was beginning to lose relevance, the Blair election campaign was just a year away, and perhaps the country was in the mood to face the future.

There was a changing mood. Tony Blair, the New Labour prime minister, was about to be voted in after 18 years of Conservative rule under Margaret Thatcher. Out with the old and in with the new. St Luke's and Ikea lit a fire under the changing tastes and attitudes and swept away Victoriana and Macmillanism. "The only thing we could do was change people's attitudes to furniture and then build the beacon brand with Ikea," recalls Andy Law, a co-founder of St Luke's.

Two years later, St Luke's ran another campaign with the strapline, "Stop being so English." It was a time when British culture was opening up and modernizing. One former St Luke's person explains: "The long stagnation of the 1980s and 1990s was over, that England of *Abigail's Party* was dead and something more cosmopolitan had replaced it."

Ikea managed to associate itself with that change, and it became associated with a more modern way of living. Perhaps the British class-ridden obsession with country house style was ready to crumble? Perhaps all those housewives in Birmingham were ready to cave in? They're probably all having barbecues now on their decking, shopping in Gap rather than Marks & Spencer, and using a Dyson to clean their wooden floors.

Changing rooms

Ikea wasn't the only brand to tap into a nascent trend. The UK's two main terrestrial television channels, BBC1 and ITV, both began to launch a number of home improvement programs such as *Changing Rooms*, which helped people redecorate and transform their rooms in a few days on a small budget. A pan-European survey by Black & Decker asks people the question, "What best represents your personality?" Every single country aside from Germany said, "my house." Ten years ago people wouldn't have said that.

In the United States, a similar wry humor has helped persuade Americans to swap some of their country-house-style patch-work quilts and lace tablecloths for sensible Swedish design. One self-deprecating ad in America, says simply: "America's a big country, someone's got to furnish it."

In mature markets, one of Ikea's pressing concerns is ensuring people view furniture like they view fashion. It's more disposable and something you replace regularly. Two years ago, Ikea in the United States recruited Spike Jonze, the director of the film *Being John Malkovich*, to write a television ad. The resulting ad "Lamp," by Crispin Porter & Bogusky, won the Grand Prix at Cannes advertising festival.

It begins with an old lamp being hauled out of an apartment and dumped on the pavement outside. Meanwhile, its former owner retreats inside to enjoy the warm glow of his new lamp. The abandoned lamp is left being drenched by pouring rain, whipped by wind, and then covered by falling darkness. A Swedish man appears from nowhere to address the camera. "Many of you feel bad for this lamp," he says sternly. "That is because you're crazy. It has no feelings. And the new one is much better."

A public debate

Sometimes Ikea needs explaining. One debate between Ikea and its ad agencies is the extent to which they let people work out

Ikea for themselves. Sometimes Ikea advertising needs to tell the public why self assembly is a good thing, why queuing is better than waiting eight weeks for delivery, and why established rules are wrong.

Despite its lower than average marketing budget, and the fact it normally only commandeers 10 percent of the marketplace, Ikea is a talked-about brand. It's often used as a reference or prototype. One reason for this is that Ikea's advertising is always a talking point, because it strives to make the conflict between its own idea and a country's taste in home furnishings. In 2000, one of St Luke's ads called "The tattoo man" was voted the United Kingdom's most hated ad.

In France, a new ad campaign called "réagissez" (react) through the agency CLM/BBDO is trying to overhaul the French's conservatism, which sees them cling onto the furniture they inherit. Pascal Gregoire, CLM/BBDO's creative director explained how this was to be achieved to *Campaign*, the advertising industry's trade magazine:

> We're trying to change the relationship between people and furniture by saying furniture will never die, so you have to change it. If you want to be the market leader, you have to push people and be different and sometimes aggressive, but always friendly and humorous.[38]

Ikea also uses a lot of local PR and tactical work to create noise around its stores. To appeal to families with young children, Ikea in the Netherlands built giant-sized furniture in parks around the country complete with storytellers to entertain intrigued families. Meanwhile, huge 12 metre yellow footprints led a path to a local Ikea store. Journalists were taken on helicopter rides to maximize the PR opportunity.

In Canada, Ikea placed furniture around the streets of Toronto with "steal me" signs next to them. In China Ikea furniture is displayed in lifts, while in the Netherlands blue and yellow dressed Abba-listening fans camped out in towns where Ikea was set to open. In Singapore, a kids television show features children broadcasting from their bedrooms, which have been redecorated by Ikea.

In the United Kingdom, before the opening of Bristol Ikea, it was made clear that beards would be banned from the store during the first few weeks, to keep numbers down and avoid overcrowding, but also to generate lots of PR. During the launch campaign for "Chuck out your chintz," Ikea built glass-walled living rooms at Liverpool Street railway station in London, complete with actors, to show people what their furniture looked like. In Paris, it hung 39 mattresses in a railway station to promote its beds.

One local, tactical ad by St Luke's to publicize the winter sales showed Ikea staff laughing at the customers who'd bought items before the sale and not saved money. All the regional managers in the United Kingdom refused to run it apart from the Newcastle upon Tyne store, which thought it was funny. It was a great success.

Ikea's relationship with St Luke's ended in 2002, six years after the "Chuck out the chintz" campaign. Ikea decided to create its advertising in-house in the future, for cost reasons and also so it could develop a more multi-channel approach. Traditional advertising is becoming less and less effective as consumers are increasingly bombarded with marketing messages.

Like many brands today, Ikea struggles to break through this clutter and noise, and is having to become even more creative with its advertising. In May 2004, in the United Kingdom, Ikea invested a six-figure sum on its first advertiser-funded program. A series of interior design shows will be broadcast on United Kingdom television channels.

Advertiser funded programming, or AFP, as it is known within media circles, is a new approach to creating television programs. Television channels are increasingly strapped for cash to make new programs, and brands are becoming frustrated with ineffective television advertising. So, in AFP, a brand will pay directly for a program, rather than pay for airtime between shows.

The programs shouldn't resemble conventional advertising, but they do enable a brand to convey a general set of values or concerns. Interestingly, *Changing Rooms*, a UK home makeover show, probably contributed more to Ikea's sales by promoting modernity and the concept of disposable furniture, than any ad campaign; and it wasn't Ikea-funded.

Elite designers

Ikea's most recent ads in the United Kingdom are led by a flamboyant, fictional designer Van den Puup, head of Elite Designers, who pooh-poohs the idea that design can be cheap as well as stylish. Van den Puup is a chubby, camp, overdressed combination of singer Elton John and designer Philippe Starck, with an accent that travels through several different European nations during one sentence. The mere sight of Ikea's cut-price efforts reduces him to fits of hysteria.

The campaign is aptly called "I hate the big stupid blue place." It began with a four-page pastiche in celebrity rag, *OK!* magazine, with a tour through Van den Puup's multiple homes and celebrity lifestyle – standard *OK!* fare. The television ads feature Van den Puup lounging by his pool in a toweling robe, railing against the fact that Ikea's products are designed well and cost so little.

On an accompanying website (www.elite-designers.org) Van den Puup muses, "The page is the egg, my pencil the sperm, the design the beautiful love child." Once more, Ikea has tongue firmly in cheek, but the irony has been lost on some visitors to the website. One angry contributor writes: "You're full of it!!!!! Elitists like you sickening bunch are exactly what turns off most of the world to the kind of claptrap you produce, and that is why a vast majority of the world turns to places like Ikea." Another posts an angry response on the website:

> Why? I think it is very sad that you have to "hate" an inexpensive furniture company just because they don't charge $8,000 for a sofa. Personally, I don't like Ikea either; but that doesn't mean that people who are less fortunate than us can't get some clean-looking furniture.

There is also an email and a telephone number for the phony designer that have been flooded with responses.

Catalog living

In the face of so much creative and award-winning advertising, it's easy to forget that Ikea's most powerful weapon is its catalog. The Ikea catalog is read more widely than the Bible. This is where the lion's share of the marketing budget is invested. It's the crown jewel of Ikea's communications. In 2004, 145 million copies of the catalog were printed in 48 editions and 25 languages. It was read by around 200m people in 31 countries. This was up from 131.5 million copies in 2003 and 96 million copies in 1999. In the UK, 13 million catalogs are distributed containing 3,000 Ikea products, one third of the total products offered.

The catalog persuades us that Ikea can tidy and transform our chaotic, hectic lifestyles. Within the pages lies the intoxicating promise that with a Mackis storage rack here and a Lyckeby box there, your dowdy, cluttered home can be transformed into a vision of stylish Swedish orderliness. The catalog proclaims:

> Possessions, like rabbits, have a habit of multiplying. The trick is to be able to find what you want, when you want it. With stylish storage and organizing gizmos galore from Ikea, life on earth is just so much better all round.

The entire catalog is shot at the Ikea studio in Älmhult, the largest photographic studio in Europe. It is 8,000 square meters and can hold 96 different room sets. It takes 35 part-time photographers over four months to shoot the 6,800 new photos for the catalog. Ikea rooms are painstakingly created in the massive studios by designers who lower ceilings, paint idyllic Swedish countryside backdrops behind fake windows, and scatter fake, brightly colored books onto Billy bookshelves. Ikea Älmhult people and their families smile up at you from the Ikea world where everything is logical, organized, and light.

Ingvar Kamprad's original vision of *Ikea News*, a brochure to entice customers to buy his mail-order furniture, has never shifted. His strategy is to over-distribute the catalog and be prepared to wait a long time before customers buy anything. Inside Ikea, the thinking behind the marketing strategy is described as the following: in the first year, you give people a catalog and they won't even open it, in the second year they might flick through, shrug their shoulders and not consider it again, in the third year they might venture to a store and have a look around but not buy anything. In the fourth year they might visit the store and buy an eggcup; and it's only the fifth or sixth encounter with Ikea that they'll buy something significant. Ingvar Kamprad is a very patient businessman.

8 The Furniture Dealer's Testament

It's a bit like being in with the in-crowd. It can get quite intense and relationships outside Ikea can break down. But you always carry an inner purpose and know what Ikea is really about. It means you can come together and do something with meaning.

> (An Ikea co-worker on working for
> the Swedish furniture dealer)

The gospel according to Ikea is carved onto tablets. The founder Ingvar Kamprad's pamphlet, *The Furniture Dealer's Testament*, is like the Ten Commandments (except he lists nine). He hangs godlike over the organization and is spoken about in pseudo-religious terms. "Once and for all we have decided to side with the many," begins his testament.[39] Ikea understands that the way to make money is to be dedicated to a vision – you don't make profit because you want to, but because there's something else driving you.

The Furniture Dealer's Testament was written in 1976 to chisel out the values and beliefs of the missionary retailer, which was struggling to retain its internal culture as it outgrew Småland. Ikea is a concept company. This "sacred concept" is repeated again and again by Kamprad and his senior team to ensure that each one of their 202 stores reflect and realize the philosophy. Kamprad crystallized his thinking into nine evangelical chapters, which are distributed with missionary zeal to all Ikea employees.

Everybody that I speak to tells me that working in Ikea is cult-like. That they're all like the Moonies, albeit Moonies that worship untreated pine and sofas called Ektorp. Ikea co-workers (what the employees call themselves) don't disagree, but they tell me it's more of a nice, friendly sect; and like a cult, they have their own language, their own way of doing things, and a code of beliefs they follow. In Sweden, things and people are either "Ikea-massigt" or they're not – which loosely translates as something which fits into the Ikea way or concept. In France, they will say, "c'est pas Ikea" or "c'est pas le concept."

It's impossible to escape the religious imagery of Ikea – you can't get away from it. There's a spiritual element that's reflected in the bright-eyed optimism of the co-workers, which you'll either find delightful or unnerving. They fervently believe that they're not simply selling chairs but peddling a whole new philosophy of home living. "We believe that Ikea is improving life by providing cheap, well designed furniture," evangelizes one Ikea lifer with misty eyes.

Ikea lifers

"Ikea lifer" is the internal term used to describe someone who's worked at Ikea for a long time. There are a lot of them. They say Ikea is like a family and that once you're in you don't really leave. "It's a bit like being in with the in-crowd," explains another Ikea lifer, who has left, but plans to return:

> It can get quite intense and relationships outside Ikea can break down. But you always carry an

inner purpose and know what Ikea is really about.
It means you can come together and do something with meaning.

I hear of one Ikea worker whose parents had met at Ikea and now he works there too. There are a lot of Ikea couples. One pair met 16 years ago, when they joined Ikea fresh from university, and are now being propelled around the organization together. Some leave and come back. Within the organization they'll be saying, "Well, Anders had his five years outside, his midlife crisis, but now he's come back." There seems to be a lot of pride in working for such a successful team – as if it's like playing rugby for New Zealand.

There's an internal saying that, "If you don't fit you quit." There does seem to be a certain kind of person who thrives at Ikea. They share traits such as being down-to-earth, not very flashy, and unimpressed by displays of status and wealth. "The Ikea way is also our own personal way of working," explain some missionary Ikea lifers. "Without thinking we know what the Ikea way is. We immediately know if a person is not right. After one day we can say, 'This guy will stay for three months max.'"

Ikea's hiring policy is instinctive. It will hire the "right" people – not always the best qualified, or the smartest, but the "Ikea" people. Nearly every co-worker I spoke to was offered his or her job on the spot. After sending in a letter, Ikea called one to say, "We like you, we like your profile and if our meeting goes well can you start on Tuesday?" "That's the good and bad thing about Ikea," elaborates another. "They either offer you something right there and then or they linger and faff around for months."

A father figure

Ikea refers to the group in terms of "we" and "us." Ikea is the collective and the only "I" in the company is founder Ingvar Kamprad, who does strike a chord as a paternal figure. Each year, the co-workers receive a Christmas present from Kamprad, which in the past has been a set of Ikea towels or a bike. In the early 1990s they all received a tape recorder with a tape of a radio interview with Kamprad that had been aired on Swedish radio. There's an internal joke that one year they received bikes as presents in Älmhult, and the next day the entire village was cycling around on identical bikes.

It is as if Kamprad is a father figure to 84,000 people. I learn of one Ikea manager in one of the Western European markets who was in the process of a messy divorce. He revealed that he was reading one of Kamprad's books to help him and to learn what Ingvar would have done in his shoes. "I've never met anyone who didn't worship him," reveals someone close to the retailer.

Kamprad's frugal and Spartan habits have trickled down to Ikea's management culture, who have famously tiny expense accounts. "Wasting resources is a mortal sin at Ikea," barks Kamprad in chapter four of his testament. "It is one of the greatest diseases of mankind. Use your resources the Ikea way. Then you will reach good results with small means."[40]

Ikea's cost-consciousness seeps into every corner of the business. One official Ikea memo was sent to its designers asking them to stop using mechanical pencils for their drawings. The powers that be had decided that these pencils were too expensive as their leads were always breaking, so they suggested their designers used normal pencils, which you sharpen manually, instead.

Ikea circulates an internal pamphlet called "Travelling with Ikea" which lists tips on qualifying for the most inexpensive airfares and lists economical, simple "Ikea hotels." All managers will fly economy class or with budget airlines, and stay in cheap, box-like motels, sometimes sharing a room. It's a kind of inverted snobbery; Ikea co-workers take real pleasure in staying in cheap hotels and eating basic café food.

One consultant, who works with Ikea on and off, recalls his utter mortification when a new PA booked him on a business-class flight while his Ikea clients squeezed into economy. Managers at Ikea do not receive the customary business perks of company cars, mobile phones, allocated spaces in the car park, and bulging expense accounts.

"We do not set any price on time," remarked one executive, questioned in a Harvard Business School paper. He once phoned Ingvar Kamprad to get approval for flying first class. He explained that economy class was full and that he had an urgent appointment to keep. "There is no first class in Ikea," replied Kamprad, refusing his request, "perhaps you should go by car." The executive completed the 350-mile journey by taxi.[41]

When Anders Dahlvig became the president of Ikea in 1999, Ikea's internal magazine ran a humorous car review comparing his car with Kamprad's car. Ikea mythology says that both owned cars that were at least 20 years old – one was a Lada and the other a Skoda. As part of the feature, the cars raced each other on a track, although neither reached the dizzy speed of 60 miles an hour.

"There are no flashy cars in the Ikea car park – there's no 'bling'," confirms one Ikea co-worker. However, some Ikea workers have learnt to be more surreptitious about their wealth, in order to fit in with the non-hierarchical ideals of the company. "I know people who drive a normal Volvo to work at Ikea and then have a Porsche at home in their drive."

Uniform humility

An influential book called *Jungte Lavin* (The Law of Jungte) was written by a Norwegian writer in the 1930s. The book sets out how no one should be seen to be better than anyone else. It's a sentiment that defines Scandinavian culture, and one that Ikea is very true to. There's also a Swedish word "odmjukhet" which implies humility, modesty, and respect for fellow humans – another important quality for an Ikean.

This is also reflected in Ikea's pride in its uniform of casual clothing. Suits are banned. Everyone at Ikea mentions this, as if Ikea was the first business to come up with the idea of dressing down at work. Perhaps it was. So the senior executives all wear jeans and open-necked shirts uniformly. I suspect Kamprad thinks it's the uniform of early pioneers.

Anyone at Ikea who has contact with customers must wear the uniform of a bright yellow shirt with name badge and blue trousers. This includes senior managers helping out on the shop floor when it's busy. The French Ikea co-workers managed to resist uniform until the early 1990s – "Is this EuroDisney or what?"[42] – and were the only country not to adopt uniform immediately. The French are now also wandering around in yellow and blue.

In France, "tutoiement" is a rule, which means that workers address everybody, including their seniors, with the informal "tu" and "toi," rather than the more respectful "vous." Similarly, in Germany the personal "du" is used rather than the more formal "Sie." Across the world co-workers are told to speak in first-name terms.

Every year, Ikea organizes "antibureaucrat weeks" that require all managers to work in the store showrooms and warehouses, to ensure they keep in touch with their fellow workers. Ikea's president Anders Dahlvig explains that it's, "so we keep in touch with the nitty gritty; stay focused on what matters to the customers."[43] Similarly, store managers are expected to step in and work on the shop floor if needed. Perhaps they will spend time in a warehouse solving a problem, or work on the cash tills when the store is busy.

Ikea is a lean organization with very little middle management. The idea is that it has just three levels of management, so if someone wants to change something in their carpet section, for example, he or she can talk to the store manager, country manager, or someone in Sweden.

Sometimes it feels as if there are just 24 people running a store the size of a space ship. The corporate offices are also very lean and tightly run. In the United Kingdom, Ikea HQ is at the top of the multistory car park at the Ikea store in Brent Park, north London. When I visited the offices, I swung on a brightly-colored Ikea hammock in the reception and read newspapers balanced on a plastic garden table.

Swedish businesses are run in a less hierarchical and more participative style than others. Leaders have to earn trust and respect, and can be expected to be questioned by their employees. "In Sweden you have to build consensus and then the organization moves. What you do find is you have people with you if you've done it well. But you can end up in endless conversations if you're not careful," confirms Thomas Gad, a Swedish brand consultant.

Reaching consensus is also an Ikea way: "They're afraid of conflict, terrified of it, everything is about consensus and agreement. There's never an open argument, things are talked around for an hour," reveals one former Ikea ad agency exec. I suspect it's relevant that "ombudsman" is a Swedish word. It comes from the Old Norse word "umbodhsmadhr" which was a trusty manager. Today "ombudsman" means someone who mediates fair settlements.

A storytelling culture

In order to perpetuate its strong internal culture, Ikea has been a seductive and accomplished storyteller for years. It weaves stories of Ingvar Kamprad's frugal ways, of Ikea's pioneering battles in the early days, of Älmhult the source of the Nile, of

Swedish modest values, and then of how the Vikings conquered the world and now how Ikea is doing the same … .

These fairy tales are whispered through the organization, they crescendo into a cacophony of noise. There are day-to-day stories and moral stories, and normally the moral is that "such and such happened because he/she/they didn't behave in an Ikea way."

"They talk things over again and again and evangelize and preach," explains one Swedish co-worker:

> They explain the context of where Ikea comes from and how it's evolved into a successful business. It's not about telling you what to do but explaining why and how. It's like those two men building – one says he's laying bricks, the other says he's building a cathedral.

As it mushroomed, Ikea has had to adopt a more formal approach to permeating its culture across the organization. In 1976, Kamprad committed his values to paper in *The Furniture Dealer's Testament*, which is now distributed to all employees.

In the 1980s, Kamprad personally trained around 300 ambassadors in a week-long seminar on Ikea's history and culture in Älmhult, which according to legend included a trip to the green shed in his garden where Ikea began. These handpicked ambassadors were then expected to disseminate their learning by acting as role models.

Today, there is a special Ikea school in Älmhult called Älmhultdagarna, where newly employed co-workers are sent for their "IKEA way" indoctrination. They see photographs of Ingvar Kamprad's upbringing in Småland and watch videos about Swedish eccentricities. Then they skip down into the local hotel's basement to walk through the three rooms depicting Ikea's history in its museum.

The Ikea way

This indoctrination (although Ikea wouldn't call it that) enables the organization to give its employees a lot of freedom, providing they always refer back to "Is this an Ikea kind of thing to do?" They have the constraints and guidance of the Ikea way, which most will feel instinctively, and the rest is up to their entrepreneurialism. It's like being given the sketchy bare-boned instructions for the Ikea flat pack and then being left to assemble it yourself.

In *Identity across Borders* Miriam Salzer interviewed Bengt, a Swedish Ikea manager, based in Canada, where he had worked since the 1980s. Bengt had been with the company for 20 years and was hired by Kamprad as an assistant purchasing agent at the beginning of the 1970s.[44]

Bengt says:

> You talk about Ikea all the time, as if there was somebody somewhere knowing everything and making decisions. As if there was some omnipotent Ikea – but Ikea is us, we who work right here. If something is going to happen we've got to do it. No one will tell us what to do or do it for us.

> There are some central decisions that we can't
> influence. The product range, the restaurant, poli-
> cies.... But I never feel we're controlled from
> above. We have enormous freedom. Ikea is not a
> company that gives you a fixed policy and says "do
> it like this now!" That wouldn't work.... For us
> Ikea is Ikea Canada. The only thing that keeps us
> together really, is our concept and our culture.

Provided store managers don't suggest foolish, sweeping changes such as the color of the store or the layout, they can be inventive and entrepreneurial. It's a delicate balancing act that Kamprad calls "freedom with responsibility." It's up to them to add some sparkle to the spartan Ikea instructions – whether that is pulling in London Zoo during half term, running bingo days, or launching a radio station.

"You get a lot of responsibility with a lot of freedom," explains one European store manager. "We have a goal but if you reach that goal they don't care how you do it – do you do it in two days or three months, they are not on your back. What's important is that it's done."

The rule of thumb is that an Ikea co-worker should know what's right and wrong in every instance. You won't get punished although you can make big mistakes within the company, but you are required to understand what Ikea is all about.

Kamprad and Ikea are famously tolerant of mistakes. In chapter eight of *The Furniture Dealer's Testament*, Kamprad states: "Only while sleeping one makes no mistakes. The fear of making mistakes is the root of bureaucracy and the enemy of development."[45] This came in handy for Kamprad's confession of an involvement with a Nazi youth organization when he was young. He has also said, "no one has made more mistakes than I have."

This corporate tolerance of mistakes has filtered down into senior management. One designer recalling an interview with the MD of Ikea UK says the very first question he was asked was, "Do you ever make mistakes." The designer admitted that he sometimes did, to which the UK manager replied: "Good, the only time you don't make mistakes is when you're sleeping."

There was another classic spread in the internal Ikea magazine, accompanied by a thundering picture of Ingvar Kamprad. The headline is along the lines of "stop being such cowards," as Kamprad exhorts the managers of the new generation to be more entrepreneurial. "This company exists because we took risks and you're more likely to incur my wrath if you don't," he shouts.

This entrepreneurial flair means there have been lots of failures. There have been ranges that come and go, new ventures that go nowhere, and countries that don't happen for Ikea. But this spirit means that unlike some other companies, Ikea internally never feels stagnant.

Ikea also keeps people on their toes and moves its most promising young co-workers around the company every 18 months or so, "so we don't grow moss," explains one. It's a transient place to work, which seems to thrive on change.

Co-workers move up and down the ranks. Some moves, which would be regarded as a demotion in other companies, are in fact promotions. For example, if someone moved from the head office to a store, at Ikea this is regarded as a step up. The ultimate experience for co-workers is getting a chance to work with logistics or in a store.

Swedish festivals

Lucia – 13 December

This festival is based on the legend of a pious girl who wanted to devote life to God instead of marriage. She was killed when she turned down the proposal of a nobleman and became a martyr. Lucia Day is celebrated with the procession of a young girl dressed in white with a crown of candles. She will bring coffee, gingerbread biscuits and "Lucian cats" (buns) with her.

Walpurgis Night – the beginning of spring

This festival dates back to the Viking era and is to honor the coming of Spring. Swedes light large bonfires and sing songs of spring.

Midsummer's Eve – summer solstice

This is one of the most popular festivals in Sweden and is celebrated with a national holiday. It's based on an old pagan celebration that was originally a fertility rite. It takes place on the longest day of the year and family and friends meet up to eat herring and drink schnapps and beer.

Smorgasbord

The Swedish language and culture is also essential to Ikea's internal workings, especially as it grows internationally. Swedish festivals are often celebrated in stores across the world. The Midsummer Night's festival, to celebrate light and summer, is a big festivity in Sweden. They make a maypole, sing, eat smorgasbord (Swedish delicacies), and drink a lot of vodka and beer. Similarly, there's a festival on the last day of April to celebrate the spring break, when the Swedes light big bonfires and fireworks to welcome spring.

Some foreign Ikea managers feel it's hard for a non-Swede to make a career, or break into the network. One Ikea co-worker said: "Unfortunately I was born in the wrong country. I've reached as far as I can," when questioned about future ambitions. Another tells me, that although you don't have to be Swedish, it helps.

Foreign managers are encouraged to learn Swedish, almost a prerequisite for advancing in the company. Former Ikea president Anders Moberg once said:

> I would advise any foreign employee who really wants to advance in this company to learn Swedish. They will then get a completely different feeling for our culture, our mood, our values. We encourage all our foreign personnel to have as much contact with Sweden as possible, for instance, by going to Sweden for their holidays.[46]

This is confirmed by a worker within the retailer: "It looks good if expat Swedes hold things like Swedish crayfish parties."

However, the bigger the organization becomes, the tougher it is to hold onto its culture. This is especially true as Ikea moves from becoming a Swedish company to an international one. Although most of the senior management remains both Swedish and male, more and more nationalities are beginning to infiltrate the upper circles.

Ikea's CEO Anders Dahlvig has publicly declared his intention to boost the diversity of management. One of the most interesting recent appointments was Kerri Molinaro, a Canadian woman and the first non-Swede to run the country operations in Sweden. She joined Ikea in 1992 and was formerly the store manager in Chicago.

Similarly, in a workforce of 80,000 there are now 500 Ikea expats helping to furnish the globe with flat pack furniture. They are often treated differently from the standard co-workers – they are paid more, sometimes provided with housing, and they travel a lot.

A graver problem though is that an average member of Ikea staff couldn't tell you what Ikea stands for and probably doesn't care. It's as if there are two tiers. There is the senior management down to store manager level, where they get the vision; and then the Ikea below that, the shop workers who interact with the public, who just don't give a damn. This causes all sorts of stresses within the organization.

But sometimes I suspect that Ikea's vision trickles down lower than it thinks. At the north London store, a flustered, bewildered check-out assistant battles with a temperamental cash till and an infinite queue of shell-shocked, weary shoppers clutching glasses and bath mats to their chests. She is wearing a plastic yellow branded Ikea watch on her wrist. "Do you have to wear that?" I ask her, astounded by the lengths the Swedish organization will go to get its staff on side. "Oh no, no, no…. It's all I ever wear," she enthuses, bright-eyed and beaming.

To the checkout

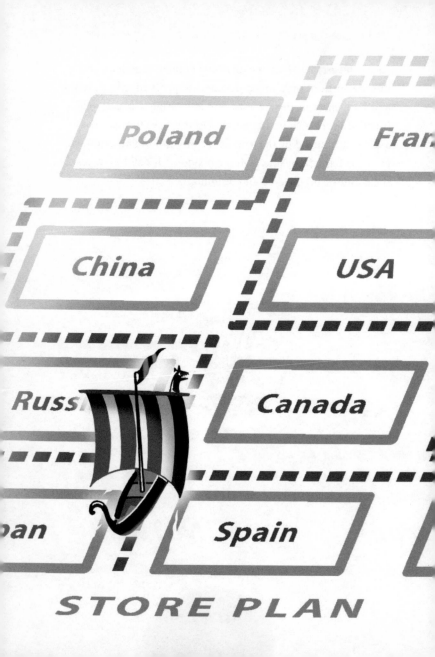

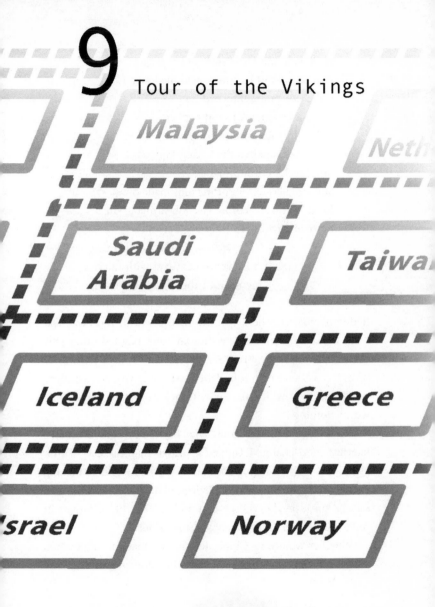

9

Tour of the Vikings

Hroþwulf ond Hroðgar heoldon lengest
Hrothwulf and Hrothgar held the longest
sibbe ætsomne suhtorfædran,
peace together, uncle and nephew,
siþþan hy forwrǣcon wicinga cynn
since they repulsed the Viking-kin
ond Ingeldes ord forbigdan,
and Ingeldes to the spear-point made bow,
forheowan aet Heorote Heaðobeardna þrym.
hewn at Heorot Heathobeard's army.

> (*Widsith*, an old English poem
> [sixth to seventh century] with the first
> mention of the Vikings by name)

It doesn't matter where you are in the world; the Ikea saga reads the same. Each of the yellow and blue painted stores sells chairs called Barkaby, Bromma, Ektorp, and Tullsta. Each store takes its customer on a roundabout, winding voyage past every single product, which begins with a kids' ballpark and ends with a hot dog.

This is globalization, Scandinavian-style. Other global brands, like fast food chain McDonald's, pledge mantras like "Think global, act local," which translates in the real world as making changes to fit in with a local environment. So McDonald's will sell flat bread in the Middle East and chicken tikka burgers in India. Ikea is less willing to make concessions.

"Whether we are in China, Russia, Manhattan, or London, people buy the same things. We have the same range everywhere

– we don't adapt to local markets. If we were to adapt, we would just became another retailer in that region or city. The whole idea is to be unique – uniquely Scandinavian and uniquely Ikea," said Anders Dahlvig, Ikea president in 2001.[47]

Internally, Ikea likes to talk of the Vikings when joking of its own flat pack empire that stretches from Pittsburgh in the United States to St Petersburg in Russia. There are now 179 stores in 23 countries, 202 in 32 countries, if you include franchises, with plans to open 20 new stores over the next 12 months. You can buy a Billy bookcase and a plate of Swedish meatballs in Malaysia, Saudi Arabia, Spain, Iceland, Israel, the Netherlands, Taiwan, Greece, Russia, Norway, Canada, France, and Poland.

Ikea's expansion model is simple and unsophisticated. You only need one set of instructions to assemble an Ikea store wherever you are in the world. It sends over products, systems, and people and then it starts selling. Abroad, Ikea is not just selling products, it's also selling its philosophy – this is how things are done in Sweden.

Every store opening begins in the same way: a Swedish breakfast, a traditional log sawing ceremony which Ingvar Kamprad often attends, with the doors open for customers at 9 am. And the openings always seem to generate a disturbing and fascinating rush by excitable new Ikea customers.

Christy Powell camped out for eight nights before the opening of a new Ikea store on Interstate 10 at Antoine in Houston, Texas. She wanted to claim the first spot in line and a US$10,000 prize, and sat through sizzling heat, a violent thunderstorm, and

the din of builders finishing the car park. By the day of the opening, the queue behind Powell had swelled to 700. After a 192-
hour wait, she bought just 12 plates and bowls for US$18 plus
tax.[48]

Or there was the couple in Canada who decided to get
married in an Ikea store. They were awarded a C$3,500 gift
certificate from the Swedish retailer, and according to reports
they were more excited about their Ikea voucher than the
actual ceremony.

Sometimes, the frenzy of a new Ikea store can lead to tragedy.
In September 2004, three men were trampled to death and 16
shoppers were injured in a rush to claim vouchers at the first
Ikea furniture showroom in Saudi Arabia. The stampede was
triggered by an offer for the first 50 shoppers to receive US$150
in vouchers. An Ikea statement said that over 20,000 people
showed up and that just two were killed.

Rioting Ikea shoppers are not unique to Ikea's newest markets,
as the launch of England's largest store in Edmonton, North
London demonstrated this February (2005). The British have
lived with Ikea's flat pack philosophy for nearly 20 years, but the
prospect of £45 special offer leather sofas led to 6,000 eager
shoppers surging into the new showroom at its midnight opening. The store was forced to close just 30 minutes later, over-
whelmed by fractious hordes fighting over cheap furniture.
Dozens of customers abandoned their cars along the road,
making their way to the store on foot in their rush to grab
bargains. The riot left six people in hospital.

American dreams

In the light of such frenetic excitement from prospective customers, it's hardly surprising that Ikea never felt the pressure to tweak its offering in new markets. Usually when Ikea expands, it just needs to open the door and boom – the sales flood in. However, when Ikea launched into the United States in 1985 it wasn't that simple.

The United States was a big awakening for the Swedish furniture dealer. After two years of trading, business was down and it was losing volumes; even a big marketing push didn't have an effect. The United States often becomes a graveyard for European retailers who are lured there by the bright lights of its huge potential. Competition in US retail is intense, and at one point it looked as if Ikea might have to offer up its own corpse.

It didn't take very long for US imitators to appear. A Californian-based retailer calling itself Stor began to emulate Ikea concepts to the nth degree. Stor sold similar designed products, had a ballpark for kids, a restaurant that sold meatballs, a similar building, and the same flags. When Ingvar Kamprad and his colleagues visited Los Angeles they were stunned to see Stor had already opened three stores.

Although Stor had copied Ikea by the book, it didn't understand its underlying thinking or why the Swedish retailer does what it does. For example, Stor decided to ditch its catalog, after being advised by a consultant that this would be an easy way to cut costs. But the Ikea catalog, which is posted to 145 million people worldwide, underpins its whole concept. Stor copied the surface, only what it could see.

Initially, Ikea decided to launch legal proceedings against Stor, as the imitation was so complete. But then, in typical Ikea style it decided to stop paying lawyers and just take Stor on, by opening four new stores in Los Angeles. A few years later, Ikea acquired its imitator, mainly to seize its locations and to ensure no other competition bought the chain.

It was easy to see why Ikea entered the United States. There are around 18 million people in New York alone, more than the population of Scandinavia, and the United States was the largest furniture market in the world, valued at around US$15 billion in the mid 1980s. But the United States didn't get Ikea – it was too unswervingly Swedish.

Initially, Ikea stubbornly refused to size its beds and kitchen cabinets to fit US sheets and appliances. The Ikea beds were sold in centimeter sizes, whereas the Americans were used to king-sized or queen-sized beds. The Scandinavian-style bookshelves were too small to hold a television for Americans who wanted entertainment shelving systems.

Ikea vases were selling out, because its glasses were deemed too small for the super-size thirsts of Americans. The European-style sofas were too hard for American bottoms, and the Ikea dining room tables weren't big enough to fit a turkey into the center on Thanksgiving. This was not the first time this had happened. When Ikea entered Germany in 1974, its desks were a flop because the Germans were used to five-legged desks and not four-legged ones.

Ikea's problems in the United States in the early 1990s

- Americans were swigging out of vases because the Ikea glasses were too small.
- Ikea dining room tables were too small for the Thanksgiving turkey.
- Ikea beds were sold in centimeters rather than king- or queen-size.
- Scandinavian-style bookshelves were too small to hold a television.
- European-style sofas were too hard and small.
- European-style bath towels were too small and thin.
- Americans keep a sofa longer than a car.
- Americans change their spouse as often as their dining room table – about 1.5 times in a lifetime.
- Americans like to drink water as they shop, so Ikea introduced water fountains around its stores.

A Swedish diplomat

In 1989 Anders Moberg, Ikea's president, took the brave and momentous decision to appoint an outsider to help take Ikea US to the next stage. Goran Carstedt was the president of Swedish car company Volvo in France and Sweden, and understood the difficulties of translating the Swedish culture into international markets. Ikea needed to find an interpretation of its concept that would be meaningful to the United States.

He wrote a letter to the 3,000 co-workers in the United States and Canada using national flags as an analogy. He told them that Ikea US was to be blue and yellow mixed up with the stars and stripes, while Canadian Ikea was blue and yellow mixed with a maple leaf. However, Carstedt's hardest task was persuading HQ in Sweden that this was a good idea. "They were afraid we were going too far and said we couldn't adapt to every market and if we went too far we'd become American," he recalls.

Aside from stubbornly not wanting to unravel its carefully constructed Swedish package for US consumption, Ikea was also aware that producing variants of its designs in each market would damage its economies of scale. When tweaking the sizes of beds in the United States, Carstedt and his team had to get around production problems, eventually finding suppliers who had numerical machines to help produce smaller quantities cost effectively.

Anywhere in the world, there is normally only a maximum of 2 percent variation in the Ikea range stocked. As soon as Ikea starts changing things it adds cost. A group of managers recently visited some factories in Poland with the founder. He wanted to know, "how can we get these mugs from US\$1 to 20 cents?" They said it was impossible. So he said, "Well what if we order 10 times as many of them – what then?"

And that's how they do things to drive prices down. It also means that there is less and less variation in the range. If you want ten mugs for the price of one, there's more pressure for Ikea to sell the same products all over the world.

There is a small bedroom table with a drawer called Kurs, which was a bestseller in the rest of the world but not in the United States. Carstedt stood in one of the stores watching people shop to try to understand why. They kept looking at the product, pulling out the drawer and walking away. He'd talk to them and ask them why. They said the drawer was too shallow and that they didn't like the fact the inside of the drawer was plastic. It took two years to change the product into a deeper drawer with better sides, because Ikea Sweden had to find an affordable way to design it, which led to sourcing some suppliers in the United States. Carstedt reveals:

> The plastic was probably a better solution but the Americans couldn't get it. In some instances, because our approach was very contrary to their way of doing things our solutions were more costly, but we gradually found ways to be cleverer and still keep the identity of the Ikea product. For four years it was a continuous adaptation process.

Some of the changes that Ikea US made have since been introduced to Europe – with great success. For example, the Americans like to sink into a large, soft sofa whereas Europeans prefer to sit on the edge. US-influenced softer sofas have become a number one seller in Europe. Similarly, large entertainment units for television systems were brought back to Europe, as were thicker and heavier bath towels.

But Ikea refused to change or adapt the look of its products for the US market. In stores based in Middle America, this was tough; although coastal cities like New York got it. Although Pittsburgh and Minnesota would have loved 18th-century-style traditional Swedish furniture, which was quite similar to Shaker-style, they did not understand the modernist, blond wood Scandinavian vision.

Once again, Ikea had to work hard to open the eyes of its customers to a different taste. It worked with US home decoration journalists in an advisory council to find out what was meaningful for Americans from the Scandinavian way of living. Similar to other countries, one of Ikea's barriers was Americans' long-term attitude to furniture. Americans keep a sofa longer than a car, and they change their spouse as often as their dining room table, about 1.5 times in a lifetime.

Ikea's system of self service, self assembly, and involving consumers in the whole retail process also bewildered Americans. This is a society familiar with slick customer service and customer focus. US customers felt as if they were caught in a trap when shopping at Ikea. One of the most frequently asked questions was how to get out.

For the first time, Ikea produced a 'one-two-three' step plan explaining how to shop at its stores, and it also published a new directory that included instructions on how to navigate the store more easily. Ikea also had to install much quicker check-out lines because the Americans didn't expect to wait in line as long as Europeans.

Ikea also had to introduce lots of water fountains throughout the store because Americans like drinking water. There had been a similar issue in Spain, where special ventilated smoking areas had to be introduced in the room sets in Madrid and Barcelona, because the Spanish like smoking.

However, most vital things the Swedish retailer refused to adapt, keeping the blue and yellow part of the Ikea formula. People kept telling it that it couldn't get Americans to put things together themselves, but it knew that if it gave that up then it would lose Ikea. So it gave them better instructions instead and offered a self-assembly service.

But Carstedt believes the most important achievement was keeping and developing the Ikea corporate culture in the United States. That was done primarily by importing experienced long-time Ikea ambassadors into key management positions. People like Christer Granstrand, Josephine Rydberg-Dumont, Mikael Ohlsson, Kenth Nordin, and others played a decisive role in Ikea US's turnaround, and now hold high positions in the Ikea group worldwide.

It worked. Ikea now has 24 stores in the United States, with four on the horizon – although most are scattered around the perimeter of the country. Ikea US also sells its products online, and employs 13,000 co-workers. It is Ikea's third biggest country in terms of sales (11 percent). In the short-term, Ikea's expansion will be the fastest in the United States. As one of its advertising slogan goes: "It's a big country – someone's got to furnish it."

Lost in translation

The US experience was not the first time that Ikea had struggled to put a Swedish accent on another country's way of living. Its first attempt to woo Japanese home dwellers to the joys of flat pack in 1974 failed. Ikea withdrew hastily, saying Japanese customers were not yet ready for flat pack living, and especially not convinced about putting their own furniture together.

This time round, 30 years later, Ikea is hopeful that it can seduce the Japanese, who have been battered by more than a decade of recession and are less convinced that they must pay high prices to obtain high-quality goods. It is set to open two shops just outside Tokyo in late 2005, with plans to open 8–12 more – half in greater Tokyo and half in the Kansai region which includes Osaka and Kobe – and employ between 6,000 and 8,000 people.

While Ikea's multitude of storage solutions will suit the urban, cramped apartments in Japan, the Swedish retailer will also have to shrink its furnishings to fit the smaller Japanese household. However, it will not be tweaking its designs, saying that Japanese style is quite similar to Scandinavian.

Ikea's biggest barrier this time around is the same as it was 30 years ago. Japan's notoriously fussy customers will not be open to the idea of assembling their furniture themselves. For this reason, Ikea Japan will be providing an assembly service as well as home delivery. The country manager, Tommy Kullberg knows the market well. He's a Swede who's lived in Japan for the last 10 years, including a stint as Sweden's trade secretary in Tokyo. The signs look good – the Ikea catalog has become the latest craze in Japan, with people swapping bootleg copies.

Chinese walls

Asia is going to be a very important market for Ikea. Sales at its two Chinese stores in Shanghai and Beijing rose by 50 percent last year, since its arrival in 1998. There are plans to open 10 more stores in the next six to eight years, with South Korea pinpointed as a potential new market.

Ikea opened its first store in Shanghai in 1998, swiftly followed by a store in Beijing the following year. A new redesigned Shanghai store opened in 2003, replacing the original. At 33,000 square meters it is four times larger than the first Shanghai Ikea, and attracted around 80,000 shoppers on its first day.

China is an important new market for Ikea, because home buying and home decoration have only very recently become cultural currencies. Changes in China's government housing policy in 1998 meant that the state no longer has to provide accommodation to its people through an employee's "work unit." The private housing market is booming. In 1999, the volume of home mortgages provided by the state's commercial banks jumped by 145 percent.

With a population of 1.25 billion, China has more consumers than the United States and Europe combined. It's no surprise that Ikea is not the only Western furniture dealer interested in this nascent market. B&Q, the United Kingdom's home improvement chain, has openly borrowed from Ikea for its stores in China, where it is called Bai an Ju. It's building two-story outlets, with building tools and equipment on the ground floor and soft furnishings like Ikea on the second floor. Ikea's bigger concern could be that many local Chinese stores are copying its products and designs.

Ikea is perceived as expensive in China, a store for the middle class. One observer noticed that many Chinese shoppers in Ikea were drawing pictures of the furniture and scribbling down descriptions of the products, but not necessarily buying them. Since its launch, Ikea has endeavored to cut prices by using more and more local suppliers. Its prices have dropped by 10 percent since launch, and Chinese sales rose accordingly by 35 percent in 2003.

Globally, Ikea expects to source about 23 percent of its products from China in 2004. Despite this, Ikea has made little attempt to adjust its range to local tastes. Out of a range of around 7,000–8,000 articles, only three have been added for the Chinese market – chopsticks, a wok with a lid, and a cleaver. However, there are some other tweaks to the Swedish template. As most Chinese apartments have balconies, there is a special balcony section in the stores. Ikea also offers an assembly service for Chinese shoppers.

This hasn't prevented a frenzied interest in the Scandinavian retailer. An Ikea ad campaign in Beijing to publicize the new store that stated, "Don't be like your parents," had to be pulled after one week because it was so successful, people were queuing for miles to visit the store.

Similarly, in Shanghai Wang Jian Shuo runs a web blog that among other things delves into his likes and dislikes of Ikea. He writes how, in 1999, as a new graduate he spent his first month's salary on a Billy bookcase. "Ikea seems to know my life better than any other furniture brand," he says.[49]

Wang Jian Shuo has noticed Ikea's prices dropping. He recalls how in 1999 Ikea was selling colorful paper boxes for 59 RMB which, he says, seemed ridiculous to the Chinese at the time. A few months ago he noticed that a flower picture that used to cost 19 RMB is now just 1 RMB.

Ikea always creates a new industry around itself of delivery drivers. An ad hoc taxi service has mushroomed outside Ikea in Shanghai – but instead of traditional Chinese taxi cabs, the rank is lined with little pick-up trucks.

Russian dolls

Although Ikea will gain long-term growth from targeting developing countries, they come with their own set of assembly problems. In Russia in December 2004, Ikea was forced to cancel its opening ceremony at a store in Khiniki on the outskirts of Moscow, after officials claimed at the last minute that visitors' cars might damage an underground gas pipe. Company managers have previously claimed that Ikea has been under pressure for not paying bribes in Russia.

The Swedish newspaper *Dagens Industri* reported that Ingvar Kamprad is set to meet with the Russian president Vladimir

Putin to discuss the problems Ikea is facing in this market. "I'm going to look Putin in the eyes and tell him that we have common interests, I'm going to say how much we've invested and intend to invest in Russia. We have a social mission here, Putin should understand that," Kamprad told the newspaper.[50]

Ikea is the biggest foreign retailer in Russia. It already has stores in Moscow and St Petersburg and in April 2004 opened in Kazan, the capital of Tatarstan, 1,000 km east of Moscow. It is also moving into the Ukraine. Moscow's 10 million population immediately understood what Ikea represented, and the increasing car ownership, ring road infrastructure, and a culture used to buying in warehouses makes it an ideal Ikea marketplace. Its first store in Moscow is visited by 4.5 million shoppers annually. However, middle-class Russians are still not admitting that they shop there.

In Russia, Ikea has to pay a lot in customs, so now its goal is to produce more things within the country to avoid those taxes. In fact, Russia's massive potential as a supplier market may be the reason behind Kamprad's interest in the market. Currently, the 25 percent tax on imported furniture means Ikea Russia is still making losses, but long-term it may become a useful source.

One of Ikea's biggest challenges is ensuring it is cheap in underdeveloped markets too. Its grand philosophy, "to create a better everyday life for the many people" dwindles to nothing, if it does not include and embrace people who live in poor countries too.

Ikea in Poland, China, and Russia is considered a dream purchase, an out-of-reach consumer desire that crunches uncomfortably with Kamprad's democratic aims. "When I hear in Poland that they dream of Ikea, something is not good," admits one co-worker.

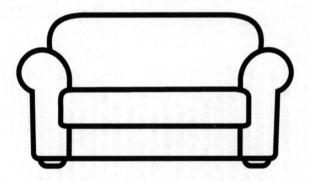

10 Ikea in the global village

> Ikea is the prototypical Teflon multinational. Like
> Ronald Reagan, known as the "Teflon president",
> there is an emerging class of global corporations
> that by virtue of cleverness, charisma or plain
> dumb luck manage to dodge or deflect the brand-
> bashing attacks launched by angry radicals.[51]

Like the non-stick coating on cooking pans, Ikea has a Teflon shield, which deflects all charges of wrongdoing. Allegations like Ingvar Kamprad's flirtation with Nazism, his alcoholism, and links connecting the furniture retailer with child labor don't seem to stick.

It's remarkable that Ikea doesn't attract more attention from anti-brand activists. After all, it's stamping the same uncompromising global footprint of furniture retailing across the world, just as McDonald's does with its fast food imprint.

Ikea's 300 million annual customers and their insatiable appetite for wooden furniture are a threat to forests, from Borneo to Russia. Similarly, one of the main ways Ikea manages to keep its prices low is by producing goods in impoverished countries like Laos, Vietnam, China, and India. You would think that the Swedish retailer would have graduated into a viable target for anyone with a grudge against big companies and global brands.

Ikea is very sensitive about the fragility of its reputation. One of the reasons that Marianne Barner, who heads up PR and communications for Ikea, refused to cooperate with this book was because (I quote from her email):

> Ikea do [sic] not want to promote themselves as a
> target for anti-globalization organizations who
> focus on big name brands like ours despite our
> many community and environment friendly
> policies and contributions.

There seems to be just one serious occasion when Ikea's own safety was threatened. In December 2002, Ikea became the target of bombers who planted devices in two of its Dutch stores, warning that another bomb would be detonated in a third. Ikea immediately closed all 10 stores across the country. Explosives were found in the Sliedrecht and Amsterdam stores, and a policeman was injured while trying to disarm one of the bombs.

Two years later, two Polish men appeared in an Amsterdam court charged with blackmailing the furniture retailer, after being arrested in Portugal the year after the incident. They had written a threatening letter in patchy German to Ikea demanding €250,000. So, in fact Ikea's enemy was opportunist blackmailers rather than anti-globalization activists.

What is it about the Ikea brand that enables it to sidestep unwanted attention? Obviously, it helps to come from a little country like Sweden rather than big, bad, corrupt America. It could also be quite simply that you never get hurt by Ikea. It does seem to be a better corporate citizen than most.

There's also of course Kamprad's vision of "design for the many" – that Ikea is always driving prices down so we can all afford faux-modernist, wobbly furniture in our homes, rich or poor. If that vision is achieved through using factories in the Third

World then so be it. At least it's helping some of the world's poor, albeit the lower middle classes in the Western world.

Ikea for kids

However, since 1992 when Ikea was tarred by a Swedish documentary showing children chained to the weaving looms of one of its suppliers in Pakistan, it has made strenuous efforts to protect its 58-year-old brand. The newly hired business manager for carpets, Marianne Barner (who now heads up Ikea's communications and CSR policies), immediately terminated the Pakistani contract and added a clause on all supply contracts forbidding child labor.

This was the beginning of a series of child labor accusations fired at Ikea in developing regions. Some stories were fabricated and some were not. In 1997, another Swedish documentary called *Santa's Workshop Ikea's Backyard* revealed the use of child workers in factories in the Philippines and Vietnam. Barner flew into investigate, and terminated the contract of the wicker furniture factory in the Philippines, but retained the contract with the Vietnamese ceramics factory.

Two years later Ikea met with UNICEF and decided that the best way to solve child labor was not through boycotts but by helping to fight the root causes of poverty and lack of education. Since 2000, Ikea has partnered UNICEF in an initiative in India's booming carpet belt, which accounts for 85 percent of the country's carpet exports and is a supplier to nearly every global retail chain. Roughly 500,000 people work in Uttar Pradesh and UNICEF estimates that 40,000 of these workers are children.

The child labor initiative aims to give financial independence to poorer women in the area, and covers roughly 1.5 million people in 650 villages in the districts around India's holy town of Varanasi. Lower-caste women pay between 20–50 rupees a month into 423 "micro credit" groups which enables them to collectively save enough to open bank accounts and borrow money at market value rather than the sky-high rates of interests from local loan sharks.

Ikea also puts children through "bridge schools," called alternative learning centers (ALCs), which can help ease them into mainstream schools. It supports around 103 schools in the area, and around 75,000 children who would otherwise receive no schooling are educated via ALCs. An estimated 21,000 kids have become literate through the scheme.

In 2000, Ikea established a code of conduct for its 1,600 suppliers called Iway – "The IKEA way on purchasing home furnishing products." It sets out rules for working conditions, minimum wages, overtime rates, trade union rights, waste management, chemical management, and emissions to air and water. And it states that it will not tolerate child labor, discrimination, or the use of timber from intact natural forests. It also asks suppliers to ensure that their own suppliers fulfill the same criteria.

Ikea's environment

Ikea grew from the pine forests of southern Sweden, and for

years it had a "green reputation" loosely based on its roots in conscientious Scandinavia. Like all manufacturers it faces increasing pressure to make products that have a minimum impact on the global village. Most famous for its wood furniture, it is Ikea's environmental policies that are under most scrutiny.

Its "green" reputation began to erode in the late 1980s when the finish on its bookshelves was found to have illegally high levels of formaldehyde. By the early 1990s, Ikea was running environmental awareness classes for 20,000 of its employees.

After conversations with Greenpeace, Ikea became involved with Global Forest Watch, which is attempting to map the disappearing forests of the world. The Swedish furniture retailer energized the project with US$2.5 million in funding, and special atlases that clearly indicate "out of bounds" areas are used by Ikea forest managers.

However, Ikea cannot guarantee that all of its timber does not come from illegally felled trees or protected forests. In the long term it is hoping that all Ikea timber will come from certified forests. It is currently working with WWF to help stop the trade of illegally felled timber along the Russian–Chinese border.

Socially responsible prices

In all these areas, no publicity is good publicity. And although Ikea's daily struggle to drive down prices for customers is key to its brand, it does not want to be seen as a retailer that achieves low prices, at any price. Sometimes, Ikea's cost-consciousness and its desire to be socially responsible walk hand in hand; sometimes they work against each other.

When Anders Dahlvig became the president of Ikea in 1999 he said that he wanted to make the company as ecology minded as it was economy minded. Often these two things overlap – if you're unbelievably tight about not wasting resources then that can be environmentally friendly too.

A few years ago, a competition was held within Ikea called Kill-a-watt. It was a cost-saving initiative that also happened to be good for the environment. Staff were urged to turn off lights, taps, and computers when they were not using them. Whichever store or office around the world saved the most electricity would win a prize.

Similarly, Ikea designers are encouraged to think of ways of designing products that take up less space when they're being transported. More efficient use of transport means more products can be squeezed into every shipment, reducing both costs and pollution.

Ikea's internal corporate social responsibility brochure on its intranet tells the story of Ikea designer Monika Mulder, and her prize-winning watering can Vallo. While conventional watering cans with their hollow bodies, long spouts, and handles are cumbersome to transport, Mulder's Vallo is stackable.

But reconciling keeping prices low at all costs and being environmentally friendly is tricky. At what point is it not ethical to drive costs down? Ikea's early struggles with child labor and its reliance on suppliers in developing markets means this juggling act will not go away.

Similarly, Ikea is already facing grumbles from some areas about its own retail model. Building huge retail outlets out of town which people have to drive to is being placed under more and more scrutiny. In the future, it's easy to see that Ikea's advocacy of disposable furniture, exchanging sofas for fads and fashion, will also be placed under the microscope. It's certainly not a sustainable way of living, and if nothing else, Ikea will be held more accountable for the way in which tired bits of furniture are discarded. It may be obliged to take back products that people don't want. Its designers will also be placed under increasing pressure to design furniture so that its different materials can be easily separated for disposal – all of which impacts its daily push to drive down costs.

Threats from all over

Fitting into the global village that it furnishes is just one of a myriad of threats hovering above Ikea like a raincloud. Although there have been few competitors trying to copy everything that Ikea does, there is no doubt that its ways are educating and informing its competitors. For example, the bare blond wood Scandinavian look has permeated all retailers. In the United Kingdom the DIY store B&Q and the supermarket Sainsbury's have produced a rash of Ikea-esque designs.

Although there's not one big competitor that Ikea needs to be aware of, there are lots of different companies nibbling around the edges of the Scandinavian furniture dealer. In the United

Kingdom, catalog shopping company Argos is selling furniture far more seriously than it used to: The furniture division of its business grew by 12.2 percent last year. DIY retailers like Home Depot in the United States are all dabbling in furniture.

In China, B&Q stores are split into two levels, with DIY tools and cement on the ground floor and Ikea-looking soft furnishings on the top floor. Meanwhile, a Danish, more grown-up version of Ikea called Ilva is poised to roll out across Europe. It's already opened in Sweden and will be opening in Manchester in 2005, with plans for another 20 stores in the United Kingdom, headed up by Martin Toogood, the former Habitat chief. Significantly, unlike Ikea it will do home delivery.

Ikea's supply economics depend on two factors – flat pack and scale. Flat pack furniture is easily replicable but scale is harder to replicate – it would take a new entrant a long time to reach Ikea's volumes. However, the real danger for Ikea comes from giant supermarkets like Wal-Mart, which is becoming increasingly interested in home furnishings. Wal-Mart enjoys the same scale benefits as Ikea because it has a finely honed juggernaut of a distribution network that it can leverage in the market.

Ikea's lack of flexibility in terms of its retail experience could make it vulnerable in the future. On the one hand you can't argue with the Swedish retailer's steadfast and stubborn approach because it has worked so far. Hence customers continue to trek a winding journey through Ikea's maze, where they must wrestle with oversized flat packages and then assemble the furniture themselves – but are we getting sick of it?

The core of Ikea's appeal is affordable design, and its low-cost proposition stems from its uniformity. However competitive threats could come from a lot of different directions. Ikea could be attacked from the low-cost angle, from the design angle, and also by making the retail experience more appealing. It's a potential time bomb.

Although Ikea customers can buy online in some markets such as the United States and Sweden, Ikea has seriously under-exploited the Internet as a sales channel. Online shopping seems to make perfect sense for a retailer that is beginning to suffer declining sales in its mature markets across Europe. The mechanism is already in place – it has its catalog and its network of distribution centers. It seems incomprehensible that customers frustrated with shopping in Ikea can't do it from the comfort of their Galant desk at home. Why is the retailer that invented catalog shopping not taking advantage of the Internet?

But Ikea likes us getting trapped like flies in the sticky web of its 190,000 square feet stores. It makes us buy things we don't want, things we didn't know we needed. When Ikea experimented in the past with high street versions of stores in Switzerland and Austria, it backfired. Sales went down overall because customers were visiting the high street rather than the out-of-town stores. They were buying wooden spoons and martini glasses from the marketplace and not buying furniture. Ikea's little stores cannibalized its sales, and I suspect management is concerned that the internet could do the same.

However, in the United Kingdom Ikea may have to compromise on the size of its stores if it is to expand across the country. The

Swedish retailer has been embroiled in planning disputes with the UK government, and has only opened one new store since 1999. The government is afraid that large out-of-town developments will kill city centers and increase car traffic. Ikea may have to alter its strategy and open smaller stores closer to town centers if it is to achieve its aim of opening 10 more UK stores by 2010.

The end of the affair?

Is our love affair with Ikea beginning to fade? It's not just the hellish customer experience; it's the design too. Perhaps the Swedish furniture dealer has become a victim of its own success? The more homes are furnished with identikit, spare, Swedish finish, the more we want to add variety to stand out from our neighbors. Many observers believe that it's time for Ikea to change. "Ikea has had such a category-killing concept that it hasn't had any call to tweak it so far. That call's on the horizon," warns Gavin Rothwell, retail analyst at Verdict Research Ltd.

The average age of an Ikea customer across the world is now 42. It's older in some markets. Ikea needs to learn how to keep attracting an aging population with maturing tastes. Older customers have got more money, want to buy furniture that's going to last, and want to be treated properly in stores. This is a real issue for Ikea, and is probably the first time it's had to adapt to market conditions. It's an issue for designers too. Ikea's furniture will need to be easier to assemble for an older generation.

Perhaps the pieces will "click together" rather than be screwed to fit using Allen keys.

Ikea design will also need to evolve for younger consumers. Will young people who grew up in an Ikea bedroom want to carry on buying furniture from the Swedish retailer? Do they want to be buying the same furniture as their parents? Probably not, and that's why Ikea was successful in the first place.

I think Ikea's biggest problems and issues come from its mature markets, like Sweden, the United Kingdom, and Germany, which have been taking Swedish furniture advice for the last 30 years. Ikea has always been a challenger brand, a rebel that persuades people to change their tastes and behavior. But how should Ikea act when it doesn't have any more difference to make? What's the next stage?

Once Ikea's traveled around the world saying "Here's a new way of doing it," what happens then? It is time for a change. But it's as if Ikea has been shouting its message so loud and for so long, that it now doesn't know what to say next. Ikea was always about pushing ideas onto people rather than listening to what people want. That was right in the beginning, because we didn't know we wanted Scandinavian design, but now it's different.

The next generation

I sense that there are probably quite a few senior managers within Ikea who know they need to shake up the company and change things, but are too saturated with work. Perhaps the death of 78-year-old Ingvar Kamprad will lead to a spate of changes. Although Ikea workers have permission from the eccentric founder to be polite radicals, some suggestions are off limits.

But nobody internally believes that Kamprad's death will lead to the end of Ikea. He has carefully prepared for this moment for many, many years, to ensure that his own death will not signal the demise of his company. Although his succession plans are shrouded in secrecy, it is widely expected that his sons will continue to be actively involved in the business.

Kamprad has three sons – Peter, Jonas, and Mathias, who are all employed in different roles with the furniture empire. So the continuation of Kamprad's dynasty, the way he likes it, seems inevitable. Admittedly, this is not the naked succession plan and nepotism that is displayed at Rupert Murdoch's newspaper empire News International – Kamprad's sons must prove themselves.

However, these three paper billionaires seem to have inherited some of their father's traits. I hear stories of the eldest Peter, who sits on the board of Ingkva, the parent group for all Ikea companies, and is tipped as the most likely successor. One of his staff tells me that he prefers to give packets of seeds as gifts, rather than bunches of flowers, as they're less expensive.

I hear from another Ikea co-worker about traveling to a meeting in a car with Peter. He was looking for somewhere to park, and kept driving around and around to find a meter with some money left on it, so it would be cheaper. They were late for their meeting.

Peter Kamprad's home life seems modest, like his father's. He wears the same jumper every winter, with holes in the elbow, and socks and sandals. His wife buys her clothes from Swedish value fashion store H&M. They drive an old Opal around town, and although Peter buys new toys for his children, he also likes to visit flea markets to buy second hand Lego for them. His father Ingvar must be proud.

There are many lessons that other brands could learn from the Ikea saga. The most important is never resting. Always looking out for the next big thing, the next idea, the next market, the next "something" that will improve business and enhance the central vision.

Led by its restless founder, Ikea has always been in perpetual motion. For example, in 1986 the Swedish furniture dealer made its first billion dollars (10 billion krona) in turnover. This would have been an enormous cause for celebration in most organizations, a chance to go out and celebrate and perhaps relax a little. At the board meeting Ingvar Kamprad simply asked his management team to take a one-minute silence to reflect on this milestone. They did, and then they got back to work.

Ikea would say themselves that most things remain to be done. Kamprad's zealous *Furniture Dealer's Testament* ends like this: "Happiness is not reaching your goal. Happiness is being on your way.... What we want to do, we can do and will do together. A glorious future!" And that's what keeps driving the Swedish retailer forwards in its relentless mission to furnish the world.

What other brands can learn from Ikea

- Ikea has a meaningful purpose. It understands that the way to make money is to be dedicated to a vision. A company doesn't make profit because it wants to, but because it offers something different.

- Ikea recruits on potential rather than experience. It instinctively knows whether an individual will fit into its way of working. Once inside, there is space for people to grow and to make mistakes.

- Ikea is driven by long-term thinking rather than short-term sales pressure. It accepts that it will lose money in emerging markets such as China and Russia, but knows that these losses will be worth it in the long term.

- Ikea understands the importance of being honest and transparent. When it makes mistakes, it admits to them, apologizes and tries to make things right.

- Ikea rarely asks its customers what they want, but uses good design, low prices, and challenging advertising to persuade them.

- Ikea turns problems and difficulties into opportunities.

NOTES

1   R. Fuchs, "Isn't it great to be Swedish," from *Visst ar det harligt att vara svensk*, Stockholm, 1991, p 171.

2   *Scotland on Sunday*, February 3, 2002.

3   Miriam Salzer, *Identity across Borders: A study in the "Ikea-world,"* 1994, p 255.

4   Ikea internal documents.

5   *Ikea Mania*, Five (UK television documentary).

6   Bertil Torekull, *Leading by Design*, Harper Business, 1998, pp 143–4.

7   *Design for Life*, BBC4 (UK television documentary).

8   Professor Christopher A. Bartlett and Asish Nanda, *Ingvar Kamprad and Ikea*, Harvard Business School Case Study, July 1996, p 3.

9   Bertil Torekull, *Leading by Design*, Harper Business, 1998, pp 4–6.

10 *Design for Life*, BBC4 documentary.

11 Oliver Burkeman, "The miracle of Älmhult," *Guardian*, June 17, 2004.

12 Bertil Torekull, *Leading by Design*, Harper Business, 1998, p 20.

13 Professor Christopher A. Bartlett and Asish Nanda, *Ingvar Kamprad and Ikea*, Harvard Business School, July 1996, p 1.

14 Bertil Torekull, *Leading by Design*, Harper Business, 1998, p 22.

15 Bertil Torekull, *Leading by Design*, Harper Business, 1998, p 25.

16 Bertil Torekull, *Leading by Design*, Harper Business, 1998, p 45.

17 Bertil Torekull, *Leading by Design*, Harper Business, 1998, p 103.

18 Oliver Burkeman, "The miracle of Älmhult," *Guardian*, June 17, 2004.

19 Bertil Torekull, *Leading by Design*, Harper Business, 1998, p 80.

20 Oliver Burkeman, "The miracle of Älmhult," *Guardian*, June 17, 2004.

21 Miriam Salzer, *Identity across Borders: A study in the "Ikea-world,"* 1994.

22 "Krybbe to grave," *The Economist*, June 12, 2004.

23 Nicholas Ind and Cameron Watt, *Inspiration: Capturing the creative potential of your organisation*, Palgrave, 2004, p 156.

24 Miriam Salzer, *Identity across Borders: A study in the "Ikea-world,"* 1994, p 256.

25 Miriam Salzer, *Identity across Borders: A study in the "Ikea-world,"* 1994, p 255.

26 Charlotte and Peter Fiell, *Scandinavian Design*, Taschen, 2002.

27 Miriam Salzer, *Identity across Borders: A study in the "Ikea-world,"* 1994, pp 255–6.

28 Miriam Salzer, *Identity across Borders: A study in the "Ikea-world,",* 1994, p 260.

29 Bertil Torekull, *Leading by Design*, Harper Business, 1998, p 62.

30 Michele Hanson "Peace, love and flat pack to all," *Guardian*, April 12, 2004.

31 Miriam Salzer, *Identity across Borders: A study in the "Ikea-world,"* 1994, p 59.

32 Extract from "The future is filled with opportunities," cited in Miriam Salzer, *Identity across Borders: A study in the "Ikea-world"*, 1994, p 63.

33 Advertising jingle for 1996 Ikea ad campaign in the UK, cited in John Grant, *The New Marketing Manifesto*, Texere, 1999, p 190.

34 Miriam Salzer, *Identity across Borders: A study in the "Ikea-world,"* 1994, p 3.

35 Human rights campaign foundation. www.hrc.org

36 *Chicago Sun-Times*, April 2, 1994.

37 John Grant, *The New Marketing Manifesto*, Texere, 1999, p 190.

38 Lucy Aitken, "Ikea: chucking out chintz around the world," *Campaign*, December 10, 2004, p 17.

39 Ingvar Kamprad, *The Furniture Dealer's Testament*, quoted in Miriam Salzer, *Identity across Borders: A study in the "Ikea-world,"* 1994, p 255.

40 Ingvar Kamprad, *The Furniture Dealer's Testament*, quoted in Miriam Salzer, *Identity across Borders: A study in the "Ikea-world,"* 1994, p 260.

41 Professor Christopher A. Bartlett and Asish Nanda, *Ingvar*

Kamprad and Ikea, Harvard Business School Case Study, July 1996, p 5.

42 Miriam Salzer, *Identity across Borders: A study in the "Ikea-world,"* 1994, p 126.

43 Nicholas George, "Ikea continues to build on global success," *Financial Times*, September 29, 2004.

44 Miriam Salzer, *Identity across Borders: A study in the "Ikea-world,"* 1994, p 178.

45 Miriam Salzer, *Identity across Borders: A study in the "Ikea-world,"* 1994, p 264.

46 Professor Christopher A. Bartlett and Asish Nanda, *Ingvar Kamprad and Ikea*, Harvard Business School Case Study, July 1996, p 8.

47 "One furniture store fits all," *Financial Times*, February 8, 2001.

48 *Houston Chronicle*, August 5, 2004.

49 www.wangjianshuo.com

50 *Dagens Industri*, December 14, 2004.

51 "The Teflon shield," *Newsweek*, March 12, 2001.

BIBLIOGRAPHY

Bartlett, C. A. and Nanda, A. (1996) *Ingvar Kamprad and Ikea*, Harvard Business School Case Study.

Burkeman, O. (2004) "The miracle of Älmhult," *Guardian*, June 17.

Fiell, C. and Fiell, P. (2002) *Scandinavian Design*. Taschen.

Grant, J. (1999) *The New Marketing Manifesto*. Texere.

Ind, N. and Watt, C. (2004) *Inspiration: Capturing the creative potential of your organisation*. Palgrave.

Law, A. (1998) *Open Minds*. Texere.

Salzer, M. (1994) *Identity across Borders: A study in the "Ikea-world,"* unpublished PhD thesis.

Torekull, B. (1998) *Leading by Design*. Harper Business.

Television documentaries

Design for Life, BBC4.

Ikea Mania, Five.